RICH IN YOUR *love*

Copper Valley Fireballs Series

Jock Blocked
Real Fake Love
The Grumpy Player Next Door
Irresistible Trouble

Tickled Pink

The One Who Loves You

RICH IN YOUR love

PIPPA GRANT

 Montlake

Published by Montlake, Seattle

www.apub.com

Amazon, the Amazon logo, and Montlake are trademarks of Amazon.com, Inc., or its affiliates.

ISBN-13: 9781542037679
ISBN-10: 1542037670

Cover design by Caroline Teagle Johnson

Cover photography by Wander Aguiar Photography

Printed in the United States of America

RICH
IN
YOUR
love

Chapter 1

Octavia Lightly, aka an Heiress with Too Many Secrets to List Here

Two months ago . . .

If there's anything better in this world than coming home to someone who missed you, I have no idea what it is.

Also?

I have no idea when I started thinking of Costa Rica as *home*, but there's this peace settling over me as I pull to a stop at the end of the road leading to my cacao farm that tells me I'm finally where I belong.

Where I'm accepted.

Where I can be *me*.

No apologies. No excuses. Just *me*.

And when the door to the villa at the end of the drive flies open and Naomi Cross comes rushing out, it's like, *This.*

This is what I've been looking for my entire life.

"We have beans!" she shrieks, holding a yellow pod aloft. "*We have beans!*"

"What?"

I leap out of the Jeep, grab my dog, and dash to my best friend across the small but lush yard.

And I do mean lush.

The land is wild and free and beautiful. It's everything I've always wanted my own life to be.

"Beans!" Naomi crows.

"Beans!" I echo. "Our beans? For real?"

Pebbles, my teacup Yorkie, howls in glee with us, and I lift her to kiss her head as we reach Naomi.

If the photographers following me all over Milan in the latest couture with my mother's handbags last week saw me leaping for joy over *beans* in this primitive slice of heaven in Central America, they'd be much more excited to snap my picture. *Tavi Lightly, vegan sugar-free fitness and fashion guru, loses it over chocolate in cotton shorts in the jungle.*

Naomi flings her arms around me, and we spin in a circle. When she lets go, I grab the yellow pod from her and kiss it, then offer it to Pebbles, who licks it, too, before making a face that makes me laugh. "Beautiful, beautiful bean!"

"Sebastián says we'll have an actual harvest this winter," she tells me.

"No way!"

"Yes! From the trees that were started before we got here."

I squeal.

Naomi squeals.

We hug and dance in a circle again.

Three years.

For three years, I've been hiding this secret from virtually everyone I know, waiting and hoping and spending money hand over fist from my trust fund to save this farm. I've expanded with every opportunity, buying slices of land around our mountain farm as they come up for sale and planting trees there, too, sneaking here every chance I've had between photo shoots and business meetings for my influencer business.

I've also gotten *excellent* at producing small-batch chocolates with beans from another nearby farm while we slowly perfect our craft.

My parents and siblings don't know. My industry contacts don't know, nor do any of the men I've dated. The five million people who follow me across all my socials don't know.

And I love it.

Not the secret part but the *belonging* part. Being just Tavi. Getting to know the locals who have worked this land with their families for decades, as well as their friends and neighbors, who think I'm ridiculous for my *day job* and who would eat raw beans before talking to reporters. Eating dinner with them at their houses and hearing their stories and realizing that life is so much more than what you can buy and how you look. Getting their honest feedback on flavor combinations and various truffle recipes at gatherings that we regularly host.

And now that our trees are making beans again, now that we're this much closer to launching our chocolate business with beans harvested on our own land, this is *real*.

Naomi and I did something.

We did something good for the land here, for the people here, and for the world.

Not that I can tell anyone.

Prance around in public telling people I bought a run-down, dried-up cacao farm out from under a mining company that wanted to strip the land and offer the locals horrible mining jobs so that I could go into the luxury chocolate business with a rando I met when she accidentally crashed my private tour bus one time, caught me eating fish and chips with a side of chocolate chip cookies, broke her leg trying to get back off my bus, and became my best friend in an unexpected but good series of events over the months that followed?

Hello. *No.*

I'm *Tavi Lightly*, with all those Insta followers who know I would *never*. I'm famous for eschewing dairy and sweets and endorsing exercise and vegetables on all my socials.

It would be on brand if I were shilling the raw cacao beans to be used in facials and as raw ingredients in organic, no-sugar-added smoothies, extolling their antioxidant powers to make skin younger and bones healthier and muscles stronger.

But I don't want to be *on brand*. My brand is something I fell into when I didn't have any better ideas after realizing college wasn't for me if I didn't know what I wanted to do with my life, nor did I have any faith that I had the skills necessary to *be* someone.

Now, I know I want to be a success of my own making, doing something I love instead of something I got into in the hopes of winning my mother's approval, something I keep doing because I'm so strapped for cash with all the work this cacao farm has taken—plus a few side charity projects that I can't fathom giving up—that I can't quit.

And running this farm with Naomi?

It's been the single biggest source of joy, other than my dog, in my entire life.

Even with it requiring every dime I can get my hands on.

I was born into money—money I can't fully access until I'm thirty next year, but still money—and I've finally found a use for it that makes me feel good.

Like I'm doing something *real*.

Something that matters to the people around me, to the locals who were struggling for work to make ends meet before we hired so many to come back to the farm and started finally paying them what they're worth. Something that matters to the earth, which won't see these twenty acres that we have now ever be deforested or mined. Something that matters to the end customers who will eat our truffles on bad days or celebrate milestones with them or give them as the perfect pick-me-ups to friends in need.

"We're doing it," Naomi cries. "We're making our dreams come true! Come inside! I have more beans from the farm across the mountain, and I promised Luciana and her daughter that next month's flavor would blow them away, so we need to get to work. Plus, we'll have to pick the final launch recipes soon if we're going to have *our own beans* this fall."

"Did we get the dried banana peels?"

"I got everything on your list, plus Maria at the market insisted I add fresh guava."

"Maria is brilliant."

"Right?"

Pebbles barks her agreement as I follow Naomi inside the small house.

There's no air-conditioning, so I flip my hair up and tie it back with a rubber band from the basket by the door.

"Did you want to rest or something first?" Naomi spins back to me. "Hello, eighteen hours of travel plus jet lag."

"I'm good."

"You're like . . . just *how*?"

"I slept on the planes. Plus, I *always* have time for the things I *want* to do."

She throws herself at me and hugs me again. "I'm so glad you gave me a chance to prove I wasn't the weirdo I looked like the day we met."

I hug her back. "You weren't a weirdo. You were exactly what I needed. Now take me to our cacao beans!"

Pebbles dances at our feet while we head to the kitchen, which takes up half the house. We're building an industrial kitchen to support the ramping up we expect to do next year, too, when *all* my cacao farms start producing en masse so that we can actually run a sustainable chocolate business.

The beautiful thing about being a Lightly heiress?

I don't need any of this to work or to make money right *now*.

We can quietly build the backbone for a small empire, paying all the staff we need and supporting the local town so it, too, can grow to support having a small chocolate empire here, without many questions.

I reach into my pocket to toss my phone aside, but before it hits the metal countertop, it starts ringing.

Naomi cracks up. "Is that the Wicked Witch of the West's theme song?"

"Yes."

I stare at the screen. *Gigi Khan.*

Her name's actually Estelle Lightly, but she's like Genghis Khan reincarnated, if Genghis Khan came back as a rich Upper East Side grandmother and eviscerated people socially instead of actually murdering them, and she insists the family call her *Gigi*, so I labeled her appropriately in my phone.

"Are you going to answer it?" Naomi asks.

My face twitches in a way that would make my mother tell me I'll get wrinkles, and thinking about my mother telling me I'll get wrinkles makes my face twitch even more.

No one in Costa Rica cares if I get wrinkles. Pebbles doesn't care. Naomi doesn't care.

They don't care that I'll age out of the influencer system if I haven't made something bigger of my name before I'm thirty, and now I'm thinking about my mother telling me not to eat any of this chocolate, because it'll go straight to my hips.

"Life is meant to be lived, not staged, Tavi," Naomi's forever telling me. And then she always points to her own hips. "And do you love me less for these?"

Of course I don't. But while I *hear* her, a lifetime of *oh, honey, I wish you'd gotten your sister's slender genes* takes some time to overcome. Especially while I need this influencer gig to pay the bills for the things that truly matter.

The song keeps playing.

Naomi's eyebrows lift. "I've never heard that ringtone on your phone before."

"She doesn't call often."

"She?"

"My grandmother." I snatch the damn phone with a sigh. "If I don't answer, God knows what she'll do."

I brace myself, blow out a slow breath, and then put on my fake happy face and brainless-social-media-queen attitude before answering. "Hey, Gigi! Oh my gosh, I was, like, just thinking about you!"

"Octavia."

Dammit. That's her *I am displeased* voice. I head back outside, because I don't want the chocolates getting Gigi vibes on them.

Talk about something that'll ruin you. "Yes, Gigi?"

"I choked and nearly died three weeks ago, and all you did was send a card. A card with a ridiculous round yellow happy face on the front."

"But you didn't die, Gigi! You lived! That's worth celebrating!" God, I hate playing the ditz.

Hate hate hate it.

But my sister, Phoebe, is the *smart, attractive businesswoman.*

I'm the chunky one who got lucky that she was already famous from the child beauty pageant scene before her hips started developing and that she can now apply enough makeup to make a living as an Instagram influencer.

And don't start with me about the Kardashians.

They don't have my mother.

"The only thing worth celebrating is that I've discovered it's time to save your soul," Gigi replies.

For once, I don't have a quick answer.

Not even a ditzy one.

"I want you on the next flight home," she continues. "Your parents, plus Phoebe and Carter, will be joining us for the next year in a small town in northern Wisconsin, where we'll all live together, work

7

together, do charity together, and learn to be better citizens of the world so that you all don't go to hell."

"Gigi, that's really sweet of you to invite me, but I have photo shoots and product testing and—"

"And I'm freezing your trust fund."

My breath whooshes out so hard I physically have to bend over. *"What?"*

"I'm freezing your trust fund."

"Gigi—"

"Tickled Pink, Wisconsin, is home to *Pink Gold*. The blueprint to saving our souls. This is not optional. If you want your little cacao farm's bills to continue to be paid, you'll get your rear end on a plane and *come home*. Now."

Oh God. She knows.

She knows.

"I—don't know—what you're talking about," I stammer.

"Octavia, do you know what it's like to choke, pass out, think you're dying, see the flames of hell looming ahead as your eternal reward, and realize you have *one chance* to straighten out this family that you've let become a group of selfish, insensitive, entitled asses?"

"Gigi."

"You have twenty-four hours. I'm not wasting any more time letting you all run about taking oxygen that could be used by people who actually stand a chance of getting into heaven."

"*I am not a waste of oxygen.* I'm doing important things here. I'm *saving* people, Gigi. I'm saving the earth and a farm and people's jobs and a town and my—"

"We'll discuss it in Wisconsin. And if you don't show up, you won't have to wonder who outed you for eating meat and sugar in addition to selling your little farm. I'll do it, and I'll do it for your own good. Are we clear?"

My eyes are hot. My chest hurts. My stomach hurts worse.

And despite the fact that I regularly run over fifty miles a week, my legs can't hold me up anymore.

My bones are buzzing bees, and my muscles are made of dust.

"Gigi, I can be a good person." My voice is thick, and I *hate* that. I hate letting my family see my weaknesses. They're the first people who would use them against me. "I *am* a good person. I do good things. I can come for—Gigi?"

I pull the phone back and peer at it.

She hung up.

She *hung up*.

"Tavi?" Naomi whispers behind me.

I swipe at my eyeballs. "I have to go. My grandmother—extortion—Naomi. Don't freak out, okay?"

The only person in the world who's ever let me just be *me*—who treats me like a sister merely *because* I'm me, the *real* me—stares back at me with round brown eyes. "I think we're past that."

"My trust fund just dried up, but it's a blip. I swear. Just—don't panic. Stay here. Don't tell anyone that anything's wrong. I'll fix this. I'll smooth it over. And everything will be okay. Okay?"

She nods.

She nods, because she believes in me.

Ironic.

I don't actually believe in myself.

But *I have to*.

This is my dream.

The people here are my friends.

This town and my farm are my home.

Naomi gave up her entire life to go on this journey with me.

I'll make this okay.

I will.

9

"I'm sure once I get back to the States, she'll realize she's being unreasonable, and I'll be back by the weekend. This will be okay. We can do this. *We can do this.*"

We have to.

We've put too much into our dream to lose it now.

Chapter 2

Dylan Wright, aka a Small-Town Plumber Who Knows How to Keep Secrets

Present day . . .

There's nothing like poker night, and tonight is nothing like poker night.

It's a little more . . . interesting.

"Who invited the tofu?" Jane Stewart mutters. She's a Black lady who can fish all of us under the table, and she gets mad when I say she's one of my favorite people in Tickled Pink, since she thinks it's all about the home brew she makes and sells in her garage.

Willie Wayne Jorgensen, a white guy a few years older than me who quietly keeps the town running by doing all the jobs necessary to keep a small town running, pulls up a chair at the card table under the buzzing light in the bunker that serves as our secret hideout. "Wasn't me."

"I would've invited my wife before I invited one of *them*," Ridhi Denning, a brown-skinned woman who suffers no fools and runs Tickled Pink's only café, says. "And she's a terrible poker player."

They all turn to me.

I lift my hands. "Don't look at me. She'd have to talk to me for me to have invited her."

The *her* in question is five feet, three inches of brown-haired, white-skinned, round-cheeked, fancy-outfit-wearing, teacup-Yorkie-carrying, perpetually working-out, vegan and sugar-free social media influencer Octavia Lightly.

And that's only half of her adjectives.

She belongs here in Tickled Pink, Wisconsin, about like I'd belong in a limo heading to a private jet about to take me to a concert I was headlining in Monaco, which isn't her fault.

Not the part where I'm not a rock star. That's all on me for poor life choices.

But the part where Tavi happens to be stuck here in Tickled Pink. Been an interesting couple of months since the Lightly family arrived thinking this was where they could improve their souls, that's for sure.

"No one invited me." She shifts the fancy bag carrying her dog to her other shoulder, and Pebbles happily turns around so she's still facing us, tongue wagging. "I followed one of you, but I'm not telling you which one. Won't do my soul much good to pit neighbor against neighbor, would it?"

She's looking at Ridhi and Jane while she talks, and I don't know if she's ignoring Willie Wayne to make it look like she just doesn't talk to men or if she tried to do for him what she tried to do for me a couple of weeks back and now can't look him in the eye either.

Frustrating, honestly.

My days of being the guy that people can't stand to look at have been over for a long time. And honestly? These days, I like getting along with people.

Even people who don't belong.

Might even have a soft spot for people who don't belong.

Like I said, not her fault she's here, and after almost two months of Tickled Pink living when she's used to big-city life on one coast or another, seems like it's starting to wear on her.

"What do you want?" Jane asks. No nonsense, that's our Jane.

Tavi flashes that smile that's all over her Instagram but that I don't see often when I swing by the school that her family's living in and fixing up. "To play."

"Four-person card game."

"I'll be on someone's team."

Ridhi pulls a deck of cards from her back pocket while she eyeballs the bunker's crude, monochrome gray kitchen setup, where we keep a stash of everything from wine to vodka.

But no food, unless it fits inside the locked fridge inside the cabinet, and even then, we're serious about crumb pickup.

Bunker's not as airtight as it was when Willie Wayne's uncle installed it forty years ago to have a place to hide from the "riffraff," aka the tourists coming to Tickled Pink to check out where *Pink Gold* was filmed, and I hear it wasn't so airtight then either. No reason to invite the critters in.

"No teams," Ridhi says.

"I'll sit out and watch if we switch this over to strip poker," Willie Wayne offers.

Ridhi pulls a face that says Willie Wayne's getting bad coffee next time he stops in her café.

Jane pulls a face that says he's getting something worse than spit in his beer the next time he swings by her garage for an after-work beverage. "Quit being a dirty old man."

He grins. "Just pullin' your chain. Akiko would kill me if she heard I watched strip poker. Not that she knows about this. No, sirree. The Tickled Pink Secret Poker Society is top secret. All the way."

All of us look at Tavi.

She keeps staring at Jane and Ridhi like she's incapable of acknowledging the presence of the rest of us in the room. "*I* won't tell. Naturally. Friends, like, keep each other's secrets." She drops her voice. "I won't even take a single selfie while I'm here. Will I, Pebbles? No, I won't. No, I won't."

The dog yips back happily at the baby talk.

"Friends don't usually follow friends into a secret bunker to crash a private poker game," Ridhi points out.

"I wasn't trying to crash! I just wanted to hang out. I've been here for, like, *months*, and Pebbles and I haven't hung out with any of you yet. I mean, other than when you're being so kind and volunteering to help us clean up the school, or when Gigi makes us subject you all to our presence at community picnics, or when we're falling on our faces during snowshoe baseball. Which I try really hard at, for the record. I *want* to be a good Tickled Pinker while I'm here."

"Because your grandmother told you to?"

"It's never wrong to make more friends."

Ridhi snorts. Pretty sure Tavi's also getting crap coffee next time she's in Café Nirvana.

Not sure she drinks it there, though. It might not be vegan and sugar-free.

I tip my folding chair back on its rear legs until I'm resting my shoulders against the cool metal wall and study the middle Lightly sibling.

She actively doesn't look back at me.

"You any good at poker?" I ask her.

She turns her head toward me, her cheeks taking on a slight pink hue, and she answers the poster of a sunny Wisconsin day plastered to the wall above my head.

It's progress.

First time I saw her after the incident that I pretend didn't happen, she ducked, turned, tried to cross the street, and almost got run over by the garbage truck. Hasn't looked me in the eye since.

"I brought cash," she tells the poster. "Is two thousand enough for a buy-in?"

Two thousand.

We usually play with fifty bucks each, and that's on the weeks we're feeling rich.

"We know you've got cash," Jane says. "We need to know if you can play or if this is going to be boring."

Tavi's dog barks twice.

"Shh, Pebbles, Mommy's got this," she says to the fluffy little creature as she scratches its head. Then she reaches up to her face like she wants to adjust the sunglasses she's not wearing tonight and smiles at Jane again. "I got stuck in a poker game in Russia once with my friend Svetlana, and I thought they were playing in rubles, but it turns out they were playing in dollars, and ten thousand dollars is a lot more than ten thousand rubles, so since none of us had more than five thousand in cash on us, we had to get our hosts drunk, which is *super* hard to do when you're in Russia, by the way, and it involved a lot of dancing and a lot of faking taking vodka shots myself, and in the end, I walked away with three phone numbers, and Svetlana got married to one of them six months later."

Willie Wayne, Ridhi, and Jane all frown at her.

I swipe a hand over my mouth to cover a grin. "All right then. Here. Sit in for me."

"*Dylan,*" Jane hisses.

"I'll spit in your eggs if you don't sit your ass down right now," Ridhi tells me.

I ignore them both and look at Tavi again as I rise and offer her my chair. "What's your poison? I'll fix you a drink."

"Oh, you don't have to do that," she replies to my left ear.

It's progress.

Don't really like it when people don't want to talk to me.

I'm about as harmless as a cotton ball—these days, anyway—unless you're a clogged toilet or a drippy sink, and I intentionally have the memory of a goldfish.

Forget all kinds of things I don't want to remember.

Like what happened that's making Tavi Lightly unable to look me in the face.

"It's the rules," I tell her. "Have to have a drink if you're gonna play poker. Keeps the playing field level."

"Level as that second pool table at Ladyfingers," Ridhi murmurs.

Tavi's nose wrinkles at the spread of alcohol on the counter. "Do you have any vegan, sugar-free light beer?"

Ridhi shuffles the deck. "We have vodka. You want to play, you'll have vodka too."

"Okay. Vodka it is." Tavi beams at Ridhi and Jane again. "And I promise I'll keep up. No questions. For real. About the game, I mean. I have *so* many questions about Tickled Pink and all of you who live here. This seems like such a great chance to get to know you better. And I really do want to get to know you all better. I was so overwhelmed when we got here, especially when I realized my new home needed *so* much work, but now it's, like, time to really dig in and be part of the community, you know?"

"Only thing you need to know is that if you breathe a word of anything that happens tonight to anyone, we'll be breathing word of what you're up to all over the tabloids."

Can't fault Ridhi for saying it.

If the rest of the town knew we ran secret poker games in a secret bunker one Thursday night a month, we'd have to find a new night.

And a new bunker.

Not as easy as you'd think. Even if there are other bunkers that people built around here over the years, like Willie Wayne's uncle did, nobody talks about them.

And considering Tavi and her whole family are all up to something more than supposedly turning themselves into good people, and everyone here knows it, you wouldn't think the threat would make her go pale, but it does. "The tabloids are great, but you should really start thinking bigger if you want to get Tickled Pink back on the map."

Ridhi splits the deck, shuffles, and bridges it. "We're still on the fence about wanting to be on that map. Bets down, everyone. Dylan, get me a bourbon on the rocks while you're up."

"Anybody else?" I ask.

"Brought my own beer," Jane says.

Willie Wayne lifts a sparkling cider. "Got my own too."

"I brought dried cauliflower sticks to share." Tavi reaches into her purse, not calling any of us on Ridhi's insistence that Tavi have vodka if she wants to play, but I'd bet she noticed. "They're curry flavored."

"If you want to live, you'll keep those in your purse," Ridhi tells her.

Pebbles barks in glee like she agrees.

Tavi makes kissy-faces at the dog. "Who's a sweet girl who loves curry cauliflower sticks?"

Pebbles gives her a doggy grin.

Say what you want about Tavi Lightly—she treats that dog mostly right.

Can't be all bad if you care that much about an animal, though I hope she feeds the pup some meat when no one's looking.

I fix drinks, pass them out, and lean against the counter, watching the first few games go down.

Tavi's truly terrible.

Takes six rounds for her to almost run out of chips, and all the while, she's asking questions about Tickled Pink like she's a travel reporter, not like she's someone who's been stuck here for months.

When I heard some rich old lady was bringing her family here to Tickled Pink because she'd decided that *Pink Gold*, the movie filmed here about a rich old lady trying to get to heaven, was the blueprint to saving her own soul, I, like most people around here, figured they wouldn't last a week.

And then I heard Estelle Lightly was planning on moving her family into the abandoned Tickled Pink high school building and fixing it up as part of their "soul journey," and I joined the chorus of people speculating they wouldn't last three days.

They've proved us all wrong. Guess you don't get rich without also having some drive, and honestly?

It's nice seeing the old high school put back to rights.

Not because I liked my time there. Or because *anyone* liked my time there.

Feels a little like all that cleaning, renovating, and fresh paint is giving us a new perspective on what we've forgotten Tickled Pink could be.

"Drink up," Jane says to her, nodding to Tavi's still-full vodka as they're dealing out the seventh hand. "Might help."

"Oh, I don't mind losing." Tavi gestures to the four chips left in front of her. "There's more where that came from."

Ridhi glances at her two cards, then shoves her own pile of chips into the pot. "If you're trying to butter us up by letting us have your money, won't work."

"I don't buy my friends, Ridhi."

"And we don't make friends with people who don't drink their vodka."

Tavi eyeballs the shot glass on the table in front of her, scoops it up, and tosses it back. "Yay! We're friends now."

Ridhi and Jane share a look.

"This is such a great town," Tavi says. "With just a little extra publicity, you could get tourism up even more. Like, enough to really maintain all of the improvements my family's making this year. I'm *super* good at helping people learn how to market themselves. I could, like, totally show you how to market the town."

"Don't know that I'd call them all *improvements*," Jane says.

"Okay, yes, the old high school doesn't need to ultimately become a museum to my grandmother's memory when she goes back to running people's lives in Manhattan instead of here, but at least there aren't any dead animals in it anymore."

"That you know of," Willie Wayne mutters.

I nudge him. There aren't any more dead animals in the school.

Unless someone put more dead animals in, that is.

He slides me a grin.

Tavi frowns at him. "If you're going to put dead animals in the school again, can you at least put them in Carter's room? It, like, would totally fit the vibe of his music."

Jane chokes on her tequila shot. "Okay, that was funny."

"Good. Don't expect it to happen again." Tavi slides her glass to Ridhi. "May I please have a refill? Because I have to talk all of you into something that none of us are going to like, or else I will *never* get to leave Tickled Pink, and I think the vodka will help. And trust me, you all want me to leave as badly as I want to leave. It's not you. It's really not. You're all lovely, and, like, the things you've put up with, like Gigi, and my parents, and Carter's quote 'music,' and Phoebe taking, like, *the* most eligible bachelor in the whole town so no one else could have him . . . I would *totes* want to get rid of us if I were you. But Tickled Pink is awesome. For real. I just have other things

I want to do with my life, and those things are far, far away from my grandmother. Which I'm *sure* you all, like, *totally* understand."

Willie Wayne shoots a look at me.

I shrug.

Pretty sure she won't be trying to talk us into the last thing she tried to talk me into.

Which I have permanently blocked from my brain.

She hasn't blocked it from hers, though. I can tell by the way she ducks me every time we're near each other, though she hasn't had any more near misses with a garbage truck or any other heavy machinery since that first time.

So tonight is already interesting.

But her tossing back a second shot?

Jane leans across the table, her brown eyes taking on a glow. "Talk, princess."

Tavi glances at the pot. "What if I play you for the inside scoop on what's going on inside the walls of that high school for the *Tickled Pink Papers* if you win and your agreement to cooperate if I win?"

"We already have spies to tell us that."

"So let's wager some favors, shall we?"

The four of us who created this secret poker society eyeball each other.

On the one hand, we're the four best poker players in all of Tickled Pink.

On the other, Tavi Lightly is a wild card.

I like wild cards.

Been a long time since I've gone down the path to digging into wild cards, but I'd be lying if I said I gave them up all the way.

Also? Wouldn't surprise me if Tavi *can* play and is losing on purpose to try to gain our trust.

Won't work on any of us—not in this bunker—but it makes me very curious.

Jane throws her hand down. "I want nothing to do with this."

I push away from the wall. "I'll fill in."

Everyone in the bunker stares at me.

Even Tavi.

Especially Tavi.

She doesn't know this, but the first time I actually saw her, *before* the incident that didn't happen, she was helping a duck cross the road near the lake.

Could've run on by.

Ignored the duck wandering aimlessly in the predawn light.

But she stopped and shooed him to the side of the road, all dressed in reflective gear, as I was heading out for an early-morning emergency job in Deer Drop.

She's the only reason I didn't have to bury a duck that day.

She thinks I remember one thing and one thing only.

I remember a little more.

And honestly?

Between the dog and the feeling that she's more than the fluffball she makes herself out to be when she knows people are looking, I'm curious what Tavi Lightly is really made of.

I like knowing my neighbors, and she's my neighbor for at least another nine to ten months, if her grandmother's plans are to be believed.

So far, nothing about Estelle Lightly suggests she'll bail early, no matter what we all thought at first.

And nothing about Tavi Lightly suggests she'll be granted one of her grandmother's *Get Out of Hell Free* cards early like her sister, Phoebe, got a couple of weeks ago.

"You really want to do that, Dylan?" Ridhi asks as I take Jane's seat.

Tavi meets my gaze, then quickly averts her eyes.

And that seals it.

I like people to like me.

I like to get along with my neighbors.

And Tavi Lightly and I need to clear the air so I can get back to being that guy I've finally made myself into—the trustworthy, dependable, nice guy next door. "Sure do."

Chapter 3

Tavi

It doesn't matter how evil my grandmother is for making us move to this little town in the middle of nowhere, Wisconsin—there is no evil that can top being woken up in the morning.

And it happens *every damn day*.

"Morning, sunshine," a deep, ruffled voice says nearby.

Okay, being woken up by the one person you need to talk to most, whom you really don't *want* to talk to at all, and whom you mistakenly thought you'd find alone when you followed him into a secret underground lair last night, is probably a worse evil.

"Mmphle," I whimper out.

My head feels like it's been put in the mouth of the world's largest, ugliest nutcracker. Something smells like goat mixed with body odor mixed with Vaseline. A strobe light flickers beyond my closed eyelids with a buzzing to go with it, and I don't know what I'm sleeping on, but I'm reasonably certain it hasn't been cleaned in a few decades and might be filled with gravel.

This reaction to mornings has nothing to do with the two shots of vodka last night and everything to do with the fact that I haven't slept more than twelve hours in a single week since I got here to Tickled Pink.

Is that polyester upholstery scratching my cheek?

Do I care?

No, I do not.

I was *sleeping*.

Hard.

I'd sleep here every night if I could sleep this hard, but longer.

"She speaks," Dylan Wright says. "Welcome back to the land of the living. Gotta get moving. I'm due in Deer Drop for a shower-valve-assembly problem, and I can't leave you here alone."

My eyelids refuse to open.

My mouth tastes like I went scuba diving in a landfill.

I'm still wearing my shirt, and I think my pants, too, and my hairstyle today will most likely be full regret.

"Affabammala?" I croak out.

"It's five thirty. And I also promised I'd get this place locked up. C'mon, princess. Time to go."

I pry open my eyelids to scowl at him.

I *hate* being called *princess* almost as much as I hate that I have to fake my way through one more morning here.

But not as much as I hate mornings.

I *hate* mornings.

I hate mornings so much that if Gigi were put in a wrestling match with mornings, I actually don't know who I'd root for. If hell is real, mine will be an eternity of an alarm clock buzzing thirty seconds after I fall asleep.

My vision is blurry, but I can still tell he's grinning at me as he prods me. "I thought you loved mornings. Always pass you when you're out running at six a.m."

My heart does a slow somersault of excitement at the idea that he sees me every morning.

And my brain translates exactly what that grin looks like when it's in its full, clear glory, and I want to scowl at him all over again, but that would take effort, and the truth is, Dylan Wright is not the kind of man you scowl at.

He's the kind of man you toss your panties at.

Not just because he's drop-dead gorgeous-handsome, which I did *not* expect to find in the Northwoods of Wisconsin, but also because he's kind and generous and easygoing in ways that I don't normally find in the men in my life.

For the record, I know attractive people exist outside my social spheres. I've traveled extensively, and I know there are attractive people everywhere.

But he's next level. He makes Calvin Klein underwear models look average. He would stop traffic in LA. If he got a job as a newscaster, the world would be saved, because no one would hear any negative reporting, even if he covered an asteroid hurtling to earth headed straight toward an orphanage full of babies and puppies. They'd be too awestruck with the gorgeous view to process a word he actually said, and all those good vibes would miraculously make the asteroid bounce off the world's good-vibes force shield.

Or possibly all my brain cells are broken by this massive crush that I have on a guy who does *not* belong in my world.

It's like he's not real, but I want him to be real, and I want to soak him up every single minute of the day until I can finally leave this town—and the people I'm related to—behind.

But Dylan is *involved with someone.*

Off limits.

Taken.

Unavailable.

And honestly?

The fact that he's so loyal only makes him more attractive, and the fact that he didn't tell me who says a lot about his character.

You don't tell Lightlys anything you don't want used against you, and you don't tell Lightlys who to hurt in the event that they need to use that information against you.

Even when my head is being squeezed like an orange in a juicer—I have *got* to get more sleep and less stress in my life—and when whatever that smell is that's lingering in this underground bunker should be a turnoff even under normal conditions, I find him absolutely charming and irresistible.

And he finds me amusing and flaky and only interested in tossing my panties at him.

Which I did *not* do, for the record.

What I did was much, much worse, and I would very much appreciate it if I could come down with amnesia.

Actually, amnesia would cure nearly everything that's wrong in my life.

I wonder if I could fake it.

There's an odd click, then a series of beeps, and then I hear a microwave whir to life. "So we're still not talking, or is it the vodka?" Dylan asks.

The question reminds me why I'm here.

"Owe me a favor," I croak.

Ten points to Tavi Lightly for pulling off the babe look while demanding restitution in a freaking bomb shelter before six in the morning.

Or not.

Is it bad that I can *hear* him grinning bigger? "So you *do* remember last night," he says.

That sentence should have much, much better connotations. "I don't drink much." Not a chance in hell I'll admit that my problem isn't the alcohol when the vodka is so much easier to blame.

"You should. You're funny when you drink. That story about the camel at that garden party in Paris—you hear a lot of things when you're the guy on call to resolve plumbing issues that you wouldn't ever dream would be real things, and I never thought I'd hear something like that."

I wince.

I forgot I told the camel story.

I always tell the lies when I'm a little buzzed, which is why I so rarely drink anymore. "What's that smell?"

It's not the weird bunker funk anymore.

It smells like—

Oh God.

It smells like eggs and cheese and McDonald's.

"That's my first breakfast," Dylan says. "I'd offer you some, but I know how you feel about meat. And eggs. And cheese. And sugar."

No, he really doesn't.

My stomach grumbles.

As if I'll listen to it. I need to skip breakfast to compensate for the calories in those vodka shots last night, and I'm supposed to convince half the townspeople today that they want social media accounts so that they can do on their own what my family is trying to do for them once we leave.

Starting with Dylan, because *duh*.

All he'll have to do is smile for Instagram in front of the newly repainted gift shop on the square, or smile while he's holding up a fish he caught in Deer Drop Lake a couple of blocks away, or smile while pointing to the WELCOME TO TICKLED PINK, HOME TO PINK GOLD, THE MOVIE, AND ITS STAR, ELLA DENNING sign that doesn't exist anymore but will be replaced soon, and people will flock here to bask in his glory.

Forget the damn old movie that Gigi's nearly recreated without finding her own soul yet. Forget the half-finished, ivy-covered Ferris wheel that my sister, Phoebe, wants to keep while building a bigger, better Ferris wheel next to it now that she's fallen in love with a local and is fully on board the *let's restore Tickled Pink to its former glory and give them the amusement park that failed when people lost interest in the movie* train.

The real tourist attraction in this town is Dylan.

Okay, probably not, but he's still my number one choice for *most likely to lure in visitors by making Tickled Pink look awesome.*

Even if that little incident with him in the high school's locker room a few weeks ago means that I would rather disintegrate and get washed down some plumbing myself than talk to him.

I mentioned my grandmother is as evil as mornings, right?

Ironic that she made us all come here to supposedly save our souls when she seems to be getting worse and worse every day.

You haven't done enough good since we got here, Octavia. Not like your sister. Look at all that Phoebe's done, and she's the least likely of all of us to have wanted to settle in to small-town surroundings. Get busy, Octavia. Give a town a little publicity, and they'll have tourists for a week. Teach a town to make its own publicity, and they'll have tourists for the rest of their lives.

The egg-and-cheese smell gets stronger while the microwave whirs.

"Not making you sick, is it?" Dylan asks.

I shake my head as I try to push myself up, and immediately regret it.

Okay, maybe this *is* a little bit of the vodka too.

Or possibly I didn't eat enough yesterday.

Or maybe it's just my life.

"Whoa there, go slow."

A warm, rough hand grips me by the arm, another providing support at my back, as I push to sitting.

While I smell like I spent the night frolicking in a sewer, Dylan smells like fresh straw and line-dried cotton. His kind brown eyes are smiling at me without mocking me, and a single lock of his brown hair has fallen across his forehead as if to say, *This is just how I feel today.*

Am I staring?

Oh crap.

I am.

I'm staring at him again.

And this is why I avoid looking at him at all costs.

When I look at Dylan Wright, small-town plumber in a run-down, backwoods slice of the world once known for a movie with questionable mass appeal, I am no longer an heiress to a worldwide consumer goods conglomerate, internationally known social media influencer, and massive secret keeper.

I'm a teenager with a crush.

I've dated rock stars and movie stars and hedge fund managers and professional athletes. My personal assistant regularly fields calls from men wanting to know if we can have a single date so that they'll get a little notoriety in the tabloids.

And I'm no fool. I know it's not that I'm the prettiest or smartest or even most interesting woman in the world. I don't have the best personality. After expenses, my social media business doesn't make me nearly as much as people assume it does. Loyalty and silence are expensive enough even before my conscience reminds me I'd be nothing without the people who make me look good. Half of what I feature on my socials are my mother's purses and shoes, which I've always done for free since her business hasn't been in the black for at least a decade, and if you tell a soul that, I'll tell the world *your* secrets too.

Also, because I can't list my faults without my brain going *there*, I can't eat carbs without gaining an inch on my hips, as my mother loves to remind me. And no matter how many times Naomi tells me that my weight doesn't define me as a person, I can't *unhear* the first lessons I got on self-worth.

But the thing is, I didn't expect a small-town plumber to be the one to turn down an offer that I haven't made—and wouldn't ever make—to much more famous, rich, and successful men.

To be fair, though, the men I'd usually date wouldn't have done what Dylan did for me and my family either.

They wouldn't know the first thing about switching out a water heater to give us real hot showers for the first time in well over a month.

And now I look like *that woman* trying to move in on another woman's man.

I grew up in a family whose dynamics were defined by the moments when my father was caught cheating, and I just found out my mother's no saint, either, despite the number of years she spent playing the scorned woman.

I do *not* want to be like them.

And I'm not doing so hot, considering I now accidentally look like I'm that apple sitting not so far from the tree.

"Okay?" Dylan asks, rubbing my back gently and sending sparks of lust all over my body with that simple touch, his voice close, still carrying no judgment, the warm tones settling the upheaval in my head and making morning a little more bearable.

Am I okay?

Not at all. "Yes. Thank you."

The microwave beeps, and I wince again.

Not because the noise hurts my head.

More because it makes him leap up, and now he's not touching me anymore.

"Ah, sorry. Hold on. Let me get that." He doesn't go far. The microwave's on the counter at the edge of the bed, which isn't so much a bed as it is a crude couch.

This whole place is tinier than my sister's new boyfriend's tree house—yes, I'm serious—but I guess you don't go big when you build a bunker.

You go survivalist.

It's a wonder the folding card table fit in here last night.

Dylan hits the button to pop open the microwave door, and saliva floods my mouth as the full scent of the microwave breakfast sandwich hits my nostrils.

"You owe me a favor," I croak out again.

He pulls the sandwich out of the microwave. "If that favor is walking you back to the school so you don't have to do the walk of shame by yourself, don't worry. I'll do that for free."

And that's one more damn thing to like about Dylan Wright.

"I'm involved with someone," he told me.

Yet he's willing to walk through town before six in the morning with another woman.

How—*how*—can anyone be that secure in a relationship that they're not worried about what that would look like?

I can't even handle the idea of being seen in public with him.

It says something, you know?

And I am *never* getting married. *Ever.*

When I have kids, I'm doing it on my own and then raising them with Naomi in Costa Rica, and they'll never, ever, *ever* know the family that I came from.

I don't know the first time I realized that money was the only redeeming quality about my family, and that *money* being our best quality meant that we were all pretty much shitty human beings.

My father, as noted, is a serial cheater who's spent his adult life working for Remington Lightly, the global consumer goods company that my grandfather founded decades ago. Dear old Dad has a law degree from Harvard and has spent his adult life doing as little as possible in Remington Lightly's legal department. He's one of those *networking on the golf course is a vital part of my job* people.

My mother's first love is her tarot cards, her second love is her reputation, and her third love is taking credit for her kids' accomplishments and blaming other people for her failures.

Until recently, my sister, Phoebe, was Robot Business Barbie whose sole mission in life was to step on everyone around her to climb the corporate ladder all the way up to CEO at Remington Lightly and look down her nose at the rest of us for *not actually doing anything* with our lives.

And the baby of the family, my brother, Carter, has spent most of his adult life living the rock star lifestyle—booze, weed, and groupies—while claiming to have writer's block for his next song. As *Carter Hardly*, he's had exactly one musical hit—kind of—and knowing our family the way I do, I wouldn't be surprised to find out he cheated to get it.

And we all basically hate each other, because who would *like* people like that?

Gigi brought us here to become a better family, and honestly, yes, I can tolerate Phoebe so much more today than I could two months ago—ever the achiever, she threw her heart and soul into fulfilling her mission so well that it actually *worked* on her, to the shock of all of us. She's traded her business suits for lady-lumberjack chic, smiles like she's found joy in her life, and is dating the town's grumpiest recluse and planning to stay here forever.

She also accidentally stumbled over me playing with chocolate, and even now, weeks later, she hasn't told a soul.

There might actually be hope for our relationship.

But the rest of them?

The past two months have reinforced that I don't want them. Nothing against Tickled Pink—the people here truly are lovely, and the town has real potential—but I *cannot* wait to leave again.

Which unfortunately requires my trust fund. So I'm stuck here for a while longer.

Dylan's lifting his brows at me, waiting for an answer.

"No, Pebbles and I can make it home okay. Thank you." Am I drooling? I think I'm drooling. Also, I should not waste my favor on jumping him and stealing his breakfast sandwich, no matter how good it smells and how much I'm struggling to keep drool from dripping out of my mouth.

I truly shouldn't.

I need that favor to be him agreeing to be a social media experiment for me, both because he's by far the most attractive man in Tickled Pink and also because the sooner I convince Gigi that Tickled Pink has a marketing strategy for the town to keep drawing in tourists after we're gone, the sooner I can get back to Costa Rica and Naomi and the farm.

"So that favor . . . ?" he says.

"I was just remembering," I lie. I need makeup and a shower and a serious pep talk before I tackle asking for that favor.

Also?

I would give my left arm for that breakfast sandwich.

He looks at me.

Then at the sandwich. "Got another one in the fridge."

"That's, like, *gross*," I make myself say.

His grin gets bigger.

And now I'm sweating.

It's fear of him seeing right through me. Definitely *not* more attraction to that gorgeous, kind smile.

And look at that. I'm still terrible at lying to myself.

"Hangovers are a bitch," he says. "Won't tell a soul if you need something to soak up what's roiling in your belly."

"I, like, don't eat meat and dairy products, and I don't know what's in those carbs. It's probably, like, half sugar."

Pebbles whimpers next to me.

Poor thing. She hates mornings too.

"And we should go," I say. "Pebbles needs to tinkle."

He squats—*gah*, the way his jeans mold to his thighs should be illegal—locks the fridge, shuts the cabinet door that hides the fridge, and rises, grabbing the still-wrapped breakfast sandwich that I would mug him for if I could do it without him knowing it was me.

"Right this way." He points to the door.

"I know how to get out." I toss my hair—it's what I'd do in any other social situation like this—and my brain howls in outrage. Right. No hair tossing until at least four miles into my morning wake-up run. "I mean, I know how I got in, so I know how to get out."

He's grinning again. "I'm following you, Tavi. Have to lock up."

Oh.

Right.

"How old is Pebbles?" he asks as I head for the stairs.

Literally no one in town has asked me that in the two months we've been stuck here. "She's four."

"Seems like a really good traveler."

"She is."

"Nice that she fits in your purse like that."

"Why are you so nice to me?" The question comes out of nowhere, and I wish I could take it back, but I'm not operating at full brain function this morning.

His steps echo on the metal stairs as he trails me up to the dark, starry morning. "Not much reason to be mean to you, is there?"

"Where I come from, you don't need a reason to be mean. Or to betray people. Or spread rumors. Or . . . well, basically do anything *but* be nice. And I . . . wasn't nice . . . to you."

"Eh. Mistakes happen. Lucky for you, you're in Tickled Pink now. We don't need a reason to be nice." He tilts his head. "Unless you're Teague."

God help me, now he's making me laugh. In the *morning*. While I can still smell the world's worst breakfast sandwich, which smells utterly delicious, and which I wish I were eating right now.

This vegan, sugar-free public persona sucks, for the record.

"Are you, like, planning to feed that thing to the wildlife?" I ask. Mental note: when I move to Costa Rica, I will no longer say *like* for any reason.

Ever.

I annoy even myself when it comes out of my mouth.

"Can't leave crumbs in the bunker. Which doesn't exist. Right?"

"I was never here."

Except for the favors.

I won favors off Dylan and Willie Wayne last night, and I owe Ridhi *something*.

To be determined.

As soon as I'm showered and ready, I'm cashing in that first favor.

Dylan Wright is about to become a social media star, because *duh*.

Of course he's the best option.

The internet won't know what hit it when a sweet, hot, dimpled small-town plumber invites them all to come visit him in his hometown.

And then—*then*—I can finally leave Tickled Pink behind and head to my own chosen home.

Chapter 4

Dylan

The Over Easy Café in Deer Drop is busy this morning, and I'm running late after making sure Tavi Lightly got out of the secret poker bunker.

Didn't mean to let her spend the night, but when she face-planted on the table right after the final round, I volunteered to get her home and close up.

Everyone else had a spouse to get home to. And I didn't specify *when* I'd wake her and get her home. Just that I would.

She looked like she needed that sleep.

And now, maybe she'll look me in the eye so we can get past that thing that I refuse to think about.

Not thinking about it right now, in fact. Right now, I'm thinking about Hannah, who's seated at a table by the window inside the café. She's already sipping her morning tea with two scrambled eggs and a slice of toast in front of her, as well as two over-easy eggs, a stack of pancakes, and a side of bacon waiting at the spot across from her on the red checkered tablecloth.

I'd rather be eating at Café Nirvana in Tickled Pink, but since Hannah moved from Tickled Pink to Deer Drop, I compromise and meet her when she's free. I'm over here often enough working jobs, so it's not like it's out of my way.

She smiles as I join her, as if I'm the best part of her day, and just like always, I get a punch to the gut that I let her get away.

Hard to call it that this morning, though.

Today, I'm having a full-on flashback to *you lost her because you never deserved her.*

Always great when teenage me puts his ugly opinions in my head, which he's been doing more and more since the Lightlys moved in.

Something about watching that old high school building come back to life is affecting me more than I want to admit.

But Hannah's always been the bright spot, even back then.

Today, her dark hair falls in spirals around her cheeks, and her light-brown skin glows more than usual. She always did seem to bloom in summer, when it's warmer. In winter, she goes into full hibernation mode, and then it's *can you go grab me more socks* or *here, warm my hands up.*

"Where were you last night?" she asks. "I tried to call to ask if you wanted to get together with Andrew and me to watch the ball game on Sunday, but my call went straight to voice mail."

"Can't tell you all of my secrets, or I'd lose my air of mystery." I grab my fork and dig into the eggs while she laughs at my joke.

Hannah and I have been best friends since third grade, when she saved me from the playground bully and I saved her from missing an assignment in art class by giving her mine to thank her.

She's seen me at my worst, and vice versa, though my worst is considerably worse than anything she's done. The fact that we're still friends says a lot more about her than it does about me.

She's the one person in the world who I don't keep a lot of secrets from.

Just that I have Tickled Pink Secret Poker Society nights one Thursday night a month and that I've been madly in love with her since about two seconds after she started dating Andrew, when I did the stupid man thing that every idiot in every romantic comedy ever does and didn't appreciate what I had until it was gone.

You know. The little stuff.

"Thanks for breakfast," I say. "I'll get it next time."

"Please. You get it every time. I got here extra early just to take my turn, and then you were three minutes late. And I repeat—where were you last night?"

"Hanging out with friends. You?"

"The usual." She laughs again. She has one of those magical fairy laughs that make you feel warm inside, and every time I think about Andrew being the guy who gets to listen to that every day—assuming he's not being his typical asshole self, and I don't call people assholes lightly, even if I seem to be the only person to call him an asshole—I want to punch him.

"So you ate dinner by yourself while Andrew worked late, binged your favorite *Game of Thrones* episodes, then went to bed with the lights on?"

"Hush." She rolls her eyes over her tea, but she's still smiling, and it makes me mad all over again that I was right.

I might not deserve her, but neither does he.

"Nailed it." I make a tally mark in the air. "That's seventy-four for me and two for you. What's wrong with your eggs? You haven't touched them."

"They sounded better when I ordered them."

I frown. "You sick?"

There are two correct answers from Hannah.

The first is *no, I ate something that didn't agree with me last night, and I'm still paying for it*, and the second is *no, but I have a big case at work today, and I have courtroom belly*.

She doesn't say either of those.

Instead, she makes a noncommittal noise, lets her eyes sparkle more, and sips her tea again.

My stomach drops like a brick tossed out of a plane without a parachute.

"No," I whisper.

Fuck me.

No.

This isn't happening.

But her growing smile says yes, yes it is.

"You wanna be my backup plan?" I asked her six years ago. "Like, if we both turn thirty and haven't met anyone else to marry and have kids with, you wanna just go for it?"

She said yes.

We started sleeping together.

"As friends," we agreed. "If someone we just hit it off with comes along, we call off the benefits, no harm, no foul."

We were on again, off again for those years we slept together, sometimes dating other people but not often.

Less and less frequently as the years went by, matter of fact.

Neither of us had slept with or dated anyone else for nearly two years when she met Andrew three days before my thirtieth birthday.

I had a ring picked out.

I had a speech prepared.

It wasn't the *best* speech—heavy on the *we've been friends forever and we're good in bed* and more or less nonexistent on the *and I care about you*—but that date was looming, and it seemed like the thing to do.

Not that she ever heard my speech.

She and Andrew started dating, and I pretended to be happy for her in public while licking my wounds in private and asking myself if it was my pride that was wounded or if it was something more.

And the first day she came over to my house, crying because they'd had a fight about which car she should buy, I realized I was *that* idiot.

I was that idiot who had willfully ignored all the signs that I was madly, completely, fully in love with her. I wasted years taking her for granted from my safe little cocoon where we got to be friends without me having to risk my heart. I was a damn fool who should've told her how special she was when she was mine, and who didn't.

Why? No idea. Maybe I still never felt like I deserved her.

Or maybe telling a woman *I love you* felt empty and meaningless after all the men my mother loved but who never loved her back.

What if I was that guy who wasn't any more capable of love than my stepfathers were?

The day after Hannah's fight with Andrew, it was all just a "misunderstanding," and they'd kissed and made up.

Six months later they got engaged.

She moved into his house in Deer Drop.

They eloped to a tropical island over the holidays and got married.

And now—

Now, I can't even think about what her bright, smiling face means, but I need to fake my way through being happy for her. "That's awesome, Hannah-Cabana. When's the little one due?"

"I have no idea what you're talking about," she whispers with a wink.

Translation: *Andrew doesn't want me to talk about it yet.*

I hate Andrew, and I don't hate many people.

Anymore.

"But," she adds, "I think it's safe to say that someone I'm married to won't be quite so concerned about what goes on my hips for the next few months."

I grunt.

"Oh, don't be like that." She reaches for my pancake and pinches a piece off. "You know he just worries about my health."

And I'm suddenly having another flashback to when I was the guy who would—scratch that. When I was the guy who *did* judge people on how they looked, who'd make comments about it in the school cafeteria or the gym or on the bus—or basically anywhere I got the opportunity.

I used to justify my snide remarks with *she was mean to Hannah* or *he told me my game sucked and deserved it* or *everyone else said the same thing*, but there's no excuse for being a dick. Still wish I could go back in time to muzzle myself, but I can't, so instead, I make a point to do better every day.

Even if it never feels like enough.

"Your mom know yet?" I ask her, though acknowledging the truth of her situation might not be better than ruminating about high school.

She sighs, then lifts a hand before I can twitch a single facial muscle. "Don't start. You know what'll happen the minute I tell her."

I smile, and I almost mean it. Eggs aren't sitting so great in my stomach, especially on top of that breakfast sandwich, but I keep eating. Long day today. Probably won't get lunch. Second breakfast is important. "I do."

"And there's no taking it back once it's out."

"She'll want you to quit your job."

Hannah slides a look out the window and sips her tea.

Peppermint.

I smell peppermint and surrendered dreams.

"You're gonna quit?" I ask her.

"I don't know. There's so much up in the air, and Andrew's mom stayed home with him, and he thinks it's really important. Plus, he travels so much. And it's not like I can't go back in a few years."

"I'm going to have it all," she told me once. "A fabulous job, the perfect husband, three kids, and a dog, and it'll be hard, but when I'm eighty-six and lording over my Thanksgiving table, issuing orders about who can put their elbows on the table and who owes me a quarter for saying a cussword, all fourteen of my grandkids will be like, *Glam-Glam has game. She's always been such a badass.*"

She said it with the kind of grin that suggested she was only serious about half of it, but I know Hannah.

I've known Hannah forever.

And I keep waiting for her to wake up and realize Andrew isn't the guy she thinks he is, and she's not living the life she always wanted.

"You're making a face," she says. "Quit making that face. I'm allowed to change my mind about what I want."

I scrub a hand over my scruff. "I know. I know. It's just—wow. This is—this is life-changing stuff."

"Yes, yes, I'm an old married woman with a 'big change' on the way, and you're still over there in Tickled Pink bacheloring it up and being the catch of the century," she teases.

If I were the catch of the century, we'd be sitting in a booth at Café Nirvana in Tickled Pink, thigh to thigh, looking at a baby registry together while our friends and neighbors tried to help, instead of her sitting across from me in a café packed with strangers, telling me she's pregnant with *Andrew's* baby.

I feel the way Tavi Lightly looked when she woke up this morning.

Ill.

Very ill.

"Fess up," she says. "You had a hot date last night, didn't you?"

"Nope."

"Dylan."

"Just hung out with friends."

"Like *famous* friends?"

"No." I pause. "I mean, yeah, Tavi Lightly was there, but she wasn't the reason I was hanging out."

"*Dylan.* You should totally go for it with Tavi Lightly! How often do you get the chance to say you dated one of the world's most famous . . . people."

People.

And not just *people* but *pause pause people.*

Right.

Social media influencer isn't exactly the kind of job people around here consider a *real* job, and *heiress* doesn't give her much credit either.

And I'm suddenly annoyed.

Ill over Hannah's news and annoyed on Tavi Lightly's behalf. She's nice enough, considering she comes from a highly dysfunctional family and has never had to learn to work for anything in her life.

Not her fault, and I'm the last person to judge anyone for what they choose to do with their life. God knows I was never perfect either. Won't ever be, much as I try.

Tavi gets points for putting her heart into everything she does around town since her grandmother made the family move here a couple of months back, though. And saving that damn duck. Humoring the local teenagers by occasionally getting mani-pedis with them on Patrice's back porch, which is where all the ladies in town go since Patrice had to sell her spa, which is now sitting vacant just off the square since the new owners—corporate types from Oshkosh—couldn't flip it. Getting involved like she has says something about a person's character, no matter how silly she might seem otherwise.

"She's not my type," I tell Hannah.

"No one's your type these days. You're working too much. It's killing your libido."

Work is definitely not the problem. "It's not killing my libido."

She frowns. "Are you in one of those *I don't deserve to be happy* slumps? Do I need to make some phone calls?"

I roll my eyes at her as I shove a piece of bacon into my mouth and try to pretend it tastes good and not like a chewy piece of three-day-old gum.

I love bacon, but it tastes like shit in the company of Hannah's news.

She'll know something's wrong and keep pressing if I don't keep eating, though. It's a rule. "When are you going to tell your mom?" I ask.

"Changing the subject? Totally unoriginal."

"So in about a year, then. *Hey, Mom, want to come over and meet your six-month-old grandchild?*"

She laughs again. "*Four*-month-old in a year. Also, you're terrible."

"Terribly right." And terribly disappointed.

Hannah was the one thing I got right when I didn't know I had it right.

No. That's not true.

I knew I got it right with Hannah. And that made her the one thing I was afraid I'd screw up when this would be a bigger screwup than anything I'd ever done.

Now, every passing day, I'm realizing she won't discover she made a mistake with Andrew.

I'm the one who's wrong.

I'm the one who's been wrong the past two years.

Six years, really.

I was never the guy she could've loved, no matter how much I've turned my life around since the days when she had no reason to stick by me but did anyway.

I was never supposed to be hers, and even if I was, I ruined that with everything I did as a kid.

Doesn't matter how many years it's been since I got my head screwed on straight. She knows more than anyone what I'm capable of when I make up my mind to be a total shit.

Who can blame her for not wanting that in her life? Or for not wanting to risk a kid with my genes?

Maybe I wasn't blind all those years we were friends with benefits.

Maybe I *did* know what I had, and I was too terrified she didn't feel the same to risk losing the one person who'd believed in me even in the years when I didn't believe in myself.

As if it mattered.

The end result is the same. She's not mine. She was never supposed to be mine.

And that's one extra pill I don't think I have it in me to swallow today.

I grab another piece of bacon, look at my watch, and make myself grunt. "Shit. Lost track of time. I gotta go. Mrs. Meierson gets cranky if I'm two seconds late." I lean across the table and peck Hannah on the cheek, like I always do. "Congrats, Cabana. Thanks for breakfast. Let me know if you need interference when you drop the news."

She gives me a look that says I'm being weird, but she'll let it go. For now.

"Enjoy unclogging those toilets."

"Always do."

Almost wish that were everything on my agenda today. But even clogged toilets wouldn't be as shitty as I feel right now.

Chapter 5

Tavi

I'm late for a family meeting.

Usually, I revel in pushing the line at being late. It makes Gigi furious. My mother freaks over Gigi being furious. My father grunts because he, too, bends to her will, though I think in his case, it's more path of least resistance than it is fear. And my brother and sister generally send me dirty looks for making things more unpleasant for all of us.

But this family meeting promises to be different from the meetings when we first got here to Tickled Pink two months ago and moved into the condemned school building that Gigi swears is good for our souls.

I don't know how mold, questionable electricity, cold showers, and dead animals in the hallway were supposed to translate to our souls improving, but Gigi doesn't like to do anything without torture.

I've spent the past two months trying to fly just under her radar, cleaning and helping at the school, running and taking selfies everywhere to keep up my reputation, blatantly defying the rule about no phones or internet to keep my socials going, schmoozing with the townsfolk who are fans and calling it community work, and sneaking off to work on my chocolate project at every opportunity.

Until my mother dropped the bomb of all family bombs and left a few weeks ago, followed closely by Phoebe telling Gigi off and walking away completely from the family business, leaving Gigi with nothing else to hold over either of them, my plans to keep all my balls in the air were working.

But now, when we gather every morning in the cafeteria for our daily save-our-souls assignments, it's just the three of us. Me, Carter, and Dad. Well, and Gigi's butler, Niles, who's her not-so-secret boyfriend, but he tends to stick to himself.

One, who can blame him? And two, Gigi isn't trying to save *his* soul. Apparently he's good enough in bed to avoid that fate.

Also?

Ew.

I keep wondering if Carter will bail, too, and go live with Mom or at least mooch her money. While he's become oddly more tolerable since we got to Tickled Pink, he still annoys me, mostly because he's a grown-ass adult who's more worthless than I pretend to be, getting preferential treatment when it comes to tasks around the school. I don't know why he's here, but I can guess it's a reason similar to mine.

Gigi's revoked access to the trust fund, and if he wants to ever get back to traveling the world looking for inspiration—or just screwing around smoking pot and doing groupies—he has to do his time with the family first.

As far as my father goes, I have no idea why Michael Lightly is still here.

Gigi can't freeze his trust fund—once we Lightlys turn thirty, it's ours, which means I was roughly ten months shy of freedom when Gigi choked—but even if she could, he's had access to it for so long, along with getting his corporate-lawyer salary from Remington Lightly, that he doesn't need his trust fund anymore. He could retire and live comfortably as a billionaire for the rest of his life. The *worst* worst thing he might have to do if she *could* hit him financially in any way is sell a house or two and a few of his cars.

The horrors.

Everyone knows he cheats on Mom, so it's not like Gigi could be lording that over him to keep him here.

Phoebe thinks Gigi threatened to get him kicked out of his golf club back in Manhattan, except he's not using his golf club membership now, and he could just buy his own golf club, so what does he care?

It's almost like he's here just to support the rest of us, which I would believe if we were any other family, but we're the Lightlys.

We don't do that.

And I probably shouldn't be late to family meetings if I ever want to get back to Costa Rica on a permanent basis.

So Pebbles and I hustle up the stairs from the locker room—yes, the *locker room*, where I shower every morning and where *the incident* with Dylan took place—and around the corner, past rows of ancient lockers that are slated for removal in a couple of weeks, and barrel into the cafeteria, hoping today isn't one of those days where Gigi makes us watch that horrific *Pink Gold* movie again.

Thank God I can play a good ditz and utilize plot summaries from the various placards that Phoebe's been getting rehung around town talking about how *this is where the blah-blah-blah scene was filmed in Pink Gold*, because I tune out and go into a meditative state every time Gigi turns it on.

Possibly it would be an okay movie if it hadn't been lorded over me as the path to my soul's eternal salvation since we got here.

I open my mouth to make excuses to Gigi for being late, and I promptly almost trip over my own two feet.

There are *five* people already in this room, when there should only be four—Dad, Carter, Gigi, and Niles.

I manage to recover quickly when Gigi opens her mouth, presumably to tell me I'm late, despite my growing horror at the unexpected fifth person sitting at the lone cafeteria table in the room built to hold twenty of them.

"God's watching, Gigi," I say before she can get a word out.

Carter sniffs at me. "You smell."

"God's watching you too."

And he's watching me watch that fifth person in the room, who should *not* be here, and who is the absolute complete and utter worst thing that could be happening right now.

"But you smell like . . ." He pauses and sniffs harder. "Bacon."

"I was doing charity work and didn't have time to wash it all off, Carter. You can't control what people around you eat." *Shit.* Did I not brush my teeth well enough after my shower? If he goes snooping in my room and finds my hidden stash of precooked bacon—which is *not* the best, but this was an emergency—I'm toast.

Lola Minelli smiles at me. "That's so kind of you, Tavi."

Yes, *that* Lola Minelli. The Lola Minelli who's not part of my family, who wasn't here yesterday, and who's sitting in my school cafeteria slash home kitchen right now, where she absolutely does not belong, for no discernible reason.

She's a social climber, attention seeker, star of the reality TV series *Lola's Tiny House*, heiress to a perfume-and-candle company, and, unfortunately, a more popular social media influencer than I am, despite the fact that I currently have a million more followers than she does.

I mean she's more popular with sponsors.

In the world of top-tier famous-for-being-famous social media influencers, there's no friendship, only competition.

And Lola Minelli is my biggest competition. I score an endorsement contract with Gucci—she gets one from Armani Beauty. She posts a picture in Seychelles wearing Bulgari sunglasses on a contract we were trying to nab, and my team goes to work trying to score a sunglasses deal with Cartier for shooting in Fiji, which we usually fail at, because I'm known for shilling my mother's purses, which are about seven levels below the Louis Vuitton and Hermès handbags that stock Lola's Hollywood Hills and Manhattan closets.

No one in the world sets my teeth on edge and makes me feel professionally inadequate quite like Lola, which is probably also my mother's fault. *Tavi, sweetheart, you could probably get a Gucci swimsuit deal for your socials if you lost a few pounds. It's just not fair that Lola's even skinnier than Phoebe, is it?*

And lest you think the rivalry is one sided, I have staff who work for Lola who assure me that it most definitely is *not*. *What do you think Tavi will do next, and how can we do it bigger?* is apparently a common question at her strategy team's regular meetings.

And her reality TV show? *Lola's Tiny House?* Don't tell me it was an accident she called it that when the one time I talked Phoebe into doing a reality TV show with me ten years ago, it was called *Tavi's Party House.*

Lola and I air-kiss in public, but the tabloids still speculate on which of us would come out on top if we had a claws-out battle on Rodeo Drive.

And if I'd known Lola Minelli would be here this morning, I would *not* have done those vodka shots last night, and I would've gone to bed around four yesterday afternoon. I haven't had enough food, enough sleep, or a long enough run to be at my best today.

Have I mentioned I hate this game?

"Lola." I lean down for cheek kisses, completely unsurprised that she smells like roses with a whiskey chaser. Her olive skin is flawless, her hair perfectly held back with diamond-studded barrettes, her brown eyes mildly bloodshot, but only if you look closely, and her lips definitely enjoy some collagen injections. "What a great surprise. Whoever would've thought we'd find you visiting Tickled Pink?"

"Oh my *gah*, when I heard Gigi was helping people find their souls, I was like, *How* could I not come? I've been on this *soul journey* after the first season of *Lola's Tiny House*, when I realized some people actually live in closets, and it's like, the universe just *gave me* this amazing *present* of suggesting that I volunteer for Gigi's program."

My heart sinks like Carter's rank on the charts when he releases a new single.

She's not passing through.

My biggest professional rival is *staying*. And not just staying but staying and calling my grandmother *Gigi* like she's one of the family.

And now on top of my headache, I want to gag. And also howl.

I miss Naomi. I miss Costa Rica.

And it's starting to sink in that I will never win my trust fund back.

Is this Gigi's goal? *Octavia, you've been such a disappointment here in Tickled Pink that I've brought in an alternate to serve as my granddaughter. I can save Lola's soul, and then I'll give her your trust fund, and then I'll give her your cacao farm, since she always does everything better than you anyway.*

It's how Gigi operates.

Find what will hurt the most to get the people around you to do what you want them to do.

It's not enough to threaten my farm.

She has to threaten to ruin my entire life.

I've wasted two months here when I should've been trying to find silent investors. The word *GoFundMe* just crossed my mind.

Oh God.

Is all of this hopeless?

I don't know if I have it in me to play nice with one more person from my old life.

Especially when that person is Lola.

She's five feet, seven inches of judgmental, backstabbing steel, with this long black hair that's so silky smooth that she got her start shilling shampoo. She's also forever wearing bodysuits that emphasize just how tiny her waist is.

If she comes back in another life, I hope she's either a dung beetle or a sperm whale.

She probably wishes the same for me.

I'm not sure which of us deserves the fate more.

Probably Gigi.

I'm going to lose my farm.

If nothing else that I've done here is good enough for her, and now she's bringing in *Lola*, who *everyone* knows is my biggest professional rival—I'm toast.

"That's so great that you're here to work on yourself with us," I gush.

Pebbles growls at me.

She hates when I play the ugly public version of me.

I swoop down and pick her up and press kisses all over her fur so no one can tell I'm on the verge of hyperventilating at the realization that I'm going to lose my farm.

No, I tell myself. *I will not lose my farm.*

And I repeat it to myself until I believe it and can actually smile at Lola.

Fake-smile, but still smile. "Isn't it the best to become better people when you're surrounded with your family and friends?"

"Oh, *totes*," Lola says.

Translation: *The rumors about my reality TV show not getting renewed are true, so I'm grabbing onto the next biggest story in the tabloids in the hopes that the publicity will change the studio's mind, or at least I'll get a few more endorsement deals bigger than yours until I find my new next big project.*

Oh, to have an optimistic bone in my body . . .

But it makes sense. If you live your life in the spotlight, you go where the spotlight is.

And lately, it's on Tickled Pink.

Between us—one of the world's richest families—moving here after Gigi's near-death, headed-to-hell experience, and then that little thing a couple of weeks ago with Phoebe's boyfriend, Teague, who's way more interesting to the entire world than you'd think a grumpy bearded fisherman who lives in a grown-up tree house would be, and also Phoebe's trick of continually falling in the lake while the locals who would sell pictures to Page Six were watching, there's definitely been an unexpectedly high level of tabloid attention here in backwoods Wisconsin.

"Lola will be an excellent addition to the family," Gigi says. "Octavia, she'll also be an excellent partner in your task of teaching Tickled Pink how to promote itself on its own."

I stifle a sigh and pretend I don't have a headache as I scrunch my nose in confusion. "Gigi, you just told me *yesterday* that that's what you wanted me to do."

"Phoebe figured out how to get involved in the community and how to put her talents to use without having to be told what to do."

Phoebe Phoebe Phoebe.

If it's not my mother telling me how skinny and pretty Phoebe is, it's my grandmother telling me how smart and driven Phoebe is.

And the worst part?

I actually *like* Phoebe now.

I sincerely doubt I'll ever say the same about Lola.

"Well, I'm *so glad* I'll, like, have such great help," I reply.

Pebbles growls again.

Lola gives me back the same fake smile I'm giving her. "Does your dog have rabies?"

"No, she just has taste." *God*, I hate living this life. I follow the statement by lifting Pebbles so we're cheek to cheek, pulling out my phone, and snapping a selfie. *Eat your heart out, Lola Minelli. You don't have a dog to make you look like you have a soul.* "Niles, do you mind if I invade your kitchen to get her a little snacky-snacky?"

"You got a new subscription box of those organic vegan treats yesterday," the older man replies. He's clearly amused by all of this, like he has no idea he's sleeping with the woman who probably gave birth to Satan in one of her previous lives. "I put them in your room."

"Oh, *fabu*. Thank you so much, Niles. I'll just get her some oatmeal now, and then we'll get the treats later."

Pebbles hates those. Can't blame her. What dog wants to eat dehydrated cauliflower and kale?

"You'll sit now and feed your dog later," Gigi replies as Niles rises and heads to the kitchen, undoubtedly because he's reading all the *fetch the hangry influencer some food* vibes coming off one or more of us. "Right now, we need to discuss how we'll be supporting Phoebe as she gets a new Ferris wheel built and opens her taffy shop."

Good *God*. She's already opening a candy shop too?

"I could, like, open an organic vegetable shop on the other half of whatever building she rents," I offer.

"Oh, honey, being vegan is *so* yesterday," Lola says. "You'd get *so* many more endorsement deals if you'd back the new *all food can be good food* movement."

"Yes, but if we don't have our principles with our platforms, what do we have?"

I have zero principles. Possibly negative principles. Secrets, though? Those I have in spades.

I turn to Gigi before she can expose any that she happens to be aware of, which is probably all of them, given what I already know she knows. Although, considering some of the things I've gotten away with since moving here, maybe she *doesn't* know all. "So if we're expanding the save-your-souls project, will Uncle George and his family be joining us next?"

It's like painting a giant red bull's-eye on myself.

And I don't care.

I'm so tired of this. No amount of Gigi pretending that she's pleased with our progress or that she's not inviting Lola here to make me *more* miserable or that she's kinder than she was two months ago will convince me that she's not the devil.

"Legit question," Carter pipes up, and I find myself in the increasingly more common but still rare position of wanting to hug my brother. "He's been to prison. Best we know, Lola hasn't."

Uncle George is, in fact, still *in* prison. Gigi hasn't talked to or about her other son since he was convicted of tax fraud.

"I did this *so fascinating* tour of a prison one time, and I accidentally got locked in *the coldest* jail cell, and, like, everyone forgot about me except my cameraman for, like, *days*," Lola offers, which is remarkably kind of her, considering there are probably beings in other solar systems who can tell Gigi's about to blow.

"Wasn't how that episode went," my father mutters.

"Octavia, God is watching you as well," Gigi says, for once not taking the bait about Uncle George, which is just as terrifying as anything else since we got here. "And I'm sure God's disappointed that you've wasted all of the gifts and resources you've been given and continuously snipe at your family instead of trying to fit in."

Shut up, Tavi. Shut up, shut up, shut up. "But being a family is, like, so hard when you've never had a good example."

That self-talk is clearly working well for me.

It's like I *want* to ruin all my dreams.

Or possibly I'm just extra frustrated because Gigi keeps changing the rules.

Your job is to sweep and mop and paint and clean this school, Octavia. That's how you'll improve your soul.

No, Octavia, your job is to get involved with community activities and help the snowshoe baseball team win.

Octavia, didn't you hear me? I said your job is to get along better with your parents.

And now, two months in, when she's changed my "job" seven bazillion times, it's *your job is to train the people of Tickled Pink to promote the town themselves, but since you didn't decide to do it on your own, I've brought Lola Minelli in for added torture.*

She put so much effort into making Phoebe's life a living hell the first month or so that we were here that she forgot about the rest of us. And now that Phoebe told her off and moved out of the school to live with Teague and then my mother left, too, my grandmother has more time to focus on her next victim.

Gigi is finally losing her cool. You can tell because it's starting to smell like sulfur and vengeance. "If you don't want to be here, Octavia, you know where the door is. And you know the consequences."

Not for the first time this summer, my gut tightens.

But unlike every other threat Gigi has made, this one comes with a look shifted to Lola. "God likes good work to be rewarded."

I knew it.

I need a new business plan for the farm and our chocolates, and I need it yesterday.

"God doesn't like bullies," Dad says, louder. "Mother, none of us will ever meet your criteria for 'being better people' if you expect it to mean that we kowtow to your ridiculousness for months on end for no reason other than to make yourself think you're right."

Gigi's death glare switches to my father. "Excuse you?"

"You can't treat *one* person like she's saved and the rest of us like we're misbehaving children when we're all doing the work."

"Are you doing the work, Michael? *Are you?*"

Lola squeaks like she can't stand conflict, despite conflict being as essential as oxygen in her—*our* line of work. "Oh, wow, being part of a family is *so hard*. It's, like, worse than economics class."

Gigi's eyelid visibly twitches.

My father glares at her.

"And they wonder why I can't write a fucking song when I'm surrounded by this," Carter mutters, as if he's actually written a song in the past five years instead of pretending he's trying to.

"We'll continue this discussion when we can all put our best feet forward." Gigi's seething. She's not yelling or growling or sticking her nose in the air, but her jaw is ticcing and her nostrils are flaring and her cheeks are going pink.

And now I'm having a solid case of the regrets.

She does *not* forget, and despite what Phoebe thinks, Gigi doesn't forgive either.

My father grunts.

Niles marches in from the kitchen with a tray laden with—you know what?

I don't think I want to know what's on that tray.

They'll call it breakfast. That's all we need to know.

Gigi looks at him, and her jaw visibly relaxes, and the pink stain fades from her cheeks. "Thank you, Niles, that looks delicious."

"Looks like what Tavi's dog ralphed up after too many of those vegan treats last week," Carter replies.

And there she is.

There's the grandmother that I know and can't stand, rising thirty feet tall and igniting her eyeballs on fire. "I'm beginning to think I should give all of your trust funds to people who actually *appreciate* what they have and who *do the work* and who show up when they don't even *have* to be here." She glances at Lola, once again reinforcing my assumption that Gigi has no interest in changing her own habits and patterns to be a better person herself.

When Uncle George went to prison, *his* trust fund—and the trust funds of all his kids—suddenly disappeared, and my father's and his family's got a little bigger.

Carter snorts. "Yeah, we're all becoming better people if we're just doing it for the money." He rises and gives me a look that I'm nearly certain means, *We're all going to hell, so this is pointless.*

It's not pointless.

I was doing good with my trust fund. My influencer salary, too, which is also taking a hit, since so few high-end companies want pictures posted of their products in places where the prettiest scenery is a murky lake.

There's only so much my team has to work with right now, and even our backup plan isn't much of an option so long as people know I'm trapped here.

"I'm *so* excited to work with everyone here for the pure joy of it," Lola says. "Everyone's so . . . unique, and they have such a fresh perspective on life."

Translation: *These people are weirdos.*

Gigi sniffs. "At least someone is doing it for the right reasons. And that always calls for a reward."

And I want to scream again.

I *am* doing good things in the world.

But I can't say that here.

Because for all of Lola Minelli's show of hating conflict, I have zero doubt she'd be the first person to throw me under the bus if she knew I sometimes eat meat, that I'd sell my mother's secrets if I thought they'd make me enough money, where I spend several hours most nights, and what all I'm up to.

I can't go on like this.

I can't.

It's finally crystal clear what I should've been doing this whole time.

I have to find an investor for my chocolate business. Someone *not* related to me or with ties to my family so that I can finally be free.

And I need to do it yesterday.

Chapter 6

Tavi

Saturday morning, I'm back to my usual self.

Ha.

Not even.

I'm *physically* sort of okay—I managed to get to bed at a reasonable hour last night, partly because I was afraid Lola would follow me if I went where I wanted to go—but mentally?

Mentally, I'm trying to find something positive about my life on a long run before the sun and the bugs are up. And that positive is checking in with Naomi, hoping for more good news. I dial her once I'm fully awake.

"First things first," she says. "Please don't kill Lola Minelli, because I need you here and not in jail, okay?"

"I'm not going to murder Lola Minelli." I pull a face in the dim light off the setting moon as I loop the far side of Deer Drop Lake, which separates Tickled Pink from their rival town. She's connected through the Bluetooth earbud that I usually hide in the basement of a local closed-up church, along with all my other secret kitchen equipment. "Maybe my grandmother for inviting her, but not Lola."

"Don't murder your grandmother either. But speaking of awful things, our taste testers confirmed that we should not, in fact, put oregano in any chocolates *ever*."

"Good to know. I got your last package but also the note that you had to go beg beans off a different farm. What's up with that?" Since I arrived in Tickled Pink, Naomi has shipped me beans and sometimes processed chocolate in boxes disguised to look like subscription boxes and influencer swag packs so that I can continue to develop truffle recipes for our taste testers while we finally work on that business plan that'll make our farm and chocolate business profitable.

I don disguises and occasionally dash over to the Deer Drop post office to mail back samples for her.

"All the staff at the farm we usually use would say is that they had an 'issue with harvesting,'" she says. "Sebastián heard a rumor that the owners might be looking at selling. And that would be *prime* real estate, *with* productive trees. Productive *organic* trees, Tavi. We seriously need to talk about this plan you have for getting investors."

"Working on it."

"I'm equal parts desperate to expand and launch and get profitable and also scared that all of this is a terrible idea. The chocolate market is crowded. It's a boutique internet world now, and if we want to stand out, then we have to be unique, and I don't know that *we're rebuilding a community through love and chocolate* is unique enough."

"It's not like everyone's doing it."

"Enough other people are, though. Some with pretty big platforms. And I shouldn't question your marketing skills. I really shouldn't. But 'we'll get a social media influencer to sell the product'? That's not enough, especially when you can't do it yourself. We need a marketing *budget*. We need a plan. We need you to sleep so your brain can work, because I know you know this stuff. *I'm a computer engineer from Nebraska.* I'm not a business-savvy chocolate goddess who can see how we can make an affordable offer on the farm next door when we don't have any income or prospects for income. That's *you*."

And once again, I realize just how dumb this whole plan was.

I'm not business savvy.

I'm not even a chocolate goddess.

I'm simply working with what *feels* good and slowly realizing that I'm a pampered, spoiled brat who's never been told no, and now that I have, I can't make it on my own.

I've lived in a bubble.

A privileged, safe, never-wanting-for-anything-that-could-be-bought-with-money bubble.

Even failing as an influencer isn't a big deal.

For one, no one knows I'm a failure. I *look* good, thanks to good photographers and makeup artists and a travel budget, and I *do* make money, but after expenses and other commitments, it's not enough to keep the farm running.

Until Gigi choked on that piece of steak, it didn't matter. I had my trust fund to use for my favorite projects. But now, all I have is my influencer salary, and guilt won't let me stop sending my regular donations around the world to support schools, shelters, and medical clinics.

I'm broke and getting broker by the minute.

"Let me make some phone calls to some people that I have a lot of dirt on." God, I hate this life.

And I hate worse that I'm saying these words to Naomi.

Ever since we met, she's believed in me. Even *when* we met, in those awkward moments as she was lying in the stairwell of my bus, her leg *clearly* broken after she'd tripped trying to get away from me, she was all, "You're so nice to worry about me," and then she told me she was so glad that I actually ate real food that tasted good, because she'd always hoped my life would be better than lettuce and beans and sit-ups, because no one should suffer like that, and then she didn't tell anyone my secret.

Not even when she went viral six months later for proposing to a clownfish as she came out of anesthesia after having her tonsils removed, and a reporter discovered she knew me, but no matter how much anyone pressed, she kept her cool and never once even hinted at the gossip that could've destroyed me.

Not. Once.

Instead, she was all over doing interviews, graciously calling me kind and pretty and her favorite celebrity that she'd ever met.

I pinged her to congratulate her on her five minutes of fame after seeing her on the *TODAY Show*, and she replied that she'd rather have her tonsils removed again than be internet famous for five more minutes, and she was just so funny and honest and *real*, while still keeping my secret, that we ended up becoming friends.

I crashed her birthday party a couple of months before my Costa Rica trip, mostly because she'd made a joke on email that her grandma was my biggest fan, and I wanted to know what a normal grandma was like.

Turns out Grandma Clementine was a hoot.

And so I invited both of them to join me for my shoot in Costa Rica and a little touristy stuff afterward.

And then the cacao farm happened.

While they were with me.

Grandma Clementine took the secret to her grave entirely too soon afterward, robbing me of more time with the woman I'd started to wish were my real grandmother.

Naomi has kept the secret ever since. She even used the small inheritance she got from Grandma Clementine to quit her job and move to Costa Rica.

"I'm young, single, and it gives my parents indigestion to think that I'm throwing my life away," she said cheerfully at the time.

And even through the hard times, with stuff like fungus and mice and other *I never even knew that was a thing on cacao farms* incidents, she hasn't once said she regrets the three years she's lived in Costa Rica.

I'm wondering if that's about to change.

"Do you know anyone who would help you because they *want* to be associated with you and who would agree to invest in our business without planning on stabbing us in the back eventually too?" Naomi asks.

That she would have hope that a person like that actually exists is one more reason I love Naomi.

I mentally flip through my contacts list, eliminating person after person, consider asking Teague for help, and immediately squash that idea too.

I hate being used, and so the last thing I'd do is use my sister's boyfriend when Teague's made it so very, very clear that he hates that he, too, comes from money.

Plus, asking favors from family is complicated.

See also: me trapped here in Tickled Pink because I tried to save the world in my own way with the family money. "I still have a few ways to keep my name out of it."

"Maybe we could use your name."

"No. That won't work. It really won't."

"Then we need Samantha."

"Oh, *hell* no."

"Tavi—"

"The last time we did that, I almost got caught." I'm running, and I'm puffing, and I'm whispering, because I do *not* want to talk about Samantha.

"You, me, a professional marketing plan, truffle samples, meetings with venture capitalists in person. I spent yesterday doing research on start-ups, and I honestly think our investors need to see both of us together for us to sell this properly. They need to know that the brains behind this operation are committed, no matter what it takes, and if all they have is your social media profile or my word that an *anonymous silent business partner without money* is steering me through all of this . . ."

I know Naomi. She didn't research *yesterday*. She's been prepping for this while I've had my head in the sand, thinking I could get my trust fund unfrozen despite the fact that I like to mouth off to my grandmother. "I know. *I know.*"

"And that means we need Samantha."

"Naomi—"

"You *didn't* get caught. She's good. You *won't* get caught. We can—I don't know, give you a cold or something. Or measles. Or northern-Wisconsin encephalomumps."

"Northern—*what?*"

"I don't know! I'm making stuff up! But I know investors need to see that we know what we're doing, and I think you have more faith in me than I deserve, and *I can't do this on my own.*"

"Oh, honey, you can. But you're right. You shouldn't have to. Just—I'm working on something that will hopefully get me out of here soon." I have nothing. I truly have nothing. Even if I make everyone in Tickled Pink a social media star, Gigi will just find something else for me to do. "Just give me one more day to—*aaaaahhh!*"

My foot connects with something squishy, and I go flying.

"Flaabbaaanagaaaah," a deep male voice groans.

"Tavi?" Naomi says.

The concrete of the lake path greets me like a fist to a punching bag, and a man groans again.

"Dylan?" I gasp.

Where am I? Am I back on the Tickled Pink side of the lake already? Or is he lost?

"Ain't no tears, like my beers, got no ears," the local plumber sing-songs in the dark.

"Tavi?" Naomi repeats. "Are you okay? What's going on? Don't you hang up on me. It took you three days to call me back after the last time you hung up on me."

"I'm good," I tell her. I think I'm good. My arms will be scratched up, and my knee is bruised, and I'm disoriented and possibly in danger of moving wrong and landing in the lake, which is Phoebe's thing, not mine, but my face survived, and I don't think I twisted anything. "I'll call you back. Or text. I didn't wait three days to text."

I hang up the phone, then use it as a flashlight.

And there's Dylan.

Curling onto his side on the path, an empty bottle of Jack Daniel's next to him.

"Are you dead?" I whisper. I know he's not. I can see his chest moving and his mouth opening, but he's not even flinching at the light.

I hate light on a normal morning, but when I'm *actually* drunk and hungover?

It's like death with a side chaser of seeing my grandmother naked.

"Whishkey don' kill the pain." He sings it. He's drunk-singing to some tune he's making up on the fly, and even totally foxed, his voice is amazing. "She'll never be mine a-gain."

Oh.

I test my body, making sure I'm not any more injured than a few scrapes here and there, and then scoot over next to him while he keeps warbling, but the words have gone incoherent.

"You got dumped?" I ask quietly, ignoring the heavy thump of my heart that has nothing to do with my jog or my farm or missing Naomi and being afraid I'll lose my farm, and everything to do with being close to the cute plumber who was number one on my list of people to find after the sun came up today, since he disappeared from Tickled Pink completely yesterday.

Or if not *disappeared*, at least avoided public places.

Good news? Lola doesn't know he exists.

Bad news? It won't stay that way for long.

"Washn't mine, but I luuuuuurrve her anywaaaaaaays." He's still singing it, but he pauses and sniffs. And then it's back to the singing. "An' you smell like potato peels sticking up a garbage disposal."

Yes.

He *sang* that.

"Thank you. You smell like a distillery. What are you doing here?"

"Live here. Not like you. You don' live here. You're press—tess—protest—"

"Trespassing?" I suggest.

"Uh-huh."

Dylan's one of the few people in town who haven't actively been suspicious or tried to get rid of my family.

Him calling me a trespasser now? That hurts.

"Did I step on you?" I ask.

"Don' care."

"You will in a few hours."

He twists and rolls over to fling an arm across my thighs and bury his face in my hip. "Quit rockin' the boat."

"We're on land, Dylan." And he's snuggling me, and God help me, I would sit like this for the next seven years, because he's adorable and as real as Naomi, and I could soak this up forever.

I like *real*.

I hate the games.

I hate hiding.

I just want to disappear back to Costa Rica, be able to afford launching our inaugural line of products, and figure out how to expand operations without the benefit of my trust fund, which is honestly terrifying.

I hate the money but don't know how to live without it.

I hate that I'll have to trust anyone we'd let invest in our business to not screw us over, and that I'll spend the rest of my natural life waiting for the other shoe to drop if we do find an investor.

I also hate that I'm letting myself run my fingers through Dylan's hair. This is what you do for a friend when he's down and out, right? I'm not coming on to him.

He's drunk. Of course I'm not coming on to him.

"You wanna talk about it?" I ask.

He's quiet for so long I think he's fallen back into a drunken stupor. But then—"She's having his baby."

The singing is gone. The slurring is almost gone.

All that's left is pain in a sound wave.

Naturally.

Cheating sucks. Even when it's part of your normal, everyday life— and it very much is back in Manhattan, and also in LA, and anywhere my parents are—it still sucks.

"Oh God, Dylan, I'm so sorry," I whisper.

"Dumb me," he mutters.

"No, it's never dumb to love someone. And you—you're such a nice guy."

He snorts. "*Not* a nice guy."

"Yes, you are, and it makes me so mad that someone would do this to you. You deserve better. Do you hear me? Don't ever settle for anyone who makes you feel like this."

He's quiet for a long time again.

"Not a nice guy," he repeats quietly.

"I didn't say you were *perfect*. I said you were *nice*. And you are to me."

More silence, but this silence comes with his arms tightening around my hips, like he's clinging to my belief in him, which is crazy.

He *is* a nice guy.

But then, the world thinks I'm a vegan and sugar-free fitness freak.

What if he has just as many secrets and failings as I do?

He sucks in a big breath. "Never told her I like the Vikings better than the Packers."

A surprised laugh bubbles out of me. "If you can't tell the woman you're dating that—"

"Not dating."

I wrinkle my nose at him. *Okay.* So maybe he's right. Maybe he's *not* a nice guy. "You have *multiple* people that you're seeing?"

Wow.

Glowers really glow in the dark. Or maybe the sun's starting to come up.

"I said I'm *involved.*" He's not slurring his speech anymore, nor is he singing, but I honestly wish he were. Instead, he's turned his face back into my hip, and his voice is undulating grief muffled by my leg as he speaks into the spandex of my jogging pants. "I'm *emotionally* involved with someone who's *emotionally* unavailable. I've seen *Love Actually*, and that movie fucking *sucks.* That dude who shows up to tell his friend that he loves her after she's married? He's a dick. Julia Roberts in *My Best Friend's Wedding*? She's a dick. I'm not a dick anymore. I try really hard to *not* be a dick *ever.* I used up all my dick on the dick meter a long time ago, and I don't have any dick left. I don't break up married couples. I don't make my friends' lives more complicated because I can't deal with my feelings. And I don't date other people to fill a void."

It takes me a minute to find the right words.

And while I'm searching, he rubs his nose against my sweaty hip. "I didn't know I loved her until she was gone. And now I can't tell her. Couldn't tell her either. Maybe I don't love her. Maybe I just love the idea of her because she was easy and there and she didn't judge me when I deserved it."

And then I find my voice, but not my brain. *"You turned down a blow job because you're in love with a married woman?"*

"I want a tomato."

"That's not an answer."

For like a *month*, I've avoided Dylan Wright like the plague after he gave us hot water in the school locker room showers for the first time since we arrived in Tickled Pink.

I was standing there with him, in the locker room showers, and he turned on the water after squatting and bending and using all the tools on his tool belt to install the new water heater, and he has a *very* nice ass and *very* nice thighs, and the way he grinned at me when I shrieked with joy and started tearing up over having hot water after living in the school without it for weeks—I thought he liked me.

I thought it was us taking the flirting to the next level after the flirting I thought we'd been doing at the bar the three or four nights before that.

I dived for him and kissed him and then squatted and reached for his belt buckle, thinking we had this connection and also that all my acquaintances in New York and LA would die if they knew I wanted to go down on a plumber, until he put his hands on my shoulders, made a noise, backed up, and said, "I prefer payment in cash."

I was impulsively trying to show my gratitude—wrongly, I know, *I know*—and he was all, "I prefer cash." Gently, but he still said it. He had to, because I was completely and totally wrong.

And then he added the kicker. "And I'm involved with someone."

I shouldn't have been upset or offended. I shouldn't.

But my brain didn't hear *I'm unavailable and prefer cash*.

It heard the same thing I've felt from my family for years.

You're not good enough, Tavi.

Me.

Tavi Lightly, international social media influencer, heiress to one of the world's largest fortunes, dater of celebrities and athletes and politicians, and a small-town plumber rejected me.

I mean, duh. Of course he did. He has principles and knows what a good family is and cares about things other than how he looks on Instagram and if his last TikTok got enough views to satisfy his sponsor.

I was so mortified I could barely apologize, and I've been avoiding him ever since.

More than avoiding him, actually.

Actively ducking him every time I saw him until I made myself follow him to that bunker the other night. I basically had to, because ducking him was the first thing he saw me do *after* the incident in the locker room showers.

And honestly? Continuing to duck him after he thought I was so desperate to get away from him that I'd step in front of a garbage truck instead of saying hi was easier than facing him.

I was raised from birth to know how to be in public with someone when I'm still mortified over something I did to them or in front of them. I know how to pretend it didn't happen. I was winning beauty pageants before I was old enough to remember the dresses I wore or the feeling of being onstage, and if I could own that world when I was three, then I shouldn't be twenty-nine and unable to talk to a regular man.

But I couldn't be around him without feeling like a bigger idiot than I've ever felt like before, and it was easier to duck and hide than it was to acknowledge that I have a schoolgirl crush on him.

Now, knowing the full story—*It wasn't you, Tavi. It's that I'm in love with someone I'll never have, and I like it that way*—I think I like him *that much more*.

Dylan Wright has a chink in his armor—maybe several, based on that little dick speech—and despite the fact that I should be offended to the pit of my soul that this nobody would reject me merely because *he had a crush on someone else*, I'm actually swooning more.

This is the sweetest chink ever.

I can't even imagine if my life were so simple that *I won't sleep with other people while I'm waiting for the one I love* was my biggest problem.

"How do men like you actually exist?"

"You're really loud."

"I'm whispering."

"And I still want a tomato." He shoves to sitting, grabs his head, and sways into me.

I reach my arms around him to steady him, my heart once again doing backflips, and he goes completely still.

Is he going to kiss me?

Or even hug me back?

Does he want some physical solace now?

Is this the moment that I finally hook up with Dylan Wright and work him out of my system by being his rebound?

No, idiot, it's the moment when you act like a good friend and get your shit together.

I suck in an unsteady breath, and as I'm tightening my grip around him, he twitches.

I drop my arms.

One rejection is enough.

I don't need to hold on for more.

He flips over to crawl on all fours off the path around the lake and up into someone's yard.

Dammit.

Celebrities and professional athletes, Tavi. You date celebrities and professional athletes. Not small-town plumbers.

My soul really could use some work, couldn't it?

"Where are you going?" I whisper as I watch Dylan crawl up the short hill. There's a house basically right above us onshore. I can only see its outline in the dim morning light, but I know the house.

It's this adorable redbrick bungalow with a wraparound porch that makes me think of Hallmark Channel Christmas movies every time I jog past it. If I ever build a real house in Costa Rica, I want it to look like that house.

That house says, *Come in and have a cookie.* It says, *We'll make you feel at home.*

I am such a sucker for *home.*

I think that's half of why I love Naomi so much. She feels like the kind of home the Hallmark Channel says everyone can have.

"Hungry," Dylan says, his voice a little more slurred now. "Can't walk. Need tomatoes."

Tomatoes.

While I, the supposed sugar-free vegan, would give my left arm for a sausage-and-egg sandwich when mornings dare invade the world too few hours after two measly shots of vodka, Dylan drinks a whole bottle of whiskey and then wants *tomatoes*.

"You can't invade someone's garden for hangover tomatoes." The things I've said since moving here.

"*My* tomatoes." He disappears in the darkness, and I pull up my phone's flashlight to follow him once again.

The man's on all fours, making his way down a row of tomato plants, *sniffing* at them.

"Just because you want them doesn't make them yours."

He grunts, plucks a ripe tomato off the vine, plops on his back in the dirt, and takes a bite like it's an apple. *"Mmmm."*

Seeds dribble out the side of his mouth.

I've seen some weird things in my life, but I've never seen a man crave tomatoes for his hair of the dog.

Actually—

Those tomatoes look really good.

Yes, yes, I'm a fake vegan. But that doesn't mean I fake that I like vegetables. They're just not *all* that I like. "It's a good thing you all know each other around here." I sit down next to him—who would I be if I left the man to fend for himself in this state?—and I pluck a tomato off a vine too.

"My tomatoes," he repeats.

I bite into the plump flesh, and the possession in his voice registers as the tangy, sweet flavor of the world's most perfect tomato hits my tongue. "Oh my God, this is good," I say.

"Course it is," he scoffs. "I don't grow shit."

It takes a minute for me to catch on that he doesn't mean he didn't grow this.

He means he wouldn't grow crappy stuff. "You grew these?"

"My tomatoes."

"This is—this is your house?"

He grunts again.

A light pops on above us, over the swing on the cute wraparound porch.

An older lady I recognize from around town peers into the darkness. "Dylan? Dylan, honey, did you sleep in the garden again?"

Oh my God.

"Yeah, Ma," he calls back.

"Sweetie, are you drunk? Oh, Dylan. Honey. Come on in, and let's get you put to bed. I'll make you a BLT while you sleep it off, and then we can talk about what happened."

"It's *one night*, Ma. We don't have to talk about anything."

"Sweetie—"

"Not alone, Ma," he calls while tomato dribbles down his chin.

Oh my God again.

He lives with his mother.

Dylan Wright, the adorable, kind, helpful, loyal small-town plumber who apparently has a guilt complex about *something*, still lives with his mother.

In the house that I sigh over every time I loop this lake in the daylight.

"I think I might see the first problem in why you didn't get the girl," I whisper to him. "But don't worry, Dylan. Tavi Lightly is on the job."

Gigi wants me to teach Tickled Pink to support itself once we're gone.

And I've just figured out my way in to doing so much more.

Chapter 7

Dylan

This is a bad idea.

Worse than bad.

Terrible.

It's been roughly forty-eight hours since Tavi Lightly tripped over my drunk ass at the lake, and after a weekend spent bingeing her TikTok and Instagram feeds, my regrets are growing by the minute.

Unfortunately, so are my hopes.

Can't get over Hannah if I don't get back on that dating horse.

Actually, I probably could. But left to my own devices, six years from now I'll still be debating if I should join a dating app when I get the news from my doctor that I have early erectile dysfunction or something.

It's time.

Tavi's called in that favor I owe her, and in the process, she's suggested this can be my push to getting back out into the world.

God help me.

"Hey, Dylan," Bridget Miller says as she swings into Café Nirvana way earlier than a teenager like herself should ever be up on a summer Monday morning. She's about three inches shorter than I am, white, with her dad's brown hair, sporting rainbow peace sign earrings in her ears and wearing a bright-purple Sparrow County High Allies Club T-shirt. Bridget has the distinct honor of having the best parents in all of Tickled Pink. She was the *whoops*-baby result of a one-night stand that brought Teague here to marry Shiloh Denning, whose mother put Tickled Pink on the map when she insisted on shooting and starring in *Pink Gold* here before I was born. A couple of years after Teague and Shiloh's amicable divorce, Shiloh married Ridhi. Now, the three of them are coparenting goals, as evidenced by how awesome Bridget is. Plus, how many other teenagers would not only be up this hour on a summer Monday but be heading straight to their stepmother's café at the same time?

I nod to her. "Morning, Bridge."

"You look like you ate pickled skunk for breakfast."

"*Bridget.*" Anya, the café's co-owner and Ridhi's sister, which makes her Bridget's stepaunt, gives her a stink eye stinkier than any skunk could.

"She's just calling it like she sees it," I tell Anya. "And she's not wrong."

I feel a little like I ate pickled skunk for breakfast.

I mentioned the *bad, bad idea* part, right?

"I heard Tavi telling her grandma she's on her way here to see you," Bridget says. A sly grin spreads across her cheeks. "So. You and Tavi, huh? That's so swag. I mean, she actually said she was going to meet 'the plumber,' and you could do better than someone who defines you like you go around showing your crack, but—"

"*Bridget,*" Anya says again.

I could date Anya. We've known each other forever. Her parents met when they were part of the *Pink Gold* catering crew, and they stuck around to raise their family here after because they liked the vibe. Anya's attractive—brown skin, wide smile, killer Yahtzee skills, curves for days—and I could probably learn to love her if I tried.

Plus, she's friends with me despite the shit I pulled on her when we were kids.

That friend part could be a complication, though.

I'm not exactly killing it in the dating world with falling for friends, but I'm older and wiser now. And as Tavi herself said the other day, I'm a nice person.

I'm not the shithead I once was, and the people in this town have forgiven me for everything from setting off firecrackers in the middle of the night on random weeknights to spreading so many rumors about Mrs. Salcedo, the high school drama teacher, that she ultimately retired early.

I push away the guilt that *still* pokes its head up when I think about all the shit I did when I was Bridget's age, and I force a smile at Anya.

This could work.

She squints at me from behind the bakery counter. "Are you okay? Bridget's not actually wrong. You look like crap. And I heard you slept in your garden the other night. That seems . . . ominous. Not that one night of getting drunk means anything. It's just . . . not . . . like you. Anymore."

Honesty. Honesty's a good quality in a life partner. It's good that she'd call me on things and that we can talk about my past. "You wanna grab lunch sometime?" I blurt.

Anya's brows twist in an Olympics-worthy performance. Bridget stares at me like I grew a shower faucet where my nose is supposed to be.

They look at each other.

Bridget makes a noise, ducks under the counter, and heads for the kitchen. "Gotta talk to Ridhi," she squeaks.

Shit.

It's bad when Bridget won't say what's on her mind. She *always* says what's on her mind.

Anya blinks at me.

Then blinks at me again.

She takes a deep breath that I know is *not* good for whatever's coming next, and she's opening her mouth as the door bells jingle again, and this time, Tavi Lightly breezes in with her eyes hidden behind massive sunglasses, her legs wrapped in purple leopard-print leggings, her shirt a black textured tank top with an extra hole to show off her cleavage. She has seven rings on her fingers, bracelets jangling together on both arms, four necklaces hung around her neck, and three earrings in each ear. Her hair's tied up in a knot at the top of her head and held there with a wire getup studded with sparkly diamonds.

If she were an actual Tickled Pink local, I'd suspect the diamonds were fake, but not on Tavi.

On Tavi, I'd bet my favorite monkey wrench those are real diamonds.

She beams at all of us while Pebbles pokes her head out of Tavi's purse and pants happily at us. "Happy Monday morning! Air smooches, Anya. Did I see Bridget come in here? Tell her I *adore* her nails. Tiger stripes are a great choice. Hey, Dylan. Are you, like, *so* excited for today or what? I'm so excited I couldn't sleep last night. I need, like, a *triple* shot of organic espresso added to my coffee today."

"Excited about what?" Anya asks while I try to clear my head.

Tavi didn't say *like* one time when we were talking at the lake Saturday morning.

Her personality didn't *bubble*.

She wasn't all *air smooches* and *I just adore your nails*.

She was—well, she was as kind as she implied she thinks I am.

A little outraged for a moment there, but kind. Like it was my turn to be the duck helped across the road, and she was just a regular woman doing what any human being would do for someone—or something—in need.

She beams at Anya. "I'm helping Dylan get a TikTok account!"

Yes, she's speaking in exclamation marks. I swear her face is dancing in them too.

The part of her face that I can see, that is.

Anya drops her rag and leans on the counter. *"Oooh."*

Bridget pops her head over the swinging doors to the kitchen. *"Oooh."*

Even Ridhi stops behind Bridget and stares at me. "No way."

"Yes way!" Tavi dials her smile up to eleven. "Won't he be fabu?"

"I'm gonna get yelled at if I say out loud what I'm thinking," Bridget says.

She gets a double stink eye from her stepmom and aunt, and I don't know if it's because Bridget's implying I'll suck or if it's because she's implying I'll have women falling at my feet in droves.

Neither makes me particularly comfortable when they're coming from a teenager who knows entirely too much about the world.

"Right?" Tavi says with an emphatic nod. "Gigi yelled at me, too, when I said what I was thinking—she was all, 'Tickled Pink doesn't need to be sexualized to get tourists'—but, like, this is the *best* plan. And then Tickled Pink will be famous all over again for *you* instead of *us*, and you'll never have to worry about tourism again after we leave."

As I said.

Bad, bad idea.

I'm not opposed to attention the way Teague is. *Was.* He's loosened up since Phoebe came into his life and then since his own secrets spilled out about his life before he moved here, which we locals are tiptoeing around for his sake.

He's a good guy. Good dad too. And he cares about Tickled Pink.

So we're letting him take the lead on how much he wants to talk about his past. Life rule—when a guy can clearly handle the hard shit, you don't dig into the things he doesn't want to talk about until he's ready to talk about them.

You accept him for the decent person he's been for as long as he's lived here, and you give him the room he needs.

As for me, this whole town—as well as a lot of the surrounding areas—already knows my past, which might be why I'm having some performance anxiety at the idea of *me* being the new face of Tickled Pink on social media.

Fix a leaky faucet, replace a sink, handle a boiler?

I'm your man.

Get fancy for the cameras?

Probably gonna be a few people who have opinions on me that I won't like and a little more of my own past coming back to bite me.

I'll deal. Not like it's a secret, and there's no place I'd rather be if I'm going to put myself on display, and there's no other town I'd do this for.

Probably be good for me, actually, to face the stuff that's been haunting me again.

Hannah's gonna think I'm a dork.

And I need to quit worrying what Hannah thinks.

She's the past.

Still a friend, but she's the past.

And maybe this'll make me expand my social sphere outside Tickled Pink enough to actually meet someone who won't make me feel like the first thing they're wondering is if my kids will turn out to be hellions just like I was.

Maybe this will work.

"Lola Minelli came in here this weekend and asked Ridhi and me to do some Tic Tacs about making coffee," Anya says with a mischievous twinkle in her eye.

Bridget takes the bait. "*TikToks*, Aunt Anya. Not *Tic Tacs*. *TikToks*."

Tavi's nose twitches. "Aw, that's so great that Lola wants to help too. It's, like, double the positive attention."

"That was *after* we gave her coffee worse than the coffee we served Phoebe when you all first got here," Ridhi says. "We're not doing videos. None of us."

"Unless they're with you," Bridget adds to Tavi.

"No. Videos," Ridhi repeats.

"But we're not telling Lola no until we figure out what she's really up to," Anya adds. "I feel like she has an agenda."

"That's really smart." Tavi beams at both of them. "You, like, never know what people like me *actually* want."

My phone vibrates as I try to stifle a snort of *straight from the lying social media influencer's mouth to your ears*, which isn't something I need to judge anyone else for, and I suddenly don't know if this is relief or more indigestion I'm feeling.

I check the incoming text message, and my shoulders hitch. "Gonna have to wait," I tell Tavi. "Got a garbage disposal emergency."

"Fantastic! I'll ride along!" And now that beam of hers is aimed at me.

It's so fake I can practically taste the plastic in it.

Shouldn't make me mad. This is her *job*. But I'm irritated as hell that the woman who'd eat tomatoes off the vine with me at 6:00 a.m. on a Saturday morning while telling me she didn't think nice guys like me could ever be real is fake-smiling at me.

"Gonna get dirty." I'm cranky. I'm never cranky—not these days—but I can hear the crank in my own voice.

Her smile doesn't falter. "The first rule of social media—be real."

Any other day, that would amuse the hell out of me. "Be real, huh?"

Her round cheeks take on a pink hue, but she lifts her chin as if she can't feel the blush spreading over her face. "Yes. *Be real* is the *best* rule."

"And that's worked for you?"

I don't like being a dick.

I don't. Not anymore.

Totally serious that I used up my allotted dickishness already in my life.

But the woman in the bunker the other morning who I swore was going to gnaw my arm off to get to my breakfast sandwich, and the woman sitting with me at the lake the next morning, and the woman who chases ducks out of the road and runs for hours every morning, and the woman who pets and kisses her dog like it's so automatic to spoil the little pup with love that she doesn't always realize she's doing it, and the woman who gets this gleam in her eyes before she steps up to bat during our snowshoe baseball games this summer, are not the same woman who's standing here telling me I have to "be real" if I want to be on social media to help my town get a little "organic publicity."

Tavi's not budging. "Not everyone can have my level of success, but you don't need to be *über*famous to help Tickled Pink."

Anya, Ridhi, and Bridget are watching us like this is a tennis match.

"Huh," I say.

"What are we doing standing here?" Tavi asks. "Don't we have some pipes to unclog? Chop-chop! Water emergencies wait for no one!"

"Except the plumber," Bridget offers.

I eyeball the three of them. "Don't," I say.

I don't say *don't what*.

They know.

Chapter 8

Tavi

Dylan's truck is clean.

I don't know why I expected it to be a dirty mess of fast-food wrappers and muddy floor mats and weeks' worth of junk mail, but it's clean, with a tomato-shaped air freshener hanging from the rearview mirror and not a speck of dust to be seen on his dashboard.

"What's *don't*?" I ask him as I strap in, cuddling my purse with Pebbles inside it.

He slides me a look, sighs, and shakes his head. "They're activating the Tickled Pink gossip chain to open bets on when we start dating. That's what's *don't*."

I stick out my lower lip, suspecting he knows I'm putting on the Tavi Lightly Show but doing it anyway because there's still comfort in my public shield. Besides, if I don't, I might have a panic attack at the idea that I'm stuck here with him all day instead of sneaking away to my own little hidey-hole, where I truly need to work on my chocolate empire. Naomi has a meeting with a potential investor on Thursday, and I have to overnight her some new truffle samples.

"You wouldn't date me?" I ask, hating myself a little more with every airheaded syllable that comes out of my mouth. "Even now that you're . . . single?"

He squints at me harder as he hits the button to start his truck. "Who's the real Tavi Lightly?"

"That is *not* an answer to my question."

"You want real from me, you have to be real in return."

"Honestly, Dylan, there's no benefit to *me* to making you internet famous. But there's all the benefit to *you*. Do you know the one thing a woman hates more than anything? It's when she realizes what was under her nose the whole time after she sees someone else going after it. Second worst? When the only thing the new *it* couple in question, featuring the guy who got away, ever tells anyone is *we're just friends*. You mark my words—the minute you hit five hundred thousand followers on TikTok for being 'the Tickled Pink Plumber who hangs out with Tavi Lightly,' telling people we're 'just friends,' you'll have your pick of every single eligible woman on the planet. And *then* won't she see what she was missing?"

He sighs.

It's not the same kind of sigh that Phoebe's boyfriend, Teague, makes, but it's also not the sigh of a man looking forward to having a socialite influencer riding along for plumbing emergencies today.

Good thing he owed me a favor. I get the feeling he might back out otherwise, and I *need* him to do this.

Success is the only metric Gigi recognizes. I need this to be so successful she has no choice but to acknowledge I've done what I need to do to re-earn my trust fund.

I'll still find an investor—what Gigi giveth back, Gigi could also taketh back againth—but I could really use some breathing room until I do.

"It's okay if you're not ready to date yet," I offer. "I guess this is like finally letting your heart break or something?" *Good job, Tavi. Play the ditz.* "Don't worry. I won't say another word about it. And we're going to have so much fun today! I promise. You won't regret this. We can even get a T-shirt store up and running for you when this takes off. It'll be, like, an alternative revenue stream. Those are super important."

He finally quits staring at me like I'm the world's biggest inconvenience, and he pulls away from the curb outside Café Nirvana.

I spot Phoebe across the street. Teague and his brother, Jonah, are next to her, and Lola's hanging out with them too.

I tense, waiting for the moment Lola glances this way and spots Dylan and realizes he's hot, but of course she doesn't look this way.

Not when Teague's brother is rich and single. Jonah's newer to town than we Lightlys are, and he's not permanent, but when he's here visiting Teague, like this week, he attracts the *most* attention.

Eye roll, as Bridget would say, though you can't argue with results.

Teague, Jonah, Phoebe, *and* Lola standing in the square?

It has a flock of tourists gathering in groups up and down the sidewalks along the square, snapping photos and whispering and undoubtedly getting ready to go spend their money in all the little stores that are still open around here.

Maybe not the tire-and-lube place that shares a building with Café Nirvana, but definitely everywhere else.

It's way more tourists than were here when we Lightlys descended on the town, but still not enough to justify Patrice reopening her spa or Jane opening a real brewpub.

Phoebe's talking to someone else in the groups, someone I don't know, while she gestures to the half-finished, reclaimed-by-nature Ferris wheel that was started like forty years ago when the town thought it would stay famous for that *Pink Gold* movie. My big sister is tall, slender, and blonde, and until the past few weeks, I never would've considered calling her a friend.

Also?

I've never actually seen her happy the way she is now.

Love's good for her.

She wears it well. And I think she knows what she has, and there's not an ounce of doubt in my mind that love means more to her than all the professional success she walked away from.

God knows we grew up craving it enough that none of us—not even Carter—would throw it away now.

Even if the love we find isn't necessarily with a person.

I can love a cacao farm. Carter can love his . . . music.

If that's what he wants to call it.

"You want me to drop you off at the school so you can change?" Dylan asks. "Might get dirty."

"No, silly. If I let you drop me off, you'll leave without me." Also, the faster we get away from Lola without her spotting us, the better.

There's that sigh again.

"You sound like Teague."

"I do *not* sound like Teague."

"Teague sighs like that all the time."

"Teague's a grumpy asshole with trust issues. A lovable grumpy asshole with trust issues, and my friend, but still a grumpy asshole with trust issues. I'm a simple guy who wants to go unclog a garbage disposal in peace while I process that I've wasted six years of my life with a woman I'll never have and probably wanted for all the wrong reasons."

I reposition Pebbles's carrier so I can turn in my seat, pet my dog, and also watch him drive. He was all in the other day, and I get the feeling he's not as opposed to this as he says he is.

This smells like cold feet. "Do you really want to unclog the disposal in peace, or are you planning on talking to your client the whole time? Client? Customer? What do you call the people whose drains you unclog?"

"They're people." He frowns. "Usually. Had a raccoon with a plumbing emergency once, but—"

"Wait! Wait! Give me your phone. I need to record this."

"Tavi—"

"Gigi's making me and Lola compete to see which one of us can get more people in Tickled Pink on social media to pimp the town, which is *exactly* why Lola's asking Ridhi and Anya to do videos. The minute she sees you, you'll be her next victim. And you should've seen the way she smirked when I said I was talking to a local plumber about getting you on social media today. She's, like, *totally* being a Meanie McJudgy-Pants."

Pebbles yips in agreement. She, too, dislikes Lola.

I put a hand on his thigh, then snatch it away as I realize what I'm doing. "Trust me. I'm doing you a huge favor. You can have me riding along today, or you'll have Lola all up in your business pretending she cares about you by the end of the day. Not that you should turn her down if she asks you out for dinner. I mean, if she offers to do for you what I'm offering to do for you, say no. Don't trust her. But if she offers to take you to dinner, say yes."

And now I'm going to throw up, but I keep talking. "The only thing better than having *one* famous influencer telling the world you're 'just friends' to get the ladies' attention is having two. You have dinner with Lola, too, and your entire reputation and dating life will be set forever."

"So I shouldn't trust Lola, but I should trust you?"

"I mean, *no*. You really shouldn't trust me either." I smile at him. "But you and I have some history, and I don't have enough friends that I trust the way I trust you, so whether *you* trust *me* or not, I promise to have your best interest at heart." That much is true.

I don't want to hurt him. I want to see him happy, if for no other reason than that I get it.

I know what it's like to want to be loved and to constantly feel lacking, and I wouldn't wish that on anyone.

Not even Lola.

"Tavi, I'm really not the playing-games type."

I sink back into the chair and find myself sighing too. "Then we shouldn't play games. You have a good life here, and my family and I have no right to interrupt it. But before you kick me out—don't you want to know what could happen? Aren't you the teensiest bit curious? How long have you been holding yourself back, waiting for someone who's never going to love you the way you want? You have a choice, Dylan. You can stay in this rut you've built for yourself, or you can take a chance and see what else the world might hold for you. I know new can be scary, but is scary wrong? What's the very worst thing that happens?"

He turns the corner just before the neoclassical high school building that I currently call home, his face telling me there's *something* going on in his head that he doesn't want to say out loud. "You didn't say *like* or use a single exclamation point in that entire little speech there."

My cheeks flame up. "So?"

"So we're back to . . . exactly who are you, Tavi Lightly?"

"Excuse me, we're talking about *you* right now, and I'm the very best thing that could've possibly happened to you in this exact moment."

"Why do you run so much?"

"What?"

"You're out running like someone's chasing you every single morning. What are you running from?"

"That's not really relevant here."

"If we're gonna be telling people we're 'just friends,' we're gonna be the 'friend' part. Not the 'just' part."

His warm brown eyes slide my direction for a second before returning to the road. He has one hand at the bottom of the steering wheel, his posture relaxed, his profile as chill as lettuce in a crisper drawer. His rugged jawline is freshly shaved, and there's a hint of a dimple peeking out of his cheek, like he's used it so much in his lifetime already that even with his face neutral, it can't fully tuck itself back in, or possibly like he's always on the verge of smiling, even when he's arguing with someone.

I told Phoebe not long after we got here that I used to wish I'd been born in another family, until I realized I could make my own family while still benefiting from the Lightly money.

But I lied.

I still wish I'd been born in a different family—Naomi's family, preferably—so that I could talk to a man like Dylan without hiding so many secrets that I should be recruited by the CIA, without the manipulation and guilt and fake connections that leave me feeling empty inside.

If I had to be born rich, I wish I'd been born rich in character instead. Rich in integrity. Rich in love.

Then maybe I'd truly mean it when I say I don't care that I'm not the smartest or the prettiest or the most personalitied.

What does it say about a person when she peaked before she was three?

To hear my mom talk about my beauty pageant days, that's what I did. Ever since then, it's been, *Be skinnier, Tavi. Smile bigger, Tavi. No, not that big. You didn't get the brains, honey, so you have to make your body work for you, though, you poor thing, you're built like your father, aren't you?*

Honestly?

I have not missed my mother since she left Tickled Pink.

I was almost glad when she hit her limits and spilled the blackmail Gigi had used to keep her here, telling us she'd cheated on Dad about thirty-one years ago and that Phoebe isn't his. I was hoping she'd follow it with *and Tavi, you're adopted*, but she didn't.

Plus, there's no denying that I have the Lightly eyes.

And my father's build.

Sigh.

"I run to stay in shape," I tell Dylan.

"Don't have to run a marathon every day to stay in shape."

"You do when your hips are inclined to spread to the width of a continent if you're not careful."

He growls.

Growls.

And damn if that dimple doesn't disappear. "If you *actually* got hit by a garbage truck tomorrow and had to tell God your biggest regret, would it be that you didn't run seven more miles every day, or would it be that you never got to experience a bacon cheeseburger in all its glory because you were too tied up in looking like some paragon of impossible perfection?"

Once more, Dylan Wright has no idea he's making me wet in the panties. "Hello, *I like vegetables.* And beans. And tofu. And I'm doing *good for the world* with my diet. Vegetables are so much better for the environment than meat is."

"Okay, Ms. Sneaked a Barbecue Sandwich at Hog Wild While Wearing Sweatpants and a Fake Nose."

I gasp, my heart rate tripling and my knees starting to quake. *He saw through the fake nose.* If he saw through it, who else did? "*What?* Oh my *God.* How dare you. I would never—"

"The wig and the Sparrow County High sweatshirt were nice touches," he adds. "But you might want to add a limp next time. Stride gives you away every time."

Dammit.

Dammit.

"I do *not* eat—"

"Not gonna tell anybody, Tavi. I'm not like that. But if we're gonna be friends, you're gonna have to be honest with me."

There's a tingling in my chest that has nothing to do with the ridiculous crush I have on this man and everything to do with the fact that he has the ammunition to destroy me.

Or possibly it's both.

"I had a bad day," I whisper.

"Damn good barbecue. Not much better to cure a bad day. Where'd you get the beater car?"

Not a chance I'm going there. "No one would believe you if you started spreading that rumor. People try every few years, and they always disappear after their five minutes of fame, and trust me, there's *nothing* like karma when you get your five minutes of fame by trying to destroy someone who's only trying to do a little good in the world."

He goes a little pale, and his cheek twitches. "True enough," he says quietly.

I stare.

Pebbles stares.

He turns a corner, his shoulders visibly tightening.

And I suddenly have so many questions. "Is there something you want to tell me before I make you internet famous?"

He shakes his head. "I'm good. Also, setting unrealistic expectations for women everywhere when you're literally *paid* to stay in shape and pretend you eat three lettuce leaves for lunch every day is *not* doing good in the world."

How is it that he's currently on my *danger, danger!* list yet also getting more attractive by the minute? "Don't try to change the subject. You realize you just called me on keeping secrets, right? And now you're keeping them yourself?"

A muscle tics in his jaw. "Not really a secret that I was a shit in high school. I own it. But I don't have time to list all of my transgressions before we get there."

"But you're not a shit now."

"People can change. I changed. I like this me, and I'm not going back."

People can change.

He has no idea how much I needed that reminder. Coupled with *who are you, Tavi Lightly?* it feels like Dylan is exactly what I need. He's my reminder that I get to be in control of who I am, no matter my circumstances.

Naomi would like him.

I like him.

"I'll give you a pass on your past so long as you don't ask me to explain why I almost ran into that garbage truck the day after that thing that we don't need to talk about ever again," I tell him. "But if I'm going to help you get back into the dating world, I think I should know the name of this woman you've been secretly in love with forever and why you think you don't deserve her."

"Prefer if you don't talk about that today either," he mutters.

"Why?"

He pulls to a stop in front of a weathered but apparently sturdy two-story Dutch colonial in one of the quaint neighborhoods in Tickled Pink, and he nods at the house. "Because I'm fixing her parents' garbage disposal this morning."

Chapter 9

Dylan

Still don't like anything about any of what I've agreed to do this morning—the social media stuff and bringing Tavi along to Hannah's parents' house—but I can't help wondering exactly how Ken and Marta will react to seeing me with one of the Lightlys this morning.

Almost feels like some of the shit I would've pulled back in high school, bringing a super popular girl I had no interest in dating over to hang out for a night in front of last week's girlfriend's parents.

That's not what this is, but for one more split second, I *feel* sixteen again.

I breathe the feeling away while I climb out of the truck, and I've barely pulled my toolbox out of the bed when the door flings open.

Marta sticks her head out. "Dylan! You didn't tell me you were bringing a helper!"

"Quit yapping at the boy and let him get in here and fix the sink, Marta," Ken yells from deeper inside the house.

"I'm not letting Hannah's oldest friend in this door without asking him how he's doing!" Marta yells back.

"If you wanted to yammer, you didn't have to put potato peels down the garbage disposal! You could've just called him!"

"Is it Hannah? Or is Hannah her sister?" Tavi whispers to me.

She's lucky I'm not the type to threaten to spill her secrets. "Hannah's an only child. And her parents know *nothing*, so pretend you've never heard her name."

"What about you?"

"Me?"

"Are you an only child?"

"Nope. Younger sister lives in Minneapolis. Older brother lives in Nebraska. Biomedical researcher and civil engineer."

That always gets raised brows and *so why'd you become a plumber when there are brains in your family?*

But Tavi doesn't ask, nor does her face.

Appreciate that, because that's not even close to the most interesting question that could be asked about my family and my sibling dynamics.

Instead, she smiles at me. And not her camera-ready smile. This one has some meat to it, like she's actually enjoying smiling. "You're a middle child too."

"Yep." I slam the tailgate shut and gesture her up the walk.

"Are your siblings horrible pests? Or do you get along?"

"That's more complicated than we have time to get into."

"Wait. There's someone you *don't* get along with?"

"You get along with all of your family?"

She rolls her eyes. "I met your mother. Your family is *nothing* like mine."

"Doesn't mean we don't have our own brand of problems."

We reach the steps—thank God—where Marta's eyeing Tavi with open curiosity. "You're—you're—*Ken*! Ken, Dylan brought one of them Lightlys."

"Tell 'em we're not interested."

Marta rolls her eyes. She's on the tall side with broad shoulders, thick hips, red hair that's faded to mostly white these days, and if she's not wearing yoga pants and some variation of a T-shirt declaring her the world's best mom, that's when you know something's up.

Nothing's up today. She's full-on *World's Best Mom*.

"Ignore him," she tells Tavi. "He's always cranky. It's the hernia."

"It's not the hernia!"

"It's the hernia," Marta whispers.

"It's not the goddamn hernia!"

"That's better than me telling them you're a grumpy old fart!"

"I'm only a grumpy old fart because I live with you!"

Marta heaves the same long-suffering sigh that my mother liked to use when one of my stepfathers would burp at the table.

"Come on in, honey." Marta pulls the door open wider and beckons us inside. "Thanks so much for coming. Hopefully we won't take too much of your time. I heard you have a big renovation job for the Olsons starting today."

"Always have time for you, Marta."

"And it's lovely to meet you." Tavi smiles her influencer smile—the one that says *I'm harmless and you can trust me because I have a cute dog and the internet loves me*, though *harmless* is definitely an exaggeration—and holds out a hand. "I'm Tavi. And this is Pebbles."

Pebbles grins too.

Deeper inside the house, Banshee growls low in her throat.

Banshee's an overpossessive boxer-Lab mix. Hannah adopted her three years ago, but when Hannah moved in with Andrew, Banshee didn't have enough room in their apartment, so the dog moved in with Ken and Marta.

Pretty sure Banshee is half of what's wrong with Ken on any given day.

I would've offered to take her myself, but Mom had a dog back then, and those two wouldn't have gotten along.

"I'll put our dog out back," Marta says. "You come on in too, honey. I'd love to hear how the progress is coming on the school. Any chance we'll all get tours sometime soon?"

Pebbles slinks deeper into the purse while Tavi follows me into the house. "No, not soon," she says to Marta, perky personality shining through like she flipped a switch the minute we got an audience. "We still have *so* much work to do."

"I heard your brother playing at Ladyfingers the other night." Marta lunges for Banshee's collar as the dog stalks into the kitchen just off the dining room, and she tries to pull the dog past the stairs toward the side exit. "He's so talented! And I saw your sister's plans for the new Ferris wheel, and I'm so glad she's keeping the old one, too, and I think you Lightlys are just the best thing to ever happen to Tickled Pink."

"Ella Denning was the best thing to happen to Tickled Pink, and don't you forget it," Ken yells.

He might love *Pink Gold* as much as Estelle Lightly does. Not many people in town still talk about the movie the way they did when I was in grade school, when it was required viewing once a year, but Ella Denning, the movie's star, will forever be universally adored. She was one of a kind.

"Ella Denning's dead, may her soul rest in peace," Marta hollers back. "And it's lovely that we have people who are willing to come here and love our town as much as she did." She grunts, then disappears down the back hall, dragging Banshee along.

I've offered to do that for her before, too, many times, and I always get told no, that it's her daily exercise.

Marta's, I mean.

Can't argue with results. She can outlift me at the gym, and I've quit trying to compete.

"Wow, yeah, I can see the appeal to the whole family," Tavi whispers to me.

"Your family's one to talk," I reply.

She rolls a single eyeball, which is oddly adorable. "People would be so much better if they weren't so peopley."

"Best part of people is that they're peopley." I pause. "Most days."

She lifts both brows, highlighting the widow's peak in her hair, and for a brief moment, I wonder if that's one of those things she likes or dislikes about herself.

Hannah always complains that she hates how her hands are shaped. "They're too big for women's hands."

"But it's how you're made," I always reply.

"Maybe not most days," I concede, "but more days than not."

She grins at me. "The Lightly family: ruining eternal optimists one at a time."

I'm shaking my head and fighting a smile as I set my toolbox on the table and head to the sink. Marta and Ken renovated the kitchen about twenty-five years ago, and the oak cabinets are showing their age. Water stained, with creaky hinges and evidence that they've had more leaks that I haven't heard about lingering under the boxes of garbage bags, cleaning supplies, and leftover plastic grocery bags beneath the sink that I set out on the floor so I can reach the shutoff valve.

"Hand me a wrench," I say to Tavi.

I don't actually need it.

I'm just curious.

She doesn't ask which one's the wrench and instead hands over the right tool.

"Just because I'm pretty in pictures doesn't mean I'm, like, dumb," she informs me, twirling her one stray lock of hair around her finger.

I stare at her a second.

She slides me a sly grin, and I'm suddenly torn between wanting to laugh and wanting to interrogate her until I know who the *real* Tavi Lightly is, even if it means I have to confess to the real me too.

There's way more going on inside that skull than the world gives her credit for.

And if I know anything about how hard a person can be on themselves, I'd be willing to bet she doesn't give herself enough credit either.

Marta bustles back into the kitchen and all but shoves her into a spindled kitchen chair. "Oh, honey, who called you dumb? Why are people like that?"

"Because they have eyeballs, Marta," Ken calls.

"Ignore him. I'm so sorry he's rude," Marta mutters. "I swear to God, if he wasn't so good in bed, I'd divorce that man."

"Other men *can* be taught," Tavi says.

I jerk my head to look at her and bang it on the top of the cabinet.

"You need one of these hex-key thingies next?" she asks with an innocent smile, holding up my key ring of hex wrenches while I rub my head and wonder when I became the grumpy, glaring type.

That's Teague's job around town.

Not mine.

Not anymore.

Now, I'm the *happy* guy.

You're also the guy watching the love of his life have a marriage and a baby with a guy who's all wrong for her after wasting years telling yourself you still had to atone for the sins of your childhood before you'd be worthy of her.

Self-reflection sucks, for the record.

"I dated Danny Santana when he was practicing for that Christmas movie where he played the plumber." Tavi beams at me with that fake smile that doesn't reach her eyes, and I have an overwhelming urge to throw her over my shoulder, march her out of here, and tickle her.

Tickle her.

What the hell?

How hard did I just hit my head?

I lean back under the sink and finish twisting the knob to shut off the water supply.

"Oh, mercy, Danny Santana's a hot one," Marta says. "Was he as good in bed as he is on camera?"

"Right here, Marta," I say.

"Oh, I know, honey, but you're a grown-up now, and a woman has needs, and you're not *dating* Tavi, so it's not like this should offend you. Wait. You're not dating, are you? *Are you secretly dating?*"

"We're just friends," Tavi says easily.

"Ooooh," Marta breathes. "That means you *are* dating, but you don't want the world to know it, doesn't it?"

I slide another look back at the women.

Tavi gives me the universal smirk of *I told you so.*

"Jesus on clam chowder," Ken mutters loudly enough for the neighbors to hear. There's a stomp, then a "Good luck, Dylan," and then the front door slams.

Marta giggles. "He'll be back sniffing for a good time before long. Having an empty nest has really been good for us. But tell me about you two. How long have you been—"

"Marta, you got a bucket?" I ask.

"You bet, honey. Just hold there for one minute while I go wrestle it up out of the garage."

I lean back, sitting on my heels, while she bustles out of the house.

As soon as the garage door slams, Tavi leaps to her feet. "Here. Take your shirt off, and put this in your ear."

I don't answer with my words.

Pretty sure my face is doing all the talking for me while I swat at the little earbud device she's shoving my way.

Pebbles peeks out of the purse, now battling for space on the table among succulents and newspapers and stacks of mail.

"It's a clean earbud," Tavi assures me. "And it'll make your voice come through clearer on the video."

"Video?"

"Dylan. You can't be the hottest plumber on TikTok if you don't do videos. C'mon. You have to talk about why you don't put potato peels down the sink and give people three tips on how to clear it out at home when they do. The lighting isn't the best in here, but my video people will do amazing things with it."

She's aiming her own phone at me.

Interesting.

"Thought you all weren't supposed to have cell signal."

"Gigi can hardly assign me the task of helping this town get on social media without cell signal."

"We're on the internet here too, you know. Patrice, who used to run the spa, even has a popular YouTube channel, but she can't upload on Wednesday nights, because that's the night Tickled Pink Floyd is uploading his videos to his favorite site."

I let that linger while Tavi's face does some gymnastics of its own.

"Like, school-janitor videos?" she asks.

Legit question. Tickled Pink Floyd—not to be confused with Deer Drop Floyd—used to be the high school janitor. And every day I'm grateful he has a big heart and forgives easily.

I grin. "Yeah. Let's call 'em that."

"I know you're trying to distract me because you have stage fright, but seriously, Dylan, there's nothing to be worried about. This isn't live, and we'll make you look *super* good."

"I thought you needed to make me look real."

"You look good real."

We stare at each other for a second, and that's when it hits me.

Really hits me.

Tavi Lightly finds me attractive.

Not convenient. Not easy. Not *just there* when there's no one else.

She *likes* me.

I genuinely thought when she tried to go down on me in the locker room that it was a thing in her world to pay for stuff with sexual favors whether you like a person or not. And I also thought she was flirting with me in the days before that because she wanted me to fix her plumbing.

Not because she liked me.

There's a reasonable possibility I assume most people don't like me despite the easygoing, friendly, happy guy I try to be.

Even people who didn't know me in my shithead years.

I shake my head. I'm reading this wrong. "Do you—" I start, but the door to the garage squeaks, Banshee erupts in a massive snarling bark-fest, and Marta huffs back into the kitchen.

"Found it!" she announces. "Turns out it was right on top since Ken dealt with *that thing* that he gets mad at me for talking about."

Tavi turns her beaming influencer smile on Hannah's mom like we weren't just standing here staring at each other while it dawned on me that someone who lives in a world of celebrities might actually like me.

Me me.

The guy who I've worked hard for years to become.

Holy shit.

Tavi Lightly likes me.

I have a completely clean slate with her, and *she likes me*.

"Marta, don't you think Dylan would be the *best* social media star? Like, he could tell everyday, normal people how to treat their pipes and do good things for their plumbing, and he could make plumbers hot again."

And now Marta's beaming too. "Oh, honey, if you'd asked me that ten years ago, no way. But today? He'd be *the best*. Who wouldn't take advice from this cutie?"

"Aww, was he slow to develop?" Tavi asks, as if I haven't told her a million times I was a total shit.

"No, he was—" Marta starts, but I cut her off.

"Marta, you know where the circuit breaker is for the disposal?"

"Oh! Of course. I should've thought of that while I was out in the garage. Not that the garage is in the circuit panel. I mean, the circuit panel is in the garage. It's in the basement. The circuit panel. Not the garage." She's weirdly adorable when she's flustered and making zero sense.

Hannah's the same.

I pretend I don't notice. "You mind flipping that for me, too, so I don't electrocute myself here?"

"Of course! Of course." And she's off again.

Tavi frowns at me. "What was wrong with you ten years ago?"

"I was a shit."

She doesn't laugh.

If anything, she frowns harder. "I know you *said* you were a shit, but I thought you meant *normal* teenager stuff. Like drinking and smoking weed and breaking into Bergdorf to steal the latest Manolos when your father cuts off your wardrobe allowance, which I didn't do, for the record—that was someone else I know but can't name because she has too much dirt on me. Is there something more you want to tell me about before we go any further?"

"That gonna change how you feel about me?"

"*Hello*, fellow member of the human race with my own issues in my past and who's currently here because my grandmother's convinced my soul is teetering on the edge of being forever damned. I just want to really, *really* make sure you're ready if people get up in your comments and DMs, trying to tear you down because of who you used to be. It can basically suck harder than a reverse hot tub jet, and there was this time that I was in Sri Lanka at a hotel where the hot tub jets got dorked up and started sucking backward, and I had a hickey on my left butt cheek for like three weeks after I got sucked into it, so I know how hard things can suck. But you're so—I mean, I didn't think—" She cuts herself off with a sigh. "Were you *really* a shit, like the bad kind of shit, or were you just *sort of* a shit and you have a massive guilt complex?"

"I was the bad kind of shit."

"But *for real?*"

"Oh, he was a complete and total shit. The highest shit on the shit scale," Marta says as she ambles back into the kitchen. She beams at me. "And look at the man he is now. We're *so* proud of him."

Tavi squints at me.

"He's proof positive *anyone* can change. Here, honey, let me hit this switch, and—yep. Got the right breaker. You won't get electrocuted now."

"Thanks, Marta."

"Anything for you. And for the record, I'd still love you even if you were still a shit. Wasn't all your fault, you know, and our childhoods shape so much of who we become as adults. What you've made of yourself despite all that—*shew.*" She waves her hands in front of her face as her eyes go misty.

"He'll make a great spokesperson for Tickled Pink, won't he?" Tavi says to her, which isn't what I'm expecting her to follow up with.

Is she being intentionally obtuse and focused just on business?

Does she not care that I was a shit? Or is she trying to pretend we weren't having a hard discussion?

Or is it because she doesn't want an audience when she might let something real about herself slip?

Whatever the case, Marta's nodding enthusiastically as she blinks away the shine in her eyes. "Oh yes. The best."

Tavi's full grin pops out. The *real* grin. "Plus, I can't wait to see the look on my grandmother's face when I tell her that she had nothing to do with saving Phoebe's soul. It's *clearly* the Tickled Pink effect, since it's been done before."

Marta nods even more vigorously. "When the kids were little, *Pink Gold* was still mandatory in the classrooms. We're pretty sure it helps make everyone around here better people for having such a great example at a young age of even the most selfish people never being too old to learn to be better."

"Oh, totes." Tavi's eye twitches like she hates the movie, and I stifle a smile.

So I'm not the only one.

It's not a bad movie. It just makes me feel like I'll never live up.

She waves a hand like she's brushing the whole conversation away. "So for Dylan's social media debut, I'm trying to talk him into taking his shirt off."

Marta goes red as one of my tomatoes.

Honestly, I think I might be going that shade of red too.

"You know he's best friends with my baby girl?" Marta says. "Even this horny old lady has some limits."

"Sometimes you have to use what's easy first, to lure people into the good stuff. Don't you want to know the next generation will keep this adorable little town going?"

"I'm not taking my shirt off." I turn back to the task at hand and crawl back under the cabinet. "I *am* gonna clean out these potato peels and get on my way, though."

"She might have a point, honey," Marta replies. "Maybe if I close my eyes, this'll work. How's the lighting? Is there enough light in here? I can get that fancy ring-light thing that Hannah got me for my birthday for when we video chat. Does he need makeup on his chest?"

"You video chat with Hannah?" Tavi asks.

"She's so busy over there in Deer Drop."

"Oh, for sure. Especially with a baby on the way."

I freeze.

Marta makes a choking noise.

And then I'm in motion, leaping to my feet, but I'm under the damn cabinet, and instead of leaping to my feet, I hear a crack, then feel a searing pain, and then everything goes black.

Chapter 10

Tavi

"I thought you meant her mom didn't know you were in love with her," I repeat for the millionth time as I pull Dylan's truck out of the hospital parking lot in Deer Drop.

I cut a glance at him, and he doesn't look so good.

Who would after suffering from a gash like that?

Also, my pulse will never recover from seeing him splayed out, half on that linoleum floor among cleaning supplies and plastic grocery bags, half under the sink, unconscious, with blood spilling out of his head.

Doesn't matter that the doctor says it's just a mild concussion, and that Dylan insists he didn't pass out but just hurt too bad to move for a minute there, and that they both say he won't even feel the cut on his head after another day or two.

I thought I killed him.

For only like three seconds, but still.

And now he's gripping the *oh shit* handle in his truck like he's on a runaway roller coaster without a seat belt, and all I want to do is get him back to Tickled Pink and safely tucked into bed, where I'll feed him chicken-noodle soup and read him books and make sure his wound stays clean and that he has soft enough pillows under his head, no matter how much I want to ask more about him when he was younger.

"But while we were freaking out about you being unconscious—"

"I wasn't unconscious."

"—I covered and said I got confused and thought you were talking about your cousin Deanna—"

"I don't have a cousin named Deanna, and Marta knows it."

"—and then I had to make up an entire branch of your family tree that poor Marta had never heard of, which probably sounded utterly insane since *you were dead and dying*—"

"*I wasn't dead and dying.* Or even unconscious. Jesus."

"—but I was still covering for you. Don't worry. I wrote it all down while you were having your head scanned, and poor Marta probably won't even remember because we were so worried about you. Are you going to puke? The doctor said I have to bring you back in if you puke."

"Stop. Talking."

The request bruises my soul. Dylan's always so nice, and here he is, needing me to shut up. I know he's injured. I know this isn't about me. But I feel a hot sting in my eyes anyway. "You sound like Teague."

"Not helping."

"If you're going to puke, I can pull over."

I thought he was dead.

For three milliseconds, I truly, honestly did.

And then the Tickled Pink Fire Department showed up—of course we called 911 even though Dylan started talking almost right away after I yammered out his made-up family tree—and the firefighters insisted he get an ambulance to the hospital.

And I will never recover.

I swear, I won't.

I'm nothing to him, and he's just a silly crush to me. I know this. *I know this.* But staring at his lifeless body for those suspended milliseconds that felt like a lifetime all wrapped up in one tiny moment made me realize just how fragile our existence can be, and I felt like there should've been something I wanted to tell him if his spirit was floating away into the ether to never return, and I didn't know what it was, and it was just—so—so futile and *wasted*.

I cut a glance at him again as I steer his truck toward the road that leads back to Tickled Pink.

He looks a little like Carter on weed.

But way more attractive than my brother.

Obviously.

"I'm sorry," I whisper.

"Not your fault."

It was.

It was entirely my fault for not picking up on the full implication of his *don't talk about Hannah at all with her parents* request.

That's exactly what he said.

Or nearabout, right?

It boiled down to *pretend you've never heard her name*, and I fucked it up good.

I'm supposed to be excellent with social cues.

"I'll drop you at home, and then I'll run out to the store for—"

"Not home."

"Not home? But—"

"Mother—hypochondriac—not home."

"If not home, then where—"

"Don't care. Not home."

I bite my lower lip.

While I've been in Tickled Pink for a couple of months, and I know a few people here and there, I don't actually know where to take him.

Especially given that I don't want to let him out of my sight.

Not while he needs to be monitored so closely.

I could take him to the school, but odds are high Lola would be there, and I will *not* survive if he decides she's a better caregiver than I am.

Teague's place is out. He lives in a tiny house in a tree, and there's barely enough room for him and Phoebe, much less the rest of us. I went to visit one time while Bridget was there, and even with the four of us spread across two different floors of the tree house, I felt so claustrophobic I had to leave after like ten minutes.

I don't know the rest of Dylan's poker friends well enough to randomly call and ask if I can camp out at their houses with him while I make sure he's not going to die. Willie Wayne *does* owe me a favor, but I'd like to save it for something else. Phoebe knows everyone in the secret poker group, but there's no way I'm risking letting *that* secret slip after already ruining one of Dylan's secrets today. Also, while she's been getting friendly with all the people in Tickled Pink, I've been doing the bare minimum as far as helping fix the school so that I could disappear to—

Oh, hell.

No.

But it makes sense.

If I want to keep an eye on Dylan *and* get my work done so I can send Naomi the truffles she needs *and* hide him from Lola for a little longer *and* honor his request that I not take him home, then my secret kitchen is my best bet.

It's in the basement of a closed-up church.

Surely, Dylan won't die of a concussion if he's in a former house of God.

There have to be some good spiritual wavelengths still hanging out in there, right?

The only question is how to sneak him in.

I'm usually ducking in after dark or before the sun's up. Never in broad daylight, and never dressed like the public version of me. Not if I can help it.

"Won't your mom hear that you were at the hospital?" I ask him. "Isn't Tickled Pink, like, gossip central?"

"I told Shiloh and Willie Wayne to squash it."

"You can control the gossip chain?"

"Mmph."

"Don't fall asleep! Not yet. Let me get you somewhere comfy first."

Pebbles whimpers at Dylan's feet.

His phone rings for like the eighty millionth time. It's definitely getting a workout.

"Do you need me to smooth things over with Hannah?" I ask. "I can do that. And I won't fuck it up this time. Cross my heart."

"I got it."

"I'm really, really sorry. And I don't say those words if I don't mean them. It's a Lightly thing."

"It's okay."

No, it's not.

It's really not.

But me repeating myself won't change anything, so I oblige his request and stop talking.

For a couple of minutes, anyway.

"Why do people even want to get married?" I ask the silence. I don't want to pester him about his past, but I can't stand the silence, and it's the first thing that comes to mind.

He sighs. "Some people do it right."

"But, like, *can* you get it right if you grew up with . . . never mind."

"Grew up with what?"

I gave him a concussion. I already blew one of his secrets, and he saw me chowing on a pulled-pork sandwich when no one else recognized me.

He could destroy me, and it would be the final blow to everything I've wanted in life.

And I wouldn't blame him.

But I feel like I owe him, and I don't owe him tearing apart the people he loves.

So I don't finish what I was going to say. *Can you get it right if you grew up with an example like Marta and Ken?*

"My parents never fought," I say quietly, "but that was because they never talked. And my dad cheated on my mom all the time, and I have no idea how much revenge cheating she did to get back at him, because it was either all before I was born, or she's just super, super discreet. And even now, with Mom bailing on us here and Dad still mowing the grass every day at the high school and barely talking to any of us, there's, like, no hint of divorce or separation or dealing with their issues."

Dylan makes a noise. I don't know if it's a *that's relatable* noise or an *oh* noise, but at least I know he's breathing and listening, so I keep talking. "And they're not the greatest parents either. Phoebe always said they didn't care about us, but she's . . . well, she's more complicated than Carter and me. Like, she was the guinea pig kid, and she'll never be my dad's favorite for . . . reasons that aren't mine to tell, and then it took me and Carter coming along before they figured out that you're supposed to do things like go to your kids' plays and send along a nanny for the occasional field trip instead of just giving her the day off."

I cut a glance at him.

He's still half staring ahead, lids heavy but eyes open. I've already said too much, so why not keep going?

"My mom played us against each other, always telling Phoebe how pretty I was for winning beauty contests while also telling me that Phoebe was the lucky one with the *skinny* genes and the business brains. I feel like she probably did it to motivate us, and she probably did have the best of intentions, but all it really did was make us hate each other."

He snorts softly.

"If I ever have kids, all I want to do is raise them. I don't want to work, I don't want to volunteer with the garden club, I don't want to have charity balls and luncheons to go to. There won't be beauty pageants, and I'll love them all for who they each are, and I'll make sure they know they're each special and perfect just how they are and that their differences should be celebrated instead of used against each other. I just want to stay home and be with my family. And I want to *be* a family. But I'm not supposed to say that out loud, because women are supposed to want the career and the clean house and the perfect kids and the friend groups and the time for fitness—we're supposed to want it all. What if my *all* is just being the person that the family I choose to have can depend on for love and affection and loyalty, and for putting them above everything else in the world, and for believing in them so that they can do amazing things instead of spending decades in therapy to try to find their self-esteem again?"

And now I've done it, and I need to stop talking.

I need to stop talking *right now*, but he's quietly listening, those warm brown eyes shifting to train on me while I drive his truck over the bridge back into Tickled Pink.

There's something so innocent and welcoming and nonjudgmental about those eyes that makes me want to tell him all my secrets.

All my fears.

All my desires.

It's those eyes that make him the hottest thing in Tickled Pink.

Not the butt. Not the body. Not the face.

I live in the upper echelons of society with the world's most attractive people. By all rights, Dylan shouldn't be any more swoon-worthy.

But those eyes—those eyes say *I can see right into your soul, Tavi Lightly, and you're perfect just the way you are.*

At least, that's what I imagine they're saying.

Acceptance isn't something I'll ever get from my normal crowd, and honestly, it's probably not something I'll get from Dylan either.

But he makes me feel like it's possible, even when every other experience in my life except for my relationship with Naomi tells me blind acceptance is a fantasy. And learning that he has his own past that's apparently messy and imperfect and that he wasn't born this way—it's like the universe is saying, *You, too, can redefine who you are, Tavi Lightly.*

But Dylan had—and still has—something I don't.

He has a community of people who love him and believe in him.

I have Naomi and Pebbles.

I'm a lot for the two of them to handle.

"Not that I'm talking about *me*," I say, hastily swiping at my hot, wet eyes while Pebbles whimpers softly at Dylan's feet. "I just saw a lot when I was growing up. That's all."

He softly squeezes my knee, and a warm glow spreads up my thigh.

He doesn't say anything. Just squeezes my knee.

But it feels like he's echoing that little message from the universe. *You can do it too, Tavi. You can define who you want to be.*

It's more than anyone else in my life would do, except Naomi, who isn't here.

Phoebe might.

She's changed since we got here, and I almost like her, but it's still new enough that I don't know how much I can trust this version of Phoebe to stay the way she is today.

"I'm sorry about your head," I say again.

"Could've been worse."

Maybe.

But really?

In a lot of ways, him being so nice to me *is* worse.

He seems like the kind of guy who's done the work to deserve everything he wants in life.

Chapter 11

Dylan

It appears Tavi's taking me to the closed-up Methodist church.

I know I didn't hit my head hard enough to hallucinate *this*. If I were hallucinating, I'd be picturing her taking me into an elephant enclosure at the zoo, or maybe to Wrigley Field for a Cubs game, which is one more item on my bucket list that I never told Hannah about.

She's a Brewers fan first, last, and forever. Talk of any other team is blasphemy.

"What—" I start.

Tavi shushes me as we stride from where she's stashed my truck in an alleyway that almost no one uses to the basement entrance of the small building. "If anyone asks, we walked by and thought we heard gushing water, so we stopped to investigate."

"I have a concussion, and the whole town except for my mom knows it." I frown again, then glance at my phone. "I hope. She hasn't called yet. Good sign."

"See? This is your cover story so your mom doesn't find out, and you can say it was your idea to come here." She leads me down the concrete stairwell, then uses a key to open the door. "How's your head?

Is this too much exertion? There's a seat just inside, and then I'll pull up—*gaaaaah!*"

Pebbles barks, and a goat answers from inside the basement.

"How did you get in here?" Tavi shrieks.

The goat bleats back at her.

My head threatens to crack in two.

"Not the chocolate!"

I'm hallucinating.

I have to be hallucinating, except my head is aching—it's been a remarkably headache-filled week—and nothing about this feels unusual.

Helped chase a deer out of Imani's house once. Was responsible for a squirrel in the high school another time. Domesticated goats in a church basement are tame after that.

Tavi shoves her purse with the dog at me, then darts into the room, flipping on more lights and illuminating a white goat gnawing on a refrigerator door handle. There are scattered spices and chocolate bars all over the floor, along with kitchen utensils and cookware and towels. Cabinets are open. Drawers too. The goat's wearing an apron on one horn, and there's a trail of chocolate footprints all over the floor.

At least, I hope that's chocolate. She did say "not the chocolate," didn't she?

"What—" I start.

"This isn't real! You hit your head too hard!" Tavi yanks on the goat's horn. "Move, you furry beast. Oh God. Oh God oh God oh God."

My phone vibrates in my pocket for the umpteenth time, and for the umpteenth time, I ignore it when I see who's calling.

My head absolutely cannot handle dealing with Hannah today.

Heart either.

And that *today* might possibly include tomorrow and extend into next week.

I don't know if she's calling to cuss me out or fuss me out or both, but either way, I refuse to answer that phone call.

"Are you one of Teague's goats?" Tavi demands of the furry beast who's now trying to lick what I sincerely hope is a chocolate truffle.

Or maybe not.

Is chocolate bad for goats?

Would it be better for the goat if that's *not* chocolate?

"Looks like." Pretty sure that's Chester. He's been mostly well behaved this summer, but that's probably because of the number of times Phoebe's accidentally let the goats out so Chester could have some fun without having to break out. "I'll call him."

Tavi makes a grunt-groan noise that's so very obviously *I don't want you to but I know it's the best thing right now* that I find myself smiling despite the chaos and my own headache.

"You're having a bad day," I say as I dial.

"Okay, *Mr. Concussion*. Yes. Me. *I'm* having the bad day."

"What's with all the chocolate?"

"No idea. Is that what that is? Looks like bean paste to me."

She's lying.

I mean, of course she's lying. Ms. Vegan but Sneaks Pulled Pork wouldn't be Ms. No Sugar but Sneaks Chocolate too.

Gasp. Shock. Outrage.

And you know what?

I *am* outraged.

I'm outraged that hiding who she wants to be is her life.

It's none of my business. It's not.

But I know a thing or two about the misery that comes when you're trying to fit into the life someone else expects you to be happy about living.

Don't care if you're acting out by being a shit or by eating chocolate. It still sucks to be shoved in a box.

"Get off electronics," Teague grunts in my ear. "Bad for concussions."

"Chester's eating Tavi's bean paste in the old Methodist church basement."

Bean paste my ass, which I confirm by striding across the small space to grab the nearest smooth chocolate bar and sniff.

If that's a bean-paste bar, I'll give my right shoe to the goat and eat my left shoe myself.

There's silence on the other end of the phone.

In the church basement, with its ancient kitchen and even more ancient, broken, builder-grade, public-building, vinyl-tile floor, however, there's chaos as Pebbles tries to leap out of the purse and Tavi wrestles the goat, her arm muscles straining like a boss, her feet wide, ass muscles clenched under those loud leggings.

She's a freaking *beast*.

It shouldn't be a surprise—she runs all the time, and her socials all feature videos of her doing resistance training between gorgeous artistic shots of her all over the world—but watching her take on Chester and actually win, all while begging the goat to please not have hurt himself by eating something that his system can't handle, is making certain parts of me sit up and take notice in ways that they haven't sat up and noticed at all since Hannah started dating Andrew.

"Bean paste?" Teague repeats in my ear.

"Dude, my head hurts. Just come get your goat." I hang up on him and pull Pebbles out of the purse while Tavi wrenches the goat across the room.

"No chocolate for you." She's grunting as she drags him while he tries to get back to the treat on the floor. "You'll die. You'll die, and then everyone who loves you will be so sad, and that's not kind, Chester. It's really not."

"Chocolate, huh?"

"*Oh my gooooood.* Stop talking. Stop listening. Everything you're hearing is a figment of your imagination. You should go lie down in the choir loft. There are some dusty chairs up there. Super comfortable. I'll bring you some food in a few. Pebbles loves to snuggle. You should go snuggle her."

My head does ache. The Tylenol the doc gave me probably won't cut it.

But distractions are good. "You eat meat *and* chocolate."

"*Please*, please don't go there." Her eyes are getting shiny again like they did when she was talking about having kids, which hit me in a raw spot that I don't like to talk about.

My mom's good people.

She is.

But she comes with her own issues, and no matter how much it makes me feel like I'm not being loyal, I'd be lying if I said my issues as a kid didn't start with her issues.

Not all her fault.

She didn't ask to be left with three small kids.

But I'd have to know my father to blame him, too, which was a good part of the other half of the reason I had issues.

Tavi plops to the floor, arms looped around the goat's chest. "If people knew—and you have no idea what's at stake here, you really don't—my life would be over. And so would the lives of a bunch of people who are counting on me to not fuck this up like I've fucked up basically everything else in my life other than smiling for a camera and fooling people into thinking I'm pretty."

"You *are* pretty."

She rolls her eyes and grabs the goat harder when he tries to sneak back to the mess on the floor. "Can we just pretend this isn't happening?"

I snap off a corner of the chocolate bar and pop it into my mouth.

And *holy hell*. "Where'd you get this?"

"Phoebe. It's Phoebe's."

She's a terrible liar. "What's Phoebe doing with chocolate?"

"No idea. She doesn't tell me everything. *Stop eating the chocolate, you damn goat!* It'll kill you! And I don't kill animals!" She sounds near tears. "Dylan. For real. Go lie down in the choir loft. I've got this, and it's not important, and if you can *please* just forget you saw anything—"

"Reminds me of this fancy box of truffles my mom got when she did some costume work for some *Pink Gold* superfan. There was one with ancho chilis in it that was just—man, that truffle changed my life."

I don't know what that look is that she's giving me as she clings to the goat, but it's either *small-town people eat good chocolate?* or *you pronounced* ancho *wrong*.

Probably.

"You really need to go lie down," she finally says. "All this excitement isn't good for your head."

"Hasn't stopped him before," Teague says behind me.

"Phoebe!" Tavi loses her grip on the goat, dives for him, and catches him again before he can get to more chocolate. "I saved the goat from *your* chocolate! And he should see a vet. *Right now.* Goats can't eat chocolate. They'll die. For real. I read it in a book."

Oh. Look at that.

Phoebe's here too.

She's hiding behind Teague, who's basically my height, a few years older, bearded, wider, and perpetually in flannel and occasionally has bouts of the grumpies whenever the rest of us in Tickled Pink do things he doesn't like.

Like welcoming the Lightlys to town a couple of months ago.

And now he's dating Tavi's sister, a slender blonde who could out-steamroll a steamroller on even her worst days. He still objects to the Lightlys overall, but less so now.

Also, watching him mouth off to Estelle is a thing of beauty. We in the Tickled Pink Secret Poker Society have secretly inducted him as a secret member, even though he sucks too much at poker to be a real member.

We also didn't tell him he's a secret member of our secret club.

That's how secret members work.

Phoebe stares at Tavi for a second, and then two Phoebes stare at Tavi. "Yes. Of course," she says mechanically, and I don't think I'm hearing her that way because I probably should go rest. I think she's actually not trying to lie well. "Thank you so much for saving my chocolate from the goat."

"C'mon, Chester." Teague grabs the goat by the horn, then gets yanked by the animal as it lunges for the chocolate mess.

"You have to hold him really tight," Tavi offers. "Hold him really tight, or he'll eat the chocolate, and he needs to see the vet *right now*."

Shit.

There are two of her now too.

"Pretty sure I know how to wrestle my own goats," Teague mutters.

"You clearly don't know how to keep him in his pen," Tavi snipes back while the goat yanks on Teague's arms again. "And now he might *die*."

Yeah.

Arms. Like four of them.

Dammit.

I lean against the counter and close my eyes.

"Dylan?" Tavi says softly.

"What's he doing here?" Teague asks.

"He didn't want to go home."

A grunt answers.

I know that grunt.

It means, *You're being a dumbass, because your mom might be a hypochondriac, but you know she'll take care of you when you're actually sick or hurt.*

I'm thirty-two years old.

I don't want my mom taking care of me.

I want—

I want something I can't have.

And I'm starting to want something else that I *shouldn't* have, because that something is complicated and tells lies and will be leaving Tickled Pink as soon as she can, and being attracted to complications and lies and people who will leave is something I left behind in my teenage years.

But right now, more than anything, I want to rest.

Chapter 12

Tavi

There are only so many things a person can do wrong in a single day before she calls it quits, and quits is exactly where I am right now.

I owe Naomi three emails and a phone call.

I owe Phoebe and Teague a massive thank-you.

I owe the goat whatever you get a goat to say *Sorry I'm half the reason you had to have your stomach pumped, but you shouldn't have been in the church basement, you goober.*

I owe Dylan apology flowers for life.

And instead of doing any of those things, I'm currently in the old high school teachers' lounge, scrubbing the sink because Gigi's decided we need a second kitchen in the school.

Clearly, a school housing *six people* needs a second kitchen.

I mean, duh.

An entire *cafeteria kitchen* isn't enough for six people.

But she says we're being environmentally friendly by using the *smaller* kitchen in the massive high school. Which doesn't explain why Gigi took Carter shopping for new appliances.

How's *that* environmentally friendly when we already have appliances that mostly work in the cafeteria kitchen?

And why does he get to go shopping while I'm stuck here scrubbing when I would really, *really* like to be checking on Dylan again and calling Naomi and, quite honestly, drowning my own sorrows in a vat of chocolate?

Freaking *youngest* child.

The babies of the family get everything.

Gigi's probably not threatening to cut off Carter's trust fund to make him stay here.

She's probably *bribing* him.

And there's no air-conditioning, which shouldn't be a problem, except it's late July, and apparently even Wisconsin occasionally gets hot in late July.

"Wow, it smells like farm animal in here," Lola Minelli says behind me. She has one of those squeaky balloon voices that I swear she's faking to make herself stand out.

On the one hand, you have to do what you have to do when you're in the reality TV and social media influencer business.

On the other hand, is that real?

Is it *really* real?

"Right?" I say, going slightly falsetto myself. "What did you do in here last night? I've been meaning to ask you all day, but I didn't want to sound rude." I hate this life. I truly, truly hate this life.

Lola sniffs delicately. "Maybe you should ask your brother."

Whether she's implying she hooked up with Carter or that Carter did something in here last night that I don't want to know about, *ew.* "Did you get the toilets scrubbed?"

"No, Gigi sent me on a different mission this morning."

Gigi.

It bothers the crap out of me that Lola moved in here and immediately started calling my grandmother *Gigi.* It should be *Mrs. Lightly* to her. Or even *Estelle.*

Gigi is entirely too familiar, and Lola's probably only doing it because she wants to get her hands on the Lightly name or money to help her out of whatever pickle she's gotten herself into as well.

"Aw, that's too bad," I tell Lola. "Usually, alternate errands to get out of getting dirty one day mean the other shoe will drop soon. Like tomorrow? Carter will probably have to crawl through the attic or something, since he's out shopping now. If I were you, I'd be hoping the toilets are the worst of what you have coming your way. I heard they found mold while they were renovating the community center, and *someone's* going to have to clean that up . . ."

"Oh, don't be silly, Tavi. Gigi says my soul's already in much better shape than the rest of yours." She sashays into the kitchen and props one skinny, spandex-clad hip against the countertop I just cleaned. "And do you know what? Because of that, I think I should help you out."

"That's so kind of you. Does that mean you're leaving?"

She titters. "Oh, you. You were never this funny when we were younger. Or maybe I just didn't know it since Phoebe always called you such a spoiled pain in the ass. I was always so glad I was an only child."

Deliver the insult with a smile, and you can say you were joking.

But I know Phoebe thought I was a pain in the ass.

She told me so herself.

Frequently.

Even that year when we did *Tavi's Party House* together.

Maybe especially that year.

"Siblings have their perks," I say through my smile. My cheeks hurt, and my teeth are gnashed together so hard that I should probably wear my night guard all day. "Grown-up siblings are actually the best. We're built-in friends now. Not so lonely, you know?"

"It's really nice to not have to be friends with people just because you're related to them too, though." She's beaming at me so hard I'm positive her cheeks hurt too. They have to. "Like being friends with you. It's so, like, *refreshing*. And do you know what? I'm in talks with my producers to do next season of *Lola's Tiny House* as *Lola's School House* instead. As soon as Gigi signs off, we'll be getting cameras and writers and directors in here. You should totally do *Lola's School House* with me. We have this great chemistry, and we could fight over the bedrooms, and over whose turn it is for the locker room shower, and over which of us left a bigger mess in the kitchen . . ."

Lola's School House? I *told* you she wants to be me.

It's my turn to titter. "That's so last season in my family, Lola. Like, you should've seen us fighting over bedrooms when Gigi moved us into the school."

"And Phoebe took the best bedroom. Naturally."

"And wasn't that great for you when you got to move into it since she already moved in with Teague in his tiny house?" I titter again. "Like, wouldn't that be funny if Teague's tiny house was canceled too? Where would they live? They'd have to move into the library here."

She glances behind herself, then slides closer to me. "You still call him Teague? Even though . . . you know."

"I still call you Lola even though . . . you know," I whisper back.

Lola Minelli was six when she petitioned the courts to change her name from Petunia Gardenia Minelli, on the grounds of child abuse.

Her mother has a thing for flowers. And her aunt was appalled and paid the legal fees.

Which is nothing at all like why Teague changed *his* name after high school.

Lola waves a hand as if she's wiping away the memory. "Totally different."

"True. He walked away from family money to make a better life for himself, and you . . . well, I guess we're lucky you have good parents who understood you needed a lot of help."

Truly, truly, truly hate this life.

"It's eat or be eaten," Phoebe always said.

I'm glad she's staying in Tickled Pink. She's a different person here, and if we didn't have a lifetime of history with both of us being much worse than the people we are today, I'd stay and be friends with her.

For real.

But disappearing to Costa Rica to run a cacao farm with my best friend is where my heart is.

Lola leans over the sink and points. "You missed a spot."

"Hey, Lola, Gigi's on her way back." Phoebe herself suddenly appears in the doorway of the kitchen. She's alone—no Teague, no goats, no random friends from Tickled Pink tagging along to gawk at the progress we've made (or haven't made) in cleaning the school. Teague's brother isn't with her, either, which must be a major disappointment for Lola.

Phoebe's also wearing her *do not fuck with me if you want to live* look, which I hear she used to use all the time in her old day job.

But she's aiming it squarely at Lola, not at me.

Lola cocks her head and gives Phoebe a blank look. "Did she *call* you?"

Lola supposedly surrendered her phone signal when she agreed to be the next contestant on *Gigi Saves the Upper East Side's Souls*, just like Gigi somehow had all our phones reprogrammed to fail to find cell signal here too.

I assume Lola's also totally cheating and on her cell phone all the time when Gigi's not looking but pretending like she's not, the same as most of the rest of us.

Except Phoebe.

Naturally.

She followed the rules until she found her backbone and told Gigi to worry about her own soul and then reclaimed her phone.

And now she's giving Lola the boss-bitch look as she nods once. "Yes, she called me, and she's curious how much progress you've made on digging through the cabinets in the biology lab."

"Oh, I got an extension on that because I'm helping make Jane a TikTok star."

"Jane," Phoebe repeats.

Lola nods, her voice going higher. "Oh yes, Jane. We made *tight* friends, and she's going to teach the next generation on TikTok how to make Jane's Garage beer. Dylan's making cameos."

My heart drops to my toes. Last I saw Dylan, his mother was shrieking and wringing her hands while Teague helped him into the house on the lake.

Phoebe folds her arms over her black tank top and taps her fingers against her biceps. "I talked to Jane this morning. That seems so out of character for her."

"She's coming around," Lola says. "Dylan too."

"You know Dylan?"

"I mean, I don't *know him* know him, but I saw his picture, and I'm famous, so he must know me, and I asked Ridhi and Anya to put in a good word for me, and they make the best coffee, and they're so sweet, so I know he'll be in. Probably tomorrow."

"Dylan's out of commission for a week."

Lola blinks.

"Impromptu vacation," Phoebe adds.

I cringe.

"So maybe you should go get started on the biology lab?"

"If you want me to leave, just say you want me to leave, silly." Lola titters. *Again.* "We're friends. We can say things like that to each other. Air smooches, Tavi. Think about my offer. It would be, like, *so great* to revitalize your career. I know it's sagging because of this little *break* here." She blows kisses to both of us, then floats out of the room.

Phoebe nods to the sink. "Nice job."

"Thank you. I scrubbed it myself."

She leans out the door, then leans back in, lowering her voice. "Did you get Gigi that thing for her birthday?"

Gigi's birthday is in October. "How am I supposed to get it when I can't get on the internet?"

"You're supposed to *make* it."

I stare at her for a beat before a snort-laugh slips out of my mouth. She grins.

Yes, we're talking total nonsense while we make sure Lola's not sneaking back to listen in on our conversation, but *you're supposed to make it?*

Never—*ever*—have we made things for *anyone* for holidays or birthdays. Or any other occasion.

Even the paintings and art projects at school when we were kids went into the *special* pile, only displayed when we needed to look like a solid, functional family.

And food?

Not a damn chance.

Even though I've taught myself to cook—mostly sweets, not gonna lie—there's such an air of *don't eat that, sweetheart—your metabolism won't support it* in our family that none of us would ever admit to cooking at all.

I sigh. Funny all gone.

Phoebe peeks out the door again. "You took Dylan to the place," she whispers.

"He didn't want to go home, and I didn't want to bring him here, and I don't know who his best friend is—I mean, I do, but I'm not talking about that anymore, because I learned my lesson—and when I asked him where he wanted to go, he was all, 'Sandy the Giraffe,' which I think was probably a combination of the concussion and the painkillers."

"He's on *Tylenol.*"

Look at that. I can still lie to my sister, and she'll believe me. The day is saved.

Not. "*I still don't know who his friends are.* And I definitely didn't think *a freaking goat* would've been loose in there! How did it even get in?"

She makes a Phoebe face that means, *It's my fault and I don't want to admit it.* "I miscounted when I put them back after I accidentally let them out last night. And you don't do a great job of locking the front door of *the place*, and Chester apparently learned how to use his horns on things."

"I never unlock the front door. I don't go *in* the front door."

She stares at me a beat.

I stare back.

"Who else has a key?" she asks quietly.

Just the owner.

Whom I will *not* be admitting to knowing.

Admitting I know Floyd—Tickled Pink Floyd, not Deer Drop Floyd, because apparently Floyd is a common name in these parts and the locals have stories about both Floyds—would be like admitting I knew he wasn't actually a ghost when we first moved in and the townspeople were testing us by making the school sound haunted.

"Who'd you rent the building from, Tavi?" Phoebe presses.

"Weird random person in a back alley." I mean, that's definitely true. But telling Phoebe how long I've known Tickled Pink Floyd wasn't a ghost won't win me any points right now.

"I can ask Teague."

"Great. One more person who will want to know secrets that they shouldn't have to carry."

"Like that's the biggest secret he's ever carried in his life."

We stare at each other another beat before I realize I don't actually know if I'm supposed to laugh or cry at that.

"How's it all coming?" she asks me.

I hold up my thumb and index finger about an inch apart. "This close."

"But not *there* yet?"

Phoebe walked in on me trying out a new truffle recipe a few weeks back, and while she's kept my secret for me—other than apparently telling Teague—and she knows that I'm launching a chocolate business, she doesn't know all the details, and I can't ask for the one thing I need.

I don't want to be beholden to Lightly money—or anything related to Lightly money—for any part of the rest of my life.

So I don't tell her I own a cacao farm that I very soon won't be able to afford.

Naomi's right.

I need help to solve this.

And she's right that I need Samantha, and I can't even process all the ways *that* could go wrong, especially now that I'm tighter with some of my family.

They might actually *notice* this time.

"Production is almost ready for launch," I tell Phoebe. "We're just hitting . . . a few little snags."

"Tell me your snag isn't worrying that Mom will find out and tell you that you're going to get fat."

I wince. "Is it wrong to say I don't miss her? I've been ducking all of her calls about some new designs she wants me to put on my socials, and I'm sure she thinks it's because she left or that I'm mad that she never told us she cheated, but I just . . . with her gone, it's like I have *peace*."

"She tried to live out her dreams through you instead of letting you learn who you wanted to be for yourself. I wouldn't miss her if I were you." She wrinkles her nose. "I honestly think she learned a lot here, and I think if you'd talk to her and set some boundaries, you two could have a real relationship, but no, I wouldn't miss her, either, right now if I were you."

And this is why I could see myself being friends with the new Phoebe. "This place has been really good for you, hasn't it?"

"Unexpectedly so." She shakes her head. "Back to *you*. Every business hits snags. You eventually learn to prepare for them. What's wrong? Supply chain? Raw materials? Workers? Quality?"

"Time. It just takes *time*. And then there's *timing*, because *perishable*."

The look she's leveling at me now tells me she knows there's way more than *time* complicating my life. "How are you paying for all of this?"

"With money, like a good businesswoman. Duh."

She stares at me for three more beats, then sighs heavily and leans out in the hallway again. "If you need anything—"

"I've got this. It's just time. But thank you."

I know there are people who'd call me dumb for not asking her for what I need, but *I can't.*

Not only would asking Phoebe for money be like tying myself tighter to the family I'd like to break free from—we're truly awful, we are, and I don't want to be like this anymore—but it would also be admitting that I can't do this to the one person my mother has always told me is better than me.

She's so smart, Tavi. Not like you.

She's such a great businesswoman, Tavi. It's a good thing the internet likes your looks.

She's so driven, Tavi. You and Carter could both learn a thing or two from her.

I have to do this on my own.

I have to prove I can be something other than a made-up face on the internet.

That I'm more than a big disappointment.

And if, while I'm at it, I can save a small part of the world—the land, the people, their history, and their future—all the better.

She shakes her head. "I seriously don't know how you do it all. Your socials are still running, *you're* still running like three marathons a day, you're cleaning this place every time I stop by, and you're building your own *thing* for yourself. Are you sleeping? For real?"

I've mentioned I hate mornings, right? "Eight hours a night!"

"Tavi."

"This one time, when I was in Singapore with Savannah Miranda, we accidentally got talked into going clubbing with some K-pop stars that I'm not allowed to name, and we were, like, up partying for six days straight, and I thought I was going to die, but then I got like three nights of decent sleep, and I was fine."

Her cheek twitches. "You know it's annoying when you vapid-so-cial-media-star me, right?"

"Like, *Phoebe*. I can't help who I am."

"I was going to offer to help you clean that sink, but now . . ."

I wave a hand at her. "I know, I know. You have a lumberjack in need of a blow job."

"And now I'm thinking about you thinking about my sex life."

"Not that different from doing a reality show together."

We stare at each other, then both grimace.

She wasn't as into the whole reality TV experience as I was, and I knew it. But I also knew Phoebe could do anything she set her mind to, and I had no idea what I was doing in college, but I knew my way around a makeup kit and a selfie stick, and if that was what I had, that was what I'd use.

"Never again," she says.

I nod in agreement. Never again with Phoebe. Not as Lola's lackey. "Not even if Gigi says it's what I have to do next to save my soul."

And then the weirdest thing happens.

Phoebe hugs me.

"I worry about you," she says. "If you need help, you know where to find me. No strings, okay? I know I've spent most of my life wanting to be Gigi, but not anymore. Cross my heart. I just want to get to know my sister and help her when she's struggling. I know it's weird, but it's also true."

She smells like peaches, and even though the hug should be awkward, it's not.

I like *this* Phoebe.

But there's still too much history with us not being the best versions of ourselves, and I still need to solve all my problems on my own.

Clean breaks don't come with strings.

Money is strings.

I *have* to do this on my own so that I'm never, ever beholden to my family again.

Chapter 13

Dylan

I'm settling into a dream about dancing sausages when my mother's voice rings in my head. "Dylan? Dylan, honey, you have to wake up. You have *visitors*. Dylan? *Dylan*. Oh my God, did you die? Are you dead?"

"I'm 'wake," I mutter before she starts yelling for someone to call the ambulance.

"Your eyes aren't open."

"Give me a minute."

"Do you want some soup? Or some fresh bread? I know you love fresh bread. I'll go make some. But you need to wake up. It's been thirty minutes."

I pry one eyelid open.

Light streams in through my bedroom window. Still daytime.

Mom bends over and aims a flashlight directly in my eyeball. "Don't close your eye, honey. I need to make sure you're dilating properly."

"I'm dilating properly."

"You say that, but you can't *see* it. I'm calling the doctor."

"Don't call the doctor."

"I'm calling the doctor and telling her that you're not cooperating."

"Mom. We've done this four times already. I'm *fine*." And I'd be better if she'd let me rest for more than fifteen minutes at a time.

Thirty minutes, my ass.

I can still read my watch, and it's been barely twenty since I managed to get in here to lie down.

Mom nudges me, but not hard. More like she's testing to make sure I'm real. "Sit up and wake up and let me check your eyeballs, or I'm calling the doctor."

My head aches, but not like I'm gonna die, so I shove to sitting and let my mother aim the damn flashlight in my eyes. Again.

Feeling like a bum for having to push back the job I was supposed to do today.

Really need to get some more help hired. This town's big enough for three plumbers, which is great for business but really bad for that sense that I'm letting people down.

Didn't used to care about that.

Weird how the world changes once you realize that your actions have impacts on other people and that you can use that power for good instead of being miserable.

"Is he awake?" Hannah asks from the hallway.

I mentally cringe. I don't want to see her.

Two weeks ago, I would've said I didn't want *her* to see *me*. Not *like this*.

But now?

Now, she's the biggest symbol of what's wrong with my life.

"He's awake," Mom reports. "And his left pupil is too slow. I'm calling the doctor."

I sigh.

Not worth arguing. Mom's gonna do what Mom's gonna do. Good thing the doctor knows her.

But when Hannah appears in the doorway, looking like she wants to kill me but can't decide for what reason, I decide maybe *I* want to call the doctor.

Being admitted and put in isolation for medical observation by professionals only wouldn't be a bad way to spend a short recovery.

Might get me back on the job sooner.

And help me avoid the ass chewing that's coming.

But you know what?

She shouldn't have told me she's pregnant.

I'm not her average *best guy friend* from grade school.

I'm the man she was sleeping with until she met her husband, and the man who's been rooting for them to break up.

If she doesn't realize that I think Andrew's all wrong for her, then maybe she's not the friend I thought she was either. And if she *does* realize that and she's pretending she doesn't, then what does that really say about both of us?

Hannah slides into my bedroom, sticking to the wall between my dresser and the doorframe.

A year ago, she would've been at my bedside, helping Mom aim that flashlight in my eyes merely to be evil, then plopping down at the foot of my bed to give me crap about hitting my head.

Today, she's vibrating with a different kind of energy I can't decipher and, honestly, don't have the bandwidth for.

"You told my mother," she hisses.

"I—" I cut myself off, because *I didn't* isn't exactly the truth.

Hannah glowers. "You told *Tavi Lightly*, who told my mother."

"Yeah." I shake my head, realize that's a bad idea when my brain sloshes against my skull, and I meet Hannah's eyes. "I fucked up. I'm sorry."

She wrinkles her nose. "You know it's impossible to stay mad at you when you just own it without making excuses."

"You're glowing. She would've known the next time she saw you."

"And that too!" She fans her face, but I don't know if it's because her eyes are getting teary or if it's because me saying she's glowing is making her blush. Could go either way today. Or maybe it's both. Either way, we're tighter than I should be with her. "You're complimenting me to get out of trouble."

"Guilty."

"No, you're not. You'd say that even if you weren't in trouble." She takes three more steps into my room, then stops. "How's your head?"

"Stubborn and thick."

"Dylan."

"It'll be fine." I wince. "Sorry about your mom's floor."

"That's what she gets for putting potato peels down the garbage disposal."

"That's not what most people get for putting potato peels down the garbage disposal. Did she get the blood out?"

"Not all of it, but she needs to redo the kitchen anyway. You know, someday we'll laugh about this." She smiles, but it doesn't make my head feel any better.

Actually, seeing her isn't making me feel any better.

At all.

She moved on while I wasn't looking. I'm not what she wanted.

It's time for me to move on too.

It's *past* time for me to move on. I've been a damn fool, thinking she'd wake up and realize Andrew isn't what she wants.

Look at her parents.

She thinks griping at each other is normal.

I don't want griping. I don't want anger. I don't want guilt and *it's complicated* and to spend my whole life chasing love in places I can't find it.

I want respect and affection and for my kids to know—

Dammit.

I want my kids to know that I love them unconditionally, without question, and that my fuckups aren't their fault, and that they can count on me and hopefully their mother for anything, even when—no, *especially* when they fuck up too.

No emotional roller coasters. No questions of *What do I need to do to be enough for my mom so she quits finding me new stepfathers?* or *What do I need to do to prove this stepfather isn't worthy?* No dysfunction.

And if they still have their shit years despite me doing my best, they'll know I still love them, and I'll be there for them.

I want what Tavi Lightly wants.

A solid, real, imperfect, but always-trying family.

Didn't see *that* coming when I rolled out of bed this morning.

"Do me a favor?" I ask Hannah.

"As if I could tell you no when you tried to bleed out through your head on my mom's kitchen floor after letting my big news slip."

"Ouch. Okay. Got it. No favors."

"No, no, I'll do a favor. I mean, so long as I'm home before Andrew gets off work. It's my night to pick takeout, and if I don't do it, he will, and he's been on this burrito kick recently, which would've been fine two weeks ago, but right now, all I want is fresh bread. Like those rolls that they used to have at lunchtime at Ladyfingers."

"The ones Jane's mom made." I smile at the memory. Jane's mom had a side business baking the heaviest, yeastiest dinner rolls, then threatening to sell them to Ladyfingers' competition anytime she raised her prices and they didn't like it.

Good lady. We all miss her.

Pretty sure she wouldn't say she misses me, but I miss her.

Hannah's smiling too. "Oh my God, *yes*. I would give my left arm for one of those rolls right now."

I reach for my phone, the automatic response to Hannah's *I would give my left arm* request, but it's not on my nightstand.

"Your mom has your phone," she says, "and I can text Jane myself to see if she'll make a batch."

"Yeah, but you're a Deer Dropper now. She'll tell you to go ask Deer Drop Floyd, since he likes to steal Tickled Pink recipes so much."

"Oh, stop. He's not that bad."

"*Not that bad? Not that bad?* Jesus, Hannah. You really are a Deer Dropper."

The doorbell rings, echoing through the house.

"Quiet," Mom hisses at it.

She used to tell the dog to be quiet or one of my stepdads to be quiet, but she's in a spot between dogs and husbands, so it's just the doorbell she can tell to hush.

"She needs another dog," Hannah says.

"Not while she's living in my house, she doesn't."

"Okay, Grumpy."

"I like dogs."

"Uh-huh."

"I like *plenty* of dogs."

"So why can't your mom have a dog?"

"Because when she finds an apartment or my next stepfather, there'll be a question of ownership, and I'm not losing another dog to my mother, who just might lose the dog to her next ex-husband."

Hannah's cheeks go pink. "Was that subtle shade?"

I blink as I belatedly remember Banshee and the situation with Hannah's parents. "Not on purpose."

"I suppose I'll forgive you."

Voices drift down the hall, followed by a short bark.

My entire body goes tense.

I know that bark.

And I know that voice.

Hannah jerks her head toward the door as Mom strides in, Tavi Lightly on her heels.

"Look at this," Mom says. "So popular with the ladies today. You should hit your head more often."

"Good plan," I agree dryly.

"Dylan Presley Wright."

Pretty sure I'd get whacked with a dish towel if she had one in her hand and I weren't laid up in bed with a concussion. "What? You said it first."

Hannah's smile doesn't reach her eyes this time. "Oof. Middle name. You're dead to everyone today."

"Please don't be dead," Tavi says. Her voice is softer and sweeter, like she's putting on the Tavi Lightly Show, and it irritates me. She holds out a bag of oranges. "I brought health food."

"That is *not* dinner rolls," Hannah says.

Tavi smiles at her. "Hi. I'm Tavi. And this is Pebbles."

"I know who you are."

Shit.

I've seen this before. Been a while—last one that clearly stands out was after the last football game of my high school career. Junior year. I was kicked off by senior year. And that day, I was dripping with sweat and anger and a mood after getting knocked out of playoff contention, and Hannah was sizing up the cheerleader from the other team who I'd been dating, probably to spite someone, and that's the same look she's wearing now.

I might have a headache, but I know what's coming, and I can still leap into the fray to try to prevent the train wreck. "Hannah, this is Tavi Lightly, newest resident of Tickled Pink, and her dog, who's the least amount of trouble of her whole family. Tavi, this is Hannah Thoreaux, who currently holds the county record for most snowshoe baseball strikeouts in a single season."

"No way." Tavi's smile ratchets up thirty-five notches, and it's so fake I wouldn't pick it up in a department store if Oprah herself tried to convince me it was real.

I also might spend too much time watching Oprah specials with my mother.

"Total girl boss," Tavi says to Hannah. "That's the best."

"Girl-bossing is when I make opposing counsel eat their briefcase in court," Hannah replies.

"She got me out of a parking ticket once." Mom beams at Hannah.

She, too, is sad that Hannah married Andrew.

Devastated, really.

Tavi joins the beam squad. "All of that, *and* you have the most gorgeous hair. And I love your necklace. It's such a unique design."

"Oh, this?" Hannah touches the steel butterfly. "There's a vendor at the Renaissance faire who makes them in bulk with premanufactured beads. Half the women in the state have one."

"Renaissance faire? *No way.* I've always wanted to go to a Renaissance faire. Is there seriously one here too? What an amazing little community."

"Yes, compared to the rest of the world, we have *so* much to offer. Eat your heart out, Milan and Tokyo."

"It's our own little slice of heaven," I interrupt. "Tokyo doesn't have the annual Christmas-light wars or ice fishing."

Tavi turns a smile to me. It's worried, but it feels more real than just about anything about her. "You'd be surprised what you can pay to make—ah, I mean, yeah, Tokyo sucks."

"Oh, Dylan, your head's bleeding on your pillow," Hannah says.

Tavi cringes, and something deep in my chest that I don't let out often flexes and growls. She's not in her normal circles here, and I wasn't clear enough when I said *don't tell them.*

Or maybe Tavi Lightly has bigger problems than worrying about a bunch of small-town secrets.

Mom hustles over to grab my head and peer at my wound. *"New bandages!"*

"Enough." I wave her away. "It'll wash."

"It's blood. *Blood doesn't wash.*"

Hannah slips her arm into Mom's. "It really does. It's okay. Here. I'll go get a clean pillowcase, and you can sit down. I know it's been a hard day for you. But Dylan's okay. I promise."

Tavi's shrinking back out of the door. She sets the oranges on my dresser. Pebbles whimpers in her purse carrier.

"I guess you're in good hands," she says to me. And I don't buy that smile for a second.

Not when it's coming with shiny eyes and a wobbly chin.

I don't get her.

I don't.

She eats meat and probably chocolate, too, when she's alone, but in public, she's a paragon of perfection.

How does she live with herself like that?

And why does she feel like she has to?

Why *can't* she go live that life she talked about this morning?

And why do I want to dig deeper into that question?

I flip my pillow upside down. "There. No more blood. I'm fine. Just need a little *rest*."

"Don't give me that look, young man," Mom says. "You are *not fine*."

She probably has a point.

I'm not fine.

My head hurts.

My heart hurts.

And I can't go work it off with a pickup game of soccer or in answering emergency plumbing calls.

But there's one thing I *can* do.

I toss the sheets back. "I'm going to sit in my garden. Alone."

"Oh, sweetheart—" Mom starts.

"Nagging's bad for concussions," I tell her.

She's not fazed in the slightest. "I'm your mother. It's what I do."

"It's a mother's right," Hannah agrees. "Mothers have *so* many rights that people forget about."

Yep.

I'm in trouble.

For the rest of my natural life.

I peck Hannah on the cheek. "Thanks for coming. You know where the door is." Then I peck Mom on the cheek. "Call the doctor. That'll keep you busy while I get fresh air."

And then I grab the oranges.

I don't know why. Maybe I'm feeling like a dick after being cooped up and fussed over all day. Maybe I'm tired of the expectations that I never fuck up because I ran through my lifetime supply of fuckups over a decade ago.

Maybe I want Tavi to get a small win, because God knows she's trying, even if she confounds me as much as the rest of them.

But when I stoop to peck her on the cheek, too, I get a whiff of something fresh and sweet, like she has chocolate buried in her hair, and I feel an unexpected pull in my cock. "Thanks for the oranges. Maybe next time bring beets too. They're my favorite."

"You don't like beets," Hannah says.

"*You* don't like beets," I throw back. "I eat mine roasted with goat cheese and walnuts."

"When?" Mom asks. "I've never seen you eat beets."

I stifle a sigh.

"My tastes totally changed with adulthood." Tavi's cheeks are glowing pink, and her voice is higher than normal. "I guess it happens all the time?"

"But *beets*?" Hannah makes a face.

Mom echoes the face.

"They're so good for you," Tavi says. "I can drop some by later."

"*I'll* get him beets," Mom says.

I leave them to discuss who will take care of my new unexpected favorite vegetable, and I head outside.

Chapter 14

Tavi

I'm back to avoiding Dylan.

It's not that I'm embarrassed that he didn't want a blow job to compensate for his concussion. I didn't go there this time.

It's more that I don't fit in his world.

His perfect, charming, normal world with people who can care about him in ways that I can't.

People who know him, who've known him his whole life. People who don't have to hide who they are to be nice to him.

Normal people.

And on top of knowing I'm not good for him, every time I see him, he does something utterly and completely charming that makes me like him even more.

A girl's gotta protect herself from all these feelings.

When's the last time I swooned just because a guy kissed my cheek? *Never.*

That's the last time.

My future is in Costa Rica with Naomi, where we'll launch a farm-and-breakfast experience as soon as we can afford it, which will hopefully be soon.

I've finally come to grips with the fact that we need an investor, and things are in motion—bigger things, *better* things—with a list of potential investors that I've curated based on knowing if they need an environmental win, if they get bored, if they need to impress or annoy someone, and if I can stand working with them.

Avoiding Dylan has been almost easy, for the record, because if I haven't been cleaning the school, I've been spending every last minute developing a solid pitch, a proposed marketing campaign, and a long-term business plan, which Naomi's failed meeting last week made glaringly obvious that we need.

I don't know if I'll get my trust fund back or if I even want it, but I know that it's my backup plan for keeping the farm running. So I can't leave here until I know the farm is safe and that I have solid footing for running the chocolate business like an actual business.

Although I'm seriously contemplating doing something I swore I wouldn't do again, given how dangerously close I came to getting caught and losing it all last time, but if this works, my days in Tickled Pink will be forever in my rearview mirror.

As will any need to hang on to hope that Gigi will give me access to family money just a little while longer.

I won't have to take any more photos of me carrying the bags my mom designs. I won't even tell my mom where I'm going.

There'll be no more exhausting myself by flying all over the world taking pictures of other companies' products whether I actually like them or not just so that I can score a big payday. I hate the job so much I've spent the past four years donating my salary anonymously to help build schools, medical clinics, and pet shelters around the world.

The donations never made me feel better. Not the way the farm does.

And once I'm on the farm, for good, when it's self-sustaining, when we know there's no longer a risk that we'll miss a mortgage payment and have to sell out to a mining company, when we're solid enough to buy the farm next door to save it, too, if it goes up for sale like Naomi thinks it will, there'll be no more adding extra miles to my morning run and extra weights to my lifting routine when a tabloid says I've gained seven-tenths of a pound.

No more cozying up to the other residents in Tickled Pink to see who'd be good on camera instead of just because they're interesting people, or having Ridhi and Anya serve me terrible coffee one day and good the next depending on their mood or when I last accidentally insulted or hurt a Tickled Pink native, or getting laughed at by Willie Wayne until he nearly has an asthma attack when I attempt to call in that favor to have him launch an Instagram account about the hidden gems in Tickled Pink.

No more mooning over Dylan Wright.

No more blackmail from Gigi.

Freedom is so close I can taste it.

And it has me letting my guard down, which is how I end up running straight into Dylan a week after the incident at Hannah's parents' house.

I'm hustling in the door at Café Nirvana, hoping they can hook a girl up with a decent vegan caramel macchiato since, to the best of my knowledge, I haven't hurt or offended anyone in a few days, and Dylan's on his way out, and we collide with an *oof* that makes Pebbles yip and shriek and dance in my purse, throwing me even more off kilter.

Dylan grabs me by the arms. Those warm brown eyes sweep over me, and his dimples pop out when he smiles. "Hey, Tavi. You okay?"

"Oh yes! Perfect. Perfectly perfect. I'm a steel door. Can't hurt me." *Shut up, Tavi. Shut. Up.*

His smile gets dimplier, and he glances at my waist. "And how about you, Pebbles? All okay?"

Pebbles barks once and grins her doggy grin at him.

"Good," he says.

"How's your head?" There. That's a reasonable question.

"All better. Even cleared for snowshoe baseball this week." His phone beeps on his belt. "And that means I'm late. Good to see you. Don't feel like you have to duck and hide next time we pass in the Pick-n-Shop, yeah?"

"Oh, I wasn't ducking and hiding. I was looking for something on the bottom row. That I dropped. Under the shelf. And I didn't see you." And again, *Shut up, Tavi.*

"You want to ride along today? Had a thought on that TikTok thing you were talking about."

"Oh, no, I can't risk giving you another concussion. And really, being famous on all the socials is terrible. You don't want that."

"I'm not going to get famous."

"You are seriously underestimating yourself. And me. Don't talk to Lola."

He laughs, and yes, I'm swooning.

"But we should do lunch," I add impulsively. "In a place. Without any hard things."

"One o'clock. Ladyfingers."

"Today?"

"Today."

"Oh, I—"

"Or I can call Lola."

"—would love to meet you at Ladyfingers for lunch today at one o'clock."

As soon as I get these pitch meetings set up with some investors, God help me, there'll be no more cracking my molars whenever Lola talks about running into "the cutest guy" who would be "so great for socials and to drop in on *Lola's School House*."

Which is what I listened to in the four minutes and thirty-six seconds that I was free in the past week, but which thankfully was not about Dylan.

Yet.

He squeezes my arm. "Great. See you then."

And then he's gone, stepping out into the morning with a whistle on his lips and a lightness in his step.

I stare for a moment—the man *does* have the best ass in Tickled Pink—and when I turn back to the counter to try to schmooze my way into a decent coffee, three sets of eyeballs are staring at me.

"So you and Dylan, huh?" Bridget Miller says. "Called it!"

Anya cackles. "We knew he was handsome, but we had no idea he was *worldly* handsome."

Ridhi glares at me. "Hurt him and die."

"She already gave him a concussion," Bridget offers.

I put a hand to my chest and act wounded. "And here I was going to offer to do mani-pedis with you tomorrow."

"You don't have time," she replies. "You have a school to clean and too much running to do. What's with the bags under your eyes? Bed too hard? Or are you accidentally asphyxiating yourself because the gas burners in your bedroom are leaking and no one knows it? Oh! Do you know who could check to make sure your bedroom's safe? Dylan."

"Or the whole Tickled Pink Fire Department," Ridhi says. "You know. The one your mother works for?"

"Dylan's a *much* better choice. Mom would be all, *We already checked this before we let your family move in because we didn't want accidental deaths in that old school building on our hands.* Dylan would be all, *Oh yes, Tavi, let me bend over and let you stare at my butt while I check things that don't need to be checked.*"

"I forbid you to continue being a hormonal teenager," Ridhi says.

"It's summer. I'm not old enough for a real job, and I'm bored. And seriously, isn't it better to make up stories about Dylan falling in love with Tavi or Lola than it is to think about him moping away in his house because he can't have *mmmph!*"

"I know who he *can't have*," I tell Ridhi, who's clamped a hand over Bridget's mouth. "You can let Bridget go. I'm not telling anyone."

Bridget twists free. "Like you told her parents about—*mmph!*"

And now Anya's muffling the teenager, whose eyes are twinkling like this truly is the most fun she's had in a week.

I look out the window. Dylan's climbing into his truck in front of the ivy-draped half-finished Ferris wheel, which the town started and abandoned somewhere between thirty and forty years ago, after national interest in *Pink Gold* fizzled out.

It feels like a metaphor for where my life is headed. *Tavi Lightly bursts onto the scene with all kinds of promises of making the community she grew up in stronger and bolder, only to wither and become forgotten and covered in vines when everyone realizes she's not what they hoped she would be.*

"How is it that the whole town knows he's in love with her, but she doesn't know?" I ask. "And can we *please* not talk about my awful slipup?"

"He's a man," Ridhi says. "*He* didn't know, and who can blame her for not wanting to wait any longer for him to figure it out?"

"So she loves him too?"

"*So* much," Bridget says.

Ridhi snorts softly. "Yes, nothing says *I love you* like marrying someone else without fighting for the one you fell in love with in the first place."

"You can't really blame her, given how he was in high school," Anya says.

Both Ridhi *and* Bridget shush her.

There's something to unpack there, but I want good coffee, and I'd rather let Dylan tell me his story at his own pace, so I don't press. "She seemed nice."

"You're seriously calling the competition *nice*?" Bridget asks.

"It's not a competition, Bridge," Ridhi says. "Love's love. Not a game."

"So, like, he could have a harem?"

Ridhi and Anya make matching noises of horror, but I love the way Bridget's eyes light up when she's pushing the limits of what the adults in her life will tolerate.

She's fifteen.

Both light-years and also a blink of an eye away from being an adult herself.

Also? Phoebe's basically in line to become her other stepmom, and the idea of Phoebe having to learn to handle a teenager is chef's kiss. And yes, I can like my sister better *and also* give in to a cackle or two of glee at the idea of Bridget giving her occasional heartburn. I'm allowed to be complicated like that.

"Could I please have one of your absolutely to-die-for vegan caramel macchiatos?" I ask Anya with the friendliest smile I can find. "I forgot my oat milk, but I have my special cinnamon."

She and Ridhi share a glance. "Are you helping Dylan get over Hannah?"

"I'm trying to be friends with more people here. Jet lag was *so* bad when I first arrived, and then Gigi put us all straight to work, and it was so overwhelming to be living in a high school that needed so much work, and also, like, *wow*, where did all the time to make friends go? So now that we're more settled, I'm trying to be more present for everyone. Like, I totally sat down with Dante and Imani the other day and talked with them all about their plans for reopening the inn once tourism is a little more up, and Akiko and I had coffee so she could tell me all about the best parts of the high school that we should restore once Gigi realizes no one will want to go see an old high school converted into a museum about her, but they'll *totally* want to see an old high school that has, like, nostalgia for a time gone by and *life* and *stories*."

And there's another shared glance.

I don't think this one means, *You've earned the good coffee that we give to your sister.*

I think this one means, *She's such a fake.*

Ridhi stares at me longer than the other two. "You owe me a favor," she finally says.

Oh, *hell.*

I think I'm actually nervous.

"She does?" Anya asks.

"Why?" Bridget wants to know.

I flap my hands. "Oh, we don't need to—"

"You owe me a favor," she repeats. "And I'm cashing in."

Chapter 15

Dylan

I'm digging into a burger at Ladyfingers, more anxious than I've been in a long time, fully expecting to be stood up for this lunch, when Tavi hustles in the door fifteen minutes late.

My pulse skyrockets. My mouth goes dry. My cock leaps to attention.

And I almost choke on the burger because I can't swallow it with a dry mouth, and I don't know what the hell's wrong with my body.

Have to take a gulp of tea to get the burger down.

All because a curvy brunette in a tight pink skirt, a low-cut white blouse, and stilettos arrived to finish lunch with me.

"Sorry," she says, completely out of breath as she drops into the seat across from me and pulls off her sunglasses. "Ridhi called in that favor I owe her, and then—"

"What's the favor?"

She flaps a hand, still catching her breath. "Oh, that. Just a—" She glances around, drops her voice, and leans closer, plumping that cleavage up even higher as her chest heaves, and I absolutely, positively cannot stand up from this booth. "She wants me to plan a surprise party for Shiloh. I guess it's one of those things Shiloh's always wanted but pretends she doesn't? And it's, like, her thirty-somethingth birthday, not her fortieth, so doing it *now* will be totally unexpected."

I shove a fry in my mouth and make a noncommittal noise.

Tavi squeezes her eyes shut and sighs. "She's setting me up to look bad because Shiloh doesn't want a surprise birthday party, isn't she?"

"Nah."

"Dylan."

"Three things you need to know. One, Shiloh *hates* surprises. Two, Ridhi won't tell you that she's telling Shiloh that you're planning a surprise birthday party, because that takes the fun out of Shiloh pretending to be mad at everyone who thinks we've actually kept it a secret. And three, don't plan anything without running it by Teague first."

Her nose wrinkles. "You want me to ask my sister's boyfriend to help plan his ex-wife's birthday party? I know they get along, but this is, like . . . weird. And I once planned a surprise birthday party for Melanie Schwimmelstein where I had to work with three different boyfriends in that week that we were setting everything up, because *oh my God*, she used to go through boyfriends faster than Periwinkle Van Doherty would go through toothpaste, and her dad was, like, dentist to who's who of the Upper East Side, so she went through toothpaste like it was champagne at the Minellis' annual garden party. She actually brushed her teeth so much she needed gum grafts at sixteen, and *how gross is that?*"

I shove another fry in my mouth and stifle a grin. She's getting worked up, and she's breathing heavily again.

She frowns at me. "Were you totally serious about all of that advice?"

"Totes."

"Oh my God, don't say *totes*. It's all wrong on you. But also, I really need help. I have too many other things going on to do this right, and it's, like, things I can't control. Like, the *other* half of the reason that I'm late is because I was chasing a goose out of the library at the school when I was supposed to be getting ready for this. *How?* How has there been *a goose* living in the school library this whole time, and we didn't know it?"

I don't know if there was really a goose, if she's really still out of breath, or if she's putting on a show to make up for being late, but it makes me feel better that she's suffering from some kind of nerves too. "Better question—how can you run sixty-eight miles a day and get out of breath chasing a goose?"

"Runs don't flap in your face, Dylan."

I grin. "See, I want to believe you, but there aren't any feathers."

"What?"

"Feathers. If you fought a goose, you'd be covered in feathers." I point to her outfit, which I should *not* be looking at again, because she has lovely cleavage and that pink neck-wrap thing that's probably called a scarf isn't hiding it. If anything, it's positioned perfectly to make people look at her cleavage.

I shake my head and remind myself I am not a man who can be distracted by cleavage. "No feathers."

"I took a shower."

"Uh-huh. French fry?" I hold one out to her, watching as lust overtakes her features.

"Oh, no, thank you. They use lard here, and I'm vegan." She turns a smile to Zoe, the lunch server today, who's sighing as she stops at our table. "Could I please have a side salad, but hold the cheese and croutons, and just bring me a little dish of vinegar for the dressing? And a Perrier, please. Thank you so much. And I *love* your button. Do they sell those over at the Pink Box?"

Zoe blinks slowly behind her glasses. "It's an autism awareness button."

"I know, but I never know where to get them, because I never see them in stores."

"You order them online."

"Oh my gosh, *duh*. Of course. Thank you. The next time my grand-mother lets me use the internet, I'm totes ordering one for, like, me and *all* of my friends."

Zoe makes a noise, then turns and walks away.

I bite into my burger.

Tavi's stomach grumbles.

"She doesn't believe you," I tell her around a mouthful of beefy goodness.

She drops her head to the table. "What's a girl gotta do to get a decent salad and make friends in this town?"

"Be yourself."

"I *am* myself."

I take another massive bite of my hamburger and watch her lift her head back up to watch me eat.

We're playing a game here, and I don't know if I'm right or wrong. How much of this is *genuine* Tavi Lightly, and how much of this is a show she puts on for the world because it's what she thinks the world wants of her?

"You ever do any charity stuff?" I ask her.

"All the time."

And here we go again.

I don't know if the defensive tone means she does it or if it means she's offended that I'm calling her on not doing it more often. "I can't really talk," I tell her. "I buy those coupon books the schools sell every year for fundraisers or the cookie dough the band kids sell, but I don't go looking for good causes, so I really only donate to things when I get something out of it."

"Benevolence and charitable giving are a massive part of what my family spends time and money on every year. It's, like, expected when you're rich. And I mean, *hello*. I just told you I'm doing something nice for someone else here."

"Because you owed someone a favor."

She *hmph*s. "What do you think we're all doing here in Tickled Pink?"

I shrug. "Heard it's to save your grandmother's soul. So is it really benevolence? Or is it what she gets out of it?"

She chews on her bottom lip, her blue eyes raking over my face. "I'm not my grandmother."

"None of us are our parents or grandparents. Not if we pay attention and don't want to be. Now, I wouldn't mind being *my* grandma. At least, the me version of her. She was a spunky, funny, no-nonsense lady. Brought snowshoe baseball to Tickled Pink, *and* she once made my grandpa go Christmas caroling in his pajamas in June."

She smiles. "Why?"

"He was being grinchy."

"Do you think that would work on my brother?"

"No."

Her laugh hits me square between the eyes. It's different from every other laugh I've heard from her lips—not that I've heard many, though I was subjected to reruns of her reality TV show a few weeks back at Willie Wayne's house, and I did spend that weekend watching all the clips on her TikTok channel—and there's something so genuine about it that I feel like giving myself a high five.

It's like I've glimpsed the real Tavi Lightly. The one who eats chocolates and who talks about being a good mom and who let me hug her when I realized how much of my life I've wasted thinking Hannah was first the easy option, then my "one."

I like knowing real people. That's half the joy of life.

Another quarter of it might be finding those real people in places I don't expect.

Like sitting across from me in a small-town hole-in-the-wall bar wearing her fashionable clothes like armor.

She clears her throat and squares her shoulders as she glances to the side.

People are staring.

"Not used to that?" I tease.

"Ha ha." She reaches beside herself, like she's looking for the dog. "Where's Pebbles?"

"Recovering from the goose incident with a very long nap in Niles's art room. How's Hannah? Is she still mad at you?"

I shake my head. "Too morning sick to be mad."

"That's good. I mean, not good. Morning sick sounds terrible. But the not-mad part. That's—oh, look at that. You're almost done with lunch. We should talk business. So I asked Bridget to spend some time researching other plumbers on TikTok to scope out the competition, since you said you're still interested in doing this, and there's one who's, like, in a band, so he's all about pipes, because *ha ha*, pipes, right?"

"Ha ha," I agree.

Tavi smiles like she knows I'm humoring her. "She says you have a much better singing voice, but obviously, I haven't heard either of you, so I wouldn't know. Then there's this other plumber who, like, dances all the time or duets people with really bad plumbing jobs, but I think we can make a lot of strides with you becoming the Tickled Pink Plumber if we focus on you giving solid advice on how to take care of your plumbing and you being your adorable self. And of course, I'll pop into your videos, so naturally, you'll take off, and after a couple videos, even without me, you'll be a star all on your own."

"That thing you said the other day—if we say we're just friends, then that's gonna make all the women fall at my feet?"

Her cheek twitches, and her bright, half-ditzy, half-businesswoman facade falters before she gives me the widest, brightest, fakest smile I've ever seen.

"Oh, totes. For sure." She nods so hard she looks like a malfunctioning bobblehead. "Lunch was a really smart idea, because now people will start to wonder. We might even make the *Tickled Pink Papers*. I mean, you're the first man I've had lunch with solo since we got here, so natch, whoever runs the local gossip sheet will be *all* over it. I give it three hours after they publish pictures of us having lunch here before Lola's asking you to dinner, and *that* will totally seal your reputation as a man in demand. I mean, if you'd want to have dinner with Lola."

She stares at me expectantly, but it's not a normal question.

It's like she's asking if I *want* Lola to ask me to dinner. Like she *needs* to know.

Holy shit.

Tavi Lightly *likes* me.

I'm thirty-two years old.

Left high school almost fifteen years ago.

But I've realized in the past two weeks or so that I still feel like that's all I have to offer women around here. They look at me and think, *Oh yes, Dylan has his life together now, but can you imagine the holy terrors that his kids will be? And what if it's still simmering under the surface and he has a relapse and I'm married to that?*

Tavi doesn't look at me like that.

She only knows *this* version of me.

There's no pressure to prove to her that I can do better. She already sees me as *better*.

She believes in the me that I am today, no question. And I know she'd listen to some of the stories of my youth and match them with one or two of her own.

"Huh." I shift in my seat.

Having Tavi Lightly help me get back into the dating game? Weird, but okay. I can go with it.

Having an unexpected crush on the woman who has more secrets than a grizzled old spy?

I'd tell myself it's novelty, but I don't think it is.

I think it's worse than that.

I think she's the fresh start that I didn't know I needed.

She claps her hands like she can't sit still. "Look at you! Here we are, just eating lunch, and this time next week, you'll be world famous and have dates lined up for the next year. It's so exciting to make a star."

I don't know why I invited Tavi to lunch today.

Seemed like a good idea at the time.

I know I don't want to be some TikTok or Instagram star, but I wouldn't mind helping people troubleshoot stuff they can do themselves, like fixing a toilet flapper valve or replacing a cartridge in a faucet to make a sink quit dripping. And if I can bring some attention to Tickled Pink to help my hometown get a little more interest once the Lightlys have moved on, so we don't have to depend quite so much on miracles to do things like getting roads fixed and the elementary and middle schools improved, all the better.

But—"Don't you get tired of pretending everything's happy and all about fame all the time?"

Her face freezes.

I mentally kick myself. Not my business.

She lives in a world I can't understand and honestly don't want to. I shouldn't judge. "Sorry," I mutter. "It's just—sorry."

She leans across the table, her voice quiet. "There are trophies in my mother's study for beauty pageants that I won before I was old enough to remember even competing in them. The first truly strong memory I have as a child was my father telling me not to tell my mother that he was having a private meeting with my nanny in his study during a holiday party. I remember the ribbons and the mistletoe and wearing a dress that my mom was freaking out about because it didn't fit as well as it had the week before when we bought it. I remember itching and feeling like I couldn't breathe, but I wasn't allowed to say that, because appearances are everything."

I want to interrupt her, but that look in her eyes—it's like she's been waiting to tell everyone everything that's wrong.

So I keep my mouth shut.

And she keeps sharing. "I grew up being told that Phoebe was brilliant and could do everything, and I better watch my weight, because my looks were all I had going for me, and even then, I needed a lot of makeup. Even as a kid. So yes, I get tired. I get *very* tired. But it doesn't matter when I really haven't made anything more of myself, does it? I need the Lightly money. I need to look like I have my shit together. And I really, really need to stay off my grandmother's radar for anything other than doing what she's ordering me to do while I figure out what I want my future to be, or honestly? I might not have much of a future."

I take another bite of my hamburger.

Not to torture her.

But more because I don't like the thoughts swirling in my head, and I don't want to say them out loud. And I don't know if that's for her benefit or mine.

Your family are dicks.

Nope. Not gonna use that one.

You're fucking gorgeous.

Probably not the best line at the moment either. Have enough experience with women to know they don't believe it, even when it's true, and it can complicate even the simplest relationship, which isn't what Tavi and I currently have.

We're both messed up is probably accurate. *You're better than you think you are, and you can do any damn thing you decide you want to do.*

She squeezes her eyes shut. "I didn't say that."

"My dad walked out when I was three, and my mom's upgraded husbands every few years since. No family's perfect."

"Sometimes I wish my mom would've left," she whispers.

That hits hard.

For all that my mom drives me crazy, she's never made me feel like she doesn't love me.

And I get the feeling Tavi Lightly doesn't have the first clue what *love* means.

160

Or maybe she knows very, very well what it means.

Maybe she knows exactly what she's missing.

"I used to plan how I would run away from home after having a fight with one of my stepfathers," I tell her. I could tell her more—and worse—but I want to make her smile again. "Or my mom. Or my brother or sister."

"You still could."

"Nah. I like it here. Good job. Good friends. *Really* good friends. And someone's gotta stick around and keep an eye on Mom."

"Octavia, I thought you were cleaning the library shelves," Estelle Lightly says beside us.

Tavi's cheek twitches again, but she aims her smile at her grandmother and reaches up to curl a finger through her hair. "Dylan and I are talking about his social media debut to help Tickled Pink get famous again."

Estelle looks at me.

She's a persnickety rich white lady with enough years under her belt of being a terror that she's still adjusting to the idea of mortality and what will happen to her soul.

And she has a way of peering at a person that would make him feel about three inches tall if he cared about her opinion.

Lucky for me, I spent enough time in principals' offices growing up and have enough confidence in myself as an adult—most of the time—that she doesn't bother me much.

She sniffs. "The *plumber*."

"Great-Grandpa Horace made us rich off of a better toilet paper. It seems so fitting."

"But will it do *Tickled Pink* any good?" Estelle demands.

"This is a whole-town effort, Gigi. Who better to focus on than a hometown hero who helps basically everyone here? Do you know *anyone* who doesn't need a plumber on occasion?"

"Does the world at large recognize that?"

"We're about to make them. Isn't the world better when we appreciate everyone for their contributions to society instead of thinking that some of us are better than others?"

"Vegan tasteless barf on a plate, with pucker juice on the side." Zoe bumps in past Estelle and deposits Tavi's salad on the table.

"Thank you so much, Zoe," Tavi says brightly. "That was *so* fast. You're amazing. Can I ask you a question?"

"Was that your question?"

"No, actually—"

"Too bad. One question per day."

I suck in a grin.

"Thank God you're not trying to put *her* on camera," Estelle says.

"She'd be great," I interject. "No one knows more about Tickled Pink history than Zoe. And she tells the fun stories."

"She's rather rude."

"She's not rude, Gigi. She's honest," Tavi says. "We're not entitled to everyone here liking us. And you yourself told Jane yesterday that her beer tasted bad when we all know you don't like beer, so it's not like Jane could make any beer that you like. *That* was rude."

Estelle's eyes narrow.

"I mean, if God has a scorecard, he'd probably call it even," Tavi adds.

I shove my last bite of burger into my mouth.

"Dylan and I are going to spend the afternoon making plans for his launch on TikTok, and maybe Insta and Snap too. I'll catch up on the library like tomorrow or something? It's not like the books are going anywhere, and the feathers are, like, not the worst thing to *ever* happen to them. I found a dried pickle stuffed in the middle of a copy of *Great Expectations*. That library has *seen* things, Gigi."

Estelle frowns. "It has, hasn't it?"

"So many things." Tavi's like a bobblehead doll again. "It can wait a few more days. It might even be better to wait a few more days."

And I'm wishing I had more things to shove in my mouth.

"That's settled then," Estelle declares. "We'll both ride along with Dylan to make plans for Tickled Pink's future."

"Gigi, Dylan doesn't have room in his truck for—"

Zoe slaps both hands on the table, appearing out of nowhere and startling both of the women as she looks at me.

I know that look.

It means one of her kids did something to her house, apparently with the plumbing since she's at my table and not stopping to chat with Manuel, our local electrician, or Steve, Tickled Pink's handyman, who are having lunch across the way together.

"Here, or your place?" I ask her, just to verify.

Her eyeball twitches. "My place."

I rise and nod, grabbing one last fry before I pull out my wallet to dig out some cash. After what I did to Zoe in high school, she gets plumbing for free, for life, no matter what her kids do. "On it. Ladies, anyone who's coming better grab her lunch to go. Time to get to work."

Chapter 16

Tavi

Sometimes I wonder how my grandmother came to exist.

How can one single person be so hell bent on causing chaos and misery at every opportunity, while pretending it's all for the good of everyone around her?

There's something to be said for learning through suffering, but it's something else entirely when the suffering is unnecessary.

Like right now.

"No, Octavia, you have to stick your hand *down the toilet*," she says imperiously.

I point to Dylan, who's siphoning water out of the toilet and into a bucket. "Dylan says that's not what we have to do."

"And what will you learn from that experience?"

"I already learned how to use a snake. What have you learned? I don't see you in here offering to stick your hand down the toilet."

"Don't take that tone with me, young lady. Your soul could use some more patience with old people."

I will not murder my grandmother.

I will not murder my grandmother.

I will not murder my grandmother.

I dig deep, deep, *deep* inside and find my inner flake. "Oh, are you old, Gigi? I didn't notice."

Pebbles half barks but mostly makes a noise like she's choking on something.

She probably is.

It's undoubtedly goose feathers.

She should still be sleeping, but Gigi insisted that if we're making Dylan a social media star, then we needed the full star power of my own feeds, and that includes my dog.

She's micromanaging my soul-saving tasks.

I wish I had the freedom to do what Phoebe did and tell her to worry about her own soul, but Phoebe also has a healthy bank account after working for Remington Lightly in mid- to upper management since she graduated college, and she's also one of those people who are smart about investments, which means she took her trust fund disbursements and invested them wisely, and now she could build her own tiny house in a tree across from Teague's if they ever need more room, in addition to funding the start of what she hopes will be a small amusement park off the Tickled Pink square.

She wouldn't have bought a failing cacao farm in Costa Rica, and if she had, she would've had venture capitalists and investors and environmentalists with grants lined up to cash in on the Lightly name before the ink was dry on the purchase contract, because she wouldn't have been attached.

It wouldn't have been a mission for her. A calling. A future.

To her, it would've been just business, which works for her. But not for me.

Gigi's giving me the flat look that used to precede irrational demands that the entire family drop everything and help her plan a gala that would outshine Viola Barker's, since we were all so much more complimentary of Viola in the press than we were of whatever Gigi had done last.

Lightlys don't do second place.

"Octavia Bianca Lightly, when I say put your hand down a toilet, you don't try to get out of it by calling me *old*."

"I didn't call you old, Gigi! I said you're *not* old!"

"If you put the word in a sentence with anyone over forty, you're calling them old."

She silently dares me to say she doesn't look a day over thirty-eight.

I silently do not take that dare.

This morning at family breakfast, she was all smiles and effusive compliments for Lola's progress, surprised compliments for Carter's impromptu voluntary scrubbing of the biology lab cabinets, nose-in-the-air compliments for Dad's meticulous care of the high school lawn, and obligatory compliments for the progress I haven't made on the teachers' lounge.

Clearly, I still have the most work to do on my soul, which is starting to piss me off.

"How do I do this selfie video thing?" Dylan asks as he rises, task complete, apparently.

God bless the man.

He knows how to play peacekeeper.

Or at least how to be a distraction.

"Here." I shift around Gigi in the small bathroom and put a hand on Dylan's arm while I press a finger to the button on his phone to reverse his camera.

He sucks in a quick breath, and that's all it takes to make my nipples hard as glass. Not that the subtle scent of hamburger still lingering on him wouldn't have affected me anyway in another minute or two.

God, that looked good.

I'm not saying I want meat at every meal—even if I can shake my mother's voice in my head reminding me not to eat anything that could land on my hips, I still *like* vegetables and beans and tofu, and I'm aware of the environmental impact of meat-production plants—but once we secure investment money and we start taking in income from alternate crops, tourism, and early-run chocolate with beans from other farms, I don't have to worry about what anyone else thinks about my lifestyle.

I don't care if I never have a million dollars in the bank again.

I just want enough to take care of the farm, indulge in making chocolate, and pay my bills.

"And that's it?" Dylan asks as he peers at the phone.

"Now you hit the record button, and—*oh my God*. You're playing with me, aren't you?"

"A little." He grins. *Gah*. The dimples. Also, his front right tooth is just a smidge crooked, and it's adorable. You don't notice until you're right up next to him, but it is. It's the little imperfections that keep making him hotter.

And I need to *not* think about Dylan being hot. We're *friends*. I'm done leaving a trail of bodies behind me when I leave a place. "You know how to operate your camera."

"I only take pictures. Not video." He moves it left and right. "Huh. Pretty intuitive. Glad it's not one of those things where you move it the way you should and you disappear off the other side of the screen. You ready to stick your hand in that toilet?"

I blink at him. He very clearly said, "You don't need to stick your hand in the toilet," after the snake didn't work.

He's grinning broader as he hits the camera button to start the video. "Hi, world. I'm giving Tavi Lightly lessons on how to do her own plumbing, and today, I'm gonna talk her through sticking her hand down a pipe to dig out the remnants of Captain America taking on a raw chicken thigh in the ocean known as a toilet bowl. You ready, Tavi?"

I'm not in makeup. Not *film* makeup, anyway. I have a tickle in my nose like I still have a goose feather up there from the fight in the library. And I know we can do a second take, so I smile anyway. "I can't wait. I've always wanted to stick my hand down the pipes that carry the things we put into toilets."

The man's smile gets impossibly broader. "First rule of plumbing: the pipes don't like sarcasm."

"Oh, *ha ha*, you."

"A'right, then." He points to the toilet. "I already turned off and disconnected the toilet's water valve. We siphoned as much water out of the bowl and tank as we could, but there'll be some spillage since we can't flush this one, so we've got towels ready. Lucky it's clean water, yeah?"

"That's the only way I'd do this."

"Go on and pry those white trim caps off on the sides there. Gotta loosen the bolts holding the toilet to the floor."

I'd tell him this video's going to be seven thousand minutes too long, but one, there's no way I'm letting him put a video of me sticking my hand down a toilet on the internet, and two, even if I did, it would go through my video-editing team first to get cut down for time and clarity.

But I should know how to do this.

In case I need the knowledge in Costa Rica. Naomi could have kids who toss things down the toilet one day. *I* could have kids one day. Or I might just have to replace a toilet bowl. These things wear out after a while, don't they?

I follow his instructions and get the toilet unbolted.

"Nice job. You feel strong enough to break the seal and lift that thing off the floor?"

Why the hell not?

This video will never see the light of day.

"How do I break the seal?"

"Straddle it there, then rock it back and forth. Just like that. Good job."

It feels like I'm doing something wrong, since I never, ever would've considered removing a toilet to be a task I'd tackle.

Something creaks, and water starts leaking on the floor. *"Gah!"*

"No, no, that means you're doing it right," Dylan says. "Grandma Lightly, grab some of those towels. Tavi, give it two more solid rocks."

Grandma Lightly.

I stifle a snort of amusement.

Gigi *hates* the *grandma* word.

"There you go," Dylan says as Gigi throws a towel on the floor without getting close.

It's a small bathroom.

I have no idea if she doesn't want to be on camera or if she doesn't fit.

"All right, Tavi, now that you've got it loose, I'll pull it off the floor—"

I twist and look at him. "I can do it."

He looks at his camera—he's holding it aimed down at us, so he's in the lower corner, his backward baseball cap hiding the remnants of the stitches in his head, and I'm in the opposite upper corner—and then he looks back at me. "You sure?"

"If I'm doing this, I'm doing this, silly. No, like, shortcuts."

"Gotta lift with your hips and legs, okay?"

I grin back at him. It's a total fake, fluffy grin. "Okay, Dylan. Whatever you say."

I should let him do this.

I should.

But I don't want to be here in Tickled Pink. I don't want Gigi being an evil overlord trying to destroy the best thing I've ever done when I'm *this close* to success—and *this close* to never having to see my family again.

She was right about one thing.

We're awful.

We're truly awful.

"If you feel a pull in your back, stop *immediately*," Dylan orders.

And then there's that.

Careful, cautious concern from someone who has no reason to let me invade his life like this.

It's a lot different from *Come on, Tavi, ten more minutes on that stair climber! I can SEE your dinner on your butt!*

I know my mother meant well. I do. But her "meaning well" fucked me up good.

Although, is he—is Dylan staring at my butt?

Oh my God.

He is.

He's staring at my ass.

His gaze lifts to mine, and *gah* again.

His cheeks go ruddy like he knows he's caught.

"Stop if I hurt my back," I repeat back to him with a smile. An *honest* smile. Dylan Wright is checking out my ass. "Got it."

I squat, grab the toilet under the bowl, and lift.

He's right.

It's heavy.

But it feels good to use my muscles for good, and fixing a plugged toilet for Zoe, the Ladyfingers server whose son is a handful and a half, is definitely good.

"You got it okay?" Dylan asks. "Here. I'm stepping in the tub. Stand back, Grandma Lightly. Tavi, put it right where I was standing a minute ago."

I lift and stand, move back two feet, and deposit it on the floor. Then I rise again and flex for the camera. "Beast mode," I say with a toss of my hair and my gag-worthy social media smile.

Dylan's still aiming his phone at both of us, video rolling, but while I can see my own face doing that half-flaky, half-sexy smile that usually gets me three or four more emails asking me to shill some other product, the camera can't see his face as he stares at me like he's seeing me for the first time.

His lips are parted, his eyes serious, lids lowered just enough to make me wonder if he's turned on by feminine shows of strength.

And that question isn't doing any good for my panties, so I shove it away. "What's next, Mr. Plumber?"

He shakes his head, but his smile isn't nearly as easy as it comes back. "Gotta peel off that wax ring, and then, if we were replacing the toilet, we'd stuff a rag in the hole to keep all those icky sewer gases out until we get the new toilet in here, but since we need to remove an obstruction, after we remove the wax ring, you're gonna go fishing for some raw chicken thigh and Captain America."

Oh, good.

The gross part.

I wrinkle my nose. "Can I make my grandma do that?"

"No, Octavia," Gigi replies.

I sigh and roll my eyes. *"Fine."*

Dylan talks me through the wax-ring stuff, which is gross, and then the problem in the pipe in the floor comes into clear focus.

"That's it, Tavi. Reach on down there and grab that raw chicken thigh."

I'm kneeling, sitting on my heels as I inspect the problem, *in a freaking skirt*, but I look up and make a pouty face at the camera. "This is why people shouldn't eat meat."

Dylan's face twists in amusement. His warm brown eyes smile at me—*I know your secret, Tavi Lightly*—and he clears his throat. "Guess you could add this to your list of reasons."

"Grab the raw chicken, Octavia," Gigi orders.

"Touching meat is against my religion." I shake my hands out and make myself huff a few times. "But fine. *Fine.* Ew. *So gross.* This is, like, *disgusting.* Ew ew *ew!*"

"It's a public service, Octavia."

If Gigi says my name one more time, I swear to God, I will throw this raw chicken thigh at her.

I reach a hand down to the open pipe, where there's fleshy raw chicken clearly stuck. I can just see Captain America's hand sticking out on one side of the pink meat.

And I take a calculated risk.

I should not do this.

I shouldn't.

I poke at the chicken, and it honestly makes me gag.

Raw chicken is gross.

Especially when it's been sitting in toilet water for God only knows how long.

"Quit poking at it and remove the obstruction from the pipe, Octavia." Gigi's getting impatient.

And I'm *done*.

I grab the chicken, gagging again, and I yank.

Hard.

It doesn't budge.

I yank again.

Nothing.

"How do you get a grip on it?" I squeal.

Yes.

Squeal.

The camera's rolling.

I can't help myself.

When I move to Costa Rica, I am *never* stepping in front of another camera in my life, unless it's to *be myself* and show how we grow and make chocolate.

"Might try some—" Dylan starts, but it's too late.

I've grabbed that chicken, and it's coming out of the pipe.

I gag once more.

I yank hard.

And then I accidentally let it fly behind me.

Accidentally.

Prove I'm lying.

I dare you.

But who'd want to?

Gigi screams.

Pebbles howls in response.

Dylan makes a choking noise.

"Captain America!" I shriek, as if I have no idea that I just threw a raw chicken thigh at my grandmother. "Don't go down, Captain America!"

"Get it off!" Gigi screeches. *"Get it off!"*

"It's just chicken, Grandma Lightly," Dylan says.

"It's in my hair!"

I silently high-five myself. Even I didn't think I could do *that* well.

And even knowing Gigi *will* exact revenge, in this moment, I feel like the queen of the damn universe.

Suck it, Gigi.

"Saved him!" I cry, lifting the action figure out of the pipe. "Look, Dylan! I saved Captain America!"

He spares me a quick glance, his lips twitching, as he climbs out of the tub. "Stuff a rag in that hole, yeah? Here, Estelle. I've got the chicken. It won't hurt you. Promise."

His phone camera's still rolling.

He got every last second recorded.

I have exactly zero dollars in my bank account designated as *money to pay a small-town cutie for a video that I will lord over my grandmother for the rest of her natural life*, but I will literally walk around Deer Drop taking selfies with people for money to cough up as much as he wants.

But I won't have to.

It's Dylan.

He's the kind of nice guy who will give it to me for free and probably make me promise I won't do any evil with it, except he'll know I'm lying when I promise, and he'll probably still give it to me for free.

Good thing.

With that favor Ridhi called in, I now have even less time to pose for selfies in exchange for money, even if I farm out most of the work of planning the party to the people on my team still making my social media feeds roll.

No matter how much I delegate, I still have to decide the *what* and the *where* and the decorations and the catering menu and the guest list.

"Oh my gosh, Gigi, are you okay?" I leap to my feet and bump into him as we both try to crowd into the small area to save my grandmother from the flying chicken thigh.

Gigi aims an eyeball of death at me while Dylan plucks the raw poultry out of her hair and tosses it in his garbage bucket.

"Don't worry," I say. "We'll call Niles. He'll know what to do."

For her.

As for me, I might be toast.

And you know what?

Totes worth it.

Chapter 17

Dylan

After the extra stop to clear Zoe's pipe and then the presence of three ride-alongs for the rest of my calls, my day doesn't end until almost eight. But instead of going home, I hit the Pick-n-Shop and wish we had an ice cream place here in Tickled Pink again. When I'm done, I head toward the school with two pints in a bag.

But I reverse direction before I've gone half a block.

I don't think I'll find what I'm looking for at the old high school.

When I reach the old Methodist church and see light coming through the door crack at the bottom of the stairwell out back, the zing in my veins tells me my instincts were right.

Tavi Lightly is up to something here.

I step softly down to the basement, then creak open the door.

Voices drift out from the cool basement. Voices and soft music.

"I'm having trouble finding mint I like around here, but if you ship it to me, it won't be fresh anymore once it gets here, and this sample has to be *perfect*."

"I can overnight it."

"Too suspicious. You can't hide an overnight shipment in a swag pack or subscription box. People are already watching me more closely."

"What if I ship it to your sister?"

"No. I want to keep my family out of this."

"*Tavi*. We don't have a lot of options here. And she hasn't told anyone, has she? Honestly, we need to just say *screw it* and go public. Did you see what happened when Charisma Bliss admitted she uses beauty products that are tested on animals?"

"You mean how she was skewered alive in the media?"

"And then how she announced she was investing in a company that truly did only cruelty-free products after hiring an entire team of investigators to vet the possibilities and exposed three other liars along the way? Hello, you saved a farm, gave a bunch of people in the nearby community solid jobs with good pay, and you know Esteban? Sebastián's right-hand man? He told me if the mining company had gotten their hands on this land, he would've had to move his family or leave them here while he went to find other work, and now instead, he's doing what he loves. And the school donations? And don't tell me it wasn't you who donated the money to fix the electricity at the church building. Your fans will rally. *They will*. We'll be okay, and with the public knowledge that you're on board, we'll have our pick of investors."

"No, we won't, because *I'm a nobody*, and you shouldn't buy friends." Tavi comes into view as I turn the corner past the closet and into the main all-purpose room. She's smoothing the top of a mold with a spreader, phone on the counter. "I know you believe in me, and God knows I love you for it, but until we have an actual product, I'm just a ditz in public who gets paid to shill products because it worked so well when I did it to make my mom happy. But *my mom's purses don't sell*. It doesn't work. I'm not Charisma Bliss. I'm not an actress who left acting for this. I'm a former child beauty queen who didn't build who I am. Someone else built me to be a puppet. I'm a *fake*. And people don't follow fakes. This has to be *the fucking best chocolate* to ever touch anyone's lips, and if it's not—"

I clear my throat, which I should've done about thirty seconds ago.

Tavi cuts herself off with a yelp, drops the spreader, and then does something I've seen her do too many times in the past month or so.

She ducks under the table. "Go away, Dylan."

"Dylan? Who's—ah, hell, Tavi, did you forget to lock the door again?" the voice on the phone says.

Tavi mutters something you never hear on her public social media videos and reaches above her, slapping the tabletop like she's looking for the phone.

"Don't hit the—" I start, but it's too late.

The chocolate mold goes flying, sending thick, melted chocolate all over the floor before it lands right side up between the table and the sink.

"Dammit!" Tavi shrieks.

"Tavi? What's going on?"

"Hi," I call into the phone. "I'm Dylan. Just a harmless small-town plumber who doesn't tell secrets."

"Oh God, we're doomed," the voice replies.

I lean over the table and dangle the bag of vegan ice cream.

Tavi's covering her face with her hands.

I want to hug her and promise I won't hurt her, but I get the feeling she hasn't had many people in her life who'd tell her that and mean it.

She'd probably think it was code for *I'm going to fuck up your world like it's never been fucked before.*

"Peace offering," I say. "I'll clean up the mess."

"Not necessary." Her voice is muffled.

"Let him clean it up and then threaten to spill his darkest secrets if he tells anyone yours," the person on the phone says. "Don't tell me he doesn't have secrets. I'm from a small town too. *Everyone* has secrets. Use it. Use it to destroy him, Tavi! Oh my God, *who am I?*"

Tavi slides her fingers apart to peer at me through one eye, then sighs and scoots out from under the table. "I know his secrets," she says as she stands.

I don't correct her.

Not very nice when she's clearly already having an off night with some confidence issues.

"You let me do the dirty work," she continues with a glance at the phone, "and you stay exactly as you were five minutes ago. I'll call you back. I have to clean up a mess before another freaking *goat* smells it and invades the kitchen and eats a faucet or something."

"Email me. I'm about to go talk to Sebastián about some things he wanted to show me, and then I'm having dinner with the Vargases. Let me know if you need me to fly in to bury a body."

Tavi smiles a soft smile that reaches her eyes and softens everything about her, but she doesn't aim it at me.

She's aiming it at the phone.

Dammit.

"You know I'd never pull you into something that ugly," she says.

"You should. I'd be awesome. No one would suspect me."

"And you wouldn't be able to live with yourself. I'm hanging up before you say something truly incriminating that makes it impossible for you to sleep tonight. Tell Sofia I said hello."

"Later, Tay-Tay. Give Pebbles my love."

Tavi hangs up, then looks at me.

And I startle even myself when I wrap my arms around her and pull her in for a hug.

She looks exhausted.

Eyelids puffy, dark circles under her eyes, and her posture is sagging.

Her body goes rigid, and I'm about to drop my arms when she melts into me, laying her face against my chest and wrapping her arms around my waist.

My heart kicks up.

So does my cock, and I have to adjust my stance so she won't feel it.

This isn't about physical attraction or about wanting her to aim one of those real smiles at me, and I have no intention of leading her on accidentally.

Even if now, I wouldn't mind leading her on.

She's flawed. She's secretive. She's dangerous, as the stitches still in my head like to remind me.

And I want to learn every one of her secrets and convince her that they're all okay.

No matter what they are.

How many people has she had in her life to tell her she's okay?

"What's this for?" she whispers.

"You look like you need a friend."

"I don't want friends."

"Why not? Friends are awesome."

"I'm not staying here. I don't want to get attached."

"Where are you going?"

She takes a deep breath, and I don't think she's going to tell me, but then she whispers, "Costa Rica."

Shit.

That's seriously *away*. "I hear it's pretty."

"I bought a near-dead cacao farm to rehabilitate it and make it profitable again with luxury truffles after I did this master class online about chocolate making and fell in love with the whole process, but right now it costs more to run it than I can afford, since Gigi froze my trust fund and is threatening to expose me if I don't stay here and play her game. I keep saying I saved the farm, but the truth is, I think the farm saved me. At least, it was supposed to. Before all *this*."

I fell for a friend once.

I don't want to offer to be Tavi Lightly's friend and then do it again, only to have her walk away too.

Not when her simple, easy belief in me is giving me a newfound confidence that I didn't know I needed.

But I can imagine what it's costing her to confess this, and for once, I believe her. "I never told Hannah that her pancakes tasted like rubber gaskets and the tree she thought was a maple that she tapped for syrup is actually an oak, and it tastes like crap."

"You could still tell her."

"Yeah, I'll put that in her baby shower gift. *Congratulations. Best of luck with the baby. Don't feed it your pancakes if you don't want it to choke.*"

She sighs and tightens her grip around my waist, nuzzling her cheek against my T-shirt while I try to get my erection under control.

Not the time, good buddy. Not the time.

"Why are you so comfortable?"

Yeah. Comfortable. That helps. I'm not *sexy.* I'm *comfortable.* I'm like an old shoe to her. Good erection. Good erection simmering down. "Good genes and old shirts."

She *hmph*s.

"What?" I ask. "What's wrong with that answer?"

"It's just so *nice.* Do you know how many men would flex their pecs and be like, *Because I work out, baby?* And here you're all gorgeous, with the best ass in Tickled Pink, and you're kind, and you're patient, and you keep secrets, and you're like, *I don't know why I'm comfortable, must be that I wear old shirts.* Old shirts. *Old shirts.*"

She thinks I have the best ass in Tickled Pink. That's awesome. "You . . . don't like old shirts?"

"I come from a world where if you get caught wearing the same thing in public twice, you're shamed for not having enough money, resources, or creativity to pick something new. But *old shirts.* It's so soft. And like *butter.* And just—just—*how?* How do you stay nice?"

"I like to like myself, and it turns out I don't like myself if I'm an asshole."

She snorts softly.

"I stole my brother's girlfriend and took her to prom. Then I slept with her and immediately dumped her too."

Her arms go impossibly tighter around me. "Would you do it again?"

"*No.*" I blow out a breath. "He hasn't been back to Tickled Pink since he left for college."

"Is he . . . nice?"

"Yeah. Decent guy. Eloped a couple years back. Mom talks about his kids. I don't get pictures."

"He's still mad?"

"Doesn't come back to town. *Ever.* Can't blame him. I wouldn't want to be around me either. And I gave my little sister's American Girl doll a swirly. She saved for *years* for it, and I ruined it because I was a shit."

I mentioned she's strong, right? She's now gripping me like she can squeeze the guilt and the shame and the past right out of me. "Dylan, you don't have to try to make me feel better by being *the worse guy.* You make me feel better by letting me be me. You're one of the good guys. You really are."

I fall silent, mostly because I need all my focus to keep myself from kissing her senseless.

Part of me wants to be mad that she doesn't care what I did wrong.

But the other part of me is stuck on the fact that, for the first time in my life, I've met someone who makes me honestly feel like I *can* let go of my own past. That I *can* expel my demons and not worry that they'll come back.

She believes in me.

We're both people with ugly pasts who are trying to do better, and *she believes in me.*

And that's possibly the biggest turn-on I've ever experienced in my life.

"I liked myself once," she says quietly. "I was doing a good thing. I was doing a really good thing. And then *Gigi* happened, and now I'm here because I can't keep funding the good things if I don't give in to her extortion and play her game until I can find an alternative revenue source, because even when I'm doing good things, I can't do it without the family money."

I want to squeeze *her* tight until I can solve all her problems the way I feel like she's solving mine. "Who cares where the money came from if it's helping the world? Tell your grandmother you're a good person and leave."

"I can't. It doesn't work like that."

"Phoebe did it."

"But Phoebe is *Phoebe*, and I'm—"

"Not going to insult yourself right now, because if you do, I'll throw more chocolate all over the floor."

I'm teasing, and I expect a laugh or even a sigh and a *don't be cute, Dylan—this is serious*, which I probably deserve.

Instead, she hugs me even tighter, lining our bodies up, and I can't hide the way I'm reacting to the physical contact.

There's no amount of hoping she'll think it's a pipe in my pants that will solve this.

But I don't let go.

I hug my friends all the time. My mom. Jane and Anya and Shiloh and Ridhi. Willie Wayne and Gibson and even Teague when the grumpy bastard lets me. Hannah, though I need to let that go.

When a friend needs a hug, a friend needs a hug.

But this is different.

This is different, because I can smell the chocolate mingling with the subtle scent of her shampoo, and her forehead is resting against my jaw, and she's gripping me like she's never had a hug before and doesn't know how to let go.

Has she had a hug before?

I don't see the Lightlys in public together often, and even when I've been in the school, I haven't noticed blatant displays of affection.

Between Phoebe and Teague, yes.

Among the Lightlys?

Not so much.

And it makes me want to show her what she's missing. Give her the most basic, simple human affection that everyone deserves.

This isn't because she's pretty. Or because I'm becoming fascinated by who she is under all the layers of social media influencer fluff. Or because I love a good puzzle, and Tavi Lightly is definitely a puzzle.

A puzzle with a good heart, with at least one friend willing to hide a body for her.

Speaks volumes about a person when they have a friend willing to hide a body for them.

I tell myself that my body's reaction is because she's *new*. Because she sees me differently than everyone here does.

Not because I'm taking her out of the friend zone.

"I'm only hugging you because I'm too tired to let go," she says.

"Okay."

She arches her body against mine, and *yep*, she definitely feels that pipe in my pants.

She has to.

How could she not?

Think about Teague having sex. Think about Teague having sex.

"I'm regenerating my energy so that I can pick up that mess on the floor," Tavi says.

"You need some mint? I have lots in my garden."

She sighs. "I—is it as good as your tomatoes?"

"Better."

"Then yes, actually. It would be better if it was from *my* garden, but I can't really be picky, and my garden is really, *really* far away."

"You want spearmint, peppermint, chocolate mint, or sweet mint?"

She lifts her face to stare at me, and she's so close I can count the light freckles on her cheeks.

Hadn't noticed those before.

Maybe they're actually chocolate.

Also hadn't noticed the way her eyes are flecked with a deeper blue right around her pupils.

Or that her eyelashes are much shorter and lighter than they are in pictures.

It's like seeing her without her armor.

She's not this untouchable enigma known around the world for having exquisite taste in clothes and food and luxury brands and for living a fancy, amazing life full of travel and exercise and vegetables and all the best of everything.

She's a lost woman trying to do her best in trying circumstances, and there goes my cock once again. Effort is sexy.

She's leaving, dumbass. Don't go there.

I did the romp-in-the-sheets-with-my-best-friend thing once already.

Didn't end so well.

And now it's been two years since I've had sex, which high school me would've choked and died over, and I'm not jumping into bed with the first woman who stares at me like she wants to lick chocolate out of my belly button.

She might think I have a nice ass, but what else do I have going for me?

Hi, I've been in love with someone I can't have for years isn't exactly a turn-on.

"You have a birthmark in the shape of a mountain on your neck." She shifts, unhooking one arm to touch the side of my neck, and a full-body shiver travels from my scalp to my nuts. "I have one in the shape of Dolly Parton's profile on my shoulder blade. I hate it. It reminds me of how much we get judged for what we look like."

This is practice. This is practice for when I step back out in the dating world. "Maybe it's your own profile."

She snorts softly, her breath tickling my neck. "I'd rather have Dolly. She went for what she wanted no matter what anyone said or called her at the time. She was the real deal. She's *amazing*. I'm just . . . trying."

"So you love-hate your birthmark?"

"I do."

"Why not call it being in the shape of someone else you love for your own reasons and just love it without complications?"

"It's very distinctive." She releases me to step just far enough back that she's still in my space bubble without actually touching me, though I swear I feel her belly still pressed against my erection, and she tugs at the collar of her shirt. "Want to see?"

Before I can answer, she pulls the shirt down her shoulder, revealing smooth, barely freckled skin over firm muscle, with a birthmark that she must cover with makeup on a regular basis, because I've looked at a *lot* of her pictures, and I've never noticed it before. Her shoulder blade is a work of art, and I have zero doubt she's spent years of her life sculpting it.

"Ah, yeah." My voice is husky, my whole body tense, and my cock aching.

This isn't attraction, I tell myself.

This is my body's reaction to being near a woman who's offered to help me get back in the dating game, who meets all the standards for beauty in the world, and who happens to currently look like she needs a hero.

I'm nothing if not a sucker for a damsel in distress. "That's definitely Dolly Parton," I finish.

"Right? I told you so."

"How about these?" I brush a thumb over the freckles on her cheek as she turns back to face me, and *bingo*.

They smear.

It's chocolate.

I smile. "Ah. *Not* freckles."

Her blue irises have disappeared behind her pupils. "Oh God, seriously?" she whispers. "How bad is it?"

I lick my thumb—not bean paste, that's for damn sure—and swipe it over her cheekbone. I'm not taking advantage of touching her delicate skin. I'm not. I swear. "I've been around worse."

Her voice drops to a whisper. "I sincerely doubt that's true, and I say that as someone trying very hard to not be an egotistical drama queen."

"Just chocolate." I lick my thumb again. It's subtle, but yeah, that's the good stuff. "*Good* chocolate."

Her tongue darts out and swipes over her bottom lip. "You can tell me if it's not good. I can take it."

"Ah, look at this. You've got some on your ear too." I need to back away. Right now.

There is zero good that can come of being this close to Tavi Lightly when she's staring at me like I'm the one thing that can make or break her entire world, her eyes getting shiny, her breath coming quicker, her pulse fluttering at the base of her neck.

"You shouldn't be so nice to me," she whispers.

"Has anyone ever been nice to you?"

She blinks quickly. "Of course. People are nice to me all the time."

It's a lie.

I know it as surely as the sun rises every morning, as surely as Willie Wayne and Deer Drop Floyd will argue over who caught the biggest fish at the lake, and as surely as I know that I should not kiss Tavi Lightly right now.

Shouldn't and *won't* aren't getting along in my brain, though.

She might feel fake, but I don't know a single person in town who can say she's said a bad thing to them, except maybe her family.

And I'm pretty sure her family's earned it.

She deserves nice things too.

I lightly rub my thumb over her chin. "You have chocolate all over your face."

"Thank you for helping get it off."

Her voice is a breathy whisper, and all that progress I was making on taming my cock flies out the window. "My pleasure. Anytime. Ah, look. It's even here."

Here.

On her lips.

Which I'm touching with my own, because *someone* needs to kiss this woman and show her she's worthy.

Kissing her sends a new sensation flowing through my entire body. Her lips are unfamiliar, but they're soft and warm and taste like chocolate. She's the first new woman I've kissed in almost six years, the first woman I've kissed at all in two years.

It's foreign.

But *good*.

And wrong—I should not be kissing Tavi Lightly—but *fuck*.

She parts her lips and deepens the kiss, and I am here for this ride.

Her body presses against mine. One arm tightens around my waist, and she slides the other hand up my chest, higher, over my shoulder, and leaves a trail of fire across my skin as she rakes her fingernails up my neck and into my hair, expertly avoiding my wound.

I should stop.

But I don't want to stop.

Jesus, I miss kissing. Kissing and touching and stroking and sex.

I miss sex.

I miss—

A dog growls and barks at my feet, and I leap back, dazed and startled, and fall back on the kitchen table, smearing chocolate all over my hands.

Tavi blinks at me.

Pebbles growls.

"Oh, sweetie, it's okay." Tavi squats and grabs the pint-size guard dog, who's baring her teeth at me like I just tried to murder her mistress. "I know, I know. You don't like being left out, do you?"

She lifts the dog to her face, letting the pup lick her all over as she turns half away from me.

"I—" I start, then cut myself off as I rub my neck, where I can still feel her fingernails.

"Thank you, Dylan," she says as Pebbles continues to lick her all over her face. I'd worry about the pup eating chocolate, but it was flecks. Barely there. And I got most of it off. "I really appreciate you trying to do something nice for me, and I promise it won't change anything. You don't need to do it again."

I want to kick something.

Both because I want to kiss Tavi again and because I don't know why.

I mean, I know *why*. Sucker for a damsel and all that. After so many years of being the villain, I want to be someone's knight.

But I like my women real. Down to earth. The kind who fit in here in Tickled Pink.

Tavi doesn't.

But for the first time in my life, I wonder if maybe, just maybe, I deserve *more*.

If it's okay to *want* more.

And she is definitely *more*.

The good *and* the bad.

"Back to bed for you, Pebbles." Tavi stands, still not looking at me, and heads to the corner, where she tucks the dog into a small travel case. "Mama has to clean the chocolate, okay? And if you're still awake once everything's spotless, then maybe you can come out and play." She hits a button on a small device I hadn't noticed, and the music starts again.

"It's her bedtime music," she whispers to me.

Her blue eyes sweep over me once, like she's seeing if I'm still in one piece, and then she makes full eye contact. "I have to get back to work, so—"

"Yeah. Work. Yeah. You need help?"

"No. Thank you. I've got it under control."

I tuck my hands in my pockets, remember they're coated in chocolate, and pull them back out.

Tavi Lightly isn't the only disaster in this room.

Pretty sure right now, I'm worse.

Chapter 18

Tavi

Oh my God, *that kiss.*

My vagina is on fire, and not like *I should see a doctor* but like *if I don't jump his bones right now, this will become a permanent case of lady blue balls, and I might never walk again.* "You don't have to do that," I say, *again*, as Dylan rises with my chocolate mold in hand and heads for the sink.

I want him to leave.

I also want him to stay and do a strip tease and pour chocolate all over himself so that I have to lick it off him.

"Can't let the bean paste stain the floor," he replies, his easy smile not as easy as it was earlier today, but he gets points for trying for normal.

"It technically *is* bean paste." I can try for normal too.

We can be friends.

We can be friends who accidentally kissed when he felt sorry for me for being such a failure at basically everything in life.

Friends who do things like bring each other ice cream, which he did, and it's sitting on the table melting in its carton. I pull it out of the bag, intending to take it to the freezer—where I would very much like to put my vagina right now, too, until she's also under control—and then I realize what I'm holding. "*Oh my God.* Did you seriously buy Soy Sweet ice cream? Where did you even get that?"

"Pick-n-Shop. They're stocking it for you." His face twitches, and once again, he tries to give me a normal smile, but it doesn't reach his eyes or his posture, which is stiff as my high school principal's sense of humor. "But if it's all the same to you, I think I'd rather have the chocolate than the . . . ice cream . . . stuff."

I grimace. "Same. There is *nothing* delicious about frozen ground soybeans, no matter what they flavor it with. I'll stop in and buy more in a few days."

For appearances.

The *only* thing Soy Sweet ice cream is good for is as organic compost. I've mentioned I can't wait to leave this life behind, right?

"Don't buy it all too fast," he says. "They'll order more."

"Oh yeah, totes," I agree. "But good job picking this up for me. Everyone will know you were bringing it to me, and then they'll start talking about us, and we can be all, *We're just friends*, because we are, and then you'll have women swarming you. I bet Lola asks you to dinner within twenty-four hours, if she hasn't already."

Dylan's face twitches. Not like Teague's is always twitching—Teague has a perpetual case of *I'm annoyed with the world*—but like he's not sure he's ready for all the women in Tickled Pink and beyond to decide he's the catch of the century.

But then he sticks a finger in the chocolate mold, pulls it out, and licks it.

And there goes my lady boner all over again.

Along with an irrational desire to go all Wonder Woman on any woman who hits on Dylan.

And that's *before* his eyes slide shut and he moans. "Holy shit, Tavi. Is that wasabi?"

I wince. "Is it bad? Too hot? All wrong for chocolate? Why am I second-guessing this? *I know it's good.* And even if it's horrible, there are people who eat puffer fish that could kill them *just to say they did it*, so of course it doesn't matter how it tastes so long as it's packaged well, and—wait. You know what wasabi is? Wait, wait. Sorry. That was offensive. *Quit making me flustered.* By complimenting my chocolate, I mean. That's the *only* reason I'm flustered."

His smile gets more real as he dips his finger in the chocolate again.

He has to quit licking his fingers like that.

If he were my usual kind of boyfriend—the convenient, *let's be fake friends when it's over*, just-in-it-for-the-publicity kind of boyfriend— then I'd be asking if he wanted to taste something else right now.

Specifically, my pussy.

But he's not my usual kind of boyfriend. Or potential boyfriend.

He's a nice guy who has a life here and who doesn't need the stain of *my* life all over him when I leave.

He's the kind of guy you want to settle down with, have babies with, and get dirty with in the sheets every night, and *good God*, have my breasts ever been this heavy and achy?

"You ever have Mexican hot chocolate?" he asks. "I'd give my monkey wrench for a truffle that tastes like good Mexican hot chocolate."

"You're a foodie." I try to subtly rub away the pressure behind my nipples with my forearm while I squat to wipe the floor. He has no idea just how much more attractive he gets every time he opens his mouth, and he keeps opening his mouth, and I have to kick him out.

I need to start avoiding him again.

It's not smooth. It's not *couth*. I was raised better than to hide from a man just because I have an irrational crush that keeps growing like a fungus.

Yes. A crush is like fungus. And not like a *good* fungus, like mushrooms, but like the kind you just can't get rid of.

"Had a stepfather once who was a chef," he says. "Arrogant as hell, but dude could cook. Your chocolates are good. You don't have to fret."

He. Has. To. Quit. Talking. "It's all in good growing, and honestly? We don't really know yet if we'll have good beans. We bought these off a different farm. You don't have to stay here and clean up. I've got it. This is, like, nothing compared to the mess I usually make. You should see what all I've cleaned chocolate off of in here. It's, like, *so* messy sometimes."

He cuts a glance at me that says he sees right through me. Like he knows I'm turning on the Tavi Lightly Show, and he doesn't want fake me.

I flap my hands. "For *reals*, Dylan. You should, like, go sleep. You had a serious brain injury just, like, a *week* ago, and then there was all that trauma with the chicken and having to put up with Gigi all day, and me too."

"We should talk about that kiss."

"What kiss? There's nothing to talk about."

"Tavi—"

"What kiss?" Phoebe asks.

Yes, Phoebe.

My sister.

The tall, slender, not-quite-natural blonde who's standing in the doorway now too.

"Would someone please lock that damn door?" And here I go with the screeching and shrieking.

Pebbles grumbles in her case.

Phoebe smiles at me.

Dylan ducks his head, clears his throat, and goes back to sampling my chocolates.

"Stop smiling," I order Phoebe.

"I'm not smiling."

I growl.

She smiles broader.

I sigh and go back to scrubbing the floor.

Tonight's wasted. No work. No recipes. No mint. And I'm running low on the raw chocolate bars Naomi sent.

She's tried helping with recipes and production, but her talents lie in helping Sebastián around the farm and in crunching numbers to tell me just how dire things are. Once we get an investor or three, we'll probably pay a professional chocolatier to help out, because I truly am running off what I learned in an online master class, and I'm sure I'm screwing things up, because that's what I do.

"Okay, okay, I'll quit smiling," Phoebe says. "I just saw Gigi at Ladyfingers, and I reminded her that forgiveness is good for her soul. You're welcome."

"Thank you," I mutter. I'm grateful. I am.

But I'm also frustrated that Phoebe can mouth off to Gigi and get away with it, when she's barely started being a nice human being, and I've put so much effort into self-improvement over the years with zero acknowledgment.

Phoebe props a hip against the table and sticks her fingers in the spilled chocolate too. "She still insists she's destroying the video of her getting smacked with a chicken thigh that came out of a toilet, which seems like a story I need to hear."

Mind made up.

We're taking that video live. "Dylan wants to be a TikTok star. I mean, the kind that does good by helping people understand how to fix little plumbing issues themselves, with lots of shout-outs to Tickled Pink so that when you're done building the new Ferris wheel, people will come."

"That's not quite—" Dylan starts.

"It's not, like, *my* fault Gigi insisted on standing in the danger zone in that bathroom today. Or that that chicken thigh had bones in it that got stuck in her hair. And do you know how wild the internet will go when Dylan's first video is of me lifting a toilet set and accidentally flinging a raw dead poultry at Gigi? Like, I'll have to do my own TikTok talking about how I gave the poor thigh a proper burial since that chicken never should've been sacrificed in the first place. Boom. Viral."

Phoebe's green eyes track me as I move across the floor, cleaning up more chocolate, wondering—*again*—how I'll sneak all of this to the laundromat without anyone asking why I have chocolate-soaked rags.

"She also said she's loaning Lola the money to buy this church because she thinks *Lola's Holy House* is a much more marketable idea than *Lola's School House*," Phoebe continues.

I gasp. "Did she tell Lola that?"

"I don't think so. Lola was busy trying to ask Teague where his brother's been hiding. But you should probably try to stay on Gigi's good side and clear out of here soon."

"No way," Dylan says. "Floyd would never sell."

Phoebe's eye twitches.

And it's not like Teague's *I hate people and the world* twitch or Dylan's *this is getting uncomfortable* twitch.

This is 100 percent a twitch of *I just put two and two together, and I am about to be very pissed at you.*

"So Dylan's offered to let me use some mint out of his garden for my next round of truffles. Do you like mint, Phoebe? I can't believe we've been sisters for like twenty-nine years, and I don't know if you like mint."

"Deer Drop Floyd?" she asks Dylan.

Either the man is completely missing the tension so thick that it's making its own gravitational pull, or he wants to see me suffer. He shakes his head at Phoebe. "No, Tickled Pink Floyd. He bought this place when it went up for sale some—you know what? I don't even remember how long ago it was. Ten years? Fifteen, maybe? Anyway, he's always talking about how he's gonna convert it to a bookshop or a nightclub or an art studio. Pretty sure he'll die before he makes up his mind as to which, and he's not one to start a project if he doesn't know he can see it through to the end. Needs a vision before he can start, and his visions have been inconsistent."

Phoebe's laser beams turn to me, and I barely avoid incineration on the spot. "How long have you been using this church basement?" she demands.

"Oh gosh, I don't know," I lie.

"Where's your rental agreement?"

"I sneaked in here. I didn't know who owned it. It was open and no one came or went, so I thought it was just fair game."

Dylan gives me a *what are you smoking?* look.

I lunge for the fridge. "So I made some sea salt caramel truffles yesterday. If we let them sit out for about thirty minutes, you can be my taste testers. Actually, does anyone want to take them home? I have these fake boxes with fake shipping labels and everything so you can say that someone mailed them to you."

Phoebe has a bone, and she is not deterred.

Actually, I'd say she's pissed. *"You knew Tickled Pink Floyd wasn't a ghost."*

I give her my best innocent look, like I never noticed that she was the one who muttered the most about *the ghost* keeping her from sleeping, or the one who seemed most creeped out about it, or the one who the locals were *totally* targeting most with all the hijinks at the school before she fell for Teague. "Phoebe, there are *so many* Floyds. I thought that the ghost at the school was, like, TPF Senior."

"TPF?" Phoebe echoes.

Dylan cracks up, and someone hold my ovaries—the man has *the best* laugh. "You have any idea how much it would make his day if you go around town calling him the Notorious TPF?"

I smile at him. "Aww, I love making people's days."

"I'm seriously regretting sticking up for you to Gigi right now," Phoebe says.

I'd feel bad, except TPF is also basically responsible for my mom leaving town. When she caught him sneaking through the halls while setting up the next haunting, she freaked out, dropped that bombshell about Phoebe's paternity and her own cheating on the whole family, and left.

As far as I'm concerned, Tickled Pink Floyd has done a lot of good in the world. Or at least for my family.

I love my mom, but I also can't stand her, and I like the breathing room since she's been gone.

She'd be the first person to tell me that making chocolates will make me fat and then make me lose my place among the top influencers in the world, and thanks to a lot of support from Naomi and my own realization that I want to be something more than a vapid face for the rest of my life, I've finally reached a place where I'm fully *fuck that* with the fat-shaming.

Most days.

Okay, some days.

Okay, *fine*.

One day, I hope to get there. I understand the theory but have yet to convince my feelings and emotions that I'm okay exactly as I'm shaped and with exactly the metabolism that I have.

In the meantime, running off all the chocolate I eat is really good stress relief.

"Do you know what else I'm doing, Phoebe?" I say. "I'm also planning Shiloh's surprise birthday party. *You're welcome.* And if you want me to do or not do anything for your boyfriend's ex-wife and the mother of his daughter for her birthday, I will totes take all of your advice, because I don't like to cause you pain."

"You're changing the subject."

"I'm highly uncomfortable with you being mad at me when you know my biggest secret, because you're usually the second person right after Gigi lined up to destroy someone."

She sighs and squeezes her eyes shut. "I don't want to destroy you, Tavi. I'm just as tired of our family being *our family* as you are, and I'm trying to do better."

"I know," I whisper. "Me too."

And now it's getting touchy feely and sappy in my chest, and I don't have time for emotions, so I glance at Dylan.

He's watching the two of us like he wants to hug us both to get us over this weird tension that always comes when we actually talk about our family problems, but he also doesn't want to interfere or get sucked into the awkward.

I clear my throat. "So you don't think Floyd will sell to Lola's producers and Gigi?"

He shrugs as he swipes more chocolate out of my mold, letting me get away with changing the subject. "Didn't think so, but I guess anything can happen."

"Is there anywhere else in town you can work?" Phoebe asks. "As the resident real estate agent in Tickled Pink, Teague will do all he can to stall Lola on having a tour if she gets wind of this even being an idea."

And this is the number one reason I might actually miss her when I move to Costa Rica.

The Phoebe of a year ago would've yelled at me for an hour for not telling her that Tickled Pink Floyd was alive and well and plotting the haunting of the high school two months ago while she was simultaneously insisting there were no such things as ghosts but also losing serious sleep over it, but this Phoebe's chill.

She gets that we both have more important things to worry about.

Truly more important things.

Like her adjusting to being part of Teague's family—a *real* family. My secret being in danger of being exposed. Gigi being an ass.

Helping Tickled Pink spruce itself up to be more attractive to tourists who might want to visit the site of the old movie and maybe even just discover a hidden gem in northern Wisconsin. Earlier, I saw three middle-aged ladies dragging their husbands along to take pictures in front of all those *this Pink Gold movie scene was filmed here* signs around town that Phoebe's cleaned up, so we know it's working on a small scale.

There's a lot to do outdoors here between the lake and the forests. Plus, I've seen a ton of cute little cabins tucked away here and there while out on my runs. They'd make great little retreats for anyone looking to get away from the world for a while. Phoebe's investing money not just in building a new Ferris wheel but also in helping the locals get their businesses—like the spa and the bed-and-breakfasts and the motel—updated or running again, and the snowshoe baseball games in the summer are fun to watch.

At least, I presume, since I've been put on display as one of the players who falls on her face in sawdust every week and haven't actually *watched* it yet as a true spectator.

"Would he be better off renting this place out than selling it?" Dylan asks Phoebe.

"That's the other thing about *Lola's Holy House*, if it happens. Teague says Floyd would get more long term if he rents the place and then sells tickets for people to gawk at the place in the church where Lola . . . did . . . whatever she intends to do."

"*Teague* said that?" Dylan and I say together.

Phoebe smiles. "Grumbled it, but those words came out of his mouth, in that exact order."

"Wow," Dylan says.

I stare at her for a second, and then I'm scowling. "It's not enough that you're the brilliant one, is it? You had to take the magic vagina to bend men's wills too, didn't you?"

She shrugs. "I don't like to be bad at things."

Dylan's going ruddy again. "You could use my kitchen," he says to me, but he has to clear his throat to get the words out.

"I can't use your mother's kitchen."

"*My* kitchen," he reiterates.

"You have another house somewhere?"

Phoebe chokes on a laugh. "Oh, Tavi, sweetie . . . you're adorable."

"Thanks, *Mom*."

She winces. "I didn't mean it like *that*."

"Sure. Excuse me, please, I need to start a new batch if tonight's not going to be a total waste."

"You know Dylan owns his house and lets his mom stay there, right?"

I turn and stare at the man who's now licking the chocolate straight out of the mold.

He freezes. "I'll wash this."

"You let your mom live with you." I probably shouldn't say it like I'm accusing him of murder, but I can't handle this tonight.

I absolutely, positively *cannot* handle him being that much more attractive.

Not after that kiss.

"She's getting back on her feet after a rough breakup." He shrugs like it's no big deal. "And I owe her for putting up with my teenage years."

"Pardon her gawking," Phoebe says to him. "It's just that both Tavi and I would probably let our mother live in a one-star hotel before we'd ever let her live in our homes."

He nods slowly. "I can see that. Especially since there's not much room in that tree house where you're squatting right now."

Phoebe's face explodes in a shower of smiles and rainbows and laughter. "Oh, stop. I'm not *squatting*. I'm paying rent in sexual favors. And speaking of . . . you never answered my question about *what kiss?*"

I take her by the arm and turn her toward the door. "Go. Away. My chocolate is very temperamental. Grab a truffle. Take one to Teague and lie to him about where you got it. Tell me what you want or don't want at Shiloh's birthday party or if I'm being set up and she'll hate it like Dylan said she'd pretend to."

"Teague knows, Tavi. He's like Gigi. *He knows all.*" She frowns. "Actually . . . he would've known you knew about Tickled Pink Floyd, wouldn't he?"

"Don't go there, Phoebe," Dylan says. "Stay happy. Forgive the man. He's had a rough summer."

"You too," I tell him. "Shoo. Go home and check on your mother. I have enough problems without you two gossiping about everything else in here. Go. *Go.*"

I don't want to be alone.

I want Phoebe to talk me through how to make my business profitable and give me suggestions for other investors that I can reach out to in case my ideas don't work. I want Dylan to tell me my chocolate is delicious.

But if there's one thing I've learned in a lifetime of being a Lightly, it's that I'm the only one I can count on.

It doesn't matter how good a kiss is. Or how much I *want* to trust that my sister has changed.

I can't.

So I'll count on me.

"You want me to take these dirty rags to my place and wash them?" Dylan asks. "Mom won't ask any questions. She'll just be happy it looks like I'm dating."

I swallow another cringe.

Chapter 19

Dylan

I'm craving chocolate.

It's been four days since I crashed Tavi's kitchen. She's followed me every day at work, taking videos, telling me to do what I'd normally do, helping with the plumbing when I've let her, falling silent until I sometimes forget she's there and start singing like I usually would while I'm alone, only to remember when she stops the video and tells me I'm better than some of the rock stars she's dated.

She's made me blush.

She's made me get irrationally angry when she talks about *oh, but it wasn't serious with him* and *we both got something out of* that *relationship* anytime one of my clients asks her about dating some famous "hottie."

She's made me want to wrap her in a hug when she gets this look in her eyes like she's trapped and frustrated and wants to be anywhere but here when she thinks I'm not looking.

She's made me want to kiss her again when she lets loose with the full belly laugh that I associate with the *real* Tavi Lightly.

I've taken her mint.

I've taken her basil and lavender.

I've been thanked and had the basement door shut—and locked—in my face, without a single bit of chocolate passed over to me.

And I'm about done.

So I'm sitting here in Café Nirvana, waiting for her to drop by for today's plans on what to record and lessons on how the hell filters work in this damn app, craving chocolate.

"How's the coffee?" Anya asks.

I smile at her. It's natural, but I don't feel it. "Good."

"You want more chocolate in it?"

"No, this is great." I'm lying.

I want more chocolate.

But I've never ordered my coffee with chocolate in it here, and it would look weird to not just ask for it but ask for more on top of asking for it in the first place, which is what I did this morning to make her look at me like she's afraid the next thing I'll do is toss an old bathtub in the lake and then bully someone into trying to row it across, with a promise that I'll toss their lunch in the lake next if they don't.

Not that I'm confessing to ever doing something like that.

And now I want chocolate again.

Mocha syrup is *not* what I want.

And I won't be telling Anya that.

Secrets and I are like acquaintances. We nod to each other in public, acknowledge that we coexist and that's cool, but I'm not gonna look up Mr. Secret and invite him to join me for dinner.

And before you call me two faced about belonging to the Tickled Pink Secret Poker Society, that's secret for a reason.

There are too many people in this town who can't handle losing and too many other people in this town who have zero poker face. And I play poker with them on occasion, too, but once a month, we save them all from themselves, and Ridhi, Jane, Willie Wayne, and I play a solid, hard-core game of poker.

Anya sizes me up like she knows there's something off about me. "You feeling okay?"

"Never better."

"You sure? You look like my mom after she eats too much chicken makhani."

"Totally fine," I insist.

"No lingering side effects of the concussion?"

"For the thirty millionth time, it was *barely* a concussion. Just felt like something different today."

"Hm."

She goes back behind the counter to wait on three people I don't recognize, but she's still shooting me looks when the door swings open.

I almost leap out of the booth, expecting Tavi, but instead, Lola Minelli marches through the door.

Dammit.

Not Tavi.

And my obsession is only because I'm craving chocolate.

Apparently lying to myself is becoming my new pastime.

"Oh my *gah*, Dylan Wright! You are just hot as a hockey goaltender after a game, aren't you? Is this seat taken. Hi. I'm Lola. We haven't met. Formally, I mean, when one of us isn't surrounded by like a million people."

She slides into my booth right next to me, and where a normal person would hold out a hand, she goes for a hug.

In the booth.

Where there's not enough room for this.

She smells like a cross between coconut oil and baby powder, and it's not a bad thing, but it's also not chocolate.

"Ah, hi." I slowly extract myself from the hug and grab my coffee cup.

Only shield I have. Sometimes, a guy needs a shield. This is definitely one of those times.

"I *just saw* your TikTok with Tavi and Captain Chicken in the toilet. You are *the best* at talking people through plumbing, aren't you? If I was ever going to fix anything myself, I would *totally* want you to be my teacher."

"Captain Chicken?" Anya glances my way as one of her customers taps a credit card against her machine.

Ridhi sticks her head over the double swinging doors to the kitchen. "I don't want to know."

"Oh my *gah*, it was, like, *so gross*. Tavi had to stick her hand down the *toilet drain* and pull out, like, this *raw chicken breast*."

"Thigh, actually," I correct.

"It's on Dylan's TikTok." Lola stops explaining to Ridhi long enough to smile widely at me. Her teeth are blinding white, and her lips are uneven, and I don't want to be here. "You were *so* patient and kind and *such* a good teacher. I thought I learned *so much* about home ownership while I was filming *Lola's Tiny House*—reruns are streaming on demand, by the way—but I never learned how to change a toilet. I could *totally* walk a stranger through doing it now."

Anya slips her phone out of her pocket, eyeballing me like I'm an alien. "You're on TikTok? I thought we all agreed we weren't doing that. You never even joined Facebook. *Or* Twitter. Or Snapchat. Or—"

I cut her off. I don't want to know how many social media sites I haven't joined. "Can't let the Lightlys be the only thing making the world want to visit us again."

"Yes, we can," Teague calls from the kitchen.

"Quit hiding and come say that to my face," I call back, a real grin finally finding its way through today.

Anya cracks up.

Ridhi makes a face at me. "Don't bait the beast. He's already mad that Shiloh and I said Bridget can take an overnight trip with a friend."

Ridhi, Shiloh, and Teague are family goals as far as I'm concerned. Having been in bad stepparent relationships, it's amazing to see the three of them functioning through shit like a team.

Phoebe's finding her footing in the group, too, with their support, and she's made it clear she wants to be part of the team and do the right thing.

It's so different from what my stepfathers wanted.

If they cared at all about us kids, they only cared that they were in charge.

"I think it's, like, *so* awesome that you're doing such a great thing for people," Lola says to me. "Understanding pipes and stuff is, like, a gift. And you give your gift to the *world*."

"*Ridhi!*" Anya shrieks while the three customers start looking at all of us like we're either aliens or way more fascinating than they expected when they walked into this little joint this morning. "Ridhi, *look*! Dylan has *two million views*. And Tavi *lifted a toilet*."

"She's such a badass," Lola says. She pokes me. "And it's so sweet of *you* to be helping her with her secret project!"

Every alarm bell in my brain goes off at once. "Not really a secret that the family's here to help Tickled Pink, is it?"

Ridhi bustles out from the kitchen.

Teague follows her with a mulish look on his face. Phoebe's right behind him, and she gives an amused eye roll, though I don't miss the look she shoots my way. "Once a grumpy troll, always a grumpy troll."

He hooks an arm around her neck and presses a kiss to her hair. "Shush."

The three people waiting for coffee look at him.

Then they look at Lola.

Then they look at me.

Then they look around like they're looking for Teague's brother, who's not in town right now, which probably explains why Lola's finally talking to me.

I'm the next-best thing.

And God help us if the three women in the café sizing me up decide the same.

They're all around fifty, I'd guess. One's shorter than the other two, who are both average height. All three are white, wearing grandma shirts that Hannah's mother has probably already ordered for herself. The shortest of the group pulls her phone out of her purse.

The one in the blue grandma shirt whispers something to the one in the rhinestone grandma shirt.

"Impressive." Phoebe's leaning over Anya's shoulder, watching the video. I can hear my own voice, then Estelle's, and Tavi's too.

And my ears are getting hot.

The unfamiliar ladies crowd around the shortest one's phone, and then I hear it again.

Anya's video is ahead, so it's no surprise when I hear Estelle's shout over the sound of my own voice telling Tavi how to unscrew the toilet.

Anya shrieks with laughter.

Ridhi snorts.

Phoebe's eyes go round.

And Teague smiles. "That should be a regular thing."

"This is even better than how Gigi described it," Phoebe whispered. "Anya. Rewind it. Play that part again."

"Did Tavi do it on purpose?" Lola slips a hand to my knee. "Did she throw that chicken breast at Gigi on purpose?"

"Chicken *thigh*," Anya says.

"It was stuck in there real good. The bone got tangled in Estelle's hair," I tell her.

"I can't believe Tavi's still breathing," Phoebe says. "Wow. I owe her a box of her favorite kale chips or something."

I meet her eyes. Does she know?

Does she know Tavi eats meat too?

She knows about the chocolate, so she has to know about the meat, doesn't she?

Considering it feels like she's silently threatening to castrate me if I so much as twitch a facial muscle, I'm gonna guess *yes*.

"Heard she likes that Soy Sweet stuff better," I say.

Lola pulls a face like she has something stuck to her tongue. "That's *so* gross. I'm so glad I don't have a problem eating a well-balanced diet from all the food groups. In public."

Ah, hell. *Distract distract distract.* "I like to garden," I tell her.

She leans closer and licks her lips. "Is that, like, *super* dirty?"

"No dirtier than plumbing."

"I like dirty."

The doors to the restaurant jingle again, and Estelle Lightly marches through the entrance.

Marches?

Glides?

Floats on the cloud of sulfur wafting up from hell to transport her where she needs to go?

She has a way of walking that says *I'm in charge, and there are so many reasons you don't want to get in my way*, while still not looking like she's barreling headfirst into any situation. Like she's in total control of her emotions, but if she unleashed them—yeah, I hope that happens far from Tickled Pink.

"You." She perches on the edge of the booth seat opposite where Lola has me trapped. "You posted a highly unflattering video of me to TikTok."

One, credit to the seventy-something-year-old woman for not calling it *the TikToks*.

Two—"I thought your whole family gave up phones and the internet."

I smile.

She doesn't.

Lola makes a noise like the guardian angel inside her got stuck in her throat trying to fly out to warn me to shut up.

"The man has a point, Gigi," Phoebe calls from behind the counter, where the noise on Anya's phone suggests they're all rewatching the video that Tavi's people apparently finished and posted.

Where *is* Tavi?

The door bells ring once again, and this time, Willie Wayne and his wife, Akiko, hustle inside. *"Dylan,"* Willie Wayne crows. "You're *famous.*"

"I—" I start.

"You really are," Lola agrees. "I knew you had star quality the minute I saw you."

I first saw Lola when I was climbing out of my truck in front of a house across the street from the school. The family had a backed-up-sewer problem. Lola had an *ew, you were attractive until I saw that your truck says you're a plumber* problem.

You see it sometimes.

They hit you with a massive smile, start to move in to talk, and spot the **Wright Plumbing** sign on the side of the truck, and their noses twitch and their eyes flare and they take a step back.

It's like they're picturing you thirty years from now with a beer belly and jeans that don't cover your crack.

Nice to get judged on how we look when we're the ones digging tampons out of someone's clogged pipes.

"You gonna go on *Good Morning America* now?" Willie Wayne asks.

"Slow your roll, Double Dub," Phoebe says, earning a high-pitched chuckle from Willie Wayne at the nickname. "One viral video doesn't make a man famous. It makes him prone to ego problems when the world forgets him in five minutes."

Estelle eyeballs me. "We already have ego problems."

"Gigi, *be human*. Monsters don't go to heaven."

"Phoebe is so mouthy," Lola murmurs to me.

The three out-of-towners are gawking.

One's holding her phone like she's trying to subtly record this.

I make the *I need to get out of this booth* gesture at Lola.

Tavi's still not here.

She posted the video, but she's not here. "I gotta get to work."

And check my TikTok account. And—

Hell.

I missed calls from my mom and Hannah. Hannah's mom. One of my uncles and two of my aunts. My kindergarten teacher, whose showerheads I replaced last week.

But not Tavi.

She has my number, and I know she has a phone.

But she's missing this morning.

Lola doesn't budge. "You look like you could use a massage. I am *so good* at finding the best massage therapists in any city. It's a gift. I'm happy to put my talents to good use for you."

"Yeah, I'm late for a job, so . . ."

I scoot closer to her again.

She still doesn't take the hint.

"Lola, let the man out of the booth," Phoebe orders. "He knows where to find you if he's interested."

"Are you sure she's done the work she needs to do to get to heaven?" Lola says to Gigi.

"I have grave doubts about everyone here this morning," Estelle replies.

"Oh, hey, is that my brother?" Teague squints out the window.

Lola shoots up out of the booth like her butt's spring-loaded. "Jonah's here? What? Where?"

"Ah, hell, I forgot. He's not back yet. Must've been wishful seeing."

I flash Teague a thumbs-up as I scoot out of the booth.

He gives me the *I hate outsiders* look in response.

Estelle rises too. She comes up to my chin, which means she's wearing heels today. "We are not done, Mr. Wright."

I slip her a card. "Sorry, Estelle. Call my answering service. I have a broken shower knob and a persnickety sink that've already waited a week longer than they should've."

And apparently a couple dozen calls to return.

And regrets to process.

And a secret-chocolate-making social media maven to track down.

"Are you coming here for breakfast tomorrow?" the youngest of the out-of-towners, who's probably close to my mom's age, asks me.

"Nope. It's against my religion to get coffee out more than once a week. Enjoy Tickled Pink. Hear there's a good sale at the Pink Box. Best shopping this side of Deer Drop Lake."

I settle my baseball cap on my head, wave to my friends, and dash out the door.

No Tavi.

No Pebbles.

And the gasp that comes from the familiar Deer Droppers heading up from the lake tells me there might not be any peace either.

"It's him, Bella! That's the cute plumber!"

Yep.

Definitely no peace.

I'm usually okay with that. Life's here to live, right?

But today, I'm out of my element without my coach.

I text her quickly. **Where are you? Things are nuts.**

She doesn't respond.

And that has me more irritated than anything.

Chapter 20

Tavi

Doing a good job shouldn't make me feel like crap.

My video-editing team back in New York did a bang-up job with making Dylan's TikTok look natural while hitting only the highlights of the chicken-thigh incident. He's so swarmed with fans at the coffee shop that he doesn't even notice when I stop in the doorway. And I have six more videos that my team sent back that'll keep his account rolling for a while, plus a virtual Tickled Pink Plumber swag shop set up for him online so that he can take full advantage of his five minutes of fame.

Bonus?

Lola's all over him.

Gag me, but also, the minute those pictures and videos get out on social media, he'll get exactly what he wants.

His choice of any woman in the world to help him get over *Hannah*.

It's exactly why I posted the TikTok to his account this morning.

So that we can move past the *he kissed me and I want him to do it again* stage and into the *he's off limits because he found a very nice, appropriate woman who wants to stay in Tickled Pink and live a happily-ever-after with him* stage.

This is a good thing.

It's exactly what we set out to do when I called in that favor and convinced him to be a face of Tickled Pink so that Gigi would quit hounding me.

And now *Lola* can do the rest of the work to make him famous, so long as he doesn't tell her my secrets.

I'm stewing so hard as I push through the girls' entrance to the school—yes, seriously, **GIRLS** and **BOYS** are stamped over the doorways on the east and west sides of the building, respectively—that I don't notice my father just inside the first classroom on the left until he says my name.

I yelp and jump.

Pebbles yelps in my purse.

Dad gives me a wary once-over. "You look tired."

He's just under six feet tall. His spray tan has completely faded, replaced with a natural tan instead. He's also let his facial hair grow wild, like he can care about the lawn outside—which is where he spends 80 percent of his time—or he can care about shaving, but not both.

And the lawn is *meticulous* now.

His brown hair is streaked thicker with gray than it was when we got here, though I have no idea if that's lack of a good stylist to dye or hide it or if he's aging faster under the stress of living with Gigi and dealing with the drama with Mom and having to pretend to like his kids again.

Well, most of us.

He and Phoebe are basically the very definition of *awkward*.

I hate that for her. It's not her fault she's not what he wants her to be, nor is it her fault that he's known for *years* that he wasn't her father and took it out on her instead of dealing with his issues with Mom directly.

I shrug at my father. "Gigi ordered brick mattresses for us. We're all tired."

"You're more tired."

I don't know who this man is.

The last time he noticed I was tired, I was about eight years old, throwing a temper tantrum while clutching my favorite stuffed bunny, and he told the nanny to do something about it.

"Busy times." I gesture down the hall. "So I'm gonna get to work. Good luck with the . . . whatever it is Gigi has you doing today."

I start back on my path to the cafeteria, not really hungry but more interested in cold, soupy oatmeal than I am in making more small talk with my father.

"If you need help, let me know," he says.

Things are just getting weird now. I glance back at him.

Does he—is he—is he *lost* without Mom here?

Can't be.

He cheats on her all the time.

Maybe he had a mistress here who broke up with him.

A very, very small part of me starts to feel sorry for him. But I still brush him off. "I got it. Thanks."

Would've been nice to have him care for the past twenty-nine years.

He's trying now, my conscience reminds me.

And that's the thing I hate about being a good person.

My conscience talks to me and guilts me and tells me I should do more, when I already do more than most of the people in my family.

"Your mom sent a box of purses for you," he says.

"I saw."

"She said she hasn't heard from you."

"No phones, Dad. Gigi's rules. Remember?"

"Yes, we're all following that, aren't we? Nice job with the plumber."

"He did that himself."

"Not the raw-chicken part."

His eyes are *twinkling.*

And honestly?

I hate that too.

I want my family to get along because we want to get along, not because we take joy in watching one of us throw raw chicken at another.

But we'll never be that family.

"It slipped." I turn back around, and this time he doesn't stop me as I head down the hallway.

I turn the corner to pass the theater, and run into Carter.

"Watch where you're going," he grumbles.

Talk about looking tired. He has bags under his eyes, his hair looks like it was used as a bed by Big Bertha, the raccoon we keep chasing out of here, and even his clothes look tired.

Maybe it's a one-hit wonder, still-trying-to-be-a-rock-star thing. "Up too late murdering people's ears?" I ask him. When Phoebe lived here, she was constantly complaining about the noise.

I probably would, too, if I were home before he went to bed every night.

One major benefit to not sleeping in general is that Carter's noise doesn't bother me.

"Don't be a dick," he says.

"I was being funny, Carter."

"No, you weren't."

I wasn't.

I really wasn't.

And this is another reason I need to leave.

I'm a much better person when I'm not around the people who taught me to be a dick.

"What's with the mood?" he asks. "You did what Gigi wanted."

I'm cringing to myself, and it's not the question.

It's the fact that Carter, who's always been the world's biggest ass-hole, is being nice to me. It's like Gigi has fully beaten him down, and I don't know who he is anymore.

Not that I knew who he was before we all got here.

"You're on the internet?" I ask.

He rolls his eyes. "We're all on the internet, except Phoebe, who's an idiot."

"She's also not living in the school anymore, so it doesn't matter if she is or isn't, does it?"

He sticks his hands in his pockets and glances toward the corner, like he's expecting Dad to appear at any minute and yell at us for not doing what Gigi wants. "Overachiever."

"Right? We could cure world hunger, and she'd have probably already done it both here *and* on some distant planet she discovered, and also cured cancer."

Not that she's into science.

She just has this drive. If she *wanted* to do something, she could.

Carter's still not looking at me. "Lola's digging."

"Duh."

"Whatever you're sneaking out to do . . . finish it."

"I'm not sneaking out."

He makes eye contact and silently calls me on the bullshit. "Yeah, and twenty years from now, I'm gonna be the next Mick Jagger."

Okay, this is new.

It's like he's admitting he doesn't think he'll make his dreams come true.

I toss my hair, because it's what I'm supposed to do, and I frown at him. "You can be anything you set your mind to, Carter."

"Yeah, maybe I'll hire someone who looks like me to do a theater tour."

My veins freeze so hard I go light headed, and it takes me a second too long to force my fake laugh. "Oh my God, that's, like, *impossible*."

He holds my gaze until even my toenails are squirming.

How the *fuck* does he know?

"Yeah," he says dryly. "Totes impossy. That's how you'd say it, right?"

"No one says *impossy*. That's a stupid word."

217

"Stupid like hiring someone to play you in public?"

"Um, totes. And why would you even want to? Someone else would get famous instead of you."

A muscle tics in his jaw.

While I look like Dad, he looks just like Mom, but in a rugged way. And just like me, if he weren't rich, he wouldn't have groupies throwing themselves at him.

We're not pretty people.

Or maybe my view of us is colored by knowing what's lurking in our souls.

"Is there any breakfast left?" I ask.

"Didn't eat with your boy toy?"

"He's not my boy toy. He's a local who needs help polishing his image to help Tickled Pink get back on the map."

"Yeah, I can see how you'd want Niles's cold oatmeal soup instead of eating with the most popular guy in Tickled Pink."

We stare at each other a beat.

"Did you just hear yourself?" I ask him.

"Most popular in Tickled Pink is still better than least popular in Manhattan."

"Is not." It totally is. I'd take Dylan over practically everyone I know back in New York.

LA too.

My brother snorts softly. "Get some sleep, buttface. It's good for your *soul.*"

Sleep would be amazing for a lot of reasons, but I can't sleep. I have a school to clean, a surprise party to plan, and a business to launch.

Getting away from my family would be good for my soul.

But I also can't do that.

Yet.

Not until new financing is secure for the farm and until we have a product to launch, which will be *soon.*

Naomi got the last samples I sent and forwarded them to the richest chocoholic I know, and we have a different meeting set with another potential investor to pitch Celebr8 Sweets.

If this works, it'll be *goodbye, old life*.

Goodbye, family.

Goodbye, influencer job.

And goodbye to this crush on a small-town plumber who kisses like a damn angel.

Chapter 21

Tavi

Filed under *things I never thought I needed to know*: cabinets are heavy.

"Niles!" I shriek. "Niles! Are you here?"

Take the cabinets down so you can paint the teachers' lounge, Tavi, I thought. *You're a beast. They can't be that heavy.*

Actually, yes, they can, and I can't see my dog, and I'm about to drop this damn thing or possibly fall backward through the open window. *"Niles!"*

"Holy shit," a voice that does *not* belong to Niles answers. "Scoot, Pebbles. What the *hell*, Tavi?"

The bulk of the weight lifts off my fingers.

"Squat," Dylan orders.

I do as I'm instructed, and a moment later, he appears over the top of the cabinet, which is now on the ground.

He glares at me, which is both hot and irritating. "Why are you doing this by yourself?"

Because I can't leave to go shopping for Shiloh's party supplies until all my freaking chores are done, and I can't get back to the church until I give Ridhi an update on plans.

Stupid favors.

Stupid better poker player than me.

"It looked like fun, Dylan. *Why do you think?*"

"There is literally not one single good reason I can think of." He sighs and rubs a hand over his face. "Just—don't do it again, okay? Get help next time."

"What are you doing here?"

"You didn't show up for breakfast."

I glance at the clock over the sink, remember it's perpetually frozen at 3:52, and check my watch instead.

Just after one. "Breakfast was like six hours ago."

"I'm aware."

"And I did go to the café, but you were busy, and I didn't want to mess with your vibe."

"You didn't tell me you were posting that video."

"I did." Oh, hell. I totally didn't. He's right. I should've, but it slipped my mind.

He cocks a brow at me, and *gah*.

Could he be any more attractive? Even when he's calling me on my bullshit, it's like he wants the best for me, and he knows lying isn't my best.

Or maybe I'm projecting.

Dylan Wright cannot possibly be all that and a pulled-pork sandwich.

No man can.

"Let's start over," he says quietly. "I missed you at breakfast, and I was worried something was wrong, since you haven't missed a meeting before, and you didn't call or text."

"Someone would've told you if something was wrong. Or you could've called me." Yes, I'm being a brat.

Yes, it's on purpose.

I need distance. I *desperately* need distance.

"I texted. And I had to get to work." He's getting a mulish look that's *also* adorable. "And fight off about a dozen women between the café and my truck."

I make myself beam and clap my hands. "It's working!"

It is clearly *not* working. Dylan's face is telegraphing utter misery.

I still keep smiling. "I'm so happy for you!"

"Knock it off."

"But I gave you what I promised. How often does a favor you have to do for someone else turn into such a good thing for *you*? And this is just the start. Pretty soon, you'll have your pick of any woman you want."

"But *I don't want any woman*." He blows out a breath. "I want—I want a *connection*. Like, you walk into a room, and *bam*. There she is. And then you start talking, and it's not just that she has a great smile or that there's nothing more attractive than a woman who'll take time out of her day to have lunch with the lonely elderly lady next door. It's that she listens and she doesn't complain if you snore or come home smelling like rotten fish. She's the first to call you out when you need it because you're being an idiot, but she'll do it kindly, and she lets you rant about how it's stupid that they put the one stoplight on Main when the corner of First and Maple actually has so much more traffic."

His ideal woman and life are so domestic and lovely that once again, that longing ache makes it hard to breathe.

Wouldn't it be amazing if life could be that simple? "I'm sure that woman is out there."

"But how do you find her when you're getting all the attention for something completely unrelated to who you really are?"

This man. I swear. "Sometimes you have to stop questioning it and just go with it."

"Is that what you do?"

"Just go with it?"

"Do you ever date anyone who gets to know the real you? Someone who doesn't care that your favorite baseball team is the Twins when you live in Wisconsin and you're supposed to cheer for the Brewers. Or someone who'll trade you all of your caramels for his morning coffee, because you don't like the way most caramels stick in your teeth, and he doesn't like coffee, and you just trade instead of mocking each other or telling each other to change."

"You never told Hannah you don't like her baseball team either? And do you not like coffee? For real? You order it every morning."

"I don't like caramels. But only when they're the kind that stick in your teeth. Honest-to-God soft caramels are fine. But that's not the point."

No, the point is, this man who kisses like a god and is everyone's best friend in Tickled Pink and who could stay famous on TikTok for *years* is too good for someone like me, and that knowledge hurts.

I wave a hand. "So you weren't interested in anyone in the first wave. Give it time. You can't force miracles."

He runs a hand over the top of the cabinet. "Are you taking the rest of these down?"

"Yep. I think I can handle it, though."

When he levels a *no, you will not* glare at me, I feel the first honest smile of the day. "You're a very good man, Dylan Wright. And good things will happen to you. Good things always happen to people who deserve it."

See also: I'm a fraud, and so of course nothing is easily falling into place with my cacao farm.

"I'm not a good person. Not all the time. And bad things happen to good people too."

"Like concussions when they make friends with the wrong people."

His lips twitch while he grabs a screwdriver from the assorted tools scattered on the counter, flips open the cabinet over the counter next to the vacant spot where the cabinet now on the floor used to be, and starts unscrewing the door. "Mistakes happen."

"*Accidents* happen. Mistakes are made. And I think you're making a mistake in being friends with me."

He shoots me another look while he scoots onto the counter so he can reach the top screw on the cabinet door.

Duh. I should've removed the doors.

It'll make the cabinets lighter.

"You think about emptying these before you took them off the walls?" he asks as he hands me a can of beans.

"Shut *up*. I get paid to look pretty, not to be smart."

"Me too."

I blink at him.

He grins. "What? A guy can't know he's pretty? I am. And I have a nice ass. You said so. And I imagine you've seen a *lot* of asses, so I trust your judgment."

"You are *not* attractive right now."

"Lies. You want to jump me. Here. Take this, and then we can pull this cabinet off the wall too."

I'm so grateful that I don't have to respond to him calling me out—yes, I *would* absolutely join the ranks of the women throwing their panties at him if I didn't know it was such a bad life decision—that I don't ask what he's handing me until I'm holding it.

"*Ew.* Is this—no, you know what? I don't want to know what this is." It might be a tennis ball that's seen better days.

Or it might've once been an orange.

Hard to tell.

He also hands over each of the shelves after he pulls them out, then points. "Hold the bottom of the cabinet for a second here. You didn't answer my question."

"I would totally not jump you."

"The one about how you know when someone's interested in you for you and not just faking it."

The cabinet gets heavier as he unscrews the second fastener, and I *oof*. "Wow, this is heavy."

He bawks like a chicken.

Softly, and good God, he's even sexy when he's making chicken noises.

I have a problem.

"How do you know, Tavi?" he presses. "What's the tell?"

"I have no idea. I don't date."

"Tabloids and all of my customers say you do."

"Have you been googling me?"

"No, I had a beer with Teague last night. Bridget was there. Root beer for her, before you ask. And she's a walking encyclopedia when it comes to the book of Tavi."

"Where was Phoebe?"

"Torturing Willie Wayne until he signed off on her plans for the new Ferris wheel? I don't know. Quit changing the subject." He leaps off the counter. "And pull."

We get the cabinet off the wall and set it on the ground next to the first one.

"Nice job," he says. "People really underestimate you, don't they?"

"You have to be good at something for people to underestimate you."

He pulls the screwdriver out of his back pocket and hands it to me. "Your turn. Get the next door. Also, ever think about believing in yourself?"

"But why, when low expectations mean you never let yourself down?" For the love of the Kardashians. How many times do I have to tell myself to shut up around him before I finally listen?

He takes me seriously when I say stuff like that, even if I add in the head tilt and the influencer voice.

"You're gonna sabotage yourself with your plans for after Tickled Pink, aren't you?"

"That's ridiculous. I'm *this close* to the life I always wanted and the life I've finally convinced myself that I deserve, and you think I'd just throw it away?"

He doesn't bat an eyelash. "That thing where I was a total shit in high school? If I hadn't been surrounded by people who believed in me and propped me up when I doubted I could turn my life around and forgave me and taught me to forgive myself, we wouldn't be having this conversation right now."

"When you say things like that, it makes me wonder if you're my project or if I'm yours."

"Maybe we're each other's."

We're both staring.

We're both staring at each other, and for the first time in my life, I have this unshakable feeling that someone sees me.

Truly sees me.

Would I sabotage an investor presentation if I was afraid it would just end in failure and that I'd let one more person down?

You bet your ass I would.

I donate my salary to preexisting charities because it's not my fault if they fuck up.

I did my part.

Not the *hard* part.

The easy part.

But the farm?

If I fuck it up, like I basically already have by relying on my trust fund instead of making it into an actual business, then it'll just prove what I've always thought.

That I suck at everything and have no redeeming qualities.

But Dylan—he sees through me.

He's staring at me like I'll be letting *him* down if I let myself down.

He has no skin in this game.

But he cares.

And oh God.

His gaze is dropping to my lips. His eyes are going dark. He's leaning in.

He's going to kiss me. Again.

I leap up onto the countertop, just like he did, but despite all the time I spend working out, I sway as I stand, and suddenly he's gripping my ass in one hand and my hand in the other, holding me steady.

"I'm not copping a feel, I swear to God," he says, his voice rough. "You okay?"

"Just klutzy."

"Have you eaten today?"

"Of course I've eaten, Dylan. It takes good food to fuel a body like mine." I had half a kale smoothie and tossed Niles's oatmeal soup in the trash when Gigi wasn't looking when I got back to the school after having an irrational attack of snarling green jealousy at seeing Dylan sitting with Lola at the café.

And that probably wasn't enough food.

"How about we go get lunch, and I'll help you finish this after I'm done for the day?" he says.

His hand is still cupping my butt.

I know he's not trying to feel me up. I know this is his instinctive reaction to wanting to make sure I don't fall. It's not sexual.

It's safety.

Okay, it's probably partly sexual too.

He wanted to kiss me.

I could feel it.

I wanted him to kiss me.

I still do.

And I still can't help wanting him to want to touch me more.

There's something undeniably irresistible about having a man see right through me, right to my biggest failings and shortcomings, and still be attracted to me.

"I have a chickpea salad in the fridge here," I make myself say. "I'll get it after this last cabinet. And my dad's around. I can get him or Carter or Niles to help me. Not because they're men, for the record. But more because they're the only other people in the school."

"Lola's here."

"No, she's helping Gigi at the community center."

"Then I passed her twin in the hallway."

I freeze. And freezing isn't good for my blood pressure when I haven't eaten enough, especially after my ten-mile run to start the day, and I sway again.

"And you're getting down *now*." He grabs me by the hips, and the next thing I know, I'm on the floor, my body lined up with his, while he scans my face as though *that's* what's wrong with me.

I'm clinging to his shoulders, and my gaze keeps drifting to his lips. *Run away with me to Costa Rica, Dylan. Show me how to be a normal woman. Save me from myself.*

Why?

Why is *he* the first man I've had a crush on since high school?

Is this a crush? Do grown women get crushes?

He's right. I should eat something.

Instead, I'm standing here clinging to him while we both stare at each other like we have no idea why we're not doing something about this already.

"A friend would answer my question about navigating the dating world as a famous person," he murmurs.

I lick my lips.

I can't help it.

Just like he probably can't help that his eyes go even darker as he tracks the path of my tongue.

"You don't *date*," I whisper. "You put on a show for the world to get better ratings or a bigger role or more publicity for your album launch or a better negotiation stance for your next sports contract. And then, if you're lucky, you find someone who's tolerable instead of just ruthless."

That's not the full truth.

Celebrities are people too.

I know plenty—I mean, I know *of* plenty of celebrities who actually fall in love.

But me?

I don't let people in. It's all surface level. I know better than to trust my world. And I don't know a single person in my world who would trust me enough to let me into theirs.

I let Naomi in more than I've ever let anyone in, because time and again, she's proved that I can trust her. She doesn't want my fame. She refused any more of a salary than she needed to live when she moved to Costa Rica to run the farm, so I know she doesn't want my money.

She lets me be as *me* as I'm comfortable being around her.

And I feel like Dylan would do the same, but I don't trust *feel*.

No matter how much I want to.

"Who did this to you?" he asks quietly.

I grimace. My family's been in town for two months, and he has to ask? "No one. It's just how I am."

He studies me for another long moment.

And now I'm squirming. "If you don't want to do the social media thing for Tickled Pink anymore, I get it. Just let me know. One viral video is like a bugbite. It's annoying for a couple days, and then it's, like, all better, and you barely even remember. But if you go big, it's a harder fall when it's done."

"I don't know what you're used to, but I'd hope you would've realized by now that I'm not out to hurt you. Some people care about their friends and neighbors, Tavi. It's what we do here. Pretend all you want with your family and with people like Lola, but I like my friends to at least be honest."

"I don't know how to have friends."

He drops his hands and steps back, shaking his head. "I'd bet there's a person *somewhere* in this world who disagrees with that."

He doesn't elaborate.

It's like he knows that if Lola's in the building, the walls have ears, though could he have mentioned seeing her sooner?

Yes, he really could've.

"I have to get back to work. You riding along? I'm snaking a bathtub. Should be nice and disgusting."

"I should go find my dad and ask him to help me finish up here, and then I have some errands I have to run, or else Ridhi will never serve me decent coffee ever again."

He nods once. "Got it. Don't hurt yourself. Pebbles wouldn't forgive you."

He stops to rub my dog's head on the way out the door, and then he's gone.

Physically.

Mentally, though, he's still up there in my head. Hanging out. Offering to be friends, when there's so little that I've ever given him in return.

I pick Pebbles up and hug her while she licks my face, offering the one constant source of unquestioning affection that I've ever had in my life. "Who's a good girl? Who's Mommy's best girl? Such a good dog. Yes, such a good dog."

Pretty sure I could've handled everything in Tickled Pink if it weren't for Dylan Wright.

I want to trust him.

I want to be his friend.

And I'm afraid if I do, he'll be my biggest regret.

Chapter 22

Dylan

My favorite thing about Saturdays is the possibility.

I'm up early, because I'm *can't sleep more than thirty minutes past my alarm even when it doesn't go off on the weekends* years old.

There's a whole day ahead of me to do anything I want, from yanking weeds in my garden to calling a few buddies for a pickup game of basketball to seeing if Hannah wants to watch TV.

I'm not calling Hannah these days.

She dropped me a note asking if I was too good for her now that I'm TikTok famous, and I haven't answered yet.

I realized I'm still using you as a stand-in girlfriend, and I can't do that anymore since you're married and pregnant and I'd like to have a life of my own isn't something I want to say out loud.

And if you can't say that out loud to your best friend, was she ever actually your best friend?

But the thing I *am* doing today?

I'm sitting on the bench by the lake at the edge of my property, sipping coffee out of a *Pink Gold* commemorative coffee tumbler that I had Ridhi fill up for me this morning.

"Do me a favor," she said when I asked for two coffees. "Make sure Tavi's not dropping the ball on the favor I asked her to do for me."

So yeah.

I'm sitting here on the lake, waiting for the sun to come up in another few minutes here, but mostly, I'm waiting for a sound that comes sooner than I expect it to.

Regular heavy breathing and a very distinctive voice.

"No, I need to go," Tavi says somewhere in the darkness. "I'm just about back to Tickled Pink. But I'm excited about our plans, even if it's a little scary. This has potential, you know? I'll call you later, okay? Yeah. Love you too, Naomi."

I catch a strip of reflective tape and her distinct outline in the first light of day as the breathing gets louder. "Coffee?" I say when she's within spitting distance.

She shrieks and throws up her hands over her face, like she's afraid I'm going to attack, and veers toward the lake itself.

"Whoa, just me." I stand, peering into the darkness. "Tavi?"

"Give a girl a heart attack, why don't you?"

"You know you can take a day off now and again."

"And you can maybe not be all creepy waiting-in-the-dark guy."

Been called worse. I sip my coffee and keep a close eye on her while she hunches over, panting.

"How's Naomi?" I ask.

"Please pretend you've never heard that name."

"We still playing this?"

"Yes."

"I have a vegan sugar-free caramel macchiato made with oat milk steamed to some magic temperature for a woman willing to sit down and talk with me like I'm a guy she trusts to keep her secrets."

She makes a noise low in her throat, and I know I've got her.

"Are you seriously waiting for me?" she asks.

"I shut my phone off." Mostly because it hasn't stopped blowing up with messages from people excited that I'm "TikTok famous," and I've seen enough comments from people in my past that I'm remembering—vividly—why I've never gotten *any* social media accounts before. "Whole day to myself. And I hear I have a friend with too much to do. Thought I'd see what I can help with."

"Why?"

"That's what you do for friends."

She bends at the waist again, holding her side like she has a stitch in it. "I'm a terrible friend."

"If you could spend an entire day doing nothing but whatever you *want* to do, what would you do?"

The outline of her face shifts in the dim dawn light, like she's staring at me and debating if she should answer that question.

I hold out the second coffee tumbler and shake it at her.

"I have to answer to get coffee?"

"Coffee's free. You have to answer for me to make all of your dreams come true."

She huffs out a small laugh. "You shouldn't offer women things like that."

"I was a shit in high school. I'm not anymore."

"I've heard rumblings to that effect."

"No, I mean, I don't make offers I won't follow through on anymore."

She pulls a foot up to touch her ass, stretching her quad. "I spilled the beans about your best friend's pregnancy to her mom, I gave you a concussion, I still chase you out of . . . *places* . . . regularly, and you still want to be nice to me."

"You know my favorite part of a banana?"

She laughs. "What?"

"Peeling it."

"I'm more like an onion than a banana."

"You *want* to be an onion. But you're really a simple banana. A fascinating, simple banana."

"This is the strangest conversation I've ever had."

"You're welcome."

She laughs again—rich and full and not holding back—and yeah. This *is* how I want to spend my day.

"Hannah thinks my garden is ridiculous," I hear myself say.

"What? Your garden is *awesome*."

"And that's why I want to spend today with you."

The confession hangs in the air. I know she's studying my profile, puzzling me out.

"Does no one here tell you you're handsome and kind and funny and a serious joy to be around?" she asks quietly.

I want to duck my head, but I don't. It's habit to own the hard stuff after this many years of working on it. "Sometimes I think they tell me that to reinforce good behavior. You . . . you don't have any preconceived notions. You don't have to humor me. You don't have any reason to build me up. You don't have to be nice to me. And you don't make me feel like I'm a project, even though I know that's what this started as. You're just doing the best you can, same as all of us, except you have a lot bigger expectations sitting on your shoulders. If I'd been a shit and also *you* in high school, there's a reasonable possibility I wouldn't even be here today."

"In Wisconsin?"

"Alive."

I sip my coffee to cover my own wince. That doesn't sound any better out loud than it did in my head.

She drops her foot and slowly approaches me at the edge of the path. "Why do you say that?"

I wiggle the coffee tumbler again.

She doesn't take it.

Clearly, the lady wants an answer before a coffee date. "All the money to indulge in fast cars, drugs, alcohol, women, which is exactly what I dabbled in in high school . . . and no support system to temper that? It wouldn't have been on purpose, but I would've self-destructed."

"Do you know what three years of hiding in Costa Rica at every opportunity with people who don't know the public me has taught me?" she asks quietly.

"That life's better when it's simple?"

"Yes, that too. But until my grandmother issued her ultimatum, it taught me that I get to forgive myself for who I used to be."

I glance at the lake, which is starting to glow a soft gray pink. "Takes work."

"Every day." She nudges me. "But you do the work. You *clearly* do the work. Give yourself credit. And when you slip, call me. I'll remind you that you deserve every good thing that happens to you, even when you feel like you don't."

"You deserve good things too."

It's light enough to see her nose wrinkle.

"You do," I repeat.

"I'm not my best me here."

"I watched you save a duck."

She squints at me. "What?"

"I left for work one morning before we met, and you were chasing a duck out of the road."

"Anyone else would've done the same."

"Would you have before Costa Rica?"

"Dylan. I'm a vegan influencer. Saving ducks is on brand."

"No one was watching. You were already saving it before you could've seen my truck coming."

She finally accepts the coffee tumbler with an eyeball of *you're ridiculous* aimed at me and a *hmm* reverberating in the back of her throat, but when she takes a sip, the noise changes to a full-on throaty moan that makes my cock hard in an instant. "Oh my *God*, this is delicious."

I smile. "Haven't had Ridhi's best yet, hm?"

"Ridhi made this? Holy shit. No wonder Phoebe calls it good coffee. Okay. Okay. I get it now. And clearly, I need to up my game for this surprise birthday party for Shiloh." She sips again. "Wow. *Wow.*"

"You nail Shiloh's birthday party, and I bet you get coffee like this every day."

She twists her neck to squint at me sideways. "You're honestly free and willing to help me today? I mean, duh. Right. Who in their right mind would be up at this hour of the day, on a Saturday, waiting with coffee, if you *weren't* planning on torturing yourself for the rest of the day too, right?"

I somehow don't think any of spending an entire day with Tavi will be any kind of *torture*. "Shiloh loves chocolate."

She eyeballs me and hums again, takes another sip of coffee, and if that's anywhere close to what she looks and sounds like midorgasm, then I am the biggest idiot to ever walk the face of this earth for turning her down in the locker room shower a month ago.

"Good *God*, that's delicious," she says. "Ten minutes. The basement. We'll plan while I work. Do *not* let anyone follow you, and if they do—"

"Say I heard water running and went to investigate."

She goes up on her tiptoes and presses a kiss to my cheek. "You're the best."

I grip her by the hips, and we both freeze.

"The s-sun," she stutters. "Have to hurry."

"You're a good person, Tavi Lightly."

For once, she doesn't argue.

Just blinks those big blue eyes at me like I'm holding her world together.

And hell if that isn't a high I don't need.
She's leaving.
But she's here now.
Today.
And that's going to have to be enough.

Chapter 23

Tavi

Chocolate and I first met when I sneaked a Twix bar out of Millicent Grover's mother's purse while we were waiting to be called back to stage for the results at the end of a beauty pageant when I was about eight, and it's been my secret lover ever since.

It's been my mission since before I knew it was my mission.

Now, since I bought the farm, whenever I'd travel away from Costa Rica to live my *real* life, I'd email Naomi and browse for truffle recipes for inspiration, and sometimes I'd walk into chocolate shops just to ask if they had any vegan, sugar-free truffles, when really, I wanted to smell that delicious, rich scent of heaven.

Most people on my support staff know I cheat on my diet on occasion, and after a lifetime of growing up with my grandmother, I learned to buy people's loyalty with compliments and air-kisses and hefty salaries and occasional loud, public professional breakups that made the other person look bad, though I only did that once because I felt so awful about it that I puked for three days afterward. Then there were the nondisclosure agreements and employment contracts and termination clauses as backup. But I still didn't ask for nearly as many truffles as I wanted to sample.

Not when my mother's voice would ring in the back of my head.

Octavia, you know what that will do to your figure.

But today?

Today, after waiting for me by the lake with the most delicious coffee I've ever had in my life, once I've finished showering and sneak into the church basement, Dylan's waiting for me with rows of open truffle boxes lying on my worktable.

I've barely shut and locked the door behind me before the decadent scent makes my mouth water. "One, how did you get in here, and two, *oh my God*, where did these come from?"

"Don't know much about getting into the chocolate game, but I know you have to know your competitors if you want to stand out."

I sniff again, then pinch myself to make sure this isn't a dream.

"I keep asking myself why you'd want to hang out with me, and I think I finally get it. It's the chocolate, isn't it?"

"We have to work on your self-confidence here."

"I was making a joke."

"Uh-huh." He points to a purple box sitting among gold, green, and wooden boxes. "This is the one I send my mom when I'm trying to get out of trouble. And that's the one I send to Willie Wayne when I need to ask him to sign off on a permit with short notice or one that he's not going to like, like when I told him we were making Jane's garage into an industrial-grade kitchen so she could sell her beer."

I'm drooling. Not even kidding, I am *drooling*. "She really needs socials if she's going to grow."

"Hasn't wanted to grow. This is a self-sustaining hobby, and she spends a lot of time debating with herself over whether she'd still enjoy it if it was her job." He points to the wooden box. "And I sent those to Hannah and the asshole when they got married. Wanted to make sure he knew that *I* knew how to send her better gifts than he does."

"You like chocolate. I mean, you *seriously* like chocolate."

"A little."

He grins again, those dimples popping out, and I have to hold myself back before I tackle him with another hug and a kiss.

Instead, I point to the table while I let Pebbles down to run around the kitchen, which I should *not* do when making truffles for public consumption, but for me to taste-test, it's totally fine. "This is not *a little*."

"Okay, Ms. Bought a Chocolate Farm." He squats to greet my dog, and my heart melts.

All of it.

"Has anyone ever told you they're glad you were a total shit as a kid?" I ask him.

He laughs. "No."

"Well, I am."

He shakes his head. "No, you're not."

"I am." I point to the boxes of truffles too. "Do you know how much work those took to go from a little seed in the ground to beans on a tree to finished product? You could've said, *Fuck it, being one of those awful overdried Halloween taffies in the orange-and-black wrappers is enough*, but instead, you took the time to turn yourself into a gourmet chocolate truffle with layers and depth. If you hadn't had your bad years, if you'd been an average kid with average problems instead, maybe you would've grown up to be a pack of M&M's. They're decent, but they're not what you send when you want to put your best foot forward. But you had to work for it. You had to pay attention to the little things. And now, you're a gourmet truffle. You deserve better than being something someone takes for granted. You deserve to be someone who's savored and appreciated for every bit of what went into making you who you are."

He's staring at me like I'm six trees short of a forest.

And now my face is getting hot, and once again, I wish mornings didn't exist.

"Never mind." I flap my hands, because I don't know what else to do with them. "I hate mornings. I don't make sense in mornings. I—"

I can't keep talking, because he's suddenly in front of me, hooking a hand behind my neck and pulling me against him for a kiss more delicious than all the chocolate in the world.

This isn't a *whoops, I fell and my face landed on your face and now our lips are smushed together* kiss.

This is a whole-body, whole-soul experience.

The rest of the world? What rest of the world?

Not when Dylan's stroking a hand over my ass, his other still holding me at the nape, his mouth devouring mine, his body pressed tight so I can feel every delicious inch of him.

I let my hands wander over his magnificent ass, and he growls low in his throat as he thrusts his tongue deeper into my mouth, tasting like he's already been sampling chocolates this morning. His erection presses into my belly, and he's not trying to hide it.

Not this morning.

But it's not the physical sensations of his kiss and his touch, not the lingering cocoa taste on his tongue, not his subtle *more* noises, that have me already soaking my panties and desperate to rip my clothes off and offer all of myself to him.

It's that he *wants* me.

It's that he could have anyone, and he's choosing to be here, kissing *me*. Holding *me*. Letting *me* stroke him and tug at his shirt and kiss him back like he's my oxygen.

"You're fucking intoxicating," he breathes against my mouth.

"More kisses."

"I love Saturdays." He helps me by yanking his shirt the rest of the way off and tossing it across the room.

Pebbles barks like she's found a new play toy, and I make a mental note to buy Dylan a new shirt later.

Maybe.

I run my hands over his chest, tracing the tattoo on his left pec. "A tiger?" I breathe. It's engulfed in flames, all monochromatic, and I want to lick it.

He angles his head to kiss my neck. "Evidence of ego, but well earned."

"You're a tiger in bed?"

"One way to find out."

And there goes that ache in my clit. And that's before he nips at my collarbone.

"I want to watch you eat chocolate," he says, his breath tickling my skin and his words making my nipples tighten.

"I—can't—"

"Fuck the noise and enjoy the chocolates, Tavi." He's kissing his way down my neck, over the strap of my halter top, and to my shoulder, his fingertips making my skin erupt in goose bumps and his lips setting them on fire. "I want to watch you enjoy yourself."

"That's usually someone asking me to make a home porno with them."

"If you want me to stop—"

"*No!* Please don't stop. I get—"

"Nervous?"

"Not usually," I whisper. "Just—now."

He's halfway down my arm, pressing kisses and teasing my skin with his fingers, but he straightens to look me square in the eye. He's so close our noses are almost touching, and I close the gap so that my eyes cross and his go double.

"Me too," he whispers back.

"Dylan. I'm just a woman. I really am."

"You're not what's making me nervous."

"But—*oh*."

I suck in a surprised breath as his brows twist, like, *Yeah*.

He rejected me not all that long ago because he was *involved*.

"You were waiting."

"I was waiting."

"If you don't want—*mmph!*"

I can't talk anymore, because there's a truffle in my mouth.

A glorious, rich, deep dark chocolate truffle.

My eyes slide shut while the flavors melt over my tongue. "Oh my God, that's good."

Dylan kisses my neck again, this time on the other side. "I want to make your eyes cross like that."

"That's—*oh my God, this is good*—very ambitious."

He laughs against my shoulder while he rubs his hands over my hips. "This is where *I love your ass, Dylan,* would be useful."

He slowly comes into focus as I let my eyes slide open, and I couldn't stop my smile if my life depended on it.

He is, without a doubt, the sexiest, kindest, *easiest* man I've ever known. "This is *really* good chocolate." I reach behind me for a box, grab the first treat I find, and hold it to his mouth. "Here. Try it."

He holds my gaze while he closes his mouth over the truffle, sucking on my finger and thumb in the process.

There's a low pull in my belly, and I lean in to kiss his neck while *his* eyes slide closed. His breath hitches when my lips touch his skin, and he pulls me tighter against him, leaving no doubt that he is *very* happy to be here this morning.

I want to reach into his pants and stroke his erection, but I need explicit permission this time.

I'm not messing up with him again.

"Yeah," he breathes. "This is really good chocolate."

"Better than mine?"

"Never."

"Liar."

"*Biased*, maybe. *Liar*, no." He hooks a hand under my leg and lifts it, nudging me to sit on the worktable. "I want to see you naked."

I hate being naked.

There's nothing that makes me feel more vulnerable than putting every physical shortcoming on display. No hiding a bloated day with a belt tied just right, no disguising my imperfections, no chance of airbrushing or photoshopping.

It's just me.

Real. Raw. *Naked.*

But this morning?

Here?

With Dylan?

It's the most natural thing in the world to reach behind my neck and untie my top.

I let the two sides fall loose, baring my breasts, my belly still covered as he cups me gently and brushes his thumbs over my nipples. "Beautiful," he murmurs.

I reach back again, this time letting my hair tie loose. "I can't reach the zipper," I lie.

His dimples pop out, that grin telling me he knows I can *easily* reach the zipper holding my shirt closed behind me. "The zipper on your shirt?"

"Mm-hmm."

"Then whatever"—he drops to one knee—"shall we do?"

I gasp as his lips close around the tip of my breast, one hand still fondling the other, his free hand now tracing my skin at the edge of my top as he searches out the zipper in question.

My clit is aching like it's near exploding, and I want to touch myself.

But more, I want him to touch me.

He eases the zipper down, and my halter top falls away, leaving me exposed from the waist up.

He grabs another chocolate from the table, catches my gaze as he licks the outside, then rubs it across my nipple before suckling me back into his mouth.

"Oh God," I whimper.

"Much better."

I have one leg wrapped around his back, and if one of us doesn't touch my clit soon, I will die.

Right here.

I swear I will. "My breast?"

"The chocolate."

I fumble blindly behind myself for the nearest box and send them all skittering across the table as I get a handful. And then I'm off the table, pushing him to his back on the floor while I straddle him. "My turn."

He props himself up on his elbows, watching while I rub my palms together, the chocolate between them, until my hands are coated in melted truffle.

"Green tea," he says quietly.

I sniff, and then I catch it.

The subtle hints of grass and tea mixed in with the heady, rich chocolate. "Are you allergic?"

He chuckles softly. "No."

"Would you rather a different flavor?"

"*Tavi.*"

"What?"

"I just want you."

I look at my hands.

Then at him.

And before my jumbled, sex-starved, overaroused brain can process what's happening, he sits up, with me still straddling him, grabs my hands, and licks my palms.

First one, then the other.

For the record, I didn't know my palms were erogenous zones.

Also, for the record, if he can make me nearly come by licking my palms, what could the man do if he licked my pussy?

"I'm supposed to be licking chocolate off of you," I whisper as I adjust myself so that my poor clit can rub shamelessly against his erection.

"It's Saturday. We have all day."

We don't have all day.

I have seventy-four million things I need to do.

But then he flexes his hips beneath me, and nothing else matters.

Today, there's no family.

There's no Tickled Pink.

No favors, no chocolate empire to plan, no secrets to fret about.

It's just me and this man who's sucking each of my chocolate-covered fingers into his mouth, one at a time, while he watches me pant and squirm at the sheer pleasure of having someone take this much time, care, and attention with me.

"Want—to do—for you," I gasp as he works his tongue between my pinkie and ring fingers.

"Shh," he whispers, and then he's holding another truffle to my mouth, this one carrying scents of curry and toasted pumpkin seeds.

I close my mouth around it, and once again, my eyeballs roll into the back of my head.

I love chocolate.

I do.

Dylan traces the tendons in my neck. "Do you have any idea—honestly—how fucking gorgeous you are?"

"It's all fake."

"Not this," he replies, flexing his hips to roll his erection against my clit.

I groan, and chocolate dribbles out of my mouth. "Oh God, I'm so—"

"If you say sorry, I *will* spank this lovely ass."

I lock eyes with him. "Will you spank me even if I don't say sorry?"

His cock surges beneath me. "Fuck, Tavi."

And then he's gripping my hair, tilting my head back while he devours my mouth again. I squirm in his lap, reaching for the button on his jeans, and then I'm on my back, Dylan between my legs, undoing the button on my bright-purple jeans and tugging them down my hips while I try to help with my chocolate-coated hands.

His shoes go flying.

So do mine.

Then his pants, and my mouth goes dry.

"Dylan," I whisper, reaching for his long, solid length. It's thick and heavy, bobbing between his thighs. He fists it as he pulls a condom from his discarded wallet, then rolls it on.

I don't know where my pants went.

All I know is that I'm lying on the floor, my legs spread, my fingers teasing my clit while I watch him quickly roll on the condom and then drop to his knees again.

He pulls my hand from between my thighs. *"Mine."*

And then he grabs one more truffle. "And yours."

I open my mouth.

He slides the chocolate onto my tongue.

And then he takes *his* tongue right where my fingers just were.

"Oh my gaaaaw," I gasp around the rich flavor as he licks my core.

I'm already so turned on, so ready, that when he twirls his tongue around my clit, I almost come off the floor as my orgasm threatens to overtake me.

He lifts his head. "Jesus. Already?"

"Not—usually—"

I don't want to come this soon.

I don't.

He strokes me with his fingers, and my hips buck off the floor again. "Oh my God," I gasp. I grab his hand. "Please. *Please.* I need you inside me. *Now.*"

I don't have to ask twice.

He shifts on the floor, and then he's between my thighs, kissing me, gripping my hips while he centers himself over me, his thick head sliding between my slick folds until he's fully sheathed inside me, and *oh my God.*

This.

This.

"Fuck," he grunts.

"You're so perfect."

"You're so tight."

He pulls out and thrusts into me again as I pump my hips to meet him, and *yes.* "Right there, Dylan. *Right—oh God, more.*"

He slams into me again.

I pull my knee to my chest to change the angle, and *oh God oh God oh God.*

"Tavi—"

"Yes," I cry.

"I can't—*fuck.*"

He slams into me once more, and everything explodes in a shower of stars as I let my climax overtake me, squeezing and spasming around his hot steel length, holding him with a leg hooked around his back while wave after wave of blissful release rolls through me.

I can feel his cock pulsing inside me, too, as he groans into my neck, his arms wrapped beneath me while he strains into me, both of us coming so hard that I'm pretty sure neither of us is breathing.

It's just raw, bare, natural pleasure.

And I don't want it to end.

The regrets are already threatening to break through.

You're leaving. You can't be his. You know he waited for the right per-son. You know he hasn't done this with anyone else. You know you're not worthy.

"God, Tavi," he whispers as his body sags against me, his chest heaving as he pants softly. "If I'd known it would be like this—"

I freeze. "Terrible?"

"So worth the wait."

His arms tighten even harder around me, which should be impos-sible. My bones are turning to jelly as the last of my spasms fade. "So worth every second of the wait," he whispers.

I squeeze my eyes shut against the heat building and threatening to cause tears.

I've never been "worth the wait."

Not personally. Not professionally. Not in bed.

"You are entirely too good for me," I whisper.

"Good," he replies. "It was all the people who were too good for me who finally showed me what mattered."

I still don't understand what he sees in me.

But for once, I push away the fears, the doubts, and the pending regrets.

"Once won't be enough," he says softly into my neck.

And despite every reason I shouldn't, I smile. "Agreed."

Chapter 24

Dylan

I'm apparently a freak.

Not because it's odd that helping Tavi make chocolate gives me a boner every damn time. Chocolate and sexy women? Yeah. Boners are natural.

No, it's my nose.

"Smell this one," she says late Tuesday night, shoving a truffle under my nose.

I take it and sniff, rub the smooth exterior and sniff again, and then I bite into it, letting the flavors melt on my tongue.

She leans on the table in the kitchen basement, watching me, eyes bright and fascinated, like she's not sleep deprived and running on fumes.

Don't tell me she's not.

I know for a fact she's in this kitchen every night until well past midnight and up hitting her favorite jogging path by five thirty. All while also spending all day working on the school, managing her grandmother, and planning Shiloh's birthday party, which is coming up two weeks from today.

"Orange and cinnamon, with a hint of . . ." I sniff again. "Olive oil?"

"I just got wet in my panties."

"I could flex my pinkie and you'd get wet."

"Also true, but *oh my God.* Do you realize you could get a job as a professional taster?"

"Because being a plumber isn't sexy enough?"

She frowns at me, and if she's not channeling her grandmother in this moment, I don't want to know what more terrifying beast she might be channeling instead. "*Dylan Alfred Wright,* there is *nothing* wrong with being a plumber, and you are a *very* good plumber, and I'm incredibly grateful you know what to do with pipes and faucets and hot-water heaters, but there's also nothing wrong with being told you have a gift that you apparently didn't know you had. *Do you understand me?*"

"Ah, Alfred isn't my middle name."

"I don't remember your middle name, so I made it up, because this is a middle name moment. *You are worthy no matter your occupation.* Are we clear?"

Her hair's tied up in a messy bun, much like it always is when she's playing with chocolate—and I say that with all due respect, since I think it's cool she loves her job this much—and she's in a pink tank top, no bra, and loose pants made of some kind of shimmery material that I have no name for.

Don't care what it's called.

I'm just glad it looks like it'll be easy to pull off her when we're done with the chocolate.

"So if we found out I had a talent for knitting, would you tell me I should leave behind plumbing and go knit?"

"Would it make you happy?"

"Ah, so you're assuming it would make me happy to sniff chocolate all day long."

Her eyebrows do a funky dance across her forehead. "I'm sorry, did you just hear yourself?"

She's so earnest I can't stop a smile. "Might not love it so much if you had to do it every single day."

"Hello, *I do it every single day*, and I love it, and I wish I had your nose." She frowns. "But for real, how do you deal with the stinkier jobs when your nose is that sensitive?"

"Used to it, I suppose."

"Could you be any more like a superhero?"

"Stop." I pluck a chocolate off the small plate and hold it out to her. "You sniff. What do you smell?"

"That one's a champagne truffle, and this one's ginger, and that one's a brown butter ganache, which I think you may recall helping make."

I remember finally carrying her upstairs to have my way with her on some dusty cushions in the choir loft when they were finally done last night. Also, I took that mental high five from high school me for scoring in a church choir loft, and I have zero regrets. "Cheating."

She grins.

It's not her public smile. Or the smile she gives to Pebbles, or the smile she aims at Bridget and the other teenagers around town.

This one is pure impish fun.

Tavi Lightly is an utter joy when she's stripped out of her makeup and the expectations of the world.

"Why don't you smile like that for your socials?" I ask her.

The fun slips away, and I want to kick myself. "Because it's easier to handle the world trying to tear me down when I know it's not *me* they're criticizing." She grimaces and turns, grabbing a box to line up the truffles for shipping tomorrow. "I get enough of that from my family."

"Your mom?"

"I know she's not trying to be cruel when she tells me what I should and shouldn't eat. She's trying to protect me from what the world would say and make me a better—no, a *more successful* person. But it just . . ."

"Makes you feel like you'll never be good enough?"

"Something like that."

"My first stepfather thought the best way to make me tough was to talk about how strong and smart my brother was so I'd want to compete and keep up."

She slides me an unreadable look. "How long was he in your life?"

"About three years. My sister turned nine, he called her a slut for wearing a skirt she'd outgrown overnight to her birthday party, and my mom finally realized she didn't want a guy like that in her life or in ours."

"So you were . . . ?"

"Ten."

"And you're going to forgive yourself for being a shit considering that's the kind of example you have?"

I eyeball her. "Somebody else say something to you?"

"Oh, no. I read the comments on your TikToks."

Jesus. Even I haven't been that brave. Actually, I wouldn't know she was posting videos to my account at all if my phone didn't regularly blow up and if I weren't getting phone numbers slipped to me every time I go out in public.

On jobs.

At restaurants.

While I'm eating with Tavi, who keeps doing that fake-smiling *we're just friends* thing, which makes my stomach do a slow roll of anger and horror and *here we go again* every time.

"Did you really plant the stink bomb that malfunctioned and festered by the girls' bathroom for five years before it just *broke* and took a major pipe with it and caused the school to permanently shut down early that last year that it was open?"

"Yep."

"And the olive oil on the stairs—"

"Yep."

"And the—"

"Highly likely, whatever they said."

"How many stepfathers had you had by then?"

"If you're trying to make excuses for me—"

"You were *a kid*."

"And I dealt with all of this a long time ago, and it's good for me to have the occasional reminder that I'm in charge of continuing to make good decisions." I nudge her. "But I appreciate you making sure I know it's okay."

She bites her lip and studies me.

I lift my brows and wait.

Don't have to wait long.

"What was your wake-up call?" she asks.

Wasn't expecting that. I suck in a big breath and blow it out slowly. Lots I don't mind talking about from my childhood. This one? It's not my favorite. "Almost drowned."

"Why? How?"

"Prank gone wrong at the swimming pool over in Deer Drop."

She visibly shivers but doesn't say anything.

So I pick up where she left off with boxing her chocolate samples. "Hear your grandma says she saw the flames of hell."

Tavi nods.

"I saw every last person I'd hurt. It was this massive kaleidoscope of my fuckups. Last thing I remember before I lost consciousness. Woke up in the hospital, eighteen years old, couldn't stop crying. Mom was there. Told her everything. And she held my hand and said, *Family forgives*. Whole damn town—they're my family. She was right. They forgave me. So now—now, I do my best to not fuck up anymore. And I don't take them for granted. And I don't judge when I see other people fucking up, because I've been there. Know what it's like. And I know you don't get through it with people yelling at you. You get through it with people supporting you."

"That's why you're so kind to me," she whispers.

255

I shake my head. "You're not a fuckup. Even when you're not being *you*, you're doing it with kindness. You know what you want to do in your life. You know why. You know how it helps the world. You're in the middle of a hiccup with making it happen, but you're still doing it."

"I'm not nice to my family."

"Define *family*."

She blinks twice, and then she flings herself at me, pressing kisses to my jaw, wrapping her legs around my hips, and then grabbing my face and holding it to hers. "You should come to Costa Rica with me."

I get a better grip on her ass—*God*, she has the best ass—and nuzzle her nose with mine, even though there's a chill spreading through my veins at the reminder that she won't stay. "Booty calls in Costa Rica? Sounds fun."

"I'm the best me there." She presses a kiss to my lips, and it doesn't matter how softly she kisses me—it always makes me hard in an instant. "I see the best you. I want you to see the best me."

"Your grandmother shouldn't have made you come here."

Her legs tighten around me. "I'm glad she did."

And then she's kissing me, long and slow and thorough, and it doesn't matter that she'll leave eventually.

It matters that she's here now.

That she makes me feel like I'm the king of the whole damn world.

And that she believes in me.

Chapter 25

Tavi

I have finally found something I hate more than I hate mornings.

I hate falling in love.

Hate it.

It's the worst. The absolute worst.

Why, you ask?

Because right now, I'm sitting in Café Nirvana with Dylan, who's spent every free minute of the last week with me, helping me plan Shiloh's birthday party, or helping me experiment with different truffle flavors, or taking my boxes of truffles to the post office for me "because I'll be in Deer Drop anyway," or very thoroughly servicing my lady bits with his hands, mouth, and wonder penis, and I'm smiling at Lola Minelli across from us and saying, "Oh, no, we're just friends."

I am head over heels in love with the man who I knew better than to let myself have a little crush on, and I have to tell the world that *we're just friends.*

"But you're so *cute* together," Lola says.

Her fake enthusiasm makes me want to gag, and I half suspect either she's reveling in the fact that after the *Tickled Pink Papers* published an edition featuring Dylan and me laughing in front of the half-finished Ferris wheel, there are rumors in the rest of the tabloids worldwide that *Tavi Lightly, internationally famous brand ambassador*, is dating a *plumber*, or she's mentally rubbing her hands in glee at the idea that we'll have a messy breakup that'll give the press something more terrible to say about me.

Maybe she's not.

Maybe she's honestly here to improve her soul.

But it's hard to trust anyone from my old world, and she is *definitely* from my old world.

Dylan squeezes my knee under the table. "You think we should date?" he asks Lola.

"*Oh my gah*, yes, *totes*."

"Just because we're cute?" he presses.

"That's, like, *the very best reason* to date. It means your souls are compatible when you're cute together. I can, like, *feel* Tavi's soul getting better every time I see her with you."

"Maybe he's not real," I say. "Maybe he's my guardian angel sent to earth in human form, and at the end of this year in Tickled Purgatory—I mean, Tickled Pink—he'll go back to heaven, and I'll get to spend the rest of my life atoning for my sins by missing him."

Anya chokes on her water behind the counter.

The forty other out-of-towners and tourists crowded into the café this morning all stare at me, too, some of them like I'm insane, some like they'd never considered that before, and one random tourist gets this weird look on her face, then pulls out her phone and starts dictating quietly into it.

I don't catch much, but I'm pretty sure I hear *book idea* and *next bestseller*.

Also, can we talk a minute about how this social media experiment with Dylan is *clearly* a success, yet Gigi is still refusing to acknowledge that I've done any work?

Soon. Swear to God, *soon*, I'll be done with this place. Everything's in place for an investor meeting with a chocoholic new billionaire who wants to do good with his money.

My nerves aren't in place, but everything else is.

I hope.

The number of things that could go wrong . . .

And the people I'll be leaving behind . . .

But I'm not thinking about that. Not yet. If I'm here, I'm going to enjoy myself. Or possibly *enjoy torturing myself* is a more accurate phrase.

I tap Dylan's arm. "We should get going. I have a consultation with a local interior designer for the teachers' lounge redesign, and you have clients who can't wait."

"Aww, you're so, like, *domestic*," Lola squeals. "Have you synced your calendars yet?"

"Not yet," Dylan replies as he scoots out of the booth and offers me a hand.

I give him Pebbles's carrying case, which he accepts with an amused smirk before offering me his other hand too.

It's like he *knows.*

He knows I've fallen head over heels for him. He knows I'm overthinking everything and can't just enjoy this for what it is in the moment. He probably also knows all my desires to leave everything here behind and move to Costa Rica are suddenly complicated.

But does he know and *care*?

Or does he know and want to spare my feelings by not pointing it out?

"Do you do emergency house calls?" asks a middle-aged guy who's probably not a local if he has to ask.

"Sometimes," Dylan replies easily.

"Leave him alone, Earl," the man's companion says. "He has to sleep if he's going to stay that hot."

"It true you kept a running tally of the girls you knocked up in high school?" Earl asks.

"*Earl.* Of course that's not true. Don't badger the poor man. How would you feel if you got famous for what happened to your dentures?"

"I can make that happen," I say sweetly.

With a smile.

Earl shrinks back. "Ain't nobody wanna hear about that. And you shouldn't wear pants so tight."

I hold my smile. It's habit at this point. But while I try to keep walking, Dylan freezes in his tracks.

"She can wear whatever the hell she wants to wear, and you can keep your opinions to yourself."

That's a new growl from him.

At least, to me it is.

It makes the hairs on the back of my neck stand up, and I don't miss the way every Tickled Pink local in the building whips their head around to stare at him.

You can *feel* the temperature changing inside the café.

It goes from *damn, it's crowded in here* hot to *oh shit, this isn't good* nuclear frost so fast you can almost see people's sweat crystallize into ice.

Dylan's not smiling anymore as he grips my arm more firmly and nudges me out the door.

"Why did Anya and Jane look like they were suddenly afraid you were going to go Incredible Hulk on that old man?" I whisper.

He doesn't answer.

He doesn't have to. Not really. I've picked up more and more on all the subtle cues around us.

They still sometimes think Dylan might do bad things.

I don't believe for one second that he would. And even if he does something *not great*, it won't be anything as bad as what he did in high school.

I peer up at him. "You really didn't have to defend me. His opinion didn't—"

"Didn't it?"

He's still growling. And he's not just scowling. He's full-on glowering.

Pebbles whimpers and sinks into my purse, which he still has flung over his other shoulder.

"Is this your temper?" I ask.

"I don't tolerate ignorant shits trying to tear other people down."

"That's not an answer."

He squeezes his eyes shut as we reach his truck, and he blows out a slow breath.

"You don't have to calm down for me. I've worked with some seriously temperamental assholes before."

"I'm calming down for *me*."

I slip my hand into his and squeeze.

"Whoa, tell me you didn't read the comments on your TikTok videos," a woman says nearby.

Dylan's cheek twitches, but he's wearing a fake smile before his eyes are fully open as he turns to the familiar voice.

Oh, hell.

It's Hannah.

"Nope," he tells her. "Café's too crowded."

She wrinkles one cheek at him as she rubs her lower belly. "That's your temper-tantrum face."

He points to his own face. "This is a smile."

She glances at my purse, still flung over Dylan's shoulder, and my dog, who's staring up at him like she wants to lick him but only if it'll help.

"That's a fake smile." Hannah steps closer and leans into him like she can read the truth of how he's feeling in his eyes.

She probably can.

261

They've been friends forever, right?

When I get to Costa Rica, I won't have to watch them together. Ever.

But the thought doesn't help.

I'll miss him.

I'll miss Anya and Bridget.

The snowshoe baseball team.

The sight of Jane and Teague and Willie Wayne out on the lake in their boats. The sight of Phoebe occasionally falling into the lake.

The half-finished Ferris wheel.

"Did someone bring up prom?" she asks him.

I lean in closer when his cheek twitches again. His nostrils flare, and I suddenly don't like Hannah for making that happen.

"Some old man told me I'm too fat to wear these pants, and it made him mad," I say. "I'd say *isn't he the sweetest*, but of course, you already know he is."

Hannah looks me up and down. "Where do you even find pants like that?"

"These?" I twist, lifting a hand to hold my hat on while looking down at the rainbow-striped leggings that make me look like Rainbow Brite's sidekick. "Oh, Gianni Versace sent them to me to test out."

Yes, yes, I'm lying.

I snagged them at the Pink Box here in town yesterday when I heard some teenage twatwaffle making fun of Bridget and her friends for wearing rainbow accessories.

Also?

The way Dylan's giving me the eyeball of *don't be a twat yourself, Tavi*, suggests he knows it as well as we all know he's faking smiling at Hannah.

I dial up my own fake smile and wish for the bajillionth time that I were in Costa Rica.

Except at this point, I'd like to take half of Tickled Pink with me—and *definitely* Dylan.

"Could you please be a sweetie and drop me off at Patrice's place?" I ask him. "She's catering my brunch with the designer."

"I'll walk you over," Phoebe says behind me.

I almost shriek with surprise, but it's not her sudden presence.

It's the no-nonsense, *someone has some explaining to do* tone.

I *hate* that tone.

"Phoebe! I miss you at the school every morning!" I smother my sister in a hug, and I'm close enough that I can hear her strangled sigh. "There's room in Dylan's truck for both of us. I'm sure he wouldn't mind giving us a ride."

I bat my eyelashes at him.

Hannah gives me the universal *what the hell is wrong with you?* look.

Dylan purses his lips together, his dimple peeking out, his eyes amused but tired. "Sure. Lots of room for both of you."

"That's okay. The walk is good for us." Phoebe holds out her hand and twitches her fingers, and he surrenders Pebbles and my purse. "Lovely to see you, Dylan. And—you too. Whoever you are. C'mon, Tavi. Can't be late. You know how much Gigi hates that."

She loops her arm in mine and tugs.

Swear I'm a human pinball this morning with all of these people dragging me here and there.

"I'll see you at lunch," I call to Dylan.

I blow him a kiss and hate myself a little for it.

What would it be like if I could just kiss him goodbye, right here on the street, and not have complicated emotions about exactly how soon I'm intending to leave Tickled Pink—and by extension, him—behind?

"I've been trying to have patience," Phoebe says as she drags me through the square, completely oblivious to the fact that the man I'm pretty sure I'm in love with is talking to the woman *he's* in love with, "but screw that. Do you have a business-and-marketing plan for your secret project? Because I feel like if you did, you wouldn't still be here."

She's a week early, which I won't be telling her. Dylan's right. It's not right to make people carry your secrets. "Phoebe. You're not the only businesswoman in the family."

"I never said I was." She frowns down at me.

It's not the same frown it would've been three months ago. That one would've been *you're annoying me, and I don't know why I have to be related to you.*

This one's *please don't reject me. I'm trying.*

And now *I'm* sighing like Dylan would. "I don't want . . . ties and obligations."

"It's not great for Tickled Pink that people are saying you and Carter are trapped here. If I can help you, I'm helping the town."

I study her as we walk.

She studies me right back.

And then I think about Dylan not talking to his siblings, and I realize I don't want that.

This Phoebe?

She's *more.*

I admire her. Not because I have to. But because she's found where she belongs and she's doing what she needs to do to fit in, just like I *want* to do.

"I . . . could possibly use an opinion or two on appealing to potential business partners."

She studies me more.

For an entire block, in fact.

"You'd turn me down flat if I offered you money, wouldn't you?"

"Yep."

"Send me what you have, and I'll meet you tonight in the place we don't talk about."

"You're not going to argue?"

"Nope."

It's my turn to study her for a block.

I don't ask if she believes in me.

I don't have to.

Somehow, I know she does.

She does, and she gets it.

She knows I need to do this on my own.

"It's delicious chocolate, Tavi," she says softly as we reach the walk-way to Patrice's house. "And I'm fucking proud of you."

Chapter 26

Dylan

Since Tavi posted the sixth or seventh video of me talking her through fixing plumbing problems, my phone won't stop ringing.

And it's no longer my friends and family.

It's potential clients.

I have this sink that hasn't drained right in a few weeks. Could you swing by this evening? My daughter will be stopping by for a visit, and she needs to know how to unclog her own pipes.

My faucets are leaking. Also, is Tavi Lightly riding along with you?

Do you know anything about why my showerhead doesn't have any pressure? I just rented this new apartment, and it's so big and lonely.

There's this weird odor coming from my dishwasher. I think it's the ghost of what you did in high school coming back to haunt me, you asshole.

Yeah, that last one's fun.

I don't return that message, but it does make my chest hurt.

"Ignore it," Teague says as I catch up to him on my way to the snowshoe baseball field just barely in time. We play for the Tickled Pink Gold Stars, with games on Wednesday nights through half the summer, and we used to be good before we let the Lightlys onto our team. Tonight's our last game.

We're playing Deer Drop.

I'm sincerely hoping the Lightlys are sitting this one out.

"Ignore what?"

"Whatever's making you look like you ate rotten sauerkraut with a curdled-milk chaser."

He doesn't look at me when he says it, but Phoebe does. "Bridget saw the trolls popping up on your TikTok," she explains.

"Trolls happen."

Now I get the full-on grumpy-dad look aimed my way. "Trolls and the people who want to tell the world about your glory days aren't the same."

And now I'm cringing. "Glory days?"

I get a rare grin, and I wonder just how much glory-daying he did himself before he left his family behind all those years ago.

Before I can ask, Lola Minelli waves at me. "Dylan! Dylan, look, I'm on your team! Isn't that the best!"

"That's my son," I hear my mother say nearby. "Yes, he got his looks from me. And wait until you see him play tonight. He's smart and talented, and he helps *so* many people."

I spot Marta with her. "I hate having split loyalties, but since Hannah moved to Deer Drop . . ."

"Dylan! Dylan, will you sign my phone case?" a teenager calls.

"Keep your head down and pretend you don't hear them," Teague says to me.

Heat is creeping through my body again, even more than should be there for a warm August evening. It's been almost two weeks since the first video, and I haven't had anything like this before. "Is this going to disrupt the game?"

Phoebe makes a strangled noise like she's stifling a laugh. "Dylan, I like you, but trust me, if Tickled Pink can get through snowshoe baseball games with my family playing, you will *not* be a disruption."

And now there's more heat for more reasons.

Of course I'm not a big deal.

I'm just a bigger deal in my own life than I've ever been before.

"Sorry I'm late." Tavi jogs up next to us. "Did you know that, like, if you don't mix a paint can well, it leaves streaky paint on a wall?"

Phoebe eyeballs her.

Teague eyeballs her.

I eyeball her.

"What?" She makes an exaggerated swipe at her face, her eyes going even bigger in a brighter Tavi Lightly Show display than I've seen since we started sleeping together. "Do I have paint on my nose? I thought I got it all wiped off. Pebbles, where's Mommy's mirror?"

"We've been painting walls in the school for almost two months," Phoebe says.

"Yes, but I've never *mixed* the paint before. But it's fine. I think streaky walls are, like, the new black." She squeals and claps, and it's so fake that I want to punch something. "Oh my gosh, are we playing a *Deer Drop* team? Is this finally our chance to show the Deer Drop Danger Ducks that we can kick their asses?"

"One time a year," Teague replies. "Why's Lola putting on snowshoes?"

Snowshoe baseball is my favorite part of summer. We dump saw-dust all over a baseball diamond and don snowshoes to play a round of softball with a sixteen-inch softball, which eliminates the need for gloves.

Good thing, too, because most of us will wipe out in the sawdust at least once per game.

Crowds are huge this summer with everyone from around the state and farther wanting to come watch the Lightlys face-plant.

Wouldn't be a bad thing if more people came back next year.

But tonight, my heart isn't in it.

I'd rather go hang with Tavi in her secret kitchen and distract her until she's tired of telling people we're "just friends."

I've done "just friends."

This is not "just friends."

And I won't be the idiot who waits until it's too late to do something about it. Not this time.

"Surely she's not playing," Phoebe murmurs as Lola rises, snowshoes on her feet, Tickled Pink Gold Stars jersey hanging from her shoulders.

And I do mean *hanging*.

She's barely three inches wide.

Not a lot of shoulder to hold that shirt up.

"They can smile for cameras, but can they actually *play?*" an unfortunately familiar voice says—loudly—from the Deer Drop bench as Tavi, Phoebe, Teague, and I arrive at our own bench.

"Andrew," Hannah hisses. "Be nice."

Tavi's head whips around so fast you'd think it was spring-loaded.

"Do *not*," I start.

"*Oh my God*, is that him?" she whispers.

I grab her by the arm. "Get your snowshoes on."

"He hit on me."

"You think everything hits on you," Phoebe murmurs.

Tavi growls at her.

Phoebe smiles. "You're right, Bridget," she calls to the teenager, who's already issuing orders to the rest of the team, since she's the best coach we've ever had. "It's *totes* fun to pick on our siblings."

"But—" Tavi starts.

"My blood pressure can't handle this," I mutter to her, which is the most honest thing I've said all day. Andrew being a sleaze and hitting on other women while married to my pregnant-with-his-baby best friend is the icing on the cake, but Andrew hitting on Tavi—swear to the holy gods of my blowtorch, it makes me want to light the man on fire. "Just—can we wait until after the game?"

"Right. Game. Of course."

"This is going to be, like, *so much fun*," Lola says. She leaps to her feet as I walk by, her arms windmilling. "Oh my *gah*, I can barely stand!"

I look at Teague.

He stares back at me.

Hell.

Willie Wayne's too far away, and he's steering clear anyway out of worry for what Akiko would think if he looked at Lola wrong— dude was addicted to *Lola's Tiny House*—which means it's on me to steady her.

"Oh, Lola, you poor thing." Tavi leaps in front of me and wraps her arms around Lola. "Here. Let me help you. You have to have really strong core muscles to stand up well in these snowshoes."

"I do five hundred crunches a day," Lola says as Tavi hugs her.

"I like kettlebell swings so much better," Tavi replies. "I'm up to like five hundred of those too."

"Oh, but you have to be careful with those," Lola says. "They can make you look fat with too much muscle."

"You steady now?" I ask Lola. "Tavi's gotta get her shoes on."

And also not strangle Lola.

"Oh, I'm *so* good, Dylan." Lola smiles at me. "And how are you?"

"Peachy."

"Your TikTok has like thirty-seven million views overall now. That's like, just wait. *Good Morning America* will be calling for sure."

"I ordered one of your shirts, Dylan," Jane's husband, Gibson, calls to me. He's a six-foot-four, bald Black travel photographer with more muscles in his left forearm than I have in both thighs together. "Gonna represent all over the world."

"Shirts?"

"Silly, your shirts," Tavi says as she pulls away from Lola. "From your print-on-demand store."

"I ordered the temporary tattoo of your face," Lola says.

"No one wants to know where you're putting it," Bridget calls. "Are we playing snowshoe baseball, or are we being old-lady gossips?"

"We're playing baseball," Teague tells her.

Bridget lifts a brow. "You're not gonna chew me out for sassing the grown-ups and insulting old ladies?"

"I'm worn down, Bridget. I am *worn down*."

"Phoebe's keeping you up too late at night?"

"I'm not worn down, and *shush your mouth*," Ridhi says. "Don't talk to grown-ups like that."

She and Anya are setting up a refreshments table next to Estelle and Niles's refreshments table. Selling out of baked goods for local charitable foundations like the animal shelters and food banks is one of the bonus perks of snowshoe baseball games. Even when we don't have extra attention from the Lightlys being here, people come out in droves from the surrounding areas to watch the players fall on their faces.

It's awesome.

Most nights.

"Tavi, *put your shoes on*," Bridget says. "I need you at shortstop. Lola, how's your arm?"

"Bridge, it's *Deer Drop*," Teague says.

Bridget grins. "Yeah, and they don't have celebrities."

Andrew coughs.

Sounds like he's covering for the word *pathetic*.

Like I said.

I don't call people assholes lightly, and he is an asshole.

"We're not handing Deer Drop a win just so you can put Lola on the team," Teague says. "Next game, fine. This game? No."

"Dad. Next game is *next season*, and Lola won't be here then. Would you please *trust me*?" Bridget doesn't wait for an answer before turning to snap at Lola. "Second base. Don't mess it up, or I'll pull you. And you better be as good of a batter as you told Willie Wayne you were."

Teague's eye twitches.

Phoebe's eye twitches.

Hell, my eye's twitching too.

"Phoebe, you're catching," Bridget says. "Dad. Pitching. Dylan, take third. Jane, first. Willie Wayne, Gibson, and Carter, outfield. Don't fight over who's where out there, or I'll bench all of you for real."

"Where am I?" Michael Lightly asks.

"You're designated hitter and our fill-in for Lola if she doesn't quit blowing kisses to the stands."

We all look at Lola again.

She pauses with her fingers smushed to her lips. "What? I, like, know to pay attention to the game when I'm *playing*."

She does not, in fact, pay attention to the game.

That's obvious before the end of the first inning.

Good news is, we make it through the top of the third inning with the score tied at zero.

Bad news is, our bench is getting frustrated.

"Bridget, I love you, and this is ridiculous," Phoebe says quietly as Lola trips on her snowshoes on the way to the plate to bat. "Pull her. Please, for the love of kittens and getting a car next summer, *pull her*."

"That's not all it takes to get a car next summer," Teague pipes up. He frowns and glances at Shiloh. "Probably."

"You're not getting a car for pulling Lola," Shiloh confirms.

"Appreciate the try, Phoebs," Bridget says. "But I'm not pulling Lola. Isn't this little project of yours about believing in people? I believe in Lola."

"Yay, I'm standing again!" Lola thrusts her hands into the air in a victory sign, takes one step, and goes down again.

The crowd roars.

And Tavi, who's been completely unable to sit still all night, sighs.

"She's doing that on purpose," she mutters to me.

"Why?"

"Because tomorrow, she'll get endorsement offers for laundry detergent and stain-resistant athletic clothing and probably something a pro football player is endorsing that they've been looking for a ditzy sidekick for in their ads."

"You live a very pessimistic life."

She slides a side-eye at me.

I grin.

Her cheeks turn pink, and she leans into me to nudge me with her shoulder. "*So* pessimistic. Like, just call me *Totes Peppimisty*."

"I think you mean *pessimisty*," Carter says from his seat behind us.

Tavi's cheeks go from pink to flaming red, which is new. "Shut up, Carter."

"Siblings don't fight if they want to go to heaven," Estelle calls. And then she gasps. "*Michael James Lightly.* Do *not* make that hand gesture. We're *Lightlys*, for God's sake."

"And you're not going to heaven either, you old witch," Michael mutters.

"I heard that."

I ignore whatever Estelle says next, because Jane's whispering something to Tavi.

I lean in.

They shoo me away.

And now heat's creeping up *my* face.

For the most part, I'm tuned in to the game tonight. But I'm aware there's a sign in the Deer Drop stands, held up by a former Tickled Pinker, calling me *Tickled Pink Dicklan*. Andrew barely missed getting on base at the top of the inning, and he cut across the diamond on his way back to the Deer Drop bench just so he could take a dig at my "desperation for fake fame." And Tavi and Lola both told me to ignore the dude in the jeans and oxford shirt lurking at the edge of the bleachers closest to our dugout.

"Keep them interested by *not* talking," Tavi said.

"Oh, I know that reporter, and he's slimy," Lola said.

So what are Jane and Tavi whispering about now?

Are they whispering about me?

Are they—I catch reference to the word *beer*, and duh.

They're whispering about the party, and I'm being a paranoid ass.

"Great job, Lola!" Bridget calls. "But try to wait to swing until *after* he pitches it, yeah?"

Teague makes a noise, but Bridget shushes him. "We're saving people's souls, Dad."

"Snowshoe baseball can't save people's souls," he replies.

"But we're overflowing the stands and selling out of baked goods, aren't we?"

Jane and Tavi are whispering again.

"Dylan! You're on deck," Bridget calls.

"Dick!" someone yells from the Deer Drop stands.

"Shut *up*," Hannah snaps back.

"He *is* a dick, sweetheart," Andrew yells from the pitcher's mound while Willie Wayne swerves to avoid getting too close to Lola as he heads to the batter's box and she sighs dramatically on her way back to the dugout after striking out.

Tavi squeezes my arm. "Don't let them get to you. I put superglue on Constance Yang's chair once in the dressing room at a beauty pageant, and it soaked through her dress and made it stick to her ass, and when they used nail polish remover to get it off, that gave her a rash, so she couldn't sit for like two weeks."

I smile at her despite not feeling it. "You're such a terror."

"*So* much," she agrees with a smile right back that I swear she's not feeling either.

Lights flicker in the edges of my vision, and I know exactly what she's thinking.

And tomorrow no one will remember, because tomorrow we'll remind the world that we're just friends, no matter what these pictures make it look like.

It's frustrating as hell that the first woman to intrigue me in years is one who doesn't want to stay and is hell bent on keeping me at arm's length.

If I told her how I feel, would it change anything?

I don't know, but I know I can't keep living like this.

"Go get 'em, sweetheart," Mom calls as I step out of the dugout. "And don't let that trash talk get to you! I'm so proud of the man you've become!"

I flash her a smile I don't feel either. "Thanks, Mom."

"Mama's boy," Andrew says out on the pitcher's mound.

I ignore him.

Out loud, anyway.

In my head, I'm about fifteen again, and that asshole is going down.

Chapter 27

Tavi

This snowshoe baseball game is awful.

I mean, not *awful* awful. We're winning one to nothing in the top of the sixth inning, but everything else is awful.

Lola's still playing second base.

I haven't had my chance to do what I need to do yet, which is giving me a knot in my stomach and making me question if I really want to go through with the plan that Naomi and I hatched to get everything lined up right for our marketing pitch on Friday.

There are more reporters and paparazzi than we've had before. The Deer Drop stands are heckling Dylan louder with every inning, with the Tickled Pink stands defending him louder and louder with every inning.

Not only is my heart in my throat over what I need to do for my cover story for the next three days, but it's also shedding tears at what he's had to go through tonight.

And it's my fault for suggesting he represent Tickled Pink on social media.

He should've told me no, but he'd rather face all of this and do good for his town than spare himself the reminders that there are people who don't like him.

Every time I think he can't possibly get sexier or more attractive, he's just *him* in the face of conflict, and yep.

Completely and totally in love with the man.

And I'm leaving.

I glance his way as we stand on the field waiting for the next batter.

"You are ten times the person any of them could ever be," I whisper with just enough volume to hopefully let him hear me and no one else. I might not get a chance to tell him again, so I need to do it now.

He scratches the back of his neck and glances away. "Haven't talked to a lot of these people since high school. It's fine."

Lola claps at second base. "High school! Oh, you must've been a cutie patootie in high school!"

"Ban the dick!" someone shouts from the Deer Drop stands.

"Shut *up*, Aiden," Hannah snaps back. "*You* set off a stink bomb in the cafeteria, and just last week you drove away from the dealership without paying for your oil change."

"Whatever, *intruder*," Aiden replies.

"In-tru-der, in-tru-der," they chant.

"Be nice to my wife," the butthole who hit on me at the post office snarls at the crowd from his dugout.

"We were talking about those rich people," someone else calls.

"At least we have manners," Dylan's mom says from the Tickled Pink stands.

Okay, she yells it.

She's totally yelling it, and it's like watching one of my own family reunions.

"Wow, this is like what half the Upper East Side families do at their own galas," Lola says. "I feel, like, right at home."

She's not wrong.

"Batter's up." Dylan claps his hands. "Eyes on the ball, Gold Stars."

"My eye is *always* on the balls, Dylan," Lola calls.

"The snowshoe baseball ball, Lola," Carter yells from the outfield. "Not *Dylan's* balls."

"I disapprove of how these heathens were raised," I hear Gigi telling someone from the refreshments tables.

Ridhi and Anya have sold out of all their treats.

Gigi and Niles are about halfway through their overpriced, repackaged Little Debbie snacks.

Deer Drop's slugger steps up to the plate.

Teague looks back at me. "Three steps back and four closer to second base."

"Big or little steps?"

"Normal steps."

I do as I'm told—easier said than done in snowshoes—and end up almost on top of second base and directly behind him. Dylan moves closer to my original position between second and third.

"What should I do?" Lola asks Teague.

"Stay. And catch the ball if it comes to you."

"You got it, Coach!"

"I'm your coach, Lola," Bridget calls from the bench.

"You got it, Coach's Dad!"

Dylan slinks closer to me.

"I can catch a ball," I whisper to him.

"It's not you I'm worried about," he whispers back.

"Dick!" someone yells again from the Deer Drop side of things.

"At least get creative!" I yell back. "You snivel-faced hider in a crowd!"

Half the people in the Deer Drop stands rise to their feet.

"Spoiled brat!" someone yells.

"Ugly!" someone else hollers.

"Stupid!"

"Lazy!"

"Your mother couldn't stand you, so she had to leave the whole damn country!"

I blow that last person a kiss, even though that one stings. "And you're welcome!"

"We're playing snowshoe baseball here, Tavi," Phoebe calls from behind the plate.

I blow her a kiss too.

The insults don't entirely bounce off like I pretend they do, but knowing I've taken the heat off Dylan helps. Every last little thing I can do before I hopefully start the next phase of my life.

Teague pitches the ball, and the batter swings and misses.

"Maybe you should worry about yourselves," Dylan's mom yells from the Tickled Pink side.

Teague points at her. "Sit down. We cheer for our own. Hard stop."

"He's so hot when he's bossy," Lola says. "I can't believe Phoebe got him first before we knew who he really was."

"C'mon, Teague, strike him out," Dylan calls.

"You got this," Jane adds.

"Did she know?" Lola asks me.

"Are you on this team, or are you on the Deer Drop team?" I reply.

Her eyes go fake big. "Oh my *gah*, right. Don't distract our team. Right."

Is she honestly this ditzy? Or is this part of the act because someone else is getting attention?

I don't know.

Not that it matters, because Teague's pitching, and that batter has murder in his eyes, and it's the sixth inning.

If I'm going to do what I need to do, I need to do it *fast*.

I focus on the batter and send a few wishes out into the universe.

Let this be my chance.

Let me follow through with it.

Let everyone forgive me for what I have to do.

Truth?

I like snowshoe baseball.

All of it. Even when I'm falling in the sawdust.

It makes me feel like a kid. Not a beauty pageant kid but a strong, athletic kid who fits in somewhere, who knows how to have fun for fun's sake, who's part of a team.

I can honestly say I'll miss this when I'm in Costa Rica.

Not that I'll ever play snowshoe baseball again anyway, even if I lived out Gigi's full sentence here. Our mandated year will be over before snowshoe baseball season starts again next year.

That gives me a pang in my heart that I wasn't expecting, and the thought almost distracts me from the whomp of the bat.

I jerk to attention as the ball goes streaking up the center—I mean, as fast as a ball that size *can* streak over a field of sawdust—and my pulse leaps as I remind myself I'm in snowshoes and move toward Lola's side of second base.

Teague dives for the oversize softball, miscalculates, and face-plants in the sawdust, much to the delight of the entire crowd.

This is it.

This is my chance.

It is now or never, and if it's never, then I'm screwing myself and Naomi and the farm over forever.

If I don't do this now, then I'm a self-sabotaging idiot who doesn't deserve my cacao farm.

I pump my knees higher.

I've played this game *six times* this summer. Totally getting the hang of these snowshoes now.

"I've got it!" I call as the batter also expertly demonstrates just how good he, too, is in his snowshoes as he huffs down the line toward first. "I've got it!"

"Oh, I can get it," Lola says.

By all rights, she should have it.

But who's going to question that I'd have a competitive streak and not trust Lola to do what needs to be done? *"No!"* I yell. "I've got it!"

I'm almost there, and that ball's slowing down, and I can get it.

I'm dashing in snowshoes like the game depends on me throwing this guy out.

And it might.

We're up by one. We can't let them on base.

Also, I have to blow this.

Shit.

"Look! I'm doing it!" Lola shrieks. "I'm running in snowshoes!"

"Let me get this!" I shriek back. "You can't throw!"

I'm there.

I'm there.

And so is Lola, which is *so freaking perfect.*

My heart is pounding so hard I might be having a heart attack.

I bend and reach for the ball, and then *Lola's* there, and I'm still running forward, except now I'm not.

Now, I'm tumbling head over ass in the sawdust all over the field.

Can they tell?

Can they tell I fell on purpose?

"My ankle," I cry out, and then I choke on the sawdust cloud swirling around me.

Something lands on top of me, and I get an elbow to the kidney—undoubtedly deserve that—and another lungful of sawdust.

"I got it," Lola cries.

The weight lifts, and I manage to twist my face in time to see Lola lob the ball nowhere near first base as I cough and cry out in fake pain again.

Mostly, I'm just coughing.

And wincing.

I have no idea if this is believable or not, but I need to be injured enough to lie low for the next three days.

This is the plan.

And the next part of the plan hinges on the performance of my life.

Dylan's dashing over to me, concern etched in his handsome face, those warm brown eyes wide and worried.

Guilt stabs me in the spleen. And a lung. And definitely in my heart.

I shouldn't do this.

Not to him.

But just like he told me he couldn't burden Hannah with the secret of how he felt about her, I can't burden him with this secret either.

The fewer people who know, the better.

Chapter 28

Dylan

It's after eleven before the lights are out at the school, which is the earliest I'm willing to sneak inside it to check on Tavi, no matter how much I've wanted to jump out of my skin for the past two hours.

Last I saw her, the Tickled Pink firefighters were hefting her into Estelle's SUV while Deer Drop took the lead on us in our last snowshoe baseball game of the season. Whole team headed to Ladyfingers, as we always do, and Lola was the only one in a festive mood while we waited for news on Tavi.

I don't think anyone else's knee wouldn't stop jumping under the table or that anyone else wanted to pace or say *fuck it* and head to the hospital in Deer Drop to check on her, but everyone was worried.

Possibly more so when I snarled at being asked if *I* was okay.

Phoebe eventually got word that Tavi's ankle's sprained.

Lola called it *convenient* that Tavi had gotten out of playing in the losing game.

I almost came out of my chair.

But I don't let my temper get the best of me anymore, no matter how much I feel about seventeen again after the heckling at the game tonight, so instead of asking her if she wanted to take it outside, I left Ladyfingers, hit the Pick-n-Shop for comfort food.

I don't know if it's for her or for me.

Might take comfort food to get through telling her how I feel.

And I have to.

No waiting. No fear that I'm not good enough for her. No logic telling me it won't work since she wants to leave Tickled Pink.

I have to tell her.

I have to take this chance.

I sneak through the dark hallways of the high school where I caused hell back in the day and creep up the stairs to the second floor, hoping Tavi's alone.

Rumor around town is that she picked the chemistry lab as her bedroom, so that's where I'm going.

I'm almost there when I hear voices.

I dive into the nearest open classroom—pretty sure I had a history class in here—and listen while Lola and Carter walk past, the beam of a flashlight bouncing off the cracked linoleum-tile floor.

"I just don't get it," Lola's saying. "I'm trying *so hard* to do what Gigi wants, and she's all, 'This is no way to get into heaven, Lola. Look at what Phoebe did. She's getting into heaven.' Phoebe called me a brat. She is *so* not getting into heaven."

"You're not here to get to heaven."

"Shut *up*, Carter. I am too."

"No, you're trying to cash in on easy fame. If you cared about your soul, you'd be volunteering at orphanages and food banks and animal shelters."

"Not everyone volunteers."

"Or you could be donating money to save the whatever."

"How do you know I'm not?"

"You offered Floyd two million dollars for his church."

"*That's charity.* And it's, like, only two million. It's not like I offered him fifty."

"Ask yourself what a guy like Floyd's gonna do with two million dollars, then tell me it's charity."

"Just because *you'd* spend it all on weed doesn't mean he would."

"You're an asshole."

"*You're* an asshole."

Their voices fade down the hall. I slip out of the classroom and knock softly on the chemistry lab door.

"Go away, Carter," Tavi calls. "I don't need your kind of painkillers."

That's as much permission to enter as I expect I'm gonna get, so I twist the knob and slip into the room, my heart in my throat.

Watching her face-plant in that sawdust, then seeing the pain on her face as she coughed it all up, and then seeing her not leap to her feet—my world stopped.

My entire world. It just stopped.

She's the woman who's shown me that *I'm okay.* That I don't have to stay trapped in old patterns that were a result of even older patterns. That I *do* get to wake up every morning with a clean slate and do my best.

That I'm allowed to look for something bigger.

To be happy. To find joy.

She's my joy.

And she's shown me that I'm good enough to be someone else's joy. That I've been holding myself back because of who I used to be without even realizing it.

I want to be *her* joy.

I glance around the room, looking for her.

Back when I had a class here, this place was lined with workstations, all of them hooked up to gas lines and sinks. I got called in to shut off the valves for gas and water the day Estelle made an offer on the place earlier this summer, but I haven't been up here since, and honestly, I was expecting it would've changed.

The moon's soft glow, illuminating the room just enough that I can navigate it, suggests that it hasn't.

The rows of workstations are still here. The cabinets are still here. Even the warning signs talking about what to do if you get chemicals in your eyes and how to shut off the gas in case of fire are still on the walls.

Crumbling and faded, but still there.

The only thing new is the privacy screen around where Mr. Lueker's desk used to sit.

"Tavi?" I whisper.

"I *said*—Carter?"

I follow the sound of her voice around the privacy screen. "I've been a dickhead a time or two, but that's a little insulting to a guy who snagged a box of the best chocolate chip cookies you'll ever taste to go along with a goat-cheese-and-beet salad."

She slams a laptop shut, which should theoretically cut the light in the room, but not with her in it.

She's my light. My hope. My fresh start. Reclining on a stack of pillows on a twin-size bed with her foot propped up on another pile of pillows and her dog snuggling next to her. Pretty sure she's in nothing more than a T-shirt and panties, but while my cock wants to go there, the rest of me desperately needs to know that she's not in pain.

"Are you okay?"

"*Dylan.* What are you doing here?" she whispers.

The next-best thing I know to do when I'm terrified to touch her but needed to see for myself that she's okay. "You didn't answer my texts."

"Gigi took my phone at the hospital."

I sink to one knee next to the bed. "Does it hurt?"

She winces and looks away. "No. I mean, yes, but, like, not bad. This one time I was in Greece with Daria Rumplestein—you know, heiress to the Rumple Shipping empire—and I slipped on some cobblestone and went tumbling ass over teacups down a hill, and I sprained my wrist and couldn't scroll on my phone for like six weeks, and that hurt a lot worse."

I tuck a lock of hair behind her ear. "Tavi—"

"Tavi?" another voice says on the other side of the privacy screen.

"*Dad.* Go away."

"Just wanted to check on you."

"I'm fine, and I have a man in here taking care of me already. *Go away.*"

There's a shuffling behind the screen, and then Michael Lightly pokes his head around. In the dim light, his beard and hair make him look more like a reclusive mountain dude than the polished uppercruster he was when the family arrived almost three months ago.

I feel his gaze on me for a moment before he looks at Tavi, who's vibrating with a new energy that I recognize all too well. "Please go away," she says, her voice clipped but controlled.

"You need any more ice or painkillers or water or food?" Michael asks her.

"I've got her," I tell him before she can answer.

He glances at her, then back to me. I wait for the inevitable—*Don't hurt my daughter*—but what I get instead surprises me. "You'll do a better job than I would." He nods stiffly. "Good night."

And then he leaves.

Shuffles back across the classroom floor without another word while Tavi and I both stare at the place he was standing.

"Did that . . . did that just happen?" she whispers.

"Guess he wasn't at the ball game," I reply dryly. I know he was at the ball game. I know he heard everything everyone said about me.

She locks eyes with me, and then she's laughing, and then she's looping her arms around my neck and kissing me while she's laughing, which is awkward but also *perfect.*

"We shouldn't do this," she says against my lips.

But I love you. I want to kiss you like this every day. I want to take away all of your pain any way I can. "I was so worried about you that I forgot goat cheese isn't vegan and brought you my favorite beet salad to make you feel better."

There's a long beat of silence.

Then—

"Does the salad have candied walnuts?"

"We might be backwoods folk, but we know our way around a beet salad."

She whimpers.

It's the same whimper she makes when I'm devouring her pussy and know *just* when to pull back to keep her from coming for a little bit longer. The same whimper she makes when I get up to put my clothes back on.

The same whimper she probably doesn't know she makes when she doesn't realize she's finished the last drop of her coffee and goes for another sip, or when we've spent the whole day with her riding along on jobs with me and I pull up in front of the school to drop her off because one of us has somewhere we have to be and we can't sneak over to the church to get naked.

God, I love her.

"You are so sweet." She strokes my cheek. "But you shouldn't be here either. When's the last time you got a full night's sleep?"

"You think I'll sleep without knowing that you're okay?"

"Dylan—"

"I don't want to hurt you. I won't touch you, I swear. I'm not here for sex tonight. But I—I need to know you're okay. I *need* to know I've done everything I can to make you comfortable."

"You didn't hurt me—"

"Tavi. I take care of the people I love. Period."

Her hand freezes on my shoulder, her eyes going wide in the dim light.

Fuck.

I swallow—hard—but I don't take the words back. "Tell me what I can do to take care of you. I have real Häagen-Dazs along with my favorite bakery cookies. I can make a call if you want a barbecue sandwich. I'll read you a bedtime story. Scratch your back. Take Pebbles out. Run over to the church and get some of your chocolates. You name it. I'm here. All yours. Whatever you need to be comfortable."

Her eyes are shining. "I do not deserve you."

"Do we need to have this talk again? I'll remind you as much as you need me to that you, Tavi Lightly, are a fucking awesome human being who *does* deserve every good thing." I pull her hand to my mouth and press gentle kisses to her knuckles. "*Every* good thing."

I don't care what she wants. She names it, it's hers.

She's staring at me like she knows what she wants, but she's terrified to ask for it, and after what feels like a lifetime, she looks away, straight at her privacy screen.

I glance at it too. It's painted with shiny butterflies that stand out even in the dark, and it feels like Tavi. An elegant splash of brightness ready to flutter away at any moment.

I rise and peer around it. "No one there," I whisper. "We're alone. You're safe."

"I don't trust that there aren't more secret passages in this school."

"Not in here. In the theater, yes. Cafeteria, yes. Gym and library, yes. There's even a secret passage from the old English room up to the art room. But if there's a secret passage into *this* room, I'm unaware of it."

"Which English room?"

"First floor, girls' hallway, second classroom on the left when you come in from outside."

"Did you use them all in high school?"

"I did."

"Does it bother you to be back in here? In the building?"

"No. I like the idea of being in detention with you."

Her laughter is music.

Swear it is.

Maybe Hannah was never my one true love.

Maybe it was that I never realized, since high school, that I need to be friends with any woman I'd date, and Hannah was convenient because we were already friends, not because she was actually the one for me.

She stuck by me through my shithead years.

Never wavered.

I'm not so sure anymore that she never judged. That she didn't get her own kind of thrill out of hanging out with Tickled Pink's Bad Boy.

But Tavi—she thinks I'm a catch. Me. Not my history. Not who I used to be. Just *me*. Today. As I am.

She's been around the whole damn world, met people in every corner of life, and she *still* tells me I'm attractive and worthy and perfect just the way I am.

She believes in me.

"Sit with me."

"I don't want to hurt—"

"Sit with me." She tugs on my arm, scooting over and shifting a sleeping Pebbles and her propped-up foot until she's made room for me on the bed.

"Stop squirming," I murmur. "You're going to hurt yourself."

She executes a move that has me wrapping my arm around her. "If we were two normal people with normal families, that would totally call for an *okay, Dad*."

I smile as I bury my nose in her hair and inhale. She smells like sawdust and antiseptic, like *life*.

"You ever worry your kids will be just like you?" I ask her before I can get off the *let's dream about the future when we have kids together* train track that my brain has suddenly jumped on thanks to the *Dad* dig.

"Every. Damn. Day. But then I remind myself that I'm not my mother. I'm not my father. And no matter what my kids look like, or what they're talented in, or *especially* if they don't know what they want to do with their lives, I will love them and accept them and be there for them. And then I realize I'll probably never have time for that, because I'll be a workaholic like my sister now that I know my chocolates are my true calling."

I squeeze my arm around her tighter and press a kiss to her hair.

I've done this with Hannah more times than I can count.

But when Tavi leans into me, my body's reaction isn't what it was with Hannah's.

This is *more*.

"You won't be a workaholic. You know what matters."

"*You* know what matters. You're the best of the best, Dylan Wright. Promise me you will *never* forget that."

I chuckle softly. "That's the last thing these walls ever would've expected someone to say to me."

"It's not your fault you didn't have the best support system when you went to school here."

"Eh. Some of my stepdads weren't so bad."

"That would be like me saying I wanted to be like one of my dad's mistresses. They're not all bad people, but if you know they'll go as fast as they came . . ."

"And you didn't want them there in the first place . . . ," I agree quietly.

"You're going to be a great dad someday." There's a wistfulness in her tone that I don't like.

It says *but I won't be here to see it.* "Tavi—"

"Thank you," she interrupts softly.

"For what?"

"For letting me in. For sharing your history and trusting me with it. For keeping my secrets about the chocolates and the church. That's—it's not something people do in the world where I came from. You've been—Dylan, you've been one of the best things to ever happen to me. And I will never, *ever* forget you."

"You don't have to forget me. I'll be right here."

She gazes up at me, and I have no idea exactly what's going through her brain, but I know she *still* doesn't believe she's worthy of me.

Her.

Tavi Lightly.

The brightest star in the whole damn universe and the only woman who's ever not just accepted me for who I am but fucking *celebrated* me for who I am and how I got here.

I know she's planning on leaving. I get that.

But she's here *now*. We have time to figure out how to make this work.

"You—" I start, but words aren't enough.

There *aren't* words.

Not words that she'll believe.

So instead, I let my body talk for me.

Carefully—I don't want to hurt her ankle—but there are still things I can do to show her that won't hurt her.

I shut up, and I brush a thumb over her jawline while I study those ever-tired blue eyes of hers.

There's no makeup. No hiding the wariness mixed with—is that hope?

Does she *want* me?

Does she still?

Am I more than *that cute plumber with the nice ass* to her?

"I admire you so much for the person you are today," I tell her.

Her nose wrinkles.

And that's it.

That little nose wrinkle of doubt is the last straw.

This woman needs to know she's worthy.

And I'm the man for the job.

Chapter 29

Tavi

Dylan's kissing me.

He knows I'm a total disaster. He knows I'm leaving, even if he doesn't know how soon. I smell like the hospital, where I bribed a nurse into letting me walk out of the exam room on crutches and pulled the privacy card to keep her from telling Gigi I'm not injured, and I definitely still have sawdust on random parts of me, and I have guilt smeared all over my soul, but I still don't stop Dylan from kissing me.

I don't want him to stop.

Ever.

Did he mean it?

Did he mean I'm someone he loves? That he feels the same way about me that I feel about him?

I should feel awful for not telling him my plans, but I can't put that on him. I can't ask him to carry one more burden for me, especially when I can't see how we can have a future.

He belongs here. I belong in Costa Rica.

But I can give him tonight.

I can give him right now and hope he forgives me if I don't come back.

My bed barely has room for both of us, but it's not too small.

Not when he's holding me this close and tasting my lips and threading his hand through my hair, teasing the shell of my ear and setting my nerve endings on fire.

"You don't have to do this for me," I whisper against his mouth.

He growls. "You think this is just for you?"

"I—" I cut myself off with a gasp as he shifts his lips to my neck.

He smells earthy and raw and like a summer night, and the realness of him is my anchor.

He's not perfect.

He's just like me.

Someone with a past, who's screwed up, who has regrets, and who's still dealing with mistakes from a long time ago.

He's my *hope*.

If he can do better, if he can find where he fits, so can I.

And the idea that he knows so many of *my* secrets, that he's seen me screw up and not keep my shit together, and he still likes me—

No, *loves* me—

It's a heady, intoxicating mix.

Usually, guys like me because they *don't* know me.

But Dylan—he knows my faults and my insecurities. He doesn't see me as some paragon of perfection. He treats me like he's glad I'm here. Like I'm welcome in his home.

Not an inconvenience.

And when his hand drifts up my thigh—I am definitely *not* an inconvenience to this man.

Not that I've thought I was the past two weeks, but tonight is *more*.

And not because I'm leaving.

But because he came to take care of me.

"Touch me more," I gasp.

"Here?"

"Everywhere."

"I don't want to hurt your ankle."

Guilt streaks through my core, but I shove it away, making myself promises that if I don't come back after my trip to Costa Rica, I'll find a way to see him again. To explain. To make it up to him. "You won't hurt me."

"Damn right. No gymnastics for you tonight. You just lie there. Let me do all the work." He skims my hip, his fingertips a light brush that sends goose bumps skittering across my flesh while he nibbles on my collarbone.

I don't know how he's staying on the bed, and so long as he doesn't fall off, I don't care.

"How's this?" he murmurs against my skin while his hand sneaks under my shirt as if he hasn't done this dozens of times in the past two weeks.

"Higher."

His knuckles brush my ribs. "This?"

"Higher."

And then he's dragging his thumb over my bare nipple, and white-hot heat streaks from my sternum straight to my clit.

"Ah, *there*," he says, as if he doesn't know exactly what he's doing.

"T-tease," I pant.

He thumbs my nipple again, and my hips almost come off the bed. "Dylan—"

"You're so sensitive."

I reach between my thighs and stroke myself.

"Ah-ah." He drops my breast to grab my hand. "Touching you is *my* job."

"But—"

He lifts my shirt, exposing my breast, dips his head to my nipple, and licks.

And *oh my holy heaven*, if this is what's waiting for me behind the pearly gates, I swear I'll behave myself forever.

He sucks my nipple into his mouth, and then he strokes my pussy over my panties, and coherent thought disintegrates behind chocolate rainbows and honey rain and divine sensations twisting and twirling deliciously deep in my core.

He slips one finger beneath my panties, and *yes*.

Yes yes *yes*.

It doesn't matter how many times this man kisses me and touches me and makes love to me.

It's always brand new, because he keeps pulling me deeper and deeper into who he is, coaxing me to let him in deeper and deeper too.

I tilt my hips to meet his hand, and he teases me, stroking my seam, circling my clit without touching it, and my body is here for it.

I want all the foreplay.

I want to grip his hair and hold his mouth to my breasts and let him explore every inch of my pussy until I'm soaked. I want to strip him and explore him exactly as he's exploring me, and I want to make him unable to catch his breath for the sheer pleasure coursing through his veins with every touch, every kiss, every lick, every nibble.

I want to stroke his cock, I want to taste it, I want to feel him inside me, and I want to drive him wild.

I want him to smell me when he wakes up tomorrow and come back for more on his lunch break.

My hips jerk against his hand.

I can't find words.

Just inelegant grunts and gasps and moans as he treats my other breast to the same luxurious, thorough worship, and his knuckle grazes my clit before he slips one finger inside me.

I'm chanting something.

It might be his name.

It might be some form of *hallelujah*, or *never stop*, or *oh my God, that feels so good*, or *you're better than a hamburger topped with a chocolate milkshake*.

What are words, really?

They're so inadequate when my body is a massive ball of primed nerves that he's playing like I'm a piano and he's a virtuoso.

"You're so tight," he murmurs as he slips another finger inside me. "Tight and hot and wet."

"Want—need—more—there—*aaaahhh!*"

He hits that spot inside me just right, and my world explodes in a Technicolor landscape of glory. My inner walls clench hard around his fingers while he teases and coaxes me higher and harder. "That's it, beautiful. Come for me. Come all over me."

My head is thrown back against the crude headboard, my eyes squeezed shut, all of me basking in the glory of this orgasm to end all orgasms.

And just with his fingers tonight.

The thought makes a mini climax erupt too. "God, *Dylan.*"

"Fuck, you're gorgeous."

All my muscles give at once, the tension leaving me and the *oh God, I'm naked* feelings taking over.

Still.

For all the times he's seen me naked, I *still* can't shut down that fucking voice.

Dammit.

I probably deserve the bad feelings, though, considering he's gazing at me with the kind of adoration I usually only see in the movies.

The kind that I've never thought could be real.

I move to pull my shirt down, but even in the dim light, he knows what I'm doing, and he catches my chin in his hand. I smell my own orgasm on his fingers.

"You *are* beautiful," he says quietly. "You're kind. You're funny. You're smart. You're strong. And you're beautiful. Exactly as you are. Anyone who doesn't see it isn't someone who deserves you."

"Stop," I whisper, the word clogging my throat.

"Front-row seat here," he whispers back. "You're fucking beautiful. And for the record, Tavi Lightly, I want to be the man who gets to spend the rest of your time here sneaking into that church basement helping you make chocolates. I want to be the man you ride along with on horrible plumbing jobs. I want to be the man you call when your family is driving you crazy and the man you call when you need help. But most of all, I want to be the man who deserves you."

Tell him, my conscience screams. *Trust him. Let him in.* "I—" I start, and then I hear it.

The click.

The telltale sound of someone sneaking out of my bedroom.

Usually, it's me making that noise.

But tonight—

"Stay," Dylan orders.

He doesn't leap off the bed.

Instead, he leaps *onto* it, expertly avoiding my fake bum ankle, and peers over my privacy screen. "Oh fuck," he whispers. "Tavi, I think we have a problem."

Chapter 30

Dylan

There are very few things I know for certain these days.

Used to be, I knew I used to be a fuckup, I'd turned my life around, and I had one *best* friend, several *good* friends, and a family that half accepted me and half rejected me. That was all on me, and I'd made peace with a lot of it.

I knew I helped people by going into the trades and being on call twenty-four seven.

I knew I owed my mom for sticking by me during my shithead years.

And I knew that most people were good.

Now, I'm not so sure I've turned my life around, and we're about to test that *friend* theory.

"Teague. Wake up, you grumpy asshole," I hiss from outside the window where I know my buddy's bedroom is.

It's midnight.

If he's asleep, he's probably naked.

Phoebe too.

And I'm not leaving the side of this tree house until he's up, even if I'm not particularly fond of being over fifty feet up in the air.

Nice of him to have stairs and a small deck on every level of the outside of this house, but I'm still not exactly in my happy place.

"What. The fuck?" he says inside, and a moment later, his grouchy bearded face appears on the other side of the screen.

"Where's Phoebe?" I ask.

"None of your damn business."

"Wha-hum?" Phoebe says inside.

"Go back to sleep," Teague tells her.

"Lola might have pictures or video of Tavi . . . ah, in a compromising position, which might've prompted both of us to babble things about—" I cut myself off with a good, solid *fuck*. Tavi was most definitely telling me my hands were better than all the chocolates she'd ever made and that she'd take me over a bacon cheeseburger, and I fucking went and mentioned the church and her chocolates. "You know what? Let's just put it at *Lola might have shit that tabloids would apparently pay a lot of money for*. We have to clear Tavi's stuff out of the church basement, and we need a place to store it."

"You know normal people sleep this time of night?" He's grumbling, but he's also moving away from the window. He gets it. More than I do, matter of fact, after how similar his childhood was to Phoebe's and Tavi's. "Five minutes. Downstairs."

It takes both Teague and Phoebe three minutes to meet me at the base of Teague's tree house, and it feels like the longest three minutes of my life.

"How much does Lola actually know?" Phoebe asks.

"Don't know, but I heard she wants to buy the church for a reality show."

"How much does Tavi know Lola knows?"

I wince. "I don't know."

"She's not planning on trying to help us move stuff on her ankle, is she?"

"I told her we had it."

Tavi sneaking around Tickled Pink in the dark is one thing.

Tavi sneaking around Tickled Pink in the dark on crutches is—

Hell.

We turn a corner, and it's clearly happening.

"What are you doing?" Phoebe hisses at her sister.

Tavi swings around and glares at her. "I'm taking care of my problems."

"We've got this. Go back to bed."

"You honestly think I can sleep right now?"

"Well, no. But you can't help either."

"Where are we putting it all?" Teague asks me.

I stare back at him. "Can't tell you."

The bunker.

Obviously.

Willie Wayne owes Tavi a favor too. I just decided she's calling it in.

"I have a storage locker in Deer Drop," Tavi whispers.

We're outside after midnight. Tickled Pink doesn't have a curfew, but it does have a lot of houses without air-conditioning, and we're definitely at risk of being overheard by some well-meaning neighbors with their windows open. One more block, and we'll be at the church.

But Tavi's slowing us down.

"Where's your truck?" Teague asks me.

"Home."

He grunts. "Fine. Borrow mine."

"You have a truck?" Phoebe and Tavi both say.

He grunts again.

"How did I not know you have a truck?" Phoebe hisses. "What else do you have that I don't know about?"

"Does the truck matter?"

"Maybe I wouldn't date you if your truck's ugly."

"Oh my *God*, Phoebe, *be quiet*," Tavi says, her voice as low as it goes.

"You're welcome for coming out in the dead-ass middle of the night to help you," Phoebe replies.

She sounds amused.

By all of it, actually. Amused that Teague has one more secret, and amused that Tavi's in a mood, and probably—

Shit.

Probably, that's what happens when you're regularly sleeping with the person you love.

How nice for her that she gets to do it without interruption while knowing that he loves her back.

"Quit being a brat," I mutter to Phoebe. "It's a bad night."

Tavi cringes.

"Not that part," I add.

"What's *that* part?" Phoebe asks.

Teague turns around and walks away.

"You getting the truck?" I whisper-hiss.

He doesn't answer.

"Aww, you two—are you? *You are.*" Phoebe squeals softly, then claps her hand over her mouth. "I totally thought you were, but now I *know* you are, and you are just the *cutest*. You're, like, totes swag."

Tavi growls at her.

I do too.

We hit the church, and I point to the back. "Go on," I tell Phoebe. "We'll catch up. I'm taking Tavi home."

"No, you're not," Tavi says.

Phoebe makes her own impatient noise. "Tavi, go home. We've got this."

"I don't need help."

The two sisters stare at each other.

Starting to wish I were back with Teague.

"You need help," I tell Tavi. "Just—c'mon. We've got this. But not if you don't *move.*"

She opens her mouth, and that's it.

We're not going to solve a thing by standing out here, so I take one of her crutches, shove it at Phoebe, and then toss Tavi over my shoulder, catching the second crutch before it can fall and wake the neighbors any more than we already have. "Downstairs," I tell Phoebe.

But when we reach the basement, it's already occupied.

Floyd leaps to his feet like he doesn't own the place. "Evenin', Dylan. Phoebe. Erm, Tavi, I'm guessing. That looks like Tavi's pants, even if I don't often see 'em from—erm—this angle."

He's an older white man with stooped shoulders who still likes cleaning up messes, which is one thing I never understood about him.

Also, I made a large number of messes for him back in my day, when he was the high school janitor and I was a pain in the ass. And he never held it against me.

Ever.

Not even when an old prank of mine caused the high school to flood and cancel school early one year long after I'd graduated.

Old coot actually *laughed* about it while I helped him clean everything up.

For free.

Naturally.

"What are you doing?" I ask him.

"Nothing." He casually shifts to block my view of the open white box of truffles.

"Floyd."

"What's going on?" Tavi asks.

"They looked good, and I didn't know why those two fancy ladies were arguing over who'd pay me more for my church, and now I find out there's chocolate fairies down here, and it all makes sense," he says.

Tavi gasps.

I grip the backs of her legs tighter.

When did she put on shorts?

And how hard was it for her to get those over her ankle?

"Those are special-order chocolates that I ordered for my grand-mother, and they take six weeks to get in and cost seventeen dollars each," Phoebe says, totally dead serious. "So we have two options here. You can forget everything you've seen, disappear from town for the six weeks it'll take us to get new truffles in for Gigi, have zero communi-cation beyond telling Teague that you're going fishing up north while my temper settles, or we can solve this immediately, right now, the Lightly way."

"He ate the truffles?" Tavi shrieks.

She's twisting, so I grip her tighter.

"Honest mistake, and it won't happen again, will it, Floyd?" Phoebe says.

The older man looks between me and Phoebe.

I shrug. "Don't look at me. I thought she was getting better."

"What's the Lightly way?" Floyd asks.

"I'm really, really pissed at you right now, Floyd, and I still wish you hadn't asked Phoebe that question, because it's *ugly*," Tavi says. "Pebbles is actually Pebbles Two. I had to replace Pebbles One after I fucked up and asked her that question."

The old man puts a hand to his heart like he believes that story. "Poor Pebbles."

"Right? I still cry sometimes."

I grunt.

She pinches my ass.

Floyd eyes Phoebe. "Are you still mad about the ghost thing too?"

"I'm currently undecided."

Teague strolls through the door, looks at all of us, and then sighs and scrubs a hand over his face. "Told you this is what happens when you try to keep a secret in this town," he says to Tavi's ass, still on display over my shoulder.

"It'll be worth it when we replace the Himalayan-gold-leaf-champagne truffles for Gigi and surprise her for . . . Talk like a Pirate Day," Phoebe replies.

Her eyebrows are saying something different, though.

They're clearly saying, *Shut up and just move things before I channel my grandmother.*

"Really looking forward to the day your whole family's souls are saved," he mutters.

With four fully functioning adults who can get up and down steps and one hobbling adult who knows where all the supplies are stashed and is remarkably adept at getting around on one leg, it takes us about thirty minutes to load Teague's truck.

He gives me the keys and a warning glare. "Hurt it, and—"

"He's not going to hurt it," Phoebe interrupts. She slips her hand into his. "C'mon. Let's go home and try this getting-back-to-sleep thing again."

Floyd mumbles something about leaving town for a few days for a fishing trip.

And then it's me and Tavi, loading up into Teague's truck. "I'm taking you back to the school, and then I'll stash these for you until we can find you a new kitchen."

She grabs my face before I can shut her inside the cab. "Thank you," she whispers.

"This is what we do for the people we love," I reply.

Her chin wobbles, and her eyes go shiny. "I do not deserve you," she whispers.

She presses a kiss to my lips, then another, and a third, and I don't care what she thinks she does or doesn't deserve.

All I care about is that right now, she's *mine*.

Chapter 31

Tavi

The airport's deserted at this hour of the night, which is a good thing.

Fewer people to see my tears.

"I told everyone it was a severe grade-two sprain," I say to Samantha as I hand her my crutches. "Just be unpleasant."

My heart is in my toes. I feel like the world's biggest jackass. And I'm on the verge of the bad kind of crying. It's only been three hours since I kissed Dylan goodbye, and already, I feel like he's completely gone.

"I can, like, *totes* do that," my doppelgänger replies with an easy nod, sounding just like me.

"Phoebe will be harder to fool this time, but if she gets suspicious, just start crying and say you're giving up on life because you're never getting out of Tickled Pink and your dreams will never come true."

"Easy."

"Carter will just think you're still weird. Gigi and I have been sniping at each other, so feel free to be catty, but not so much that I'd get extra soul duty. Volunteer at the cat shelter or something with Bridget. She'll love that, and you can sit down the whole time, but definitely wear sunglasses anytime you're with her and make a show of being in pain if she acts suspicious."

"So just like last time, but with a horrid injury."

"Yes. And if Dylan Wright stops by—"

"Hello, cutie." She grins at me.

It's eerie how similar our grins are. She has to wear a prosthetic nose, colored contacts, and a wig to fully complete the look, but otherwise, we could be twins.

Swear to God, some days I wonder if my father had an affair with my mother's doppelgänger.

Samantha's been filling in for me on my various socials for years—usually just in pictures if I'm double-booked for shootings or for random other reasons, but occasionally in a video where all I have to do is sound like a flake—and she spent three days earlier this summer acting like me at the school itself.

Phoebe got suspicious.

No one else did.

"Avoid Dylan at all costs," I tell her. "We—we've been sleeping together, and I . . . I like him."

I finish on a whisper.

"Aw, Tavi, he seems so nice. That's awesome."

I don't tell her not to sleep with him.

That part is understood. "It's not awesome. It's—look, just avoid. No stepping in front of garbage trucks this time."

She grimaces. "Not my best moment."

"Made it easier for me to avoid him until I couldn't, though. Appreciated that. Just—if he stops by, cry and tell him you're on your period and you want to be left alone to *think about things*."

Her nose wrinkles. "Men should really not be afraid of periods."

"I'm tired. It's what I've got."

"Is Niles still cooking?"

It's my turn to grimace.

She makes a noise in the back of her throat. "I'm going to start requiring hazard pay."

"I know. Believe me, I know. I'll be back in forty-eight hours. Seventy-two max. If Lola starts asking where I disappeared to tonight, tell her I needed fresh air and wanted to be alone because I hate the weight I gain when I'm injured."

"Whoa. You seriously want me to give Lola ammunition against you?"

"I'm out of ideas, Sam. Fresh out. If you have a better idea, text me. Keep a log so I know what I did and said while I was gone."

"Always do." She lifts her brows, like she's waiting for something.

And then I realize what she's waiting for.

Oh God.

I'm going to cry the entire flight.

I lift my purse and rub my face against Pebbles's face. "Mama loves you, sweetheart. Be a good girl for Samantha, and do everything she says, and I'll bring you back the best, best, *best* treats money can buy, I swear I will."

And if tomorrow's presentation to one Mr. Fitzwilliam Hawthorne goes well, then Samantha will be boarding a plane to Costa Rica to deliver my dog to me before I call and tell my grandmother I'm done.

Pebbles licks my face.

I scratch her ears.

She wags her tail.

I kiss her head and drop tears in her fur. "Last time, baby. This is the *last time.*"

"She'll be fine, Tavi," Sam whispers. "I've got her."

"Thank you," I say softly.

"No, thank *you.* I couldn't afford Mom's care if I didn't have this job."

And that's why I trust her.

Well, that and the ironclad nondisclosure agreement, and she knows I know her green card is fake.

I'd never use that against her—she's saved my life more than once—but my reputation says I would, and I don't correct it.

I've mentioned I hate this life, right?

Except for Dylan.

I most definitely love Dylan, and I don't know what to do about it.

Something else I love—and know *exactly* what to do about?

Arriving just about eight hours later at a private airstrip just outside San José, Costa Rica, and stepping off the plane to the sight of Naomi and Sebastián.

"You're here!" Naomi cries.

I fling myself at her, hugging her tight, and I'm suddenly stifling sobs again.

"Oh, honey, no, no tears," she whispers.

"This is the hardest thing I've ever done."

"Pebbles will be okay, and Sam's a pro, and we're going to nail this presentation."

I meant leaving Dylan.

But I can't say that to her, because I don't know how I left part of my heart in Wisconsin.

Nothing about that sentence makes sense.

But it's true.

Naomi and my found family here accept me, no question, no doubts, for exactly who I am. I don't have to pretend. I don't have to look good. I don't have to compete for their love, and when I fuck up, they forgive me.

They even forgive me for still learning how to forgive them when they fuck up too.

And I thought this would be the only place in the world I'd find that acceptance.

But that was before a small-town plumber with dimples and warm brown eyes sneaked into my heart and showed me time and again that we all get to define who we are.

Even if that means *re*defining who we are when we don't like the path we're on.

"I'm tired," I confess to Naomi.

That is so very true it hurts.

"Of course you are. When's the last time you got more than four hours of sleep? Come on. We have a little house we're renting in town here, and you can rest and relax and let me learn this presentation inside and out. Did you bring the truffles?"

One more thing to feel guilty about.

I lied and told Dylan I needed most of the boxes of truffles that Floyd didn't eat so that I could mail them today, and that I absolutely refused to let him do it for me since I couldn't live with myself if he were called names in public again just because I made him let me make him into a TikTok star.

I'd feel better about myself if I'd said *so I can get them where they need to be.*

Three months ago, the ends would've justified the means.

I don't care if I lie to Gigi. I don't care if I lie to my father or to Carter.

But I care if I lie to Dylan.

I don't want to lie to him.

I don't want to have secrets.

But I don't want him carrying *this* secret. It's not fair to ask that of him when we're not serious, no matter how awful I feel for keeping it from him.

I check my phone.

Last update from Sam reports that no one in the school wants to be around her because she's complaining she's bored and that her ankle hurts and that nothing tastes good because of the painkillers.

I really played up how much I wanted to taste good soybeans, she texted. Also, Lola totally went through your room sometime last night. I found beef jerky planted in the vegan protein bar boxes and a listening device planted under your bed.

I'm not scared.

I'm *furious.*

"Naomi?"

"Uh-oh," she replies.

"We're going to kill it with this presentation, and then we're going to kill Lola Minelli."

Chapter 32

Dylan

Work sucks ass today.

No nicer way to put it.

I'm running on two hours of sleep, blue balls, and three truffles that I stole from Tavi's stash as I was putting it into Willie Wayne's bunker last night.

And do I get the easy day today?

No, I do not.

Some Deer Drop dummy's sewer lines are backed up because of God only knows how many months' worth of tampons and those damn flushable wipes that aren't flushable at all, and I spend the morning snaking shit that would've made me gag in my younger plumber years.

Still not all that pleasant, but it's clinical now.

When I get back to Tickled Pink on my way to clean up before poker night, my route takes me past the church, and *Jesus*.

Teague's showing the place to Lola and two dudes in suits that I don't recognize.

We always wondered how Teague survived, since his only discernible job is being Tickled Pink's resident real estate agent, and God knows houses don't go fast around here. Has goats. Grows food too. Fishes a lot. Lives in a tree house. Doesn't need a lot of electricity or water.

When we found out he was an heir to some big oil fortune earlier this summer when his long-lost brother came to find him, we wondered if he'd been secretly living off a trust fund, but turns out the dude's a minimalist and doesn't need a lot to survive.

Puts most of his money into Bridget and the town, and that means the rest of us put our time and effort into taking care of him the best we can.

Teague lifts a hand to me as I pass by, so I slow and lower my window.

"Dylan's the local plumber," he tells the suits. Then he looks at me. "You been in here recently?"

"Thought I heard water gushing," I reply. "Turned out one of Teague's goats locked himself inside. Wouldn't surprise me if the pipes go, though. Place has been empty for twenty years or so. No maintenance."

The suits smile, look at Lola, and smile broader. "That's the best news we've had all day."

Teague scowls at me.

I give him the *warn a small-town guy who doesn't know any better next time* glare.

I didn't know I was supposed to make it sound *good*.

Probably should've, now that I think about it.

All of America would tune in to watch Lola Minelli dealing with exploding pipes in a church.

"Exploding pipes will cost you extra," Teague tells the producers.

"You that plumber from TikTok?" one of them asks me. His gaze flicks over my face. "Ever think about doing TV for real? With a face like that—"

"Right?" Lola squeals. "That's what I keep telling him."

"No." I wave, roll up my window, and head away from the church.

Don't have anything else good to contribute, and I need to see Tavi. She hasn't replied to any of my texts, which isn't unusual.

She's usually working with her family and can't get to her phone.

But I don't know what her day's been like today, when she's supposed to be staying off her ankle.

"Hey, Dylan," Bridget calls as I swing out of my truck near the boys' entrance to the school. She's out Rollerblading with two friends. "Your TikToks are killing it!"

"When you grow up and become a plumber, your TikToks can kill it too," I call back.

"Ew, no," one of the teenagers says.

"I'm gonna be the first astrophysicist to go viral for my mad guitar skills," Bridget tells me. "They're, like, *swag*."

"They totally slap," the third teenager agrees.

"Dylan! Oh, thank God I caught you."

I turn and glance at the other side of the street, where Mrs. Pennyworth is waving a towel out of her kitchen window.

"My garbage disposal just made a weird noise, and I'm hosting Erica and her new boyfriend for dinner in two hours. Do you mind taking a look? I can wait a few minutes if you want to get Tavi and do a video here."

I flash her a thumbs-up. "Let me go see how she's feeling."

I jog into the school and run straight into Estelle.

She looks down her nose at me, which is both disconcerting—she's a good four inches shorter than me—and also annoying. "Mr. Wright."

"Mrs. Lightly."

"I notice you didn't knock."

"Someone said there was a gas leak in the chemistry lab."

"Fascinating, considering that's Octavia's bedroom."

"Is it?"

She frowns.

"Right. Should've known that, since we're friends. Friends definitely tell each other where their bedrooms are in school buildings." I give her a lazy salute and slip around her. "I'll let you know if I find anything dangerous."

"I didn't bring my family here to leave all of my granddaughters behind," she says behind me.

"Tickled Pink's pretty awesome. They could do worse."

I don't tell her Tavi's not staying.

She knows.

No sense in getting my own hopes up by letting Estelle into my head.

I swing around the landing and head up to the second floor, passing Michael Lightly on the way.

He frowns at me. "She's in a mood."

"Your mother?"

"My daughter."

"Maybe she needs a hug."

"Little late for that."

He puts his head down and marches down the stairs.

I have regrets in life, and I've figured out a few things later than I probably should've, but if I ever have kids, I won't wait until they're almost thirty to hug them.

And my mom might drive me crazy some days, but I have zero doubt she loves me.

It's been the one constant.

What would Tavi be like if she'd had my mom instead?

What would she be like if she'd been allowed to find what she wanted for herself instead of being thrust into the limelight before she could choose it for herself?

I finish climbing the stairs, stride down the hallway, knock once, and let myself into her room.

"Go away," comes her muffled voice.

I ignore that too. "C'mon, sunshine. We can turn this around."

She grunts.

Maybe she's finally catching up on some of that sleep she needs. "Do you need a bedtime story?" I whisper.

"No."

She's lying facedown, her ankle wrapped in multiple flexible cold packs and propped up on six pillows. Her hair covers her shoulders and the purple tank top she's wearing, and her arm's hanging off the side of the bed.

My heart tugs as I approach her and squat so that we'd be at eye level if she turned and looked at me. "Can I get you anything?"

"No."

"Open a window?"

"Nuh-uh."

"Did Lola do something?"

"Go away."

I rub my chest, where my heart's starting to beat erratically. Did I do something wrong when I cleared out her chocolate last night? Or is this just Tavi when she's down?

I've seen her down.

Fuck.

Is she *defeated*?

"I can't make you big sweeping promises that everything's going to be okay," I say quietly, "but I believe in you, Tavi. If there's anything you need, or anything I can do, or anyone I can call, let me know, okay?" I brush her hair aside to lean in and kiss her shoulder.

She shivers and squirms. "Go away."

But that's not what turns my blood cold.

Her birthmark is missing.

How the *fuck* does a birthmark go missing?

"Tavi?"

"I *said*, go away."

I stare.

Then stare harder.

Is she wearing makeup? Am I looking at the wrong shoulder?

Wait.

That's not her shoulder.

It's not—it's not *strong* enough.

"You said," I say quietly.

"Yes. I said."

Jesus. That's not her voice either. "And who, exactly, are you?"

She doesn't move.

She doesn't even breathe.

Time stands still, my question hanging in the air between us, until she slowly rolls her head to the side and attempts to eviscerate me with a glare. "What kind of question is *that*?"

I blink.

Then I blink again.

She looks like Tavi.

She does.

The eyes, the nose, the mouth—but her ears are wrong.

Her ears are wrong.

I blink and rub my eyes one more time. "Who—"

"Shut up," she whispers. "Lola could be listening, or Carter, or Gigi, and you do *not* want to fuck this up, or I will fuck *you* up, because that's what you do for your friends."

I swallow. *Hard.* There are so many questions. *So* many questions. "We should have breakfast tomorrow."

"No."

A low growl wells up in my throat.

She matches it with a glower in her eyeballs. "Maybe, like, in a few days. When I can walk again."

Is that code? Does that mean Tavi's coming back? The *real* Tavi, not this freaky look-alike?

Is this a dream? Am I hallucinating?

"And don't, like, go ask Phoebe what's wrong with me," she adds. "She, like, doesn't know me nearly as well as this *new Phoebe* thinks she does."

And I'm officially creeped out.

This woman is *not* Tavi.

But if it weren't for the missing birthmark, she might've actually fooled me.

Also?

What the ever-loving fuck is going on?

Who—*who*—is this woman? Why does she look like Tavi?

And the very most important question of all—

Where the hell *is* Tavi?

Chapter 33

Tavi

I'm getting dressed for drinks with our prospective investor when I decide it's a good idea to check the comments on Dylan's latest TikTok.

I miss him.

I left Tickled Pink *today*—super early today, like so early it barely qualified as today, but still *today*—and while Costa Rica has been the place where I've felt most at home the past few years, today, right now, it's lacking.

Not because I'm in the city instead of on the farm.

But because he's not here with me.

Stupid, right? He can't just move to Costa Rica with me. He loves Tickled Pink. And they love and need him. In a lot of ways, I think he needs them too. They're his family. The people who have stuck with him and forgiven him and worried about him and done family the right way.

His smiling face pops up in his TikTok profile, and I both smile and fight back tears.

I wish he were here.

"Tavi?" Naomi says behind me.

I sniff deeply and blink quickly to suck back in all the feelings and close the app before I make eye contact with her in the small mirror over my wobbly dresser in the rental house's bedroom. "Hey."

"You okay?" she asks.

"Yes. Yes! Nervous, but totally okay."

She eyeballs me.

I force a smile as I turn to face her.

Her eyeball gets eyeballier. "You miss Dylan."

"I—he—we—"

"Fell in love," she finishes for me.

"No."

She quirks a brow at me, and I know exactly what that brow quirk means. It means, *You're a flake, Tavi, and you go where the wind blows you, and now you're thinking about giving up everything we've worked for to go try out being in love with a small-town guy.*

Okay, it doesn't. She wouldn't say that.

I'll say it about myself for her, though. Until the farm, I was forever finding new hobbies, new places to travel, new guys to date, and new angles for all my socials. "Naomi. I am *not* abandoning you. I'm not staying in Tickled Pink. I'm *here*. Men come and go. The farm—you—this life—I—"

"Much as I hate the idea that women are supposed to stretch to have it all, if there's any one person in this world who can do it, do it well, and still thrive, it's you. We'll figure it out. Don't give up on love. Don't *ever* give up on love. It's the one thing that matters most."

"I love *you*."

"Not the way you love Dylan. And that's okay. That's how it's supposed to be."

"*Naomi.* You and I—we've worked *so hard* to turn the farm around, and we're *this close* to taking this from a little hobby to save a small slice of the earth to something bigger, something real, something that *matters*, something that gives me a purpose and makes me feel like I belong for the first time in my life, and I'm not throwing that away for both of us just because I have a crush on a man."

"A crush."

"Yes. A crush."

"*Tavi.* The farm will still be here if you take a chance and tell that man that you love him."

He took a chance last night and included me in the *people he loves.* But does that mean he's *in love* with me or that I count as his family now?

I don't know.

"I can't," I whisper.

She studies my face, and I duck my head so she can't see what I'm feeling.

What I'm afraid of.

"I don't know how to love myself," I tell the floor, my voice barely audible even to myself. "Who am I to think I'd know how to love or be loved by someone else the way they truly deserve?"

She doesn't answer but instead walks into my bedroom and wraps me in a tight hug. "I love you," she tells me. "And I know you love me. And you love Pebbles. You loved Grandma Clementine. You love your new friends in Tickled Pink. I can *hear* it when you talk about them. Love doesn't have to follow rules. It just *is.* Don't get up in your head about it. Just let it be."

"But he's not *here.* And I want to be *here.*"

"Have you asked him if he'll come?"

"Of course not. He has a solid business in Tickled Pink, and the people there need him, and—"

"And maybe he needs you more than they need him."

"But—"

"No buts. You have a beautiful soul, a massive heart, and the best boobs in existence."

I sputter out an unexpected laugh. "My *boobs?*"

"Um, *hello*? There are entire Instagram accounts dedicated to your boobs."

"There are not."

She huffs and pulls back, and a second later, I'm staring at a list of Instagram accounts that are all some variation of *Tavi Lightly's Boobs*.

"But—"

"And the heart and soul, Tavi. You have a good heart and a good soul, and you're a kick-ass businesswoman to boot."

"I'm broke."

"Because you donate your entire salary to charity. Not because you don't make money. And if I ever meet your grandmother, I'm going to look her in the eye and tell her she's still going to hell, because she's kept you from being the amazing person that you are by trapping you somewhere that held you back."

I don't know that being in Tickled Pink has held me back.

If anything, it's taught me that it's time to truly set myself free.

There was magic in saving the farm, but there will be even more magic in making it self-sustaining instead of relying on my trust fund to keep it going.

And honestly?

I think I miss Tickled Pink too. It has its own kind of magic.

I pull back and swipe at my eyes, grateful for waterproof mascara. "We're making something amazing, aren't we?"

"We already have." She beams at me, glances down at her phone, and starts to swipe Instagram shut, but then she freezes.

And frowns.

And shoves her phone in her pocket.

"What?" I ask.

"Trolls." She spits out the word like it tastes bad, and the tips of her ears go pink.

In other words, she's lying. "Naomi."

"This is not the most important thing we need to worry about today."

I open my own phone and swipe to Instagram.

And then I choke on air.

I'm tagged in a post from two hours ago. In Tickled Pink. By an account I don't recognize, which means it's probably one of the ever-growing number of tourists who keep showing up in town.

It's a picture of Dylan carrying me over his shoulder out of the school building, ankle bandaged, wearing my rainbow leggings, with the caption OMGeeeeeeeee!! I just saw The Tickled Pink Plumber carrying Tavi Lightly to his truck! THEY ARE SO DATING!

Except he's never carried me out of the school building in rainbow leggings, nor have I had my ankle wrapped in Tickled Pink in daylight hours.

"He kidnapped Sam," I whisper.

"Tavi, she's a pro. She's got this."

"But what if *he knows*? What if he figures out she's not me? What if—" I swallow hard and don't finish that.

What if he *doesn't* know it's not me?

Naomi bites her lip. "Have you heard from Sam?"

I shake my head.

"Me neither." She hugs me again. "So we're going to put all the positive vibes out in the world, trust that she has this and that he's worthy of you and won't do something stupid, and we're going to go charm the pants off this British billionaire who's looking to do some good with his new inheritance."

Right.

That's what I'm here for.

To secure financing for the farm from Fitzwilliam Hawthorne so that our little community can keep thriving on chocolate.

"Okay. Okay. Let me touch up my lipstick, and then we'll go kick ass."

Ten minutes later, I'm still a disaster in my head, but that's nothing new when it comes to work situations.

I can do this.

We head out, walking to the hotel in the warm evening without fear of being recognized. I'm in a business suit and kitten heels, my usual glitzy sunglasses swapped for fake reading glasses, my hair swept back in Phoebe's favorite style, and my usual Margot Lightly purse upgraded to a Coach messenger bag with our sales pitch inside.

Naomi's utterly perfect in twill pants and a soft silk blouse, her wild curls framing her face, her makeup light, her messenger bag carrying truffle samples.

We can do this.

We can woo investors with the best of them.

We have to. The whole farm is depending on it.

Naomi smiles at me as we push into the door of the small hotel. "We're going to kick ass," she whispers.

I smile back.

And then I hear it.

That voice.

The voice that I hear in my head every time I eat anything, every time one of my outfits feels a smidge too tight, every time I start to doubt that I, too, can be a successful businesswoman in my own right.

My mother.

My mother is *here*.

"*Tavi.* Oh, my *baby*. Come to Mama. We're going to fix everything."

My mother's alone at the small hotel bar.

And when I say *alone*, I mean *alone*.

No one else is here in the entire room.

Including the heir we're supposed to meet for our business presentation.

"Oh, my sweetheart, I missed you." As always, she's a knockout. Her light-brown hair's been touched up with blonde highlights and falls in soft waves around her smooth face. Makeup on point. Flowing sundress that I should probably recognize as one of her favorite designers, who I refuse to name because he only dresses *skinny* women.

She grabs me in a hug while I stand motionless.

"Hi, excuse me, are you really Tavi's mom?" Naomi asks.

Mom pulls back and aims her dazzling Margot Lightly special smile at my best friend and business partner. "Yes, and who are you?"

"I'm inclined to hit you, which would be the first violent thing I've done since I pulled Bella Roberts's hair in the second grade after she called my best friend fat."

I wrench out of my mom's grip and grab Naomi by the hand. "No international incidents. Yet. Maybe *after* our meeting."

"Oh, sweetheart, I canceled that for you."

I gasp.

Naomi gasps.

"Okay," I hear myself say. "You can hit her."

Chapter 34

Dylan

It's been fifteen years since I've been this much of a mess.

It's also been fifteen years since I've done something this unhinged.

"Dylan! Let me down!" Tavi-Not-Tavi shrieks as I carry her over my shoulder down the bunker steps.

As soon as I grabbed Pebbles out of her room, verified that the dog wasn't also a fake Pebbles, and started marching away, Tavi-Not-Tavi got super interested in following me.

While hobbling.

On the wrong ankle.

She didn't argue when I flung her over my shoulder and marched her to my truck, me still carrying Pebbles. Nor did she have much to say once I hit the gas, me seething, her petting the dog, who clearly likes her.

"Who are you?" I repeat as I shove into the bunker with her.

It's the only place I can think of where I know we can talk privately without being interrupted.

"He brought the tofu again," Willie Wayne says.

"Who cares?" Ridhi replies.

Jane sighs happily. "The only thing I care about is finding out who the chocolate fairy is and getting more."

Christ.

It's poker night.

All Tavi's chocolates and supplies and equipment are here, and *I forgot it's poker night.*

"You know where we can get more?" Willie Wayne asks. "I'm trying real hard to be mad that this might attract mice, but—"

Ridhi interrupts him with a moan as she licks a truffle.

Just licks it.

And her eyes roll back into her head. "This stuff should be illegal."

"It's so good." Willie Wayne's spread eagle on the couch, admiring a truffle like it holds the key to happiness. "And it might be worth it."

Tavi-Not-Tavi makes a noise. "What did you do?" she hisses as she thrashes on my shoulder.

Pebbles whimpers under my free arm.

"Whoa." Willie Wayne sits up and studies me.

Ridhi looks twice.

Jane makes a muffled noise, then dives for the door and slams it shut.

"Sit," Ridhi orders me.

"I don't know who pissed you off, but whoever it is, we're talking it out before we leave this room," Jane adds.

Willie Wayne holds out the truffle in his hand. "Here. Eat this. It'll help."

"It won't fucking help."

Three sets of eyebrows lift in unison.

I set Tavi-Not-Tavi on the floor.

Three sets of eyeballs look at her, then immediately shift back to me.

"Did she knock you up?" Jane asks me, totally deadpan.

"Cheat on you?" Ridhi chimes in.

"Tell you she paid a service to inflate your TikTok views?" Willie Wayne guesses.

Tavi-Not-Tavi gasps. "Willie Wayne, I would, like, *never.*"

"How the hell do you know who he is?" I snap.

Her brows go up, and she gives me an eerily accurate impression of Tavi's *duh* look. "Because I, like, *live* here?"

Am I losing my freaking mind?

Is this really Tavi?

Am I sabotaging this just for the hell of it?

I spin her around and tug her tank aside to peer at her shoulder blade.

"Dylan," Jane snaps as Tavi-Not-Tavi jerks away.

"She's missing her birthmark." I want to howl. Am I losing my damn mind, or did something happen to Tavi? "And her ears are wrong. *This isn't Tavi.*"

My friends don't laugh.

They stare at me like I'm definitely losing my marbles, but they don't laugh.

"How's Shiloh's party coming?" Ridhi asks her.

"Totes perfect! I, like, complained about my mom while Bridget and I were having our toes done the other day, and she was all, 'My mom is so cool,' and gave me extra ideas for games and party favors without even knowing she was doing it, and the cake's ordered, and the community center will be almost done, so we'll, like, pull the fire alarm Tuesday night and have the whole station respond to get them all there."

How does she know all of this? Is this really Tavi? Or is this all a bad dream?

"How's my TikTok account coming?" Jane asks.

Tavi-Not-Tavi laughs. "You didn't want one, silly. Remember?"

"How did *Lola's Tiny House* end?" Willie Wayne asks.

"Um, do I care? No."

"Aha! You—no, wait, that's Phoebe who's addicted to that show. Dylan. Here, my man. Have some chocolate. It's really good chocolate. Don't write it off like it's your average Hershey bar."

"I know it's good chocolate. But *this isn't Tavi*."

Am I losing my mind?

Jesus.

What's wrong with me.

"He's right," Jane says. "She's good, but she's not Tavi. Tavi's got more . . . it's like the smell of desperation warring with hope and an unmet need to be loved about her. You can't mimic that."

"Like, *totes*," Ridhi agrees dryly. She points at Tavi-Not-Tavi. *"Sit."*

Jane crosses her arms. "And talk."

Tavi-Not-Tavi looks at me. I don't know if she's asking if it's safe to talk in front of them, if we're going to murder her and hide her body, or if I have regrets yet about bringing her here, but I know I want answers. "Where *the fuck* is Tavi?"

Pebbles whimpers at my feet.

"This isn't my story to tell," Tavi-Not-Tavi whispers.

"Ppfffft," Jane replies.

"And who do you think *we're* going to tell?" Ridhi asks. "Also, if you tell a soul this bunker exists, you're gonna need the fire department a lot sooner than Tuesday night."

"What happens in the bunker stays in the bunker," Willie Wayne agrees. "Akiko thinks I'm bowling in Deer Drop."

"Gibson's on assignment in Argentina and thinks I shut my phone off for *Ted Lasso* bingeing on Thursday nights," Jane says.

Ridhi nods. "Shiloh's at the fire station, and Bridget's cockblocking Teague."

"And I'm taking you to Estelle next if you don't fucking *talk*," I growl.

"She's at a business meeting," Tavi-Not-Tavi whispers.

Willie Wayne drops the truffle he's holding.

"Holy shit," Jane murmurs.

Ridhi grabs the nearest folding chair and sits like her legs don't want to hold her. "I will never understand rich people."

"What's your name?" I ask.

"None of your business."

Willie Wayne bolts up out of his chair. "*She didn't sprain her ankle!* This is just like when Lola faked a broken arm so that she could get someone else to cook for her on *Lola's Tiny House*. *She didn't sprain her ankle*, and we freaking *lost* because she left the game!"

"She's sorry," Not-Tavi says.

"Where is she?" I repeat.

"Even if I knew, I wouldn't tell you." Not-Tavi tosses her hair. "She's a good person doing her best in shitty circumstances, and I hope she never comes back." She gives me a half smile that feels almost real on the sympathy. "No offense. It's not about you. It's really not."

Of course it's not.

I'm nobody.

A small-town plumber who was a nice distraction while she was trapped here. "She's not coming back?"

Not-Tavi shrugs. "She says she is, but if I were her, I wouldn't. Again, no offense. She likes all of you. Like, *way* more than I've ever heard her talk about anyone else in her life except for one person."

Naomi. Her friend Naomi.

"How often have you been here?" Jane asks.

"I respectfully decline to answer that question."

"Does Lola have a doppelgänger too?" Willie Wayne asks.

Jane throws a truffle at him. "Do you really think she'd know? What do you think there is, Doppelgängers R Us on a secret corner in Hollywood?"

"*Don't waste truffles.*" He lunges for it and recovers the truffle he dropped at the same time.

Ridhi's fanning herself like she, too, is realizing this is super fucked up and can't quite get a grip on it. "How did you even get this job? Are you wearing a *Scooby-Doo* mask, or do you *actually* look like Tavi in real life?"

Tavi-Not-Tavi growls. "Can we talk about the more important part? Like how if any of you breathe a word of this and hurt Tavi, you'll regret it for the rest of your lives?"

"No one's hurting Tavi."

"What's this business meeting about?" Jane asks. "What *business*? And where the hell did these truffffffffffuuck. *Are you serious?* Shit. I mean, we all assumed she eats decent food when no one's looking, but *are you serious?*" She points at me. "And *you knew.*"

"Stop," Not-Tavi says. She wrinkles her nose, but it doesn't wrinkle with her. "Can we all please agree that I need to stay away from Tavi's family until she gets back or fires me because she doesn't need me anymore? If *you* figured it out, they might too."

I stare at Not-Tavi, and the truth sinks in.

Tavi, the real Tavi, isn't coming back.

Her truffles are fucking awesome. She's smarter than she gives herself credit for. And she doesn't want to live here for the rest of her life.

Of course she's not sitting around waiting for Estelle to give her back her trust fund.

She's out there trying to find another way to save her farm.

"What about Pebbles?" I ask. "What happens to Pebbles if she doesn't come back?"

"She'll appreciate your concern," Not-Tavi says, "but you don't have to worry."

She's wrong.

I do have to worry.

I have to worry *very much*.

Chapter 35

Tavi

I woke up from a short nap this afternoon feeling like the goddess of chocolate, but now I'm a hollow chocolate bunny.

"Octavia, open the door," my mother calls from outside our little rental house. "I told you. I'll give you all the money you need so that you can get away from your grandmother's ridiculous scheme. If you've found what makes you happy, then I want to help you be happy."

"She really canceled our meeting with him," Naomi whispers.

Her face is lit only by the glow of her laptop as we sit together on the double bed in her bedroom, and I'm pretty sure she'd only look even more grim if the lights were on.

You'd think it would be the opposite, but right now, I can convince myself she's telling a terrible ghost story rather than the truth.

"I can't do it, Naomi," I whisper. "I can't take her money. And I don't know where that leaves us."

She stares at me over the laptop, her cheekbones lit up but her eyes shadowed. "We'll tell him there was a mix-up."

"He might be new to having the money in his bank account, but he knows better than to do business with people who flake on him. It's Rich People 101, and he was raised by rich people."

"But he was so nice—"

"That might work for us if he were a woman," I mutter darkly.

She grimaces. "Okay. Okay. New plan. We still have our next-tier investor list to reach out to. You can go back to Tickled Pink while—"

"Naomi, *Dylan knows*. He won't tell Gigi, but he knows, and he hasn't texted me since before—"

I stop talking, because I cannot contemplate the rest of that sentence. *Since before he probably figured out I lied to him.*

"I can't go back to Tickled Pink," I whisper. "I can't do it. I am *not* the person I want to be when I'm around my father and Carter and Gigi, and *I can't do it.*"

"And I don't want you to." She squeezes my hand. "It's so hard seeing you miserable. And it's so complicated when you've also been so happy at the same time."

"But what are we going to *do*?"

"Tavi, my love?" Mom knocks on the bedroom window. "Sweetheart, I'm here to *fix things*. I know I was a terrible mother. I didn't know what I was doing, and your grandmother has judged me for *one little indiscretion* my entire life, and I let it get in my head when I should've ignored it and paid better attention to you and your brother and sister. I know I can't change the past, but I want to make it up to you. I want to be in your life the way you *want* me in your life, not the way I think I should be in your life."

My heart feels hollow and full at the same time, and I don't know what to do with that. I march to the window and fling it open. *"You canceled the meeting that would've saved my life."*

Her eyes go wide, and her mouth forms a perfect O.

My temper spikes through the roof. "You're standing there, saying you want to help me live my life my way, *but you keep putting yourself first.*"

Her chin wobbles.

Her eyes go shiny.

And I won't do it. I won't carry her guilt. Being angry might not be *nice*. But after what she did, I have every right to my anger.

Naomi slips an arm around my waist. "You need to leave," she tells my mother.

"I did it again," Mom whispers. "Oh my God, Tavi, I did it again."

My lungs are too tight. My throat is clogged. My eyeballs are on fire. "Yeah, Mom. You fucking *did it again.*"

Naomi pulls me away from the window, shuts it, then closes the blinds. "You can yell at me if you need to get it all out," she says softly. "Don't bottle it up. Don't let it fester."

"I'm—just—so—*mad.*"

"You should be. *I'm* mad, and I don't have almost three decades of baggage with her."

I make myself unfist my hands and swipe at my eyes. "I don't want to be angry. I want to *fix this.*" And I want to talk to Dylan.

Tell him what happened.

Hear him tell me the same, that *it's okay* to be angry. That I'll still be one of the people he loves no matter what.

But I can't. *I can't.*

Naomi gives me a gentle push, and I fall to the bed.

"You know there's one person who would understand more than anyone else," she says.

"I can't call Dylan. I betrayed him. I lied to him. And if he doesn't realize that's Sam and he tries to seduce her—"

"No, Tavi. I mean your sister."

I blink at her.

Then blink again.

"She's changed." Naomi shrugs.

She's right. Phoebe's changed. And she *would* understand. She'd be outraged with me, and then she'd offer me money, and—

Fuck.

And then it gets complicated all over again, when we don't need complicated.

"I don't want investors," I say quietly. *Oh my God.* Did my mother actually do me a favor? "I don't want—no, I *can't* live my life beholden to other people because of their money. Phoebe might help no strings attached. Honestly? I think she would. But I have to do this *for me.* With the resources I have."

And what do I have?

I have *me.*

"Where are the truffles?" I ask Naomi.

She lifts her bag.

"I need a cheeseburger."

"I know. I could seriously go for a grilled cheese right now too."

"No, I mean, *I need a cheeseburger.* And a milkshake. And truffles."

Her brows squeeze together. "Okay. There's a place a couple blocks from here. I can call in an order."

"And a glorious pile of french fries dripping in cheese and bacon bits too. And—and—and *cheesecake.* Topped with chocolate chip cookie dough."

"Oh, sweetie, it's going to be okay." She pulls out her phone. "I promise, this *will* be okay. But cheeseburgers first. I'm on it."

She has no idea the thoughts swirling in my head. I can't tell her either. She'd try to talk me out of it.

And she can't.

Mind made up.

Octavia Lightly, bullied granddaughter, fake social media star, neglected daughter, and lonely little rich girl, is dead.

It's time for the real Tavi—the good friend, the humanitarian, the chocolate goddess—to rise from her ashes—or go down in flames trying.

"Naomi?"

"Hm?"

"If this doesn't work, I just want you to know that you are one of the very best things to ever happen to me."

"If what doesn't work?"

"Me."

Chapter 36

Dylan

The last thing I expect to see when I walk out my front door Friday morning is Phoebe Lightly storming up my path. "Are you okay?" she asks.

I lift my brows and pretend I have no idea what she's talking about.

After getting Not-Tavi, who *still* refused to give us her name through our entire not-poker night, settled at Jane's house to hide from the Lightly clan, I stepped into Ladyfingers, spotted Carter strumming his guitar, and promptly left there too.

My mom thinks I got dumped.

Maybe that's what has Phoebe looking like she drank sour milk.

Maybe she thought I was good for Tavi and she's sad for me too.

Who knows?

She shoves her phone at me. "You haven't seen this?"

I glance down. "The TikTok app?"

She growls and hits a button, and a video of Tavi springs to life.

I don't know where she is. Looks tropical. Bright-green trees behind her, and she's sitting at a table that looks like it's made of straw.

Her makeup is uneven.

And she's picking up a massive cheeseburger. "Confession," she says, "I hate bean sprouts. They taste like mud water."

I choke on air as Tavi takes a massive bite of the burger.

"Also?" she continues around a mouthful of beef. "I pulled a muscle in my butt two years ago, and I haven't been able to do more than twenty squats in a day since, and I skip ab day at least three times a month. I run because I'm trying to run away from the people I'm related to and the hoops they make me jump through just so I can feel loved."

"What—" I start.

Phoebe shushes me.

Tavi's video keeps rolling. "I eat chicken. I eat cheese. I love hamburgers. And I bought a run-down cacao farm to try to save it three years ago, and I make the most delicious truffles, all full of sugar, and I eat them and I love them. Life isn't supposed to be about how you look. It's supposed to be about who you *are*."

Holy shit.

Holy fucking shit.

She's not hesitating as she speaks to the camera. "I've been lying to you for years. I'm not successful. I'm not pretty. I don't like my mom's handbags. I'm not even rich. All of my money? It comes from a trust fund, and that's gone now. *Poof!* I'm supposed to be in this little town in Wisconsin right now, sucking up to my grandmother so that I can get my trust fund back, but I'm not. I hired someone who looks like me to stand in for me so I could take a trip to check on my farm, *twice*, and *my family didn't even notice*."

She grabs a truffle, shoves it in her mouth, and moans.

My heart's in my throat. I'm so damn proud of her that it might burst, and also furious that she didn't trust me enough to tell me she was leaving town, and more than a little worried about what else is going on in her head and how bad things are wherever she is that she feels like she has to do this.

Her eyes slide closed, and she whimpers softly, the same way she does as she's coming down off an orgasm, and now my dick's hard too.

"Wait—*twice?*" I say to Phoebe.

She shushes me once more as Tavi's gorgeous blue eyes slide open again, and she stares directly out of the phone screen. "So here's my last note to my family: I'm not coming back. I don't want your money. If I want to eat a truffle, I won't worry about how it'll sit on my hips for the rest of my life, and you don't get to define whether or not I'm a good person. For those of you who aren't my family, there's a link in my bio if you want to talk about investing in Zero Ducks Chocolates."

Her voice wavers while my heart takes a roller coaster ride.

Was that a subtle nod to me telling her I saw her saving the ducks? Or not?

She shakes her head and reaches for a cup, tilting it toward the camera. "That's what I have left to give. Zero fucks. But you can't put that on a chocolate wrapper, can you? Also, this is totally a cookies-and-cream milkshake. And you know what? All of you watching right now? Don't let other people put you down. You are *awesome*. You're perfect exactly the way you are, and the only thing I'm doing here today is dropping truth bombs, so you can take that to the bank. Surround yourself with people who believe in you, and fuck anyone who doesn't. Do you. Do *the hell* out of doing you. Give zero fucks. And that's the last piece of advice you're ever going to get from me." She puts the straw in her mouth, sucks, moans again, and then her arm blocks the view as she shuts off the video.

It immediately starts up again, but Phoebe switches the phone off and looks at me.

I slowly sink to the steps, pride for her warring with injured pride for myself.

Talk about taking charge of your life. *Jesus.* She's fucking amazing.

But she also didn't say anything about me.

She hasn't texted.

She hasn't called.

And—*twice*?

When did she swap places with her doppelgänger here before?

My phone buzzes in my pocket. Then again. And a third time.

I pull it out, hoping it'll be Tavi, but it's not.

It's friends and family and clients, more piling up by the second as my phone blows up once more.

"Did she tell you she was leaving?" Phoebe asks.

I shake my head.

"Tell me you didn't sleep with that woman who was posing as her yesterday."

I scowl at her. "You knew?"

"No. I should've, but *oh my God*, even with the world I grew up in, I didn't see that coming. She was off, but—I should've known. I should've. A few things make a lot more sense now. Did you know? Did you realize it wasn't her?"

I don't answer.

It's none of her business.

"Dylan." Mom hustles out of the house. "Oh, *honey*. Did you see Tavi's TikTok?"

I look at Phoebe again. "What'll happen to her?"

"From Gigi? No idea. She's a loose cannon. From the world? She'll have people who hate her and people who defend her. She'll get endorsement offers from companies looking to cash in from the news that she eats meat and sugar and lies in public. Probably a lot of investment offers for the farm. Zero Ducks. That's so Tavi."

"So she—she doesn't have to come back."

I didn't know it was possible to feel this level of grief with this level of pride.

Of course she's getting investment offers.

I've gotten investment offers based off a handful of TikToks going viral. Tavi Lightly? Imploding her brand like that and being the bold, badass lady boss that's been hiding under all her flaky public layers for years?

She'll never have to worry about her farm again.

"Don't think for one minute her leaving is about you," Phoebe says quietly. "Our lives—the way we were raised—the things we were taught—she hasn't let me all the way in, but I promise you, she didn't leave here as happily or as easily as she would've a month ago. You matter to her. Give her time. If I know *anything* about business and publicity, she has her hands full right now."

"Oh my," my mom whispers.

I glance up at her, and she immediately shoves her phone in her pocket. "Nothing. It's nothing."

Phoebe sighs. "And speaking of publicity, here's the bigger reason I'm here . . ."

I wait, my heart in my throat.

"There's a very high likelihood that since Tavi discovered you and helped make you semifamous, you'll get a few more nasty comments on your social media feeds for being associated with her. Especially since someone posted a picture last night of you carrying her out of the school. It's not like the *Tickled Pink Papers*, where we could control how much it spreads. It was an outsider. The world's going to put two and two together and realize that wasn't actually Tavi, and it looks like you didn't know."

Fuck.

Did Tavi see that too?

I drop my head into my hands and tell myself she's not sitting somewhere in Costa Rica thinking I could know her and love her and not realize that woman last night was a fake.

But does she know I love her?

Does she?

"I know *she* won't take my money," Phoebe continues, "but I'm happy to hire you an assistant for as long as you need to deal with the potential fallout. I know someone who's good with PR. She'd probably be willing to work for the whole town for a while."

I glance up at her. "Like Tavi and Lola were supposed to."

She rolls her eyes. "Don't go there. Tavi didn't *want* to be an influencer any more than I *want* to fall in Deer Drop Lake again. She's doing what she's supposed to do in Costa Rica. So let me do what I do best and micromanage the rest of you, mmkay?"

"I don't care what they say about me, and if Tavi thinks for one minute that I would've slept with a woman who wasn't her—"

"Dylan, we Lightlys have trust issues. She'll know. And I highly doubt she would've hired someone to play her without making sure that person knew to keep her hands off Tavi's man."

"You."

I look past Phoebe at the sound of Estelle's voice. The older woman is charging up my walk, fury evident in her tight features and clipped walk. "Where is she?" Estelle demands.

"Not the way to heaven, Gigi," Phoebe murmurs.

Estelle ignores her and glares at me with the heat of a thousand suns. "Where. Is. That. Woman?"

I rise and glare right back. "Leave," I growl.

"You will tell me where that woman is right now, *or else.*" The damn woman stands even taller, and I feel something primal and ugly and irrepressible that I haven't felt in years.

I feel rage.

Pure, undeniable, furious rage. I take a single step toward her and stop.

"Dylan," my mother whispers.

I think.

Can't fully hear over the roaring in my own ears. "You are a fucking nuisance," I growl at the old lady. "Do you have any idea how many people you've hurt by trying to play God? I'm *glad* Tavi's gone. I'm *glad* she's done with you. You don't fucking deserve her. You think you saw the gates of hell when you almost died? You don't know hell. You don't have a fucking clue what hell really is. You have twenty-four hours to publicly apologize to your entire family, leave Tickled Pink, and transfer Tavi's entire trust fund back to her with zero obligations, terms, or restrictions, or I will make every last minute of your life a living, breathing, inescapable hell. Are we clear?"

Her eyes flare wide, and she stumbles three steps backward.

"Dylan." My name in my mother's voice echoes through the tunnel of rage flowing through my veins.

Should I shut up?

Go meditate?

Take a run?

Talk to a friend?

No.

Not for this.

This is Tavi's *life*, and *fuck* if I'll stand aside one more minute to let this demon in a grandmother's clothing hurt the woman I love.

I don't care if Tavi doesn't come back.

I can deal with the pain if I know she's safe.

But I can't deal with myself if I don't put an end to Estelle Lightly's reign of terror.

"Are. We. Clear?" I repeat to the ever-shrinking older woman.

"Sounded clear to me," Michael Lightly says. I jerk my head up, surprised to see more people funneling down my driveway and onto my walkway.

Tunnel vision.

I have tunnel vision when I'm pissed.

And I am *so fucking pissed*.

Michael takes a step back, too, holding his hands up as if to say, *I'm harmless. I'm on your side.* "If she won't help, I will. I might look useless, but I know a thing or two about financial law and loopholes. Found what I needed. I can get Tavi her trust fund back if my mother doesn't come to her senses."

"Happy to help with hell," Carter adds.

"Oh my *gah*, Dylan, you are, like, *a hero*." Lola swipes at her eyes. "I'm so glad Tavi has you."

"He's not being unreasonable, Gigi," Phoebe says. "Tavi *is* a good person. She *is* doing good things in the world, and she was before she got here. I deserved all those times I fell in the lake and more. But Tavi? She's always known who we are. Looks a lot like you couldn't stand the fact that she taught *herself* to be better than we were raised. That's not really the path to heaven, is it?"

I can't stop clenching and unclenching my hands. My chest is heaving. I want to throw something.

Preferably Estelle.

Right into the lake.

"I'm going to go sit in my garden." I sound like a fucking demon myself. "Apologize. Leave. Trust fund."

I turn on my heel and stride off my driveway and toward the back of my house, but I don't make it four steps before Hannah's in my way.

Jesus fucking Christ. "Move."

Her brown eyes waver, and she visibly swallows. "Oh God, Dylan, don't—"

"Go home. You're married with a baby on the way. I am *not* your project anymore."

Your project.

I was Hannah's project. I was. I was a habit. A project. And then she was done with me.

Then I was Tavi's project.

But Tavi—

Tavi makes me okay. *All* of me.

Not because I'm her project but because she *gets* it. She's everything that's ever been missing in my life.

And I hope—*I hope*—that I'm everything she needs to complete hers.

I turn and point at Phoebe.

Teague's arrived too. He growls at me.

I growl right back, then point at Phoebe again. "You. With me. Be useful."

Teague growls once more.

And I don't care.

I don't fucking care.

I need to get to Tavi, and I will take advantage of every resource at my disposal to find her. *Now.*

Chapter 37

Tavi

There are people here, but I don't know who they are, because my ears are crossed.

Happens in mornings sometimes. It's like my eyes being crossed, except with my ears.

Also?

I hate that I still hate mornings in Costa Rica.

But. *But.*

I imploded my life, so I don't have to get up, ever again, no matter what the voices say. I can sleep for *days*. That almost makes me smile as I roll over in bed and come nose to fur with Pebbles.

"Mmphle," I murmur into her tiny little body. She squirms and licks my face.

And then I freeze.

Make myself pry open one eyelid and peer at the blurry, furry figure currently trying to climb my head. *"Pebb?"* I croak.

She yips.

Am I dreaming?

Is Pebbles *here*? She's supposed to be—wait. *Wait.*

I bolt straight upright, feel my brain bounce against my skull, and then feel it scream in protest. My brain is *loud* this morning. So loud it's drowning out the soft hum of voices somewhere beyond my bedroom at the farm. And my head is swimming. And it's hot in here. And I don't remember the last time I ate, but I remember it was delicious.

Not delicious enough to keep me from falling back against the bed with a groan, though. Mornings are the work of the devil.

"You're awake," a husky voice says nearby.

Pebbles leaps back onto my chest and licks my neck while I process that sound.

I am definitely dreaming.

I have to be.

Because there's no way Dylan's in my bedroom in Costa Rica.

Am I in my bedroom in Costa Rica? Did I fly here? Did my mother ruin my business meeting? Did I post that video telling my family to fuck off and confessing all my sins to the world before insisting Naomi drive me back to the farm so I could die here in peace?

Or was it all a dream?

I'm not still in Tickled Pink, am I?

"Naomi says you haven't had anything to drink or eat since you went to bed the night before last," Dylan says. "C'mon, Tavi. You can go back to sleep after you have some water and a little food."

I force myself to pry both eyes open, and a sexy, rumple-haired, five-o'clock-shadowed, dimpled plumber with the kindest worried brown eyes slowly swims into focus before Pebbles climbs onto my face, blocking my view.

My heart hiccups. My eyes burn. My throat gets thick.

If *this* is a dream, I'm disowning my subconscious and never sleeping again. I try—and fail—to lift my dog away. My arm's asleep, and I can't figure out how to work the other one. "Dylan?"

"I'm right here, my beautiful badass."

Pebbles disappears, and there he is again, squatting at the side of my bed so that we're eye level.

There's a breeze rolling in through the window, fluttering the light curtain, the shadows suggesting it's much later in the day than I thought it was. A monkey chatters somewhere outside. The scent of fresh bread wafts into my room.

And there's Dylan, touching a hesitant hand to my hair. "Hi," he whispers.

"You're here," I whisper back.

"I'm here."

"But . . . *why?*"

"I take care of the people I love. I didn't know how to do that without being here with you."

My eyes burn hotter. "I lied to you."

"I forgive the people I love too." One side of his mouth hitches up.

I do not deserve this man. I don't.

"Drink." He holds a straw to my lips. "We can talk later."

I obey for a short sip of coconut-flavored water, tingles racing up my arm as it comes back to consciousness. Pebbles wriggles and twists in Dylan's other arm. "Sam," I blurt.

"She's here too. Safe and sound."

Thank God. I let my eyelids flutter closed while my eyes leak. "Good."

"More water, Tavi. And Juliana sent banana bread."

I whimper. Juliana's one of the locals who welcomed us with open arms, and she makes the best banana bread.

"Smells better than microwave breakfast sandwiches," he adds.

"I don't deserve you."

He growls softly, and my nipples stand at attention. "Pebbles, go find Naomi," he says.

The bed sags next to me, and then his body lines up with mine. "Open your eyes," he orders.

I pry them back open. My cheeks are wet. My mouth is dry, and my breath smells awful, even to me. I still can't move my arms.

And Dylan's right there, nose to nose with me, those beautiful brown eyes deep and serious. "You deserve every good thing in the whole fucking world."

I blink back tears again. *"I lied to you."*

"Did you?"

"That was Sam who almost stepped in front of the garbage truck that first time you thought you saw me after the locker room thing," I whisper.

He blinks once, then grins. "So you kept ducking me because she started it."

This man. He *gets* me. "I faked my ankle injury, and I knew for a week I was leaving and didn't tell you."

"You never told *me* your ankle was hurt. Did you not tell me you were leaving because you didn't trust me or because you didn't want me to have to carry the secret?"

"Stop it."

His brows go up.

"Stop excusing me for doing terrible things," I whisper.

"Will you trust me next time?"

"There won't *be* a next time. It's over. I'm not going back. I *refuse* to go back. I hate being somewhere that I have to play all of those games to please people who will never be happy, no matter what I do. I'm never going anywhere or doing anything where I have to lie to anyone ever again."

"Your grandmother's leaving Tickled Pink."

My gasp of surprise comes all the way from the deepest part of my soul. *"What?"*

"And your father filed legal paperwork to remove her as the custodian of your trust fund so that you can get it back."

"I don't want their fucking money."

"He told me to tell you that you can have a third of his too. All he asks in return is that you let him know sometime where you donated it."

I stare at him, more tears leaking out of my eyes. *"Why?"*

"Seems he paid enough attention to know a little something about who you are and what you'll do with money you don't want. Carter's getting a third, and Phoebe's getting the other third. Guess it's true what they say about money not buying happiness."

"He's giving some of his trust fund to Phoebe?"

"Yep."

"Does she know?"

"According to the *Tickled Pink Papers*, he made her cry over lunch at Ladyfingers. Then they shared an awkward hug at the end of the meal."

"Oh my God."

"He's staying in Tickled Pink. Says he's not done with whatever he needs to do. Heard Carter's been released to do whatever he feels like he needs to do too."

I squeeze my eyes shut.

I will not be jealous of my brother. I will not be jealous of my brother.

"Tavi," Dylan whispers.

I squeeze my eyes shut harder.

I don't want him to see me being a terrible person. *Again.*

"You remember what you told me about cocoa beans growing into trees?" He brushes a kiss to my forehead. "I hate that they hurt you, but I'm so fucking proud of everything you've done to turn yourself into that delicious truffle that you are today. You're fucking amazing, Tavi. So fucking amazing."

"I love you," I blurt.

His body sags. "Thank fuck," he whispers, his voice thick. Then he's pulling me close, my nose smushed against his soft T-shirt, kissing my hair, my ear, my temple, while his arms tighten around me. "I love you too. So much. *So* much."

I'm what I would've formerly called a disaster. My hair's a mess. No makeup. I can finally move my arms again, but they're still tingling from getting blood flow back. I'm ugly-sobbing, because that's apparently what you do when you realize there's someone who sees all the not-perfect parts of you and chooses to love you—all of you—not just *anyway* but *because* they know all those not-perfect parts help make up all of who you are.

But I won't call myself a disaster.

For the first time in my life, I'm simply *real*.

And he sees me.

And he loves me.

The *real* me.

I didn't need to go to Tickled Pink to find my soul.

I needed to go to Tickled Pink to find *me*.

"*Oh my God*, are you hurting her?" Naomi shrieks. "I told you to let her sleep! She hasn't slept in three months! Stop. *Stop!*"

Dylan freezes. I fling my arm around him and squeeze him tight. "He's not hurting me," I sob.

"*You're crying!*"

"*I'm happy!*"

"Oh." There's a very long pause. Then—"Is this always what you do when you're happy?"

"I don't know."

"Well, this is suddenly complicated. Do I tell you more good news now, or do I wait until you're not crying?"

Dylan shifts on the bed, turning me so that I can see Naomi while he peers over his shoulder at her too. "Might as well test it. We should know what we're getting into."

Naomi grins. "We have our choice of financial backers for Zero Ducks Chocolates, and none of them are related to you. But we might not need them at all, since I put a 'Donate to Help Save the Zero Ducks

Farm' button on your links page, and people like the Tavi Lightly who doesn't give any ducks. So basically, you saved the farm."

I stare at her.

She grins bigger.

Dylan aims his dimples at me too.

"We saved the farm?" I whisper.

"*You* saved the farm," Naomi replies. "There's a lot more—like inquiries about joining our marketing and PR teams whenever we get those up and running, and Fitzwilliam Hawthorne dropped by yesterday while you were sleeping to try our truffles and wants to help us expand, too, but it turns out he dabbles in making chocolate, too, and I don't know if we can handle two chefs in the kitchen, but— okay, I'm shutting up now, because you look like you're going to cry yourself inside out. Point is, good news. Go back to sleep. Or kissing Dylan. Or whatever. The rest of us have the farm under control until you're ready. I'll tell Sam you said hi. She's hanging here for a few days. And we'll take care of Pebbles. You just worry about you. Okay. Okay. Bye."

"Naomi."

"What?"

"Ask Sam how much money she needs to take care of her mom for the rest of her life. I got my trust fund back, and I—I—"

Shit.

I can't say it.

"No crying," Naomi orders. "That's so horribly mean of you to burden Sam with financial security for herself and her mom. Just awful, Tavi."

I stare at her for a second.

She quirks a grin, and it's so perfectly Naomi that I actually crack up.

"And now that we have that settled . . ." She pulls the door shut.

I look at Dylan, who's up on one elbow on my bed, watching me with concern etched in his eyes, his hair tumbling over his forehead, his shirt rumpled, and every bit of his aura hugging me tight.

For a split second, I think I might burst into tears all over again.

But I don't want to cry.

I want to do something else.

Chapter 38

Dylan

Tavi's always been beautiful, but with her eyes lit up in sheer joy and that smile threatening to burst, she's gorgeous.

She scoots closer to the center of the bed, giving me more room as she crooks a finger to beckon me to follow. "You're my favorite part of today."

My heart has never felt more full.

More *right*.

I follow her deeper onto the bed, watching her breasts sway under her Tickled Pink T-shirt, wondering what she's wearing under the light sheet covering her from the hips down. "You're my favorite everything."

"Thank you for believing in me."

It's the last thing she says before wrapping her arms around my neck and pulling me down for a long, slow, deep kiss that has my head spinning. She's raw and earthy and warm and soft, and she's *mine*.

Mine to protect.

Mine to support.

Mine to love.

Her hands slide down my chest and slip under the hem of my shirt. "I wanted to tell you, but I didn't want to ask you to keep that secret," she says against my lips.

"I know, Tavi. I know."

"You make me feel like I can do anything."

"You can."

Together, we pull my shirt over my head, and then she's kissing me again, her hands roaming over my bare skin like she needs to reassure herself that I'm all here, like it's been so long since she touched me that she has to memorize the feel of me all over again.

Or maybe that's why I'm touching her bare skin under her shirt.

To assure myself that *this* is my Tavi.

To prove to her that I'll be here, by her side, no matter where she is in the world, no matter if she finds a new mission in life once Zero Ducks is up and running.

Somehow, I don't think she'll be satisfied saving one little piece of the earth.

I suspect she'll want to save it all.

"Oh God, Dylan, I missed you so much," she gasps as I find the tips of her breasts and brush them with my thumbs.

"I was with you the whole time. You have my heart, Tavi. You always have my heart." I push her shirt up and worship them with my mouth instead, then twist her by the shoulder, tug her shirt the rest of the way off, and kiss that beautiful birthmark on her shoulder blade. "And I missed you too, Dolly."

She laughs.

God, she has the best laugh.

"You missed Dolly?"

"I am *so* happy to see her again."

She wriggles until she's pushing me back onto the bed, straddling me in nothing but her simple white cotton panties. "I love you," she whispers.

I palm her cheek. "I love you."

She bends and kisses my neck, my collarbone, my tattoo, and then her fingers are on the button on my shorts. "And I think it's about time we try this again, don't you?"

She doesn't wait for an answer before she's reaching into my shorts to stroke my cock.

My eyes slide shut, and I tilt my hips into her touch, losing myself in the feel of her hands and the cool breeze on my suddenly bare skin. She tugs my shorts down, one hand still stroking me, and then she licks me.

My hips buck off the bed, and I almost come on the spot. "Oh, *fuck*, Tavi," I gasp.

For all the times we rolled around in the choir loft, she didn't try to go down on me again.

"Do you want me to stop?" she whispers, her breath hot against my cock.

I grit my teeth and fight for control.

One lick.

One goddamn lick, and I'm nearly coming. "I want you to do anything you want to do," I tell her.

"Anything?"

"I'm yours, Tavi. All yours."

"Good." She licks me again, then sucks my head into her hot, slick mouth, swirling her tongue around me, and *oh my fucking heaven*.

I curl my fists into her hair while she rides me with her mouth, my neck straining with the effort of not blowing my load.

This feels so good.

So fucking good.

Her mouth—her tongue—the way she sucks and licks and bobs—"*Tavi.*"

She sucks me deep into her mouth again. "Hm?"

"Not—want—out—you—"

357

She sucks harder.

My balls tighten and my cock aches and every ounce of me wants to let go.

I wrench open my eyes and look down at her.

She lifts her eyes, her mouth still wrapped around my cock, and she smiles at me with those baby blues like she knows exactly what she's doing.

"Want—you—feel good—too," I grunt out as I struggle to keep my hips from bucking.

She presses her tongue against the underside of my dick, and I go light headed from the effort of not coming.

This woman—I plan to make love to her every single day for the rest of my life.

I can come.

I can.

But I want to come with her.

So I grunt again, and with superhuman strength, I twist my hips and pull out of her mouth.

"Dylan," she chides, lips going pouty, but her eyes are still sparkling with amusement and something else.

Desire.

"Strip your panties off." My voice is hoarse and my boner is howling in outrage, and when Tavi pushes up onto her knees and hooks her thumbs into the waistband of her simple panties, my mouth goes dry.

"Like this?" she asks, rolling her hips side to side, and she inches her panties down bit by bit until I can see all of her pussy.

I grip my cock, still wet from her tongue, and order him to wait. Her breasts are full, tipped with dark-pink nipples, her chest rising and falling, her eyes getting dark with need.

"Oh, are we doing this?" she adds, slipping two fingers into her own pussy.

I growl.

I *cannot* hold out much longer.

Need to be inside her.

Need her *now*.

I snag her by the waist and pull her against me, twist, and then she's beneath me. "I love you," I tell her.

She wraps her legs around my waist and tilts her hips, rubbing her pussy against my cock. "I love you."

I love you.

So few letters to convey the biggest joy in the world.

She squeezes those strong legs tighter, rolling her hips as I shift to position myself at her entrance. "I can't go slow," I tell her.

"I don't want *slow*. I want *you*."

It's all the permission I need to slam into her, a shudder ripping through me as I realize I'm home.

Tavi is home.

"Oh God, *Dylan*," she gasps as I pull out and slam into her again. "I love you. *I love you*."

"Love—you," I grunt, pumping faster and faster, my cock aching harder and harder. "Love you—so—much."

She matches my rhythm, her eyes glittering and dark, her lips parted, making those noises I love so much when I find the right spot and stroke her there over and over until I'm sweating and gasping from holding back my own release.

"There, Dylan. *There*. Oh my God, I love you. I love you so much."

I slam into her once more, and then she's crying my name as her walls squeeze around me, and I finally let go with a roar.

Fuck, she feels so good.

So right.

So worth every minute of my life to find *this* moment.

I'm coming fast and desperate, spilling all of myself deep inside of her, my cock pulsing harder than I've ever come before. "Love you," I gasp.

I can't stop saying it.

I love her so much. I *need* her so much.

She's made me believe I *am* the man I want to be, and she makes me believe I can do anything.

I collapse on top of her as small aftershocks run through my body, and a moment later, her legs fall slack and her head drops back to the bed.

"Dylan?"

"Yes, my love?"

"That was incredible."

"It's all you."

She laughs softly. "I think it's *us*."

"I suppose the point could be argued."

"I want to go to sleep," she whispers.

"Food and water first."

"Stay with me?"

"Forever, Tavi. I'll stay with you forever."

Chapter 39

Tavi

It's remarkable how much can change in just a few months.

The things that matter. Where my heart is. What I want to do with my life.

I thought I had it all figured out before Gigi called and demanded I move to Tickled Pink if I wanted to keep my trust fund, but life changed, so I changed.

And I don't regret a minute.

Not even the especially wild whirlwind that's been the last several days. Hard to believe it wasn't quite a week ago that I faked my sprained ankle and thought I'd never be back in Tickled Pink again in my life.

"You're on my shit list," Shiloh Denning tells me with a scowl.

I smile.

Not a fake smile either.

The *real*-me smile. "I heard I would be. Happy birthday."

Bridget giggles next to me. "Don't listen to her," she whispers loudly. "She *loooooves* it."

"If she doesn't now, she will once she gets all of her birthday presents," I whisper loudly back, gesturing to a table near the door that might not be big enough for all the gifts people have brought. "I brought her an exclusive private batch of Zero Ducks peanut butter cups."

Heard a very reliable rumor that peanut butter and chocolate are her kryptonite.

Shiloh grunts and stalks away to glare at Jane and Gibson, who are running the beer taps and the music in one corner of the largest room in the almost fully renovated community center. Multicolored streamers and balloons line the walls and ceilings, fanning out from a disco ball slowly spinning in the center of the room.

The caterers have tables lining two of the walls with everything from fried cheese curds, which I will 1,000 percent be trying tonight, to stuffed brie bites and shrimp cocktails, which I will also be enjoying without hesitation. It's a low-key menu compared to what I would've had catered if I were throwing a party for an acquaintance in New York or Los Angeles—not to mention the overabundance of meat, fish, dairy, and sugar—but it fits here.

The cake, though—for the birthday cake, I totally called in a favor. A *big* favor.

Not everyone gets a birthday cake flown in from LA's top baker, but cake isn't something you scrimp on.

"Oh my *gah*, Tavi, I didn't think you'd come back, but *here you are*." Lola launches herself at me and hugs me tight. It's a little like being hugged by a gazelle that smells like she slept in a rosebush.

My eye twitches, but I ignore it and hug her back. "Thanks, Lola."

"When I found out your grandmother had put those listening thingies in your room, I got *so mad*. Like, what kind of grandmother *does* that? I thought she was so nice, inviting me here, and then—"

"And now she's gone," Dylan interrupts, slipping a hand to the small of my back as he joins me in the main room of the community center that Gigi insisted on renovating before she departed Tickled Pink a couple of days ago.

I look up at him. "*Gigi* put those listening devices in my room?"

"That's what Teague told me. Guess he got a chance to talk to her before she left. Fried cheese curd?" He lifts the plate.

Lola squeals. "They are *so good*, Tavi. Like, *oh my gaaaah* good."

I eyeball everything on the plate he's brought. Small round fried things—definitely fried cheese curds. There's a pinwheel-looking thing that seems to be made of deli meat and cream cheese, and I won't lie—I have a minute of *I approved that on the menu?*

But these are the birthday girl's favorite foods. As are the veggies and ranch dip. The cheese cubes. Something that looks like a miniature shrunken hot dog wrapped in bacon.

My hand hovers over the plate. "There's too much to choose from."

"Definitely the cheese curd." He plucks one off the plate and pops it into my mouth, and *oh my God.*

Lola's right.

Melty cheesy goodness inside a perfectly fried shell? I whimper.

Dylan makes a strangled noise and lowers the plate to his waist.

Whoops.

Here I thought shower sex in his perfect little Hallmark Channel house right before the party would keep him from having any obvious issues in public.

He clears his throat. "You're staying, Lola?"

She chews on her bottom lip and glances between us, and for the first time in my life, I see her in a different light.

She's lost.

She's completely and totally *lost.*

She *is* me. The me I used to be, anyway.

All this time I've hated her for being my competition, when really, we're not all that different at all. We were taught to compete against each other.

What if we'd been taught to support each other instead?

"You should stay," I tell her. "Tickled Pink is—it's got this *magic*. For all of the places in the world that I've been—that we've *both* been— there's nowhere else like it, is there?"

She shifts a look around. "You know the *Tickled Pink Papers*?" she whispers.

I nod.

"I tripped over a goat in the square the other day while I was . . ." She drops her voice even lower. "While I was wearing a *wig*, with, like, *tons* of people around, like some tourists and, like, some locals, and my wig *totally* fell off, and everyone was super nice and friendly, and then the next day, there was a new *Tickled Pink Papers*, and it was, like, all about how Phoebe dumped soup down her blouse. Not a word about my . . . issue. Even though I think I know who prints the *Tickled Pink Papers*, and they were there, and I know they got a picture."

"People here have good hearts," Dylan says. "We're not one size fits all when it comes to dealing with intruding rich people."

I woke up in his arms yesterday morning, realized what day it was, and told him we had to come back here, that I had to finish up Ridhi's favor myself despite how much I passed off to my socials team. Naomi wanted to come, too, but she's tied up with Fitzwilliam Hawthorne, who's passed all my initial gut checks and who actually knows a thing or two about chocolate, even though I suspect we'll have a few arguments here and there about recipes and flavors of the month.

But also?

I'd rather have one more person on my team who I appreciate and respect and who wants Zero Ducks to succeed than insist I do it all by myself.

I *like* being part of a team.

I also like being in Tickled Pink. It's different being here when I'm here because I *want* to be and know that I can leave anytime.

It's also different being here and letting myself look at the town through Dylan's eyes.

He says he'll move to Costa Rica for me.

I feel like we can find a better compromise than all in at one place or the other. This is his home, after all. And he still loves it.

And I do want to show it to Naomi someday.

"That's like . . ." Lola shoots a glance at me. "People aren't nice like that where we come from."

"They aren't," I agree.

"I want to be around nice people. I want—I want what you have. Friends that you can really count on. Siblings who have your back. Knowing who you are."

I surprise myself by hugging her again. Is she playing me? I don't know. But I know what it's like to be lost. I know what it's like to hate the role I have to play. If there's any kernel of truth in anything she's confessing right now, then doesn't she deserve another chance too? And if she is playing me, the joke's on her.

Lola Minelli can't hurt me.

No one can unless I let them. "You know my family was never perfect, right?"

"But look at you now. You and Phoebe and even Carter . . . and, like, my father would *never* stand up to my mother if she ever took away my trust fund." She pulls back and waves her hands at her eyes. "I'm happy for you, Tavi. And you give me hope. Thank you. I'm going to go . . ."

She flaps her hands somewhere across the room, like she's embarrassed herself and wants to leave but can't find a quick escape, and a flash of blonde catches my eye across the room. I stifle a surprised gasp and inch closer to Dylan.

"Is that your mother?" he murmurs.

I nod as Lola waves at someone and dashes off.

"What's she doing back here?"

"Looking for where she fits," Phoebe says on his other side. She peers around him at me. "Apparently she's been lost without Dad, and whatever you said to her in Costa Rica was a wake-up call."

I process that for a minute. I was so mad I don't even remember what I said. It's like this blank spot in my head.

I haven't seen my dad since Dylan and I got back early today either. Partially because I've been busy, and partially because I don't know what to say to the man who's waited thirty years to show the first bit of interest in being a father.

Do I want to see my mom if she's willing to accept me—no, *celebrate* me for who I am?

I don't know.

I know so many of my issues with her are things I can't fix, but I also know she never knew any better. My mom coming back to Tickled Pink voluntarily?

This is unexpected.

It's like a vegan sugar-free social media fitness guru throwing it all away in the name of chocolate and cheeseburgers.

And speaking of—I grab the pinwheel thing to test it out. "How are you and Dad?" I ask Phoebe before biting into the thing.

"Weird," she replies. "Like maybe we could become adult acquaintances who might possibly have made the wrong assumptions about each other for a very long time and who are willing to acknowledge that we could have some kind of a relationship if we give each other the benefit of the doubt."

I nod as I swallow the odd but strangely good concoction. "That would be an improvement, wouldn't it?"

"You don't heal thirty years' worth of shit in a summer. But it's a start."

I nod again.

I don't think Gigi knew what she was doing when she ordered all of us to come here, but it's turned out pretty well for both Phoebe and me. And maybe it'll end up being good for our parents in the long run.

Possibly Lola too.

And honestly? I hope it does.

"I take it Carter left town?" I ask.

"He says he's staying at the school now that there's only Lola intruding on his time and he doesn't think she'll stick around. And speaking of," she adds as Teague joins us, "Gigi asked me to give you this." She slips a small, elegant envelope out of her back pocket. "Completely up to you if you read it or burn it. I didn't snoop. I have no idea what it says."

I take the elegant linen envelope and glance down at my own outfit.

Halter top cropped just above my belly button, tight black pants, and stilettos.

Not a pocket in sight, and I left Pebbles at Dylan's house, so I'm sans bag as well.

"Want me to hold that?" he asks.

"And maybe read it and tell me if I should too?"

He kisses my temple. "If that's what you want."

"Is that totally wimpy of me?"

"You don't have to open yourself up to letting the same people hurt you over and over again, Tavi."

"You're a very smart man."

"He is, isn't he?" His mom beams at me as she approaches us too. She's informed us that she's moving into an apartment with a friend—a single *lady* friend, she says—to give us more privacy when we're in Tickled Pink. And while I know she'd probably be happy to have Dylan dating *anyone* at this point, I also think we'll become real friends very quickly. "And so happy. Look at that face. Don't you want to just eat it up, it's so happy?"

Oh, she made him blush.

This is truly adorable.

I go up on my tiptoes to kiss his cheek. "I do, in fact."

"Enough, both of you. Tavi, eat. Mom, Marta's waving at you. Go say hi."

She squints at him. "Marta told me you told Hannah she should go to marital counseling with Andrew."

"Yep."

"That's borderline rude, Dylan."

"People shouldn't constantly bitch about the people they're married to and having babies with, and I wouldn't be a good friend if I didn't express some concern about that."

"You're staying friends?"

"We're staying people who used to be really close but have very different lives now."

I squeeze his waist.

Am I jealous of Hannah? I have my moments. Still human here.

But am I worried that Dylan would cheat on me with her or leave me for her?

Not at all.

"For what it's worth," his mom whispers with a wink at me, "I always hoped he'd do better. Good to see he was holding out for it."

"*Mom.*"

"I'm going, I'm going." She hugs me quickly before dashing off to chat with Hannah's mom.

We spend the next couple of hours mingling with the party guests. Dylan keeps a full plate in front of him at all times for me to graze off, laughs and jokes with his friends and neighbors, and growls anytime anyone asks me anything that could be viewed as judgypants about my diet.

Shiloh seems to enjoy herself.

Ridhi informs me my debt has been paid and that I even earned myself a coffee on her tomorrow morning. Vegan or otherwise.

That envelope in the back of Dylan's pocket sits on my mind the entire time.

Pretty sure he knows it, because shortly after Shiloh blows out her candles, he nudges me out the back door.

There's a patio back here, with groups of people hanging out at the wrought iron tables beneath strings of fairy lights. We find a quiet bench barely still under the light, and he silently hands me the envelope.

"How did you know?" I ask him.

"You kept staring at my ass and frowning. It usually makes you smile."

Okay, *that's* worth a smile.

He wraps an arm around me while I lift the flap and pull out a matching linen note.

> Octavia,
> It's never easy to admit when I'm wrong, but I have been wrong about you. I put my desire for control above my willingness to see you for the kindhearted human being that you've become in your years away from the family. Instead of looking deeper when I insisted you come to Tickled Pink, I let myself believe you were nothing more than the spoiled brat I would have been in your shoes, and that the image you presented to the world was all there was to you.
>
> I owe you an apology.
>
> Your trust fund has been released. I've temporarily left Tickled Pink for a private soul-searching retreat without attempting to run anyone else's lives, and to give you time to make decisions about your future without interference or judgment.

I hope to someday earn your trust enough to fully hear your story and how you came to rise above all that you were raised to be.

Gigi

I read it three times, my heart pounding first in fear, then in vindication, and finally in sadness before I hand it back to Dylan.

He doesn't say anything. Simply kisses my hair again and waits.

"I want to be furious with her," I finally say, "but if she hadn't been such a controlling, manipulative asshole, I wouldn't have you."

"Maybe don't tell her that if we ever see her again."

I laugh. "That part was understood."

"Tavi?" someone hisses behind us. *"Tavi. Dylan."*

We both turn.

Willie Wayne's lurking in the shadows, making the *come here* gesture. I lift my brows at Dylan.

He shrugs like he has no idea what's up, but he rises, pockets Gigi's letter again for me, and offers me a hand.

"Quick," Willie Wayne hisses.

We slip off the patio and into the darkness. Willie Wayne grabs each of us by the arm and tugs us deeper into the shadows, out into the woods behind the community center. "Don't trip," he whispers.

"Some light would help," I whisper back.

"Don't sound like Phoebe. You'll ruin it."

"Don't be a dick, Double Dub," Dylan whispers.

We take three more steps, and then a flashlight flicks on and shines right at us.

I wince and throw up an arm. "Where are we?"

"Hurry up," Jane hisses. "Before someone sees."

Wait. Jane's here?

She points the flashlight at the ground, and the light gives off enough of an ambient glow to illuminate one other person with her.

"Ah, hell, you aren't," Dylan says.

"Shush. You don't get a vote," Ridhi replies.

Willie Wayne shoves me forward.

Jane links her arm into mine. Ridhi does the same on the other side.

"Am I in trouble?" I whisper. "I thought you liked the party."

"Shush," she repeats.

"Octavia Lightly," Willie Wayne says in front of me, holding the flashlight now high enough to illuminate all of us, "in recognition of your outstanding service to the people of Tickled Pink, your easy acceptance of all of us who don't fit a standard mold, the fact that you make the best chocolate in all of existence, and in gratitude for your silence in regards to the Tickled Pink Secret Poker Society, by the power vested in me as president of the TPSPS, I hereby present to you your own key to the bunker."

My jaw drops, and once more, my throat clogs and my eyes get hot.

Dylan's grinning at me.

Jane and Ridhi both drop my arms and do a quiet golf clap.

Willie Wayne hands Dylan the flashlight, then steps forward to hang a ribbon around my neck, an old key dangling from it. "You're gonna have to take that off before you go back to the party," he whispers.

"Naturally."

He shakes my hand. "Welcome to the Secret Poker Society. Your job is refreshments and not talking during games. Or playing, if we're being honest. You're really bad."

Jane hugs me. "Don't fuck this up."

Ridhi hugs me too. "Be good to Dylan too."

Dylan hugs me, whispers, "Guess you're right. We definitely need to split our time between your place and mine," and then kisses me.

"And none of that in the bunker," Willie Wayne adds.

"Unspoken rule," Ridhi says.

Jane pokes us both. "Make us say it again, and we'll move the bunker and change the key."

I contemplate the logistics of that for half a second, and I snort-laugh and pull out of the kiss.

"We'll also move the bunker and change the key if you don't bring Dylan home to us often enough. We need this guy around here too. Understand?"

Dylan goes momentarily stiff, and then he releases me to hug Willie Wayne.

That man. He's still figuring out how much he's loved here.

I thought I knew what home was, but I really only knew part of it.

Naomi and the farm will forever be my home.

But Dylan is my heart, and Tickled Pink is the other home I never knew I needed. I intend to spend every minute of the rest of my life making sure everyone I love knows how much they're loved too.

Epilogue

Dylan

Travel's never been something I've done frequently, and vacations have usually been a week here or a week there.

Spending three weeks in Costa Rica with Tavi, learning all about her farm, getting to know Naomi, and meeting the locals, who adore both of the women, fills my soul with more joy than I ever thought possible. I miss work, though I suspect I'll find plenty of people who need plumbing help around Tavi's farm as I spend more time there.

For now, we're back in Tickled Pink for the next two weeks. I've spent the morning on jobs that the plumbers in Deer Drop who I called for backup haven't gotten to yet, followed by lunch with my mom at Ladyfingers talking through the applications I got for a full-time employee to cover when I'm gone with Tavi and help when I'm in town, and now I'm paused in the square, looking at the new construction that's started for the Ferris wheel that Phoebe's putting in.

"Looks good," Teague says, stopping next to me.

I flex my muscles. "I do, don't I?"

No one gives the *don't be a dumbass* look like Teague Miller. I've missed him.

I grin at his royal grumpiness. "Still can't take a joke?"

"You're sleeping with my girlfriend's sister. You're officially on my potential shit list."

I give him back a taste of his own medicine with a glare. "You know what? *Same.*"

He grins back at me.

Fine. He can win this round.

"Heard Phoebe talked Floyd into renting her the church for a candy store," I say.

"Yep." He nods to a clump of tourists gathered at the fence blocking the construction zone. That's different too. Summer's nearly over, Estelle Lightly's still gone, yet the visitors are sticking around. "Told him she'd cut him in on the profits, too, if he manages the maintenance and cleaning for her."

"He take the deal?"

"Still thinking about it. Like Tavi's still thinking about if she'll let Phoebe sell Zero Ducks Chocolates in the candy store."

"She has a lot of offers."

"Phoebe's not gonna screw her over. And it'd be good for Tickled Pink."

"So you're adjusting to life with outsiders?"

"Easier with Estelle gone."

"Think she'll come back?"

"Yep."

"Damn."

"Yep."

Carter Lightly strolls up next to us. He nods to Teague, who nods back. Then he looks at me. "Heard you need an apprentice."

"Yep. You know someone?"

He stares at me. Has Tavi's eyes. Phoebe's build. Unruly brown hair. And an air about him that I recognize entirely too well, even if it's been a few years. "Me."

I do a double take.

Tavi hasn't talked about him much. Mostly just, "We're not tight, and he left New York as soon as he could, too, so maybe there's hope for him and he just doesn't let us in."

"Is your grandmother still keeping you here?" I ask him.

"Nope."

"And you want to learn to be a plumber."

"Yep."

I glance at Teague.

He looks just as mystified as I feel.

But who am I to judge anyone?

"How about you ride along this afternoon, and we—"

"Teague! Dylan!" Willie Wayne comes flying down the street, completely out of breath. He waves, hunches over, then waves again, this time behind himself. "Phoebe. Tavi. The church."

I don't stop to see if Teague follows.

Carter, either, for that matter.

If Tavi needs me at the church, that's where I'm going. *Now.*

I dive into my truck. Carter dives in too. Teague squeezes in with both of us, and the door's barely shut behind him before I'm roaring down the road.

The three blocks take an eternity, and when I get there, I slam on the brakes in the middle of the road, barely remember to put the truck in gear, and sprint up the steps, battling with Teague to get there first.

I burst inside, lungs heaving, heart in my chest, and then I hear it.

Laughter.

Not just any laughter either.

I'm talking full-belly, raucous, guffawing laughter.

All coming from the two sisters standing beside a taffy-pulling machine sitting where the preacher would've stood back when this was an actual church. "What—" I start.

Teague makes a noise but doesn't say anything else.

Our girlfriends have wrapped themselves together in a massive batch of taffy candy.

"Teague," Phoebe calls between gasps of laughter. "Do you—pocketknife?"

"How—" he says, then cuts himself off with a shake of his head.

Tavi's trying to wipe her eyes, but her arms are completely tangled in the long, thick pink rope that's rolling off a second machine with long rotating wooden cones. "We did it wrong," she gasps. "We needed the cutter at the end!"

"Don't turn that way!" Phoebe shrieks at her.

Tavi lifts part of the taffy rope and drapes it over Phoebe's head.

"Stop," Phoebe cries. She's trying to duck out of it, but that only seems to be making it worse as more taffy rope rolls off the roller machine.

They have taffy in their hair. Coating their clothing. Draped over their shoes. Around their necks.

Carter's staring while Teague and I cross the open floor to get to our ladies. "And this is why I said to wait for the person who'll show you how to use all of this equipment," Teague says, but his lips are twitching, and I give it thirty seconds before he's rolling with laughter too.

"Chocolate in the bedroom, yes. Taffy, no," I tell Tavi.

Her eyes are shiny with tears of laughter, and she's so damn gorgeous it almost hurts. "But I could tie you up."

"*Gah*, my ears," Phoebe says. "Oh my God, my stomach hurts."

Teague takes a pocketknife to one part of the taffy rope while I kill the power to the roller machine, then get to work helping pull it off and around the women to untangle them.

"Carter!" Tavi shrieks. "Stop taking pictures and come get us out of here!"

"I can't believe you two are the *smart* ones in the family," he mutters.

"We're the *fun* ones," Phoebe replies.

Tavi looks at her and snorts with laughter all over again.

Teague chokes on a laugh too.

Even Carter smiles.

They are, though. They might not have been a few months ago when they landed in Tickled Pink, but today?

The Lightly sisters are most definitely "the fun ones."

And I might be nothing more than a simple small-town plumber, but Tavi makes me feel like the richest man on earth.

I'll forever be rich in her love.

Wouldn't want my life any other way.

AUTHOR'S NOTE

Dear reader,

I had so much fun and all the feels while revisiting Tickled Pink, Wisconsin, and I hope you did too. Tavi and Dylan will forever hold a special place in my heart for reminding me that while we all screw up from time to time, life always holds new chances and opportunities, and also that it's sometimes most important for us to forgive ourselves first.

I promise to set a good example and make Tavi proud by forgiving myself for those four pounds I gained while sampling chocolates as part of my research while writing this book.

If you're new to the Pippaverse, I hope you'll check out my website for a full list of books, and if you're really ready to dive in for more fun and feels, sign up for my newsletter for regular visits with various characters from the Pippaverse, behind-the-scenes peeks, book recommendations of my favorite reads, and more fun.

Keep reading, and be fabulously, fearlessly you.

Pippa

ACKNOWLEDGMENTS

I can't start a list of acknowledgments without thanking *you* for returning to Tickled Pink with me! It's been a joy to explore this world, and I hope you've loved it too. Also, you're amazing, and you totally deserve that special treat you've been eyeing.

To Maria Gomez and Lindsey Faber, thank you for trusting me when I say things like, "This book doesn't have an ending yet, but that's what revisions are for, right?" I'm so grateful for your wisdom, your guidance, and the love you have for my characters. You've changed my writing world for the better, and I'll forever be grateful.

Jodi, Beth, and Jess, were it not for you, I'd probably be walking around the grocery store without pants on, muttering questions to random other shoppers about which aisle they store the plots in, because my brain could not keep up with both my business life and my personal life without the three of you to keep me organized. Thank you for holding me together and for your friendship and love.

Massive thanks to Becca Syme for creating the Better Faster Academy and helping me embrace my process, and to Elli at the Better Faster Academy for letting me borrow your brain.

To Jenn, Jenny, Tammy, Joyce, and the Pipsquad—thank you for your love and dedication to the Pippaverse! Without readers and friends like you, believing in me and cheering me on and sharing random memes that inevitably spark plot bunnies, this book wouldn't exist.

To Julia Kent and Blair Babylon, thank you for the Zoom writing sessions that kept me on track, to Kait Nolan for being a constant sounding board about everything from life to books to furniture, and to LJ Evans for always popping up in my DMs to check on me.

And always saving the best for last, a massive thank-you to my hubby and our kids for not blinking when I race out of the shower in a towel, yelling, "I NEED TO WRITE THIS DOWN!" or when I zone out at dinner and then randomly crack up while blurting, "The glitter bomb!" Thank you for letting me be me. I hope I always remember to honor that by letting you all be you too.

EXCERPT FROM *THE LAST ELIGIBLE BILLIONAIRE*

Hayes Rutherford, aka a Billionaire in Need of a Fake Girlfriend

All I wanted was six hours of sleep, alone, before digging into the inconsistencies that everyone else in Razzle Dazzle's corporate real estate division overlooked to figure out why we seem to have a small leak in our bank accounts.

Instead, I have a modern flower child with the world's most obnoxious dog making a mess of my house while my mother's on her way here to convince me to marry a Wall Street heiress who needs a husband who won't mind when she flies off to visit her secret lover in Cambodia.

"Does your eye always twitch like that?" Begonia asks. She's flitted into the living room, where she's gathering scattered clothing and paint rags, slowly but steadily erasing the evidence that she was ever here. "You seem like you're under an unhealthy level of stress. *Way* more than I'd expect for you finding an unexpected guest in your house. Is everything okay?"

I open my mouth to ask what a *healthy* level of stress would be when finding a squatter in the house where I intended to be by myself for the next two weeks, but before the words can form on my tongue, the back door swings open again, and her dog trots in, carrying a wooden statue in its jaw.

"*Marshmallow!*" she chides.

He drops the statue, sits back on his haunches, and regards her with a faux innocence that's utterly diabolical while I process the rest of what I'm seeing. "What the *hell?*"

Begonia falls to her knees and grabs the small wooden statue. It's roughly eighteen inches high, and rubbing its head as she's doing will *not* fix what that dog has done. "Just needs a little polish and freshening," she says brightly.

"*Maurice Bellitano carved that.*"

She goes pale. "*The* Maurice Bellitano?"

"That's *my grandfather.* Your dog *chewed off the head of Maurice Bellitano's carving of my grandfather.*"

"Oh, god," she whispers.

We both stare at the statue in her hands.

While my grandfather was more rotund than the slender statue, the high-waisted suit pants, the suspenders, and the loafers are undeniably him.

The head used to be as well, but now there are gnaw marks in my grandfather's eyeballs, his nose is gone, and the scally cap he always wore is missing half its brim.

I shift my attention to Begonia.

Her expression leaves *zero* doubt that she knows exactly who Maurice Bellitano was, and exactly how priceless that piece of wood in her hands is. "Oh, no no no . . ."

And now my head is going to explode.

When my mother sees this—

Wait.

Wait.

I look at Begonia, a squatting divorcée with her poorly disciplined dog and her glowing hair and her disaster all over my entire house.

An idea takes hold at the root of my brain.

It's a terrible idea.

Worse than terrible.

The consequences, the repercussions—if this backfires, it could do far more harm than good, and cause more problems than the situation I'd like to extract myself from.

But if it works, it could give me exactly what I've wanted and needed for months.

Years, even.

"Do. Not. Move," I order. "Do not think. Do not breathe. Do not *move*. Do you understand?"

She's kneeling on the floor, one hand on her dog's collar, the other gripping my grandfather's chewed head, staring at me with wide-eyed fear again. "My brain and my instincts are very much at odds over understanding right now, if I'm being perfectly honest."

"And for the love of god, *do not talk*."

I need to think.

And I need to do it quickly.

Excerpt from The Last Eligible Billionaire, *copyright © 2022 by Pippa Grant*

AUTHOR BIO

Photo © 2021 Briana Snyder, Knack Video + Photo

Pippa Grant is a *USA Today* bestselling author who writes romantic comedies that will make tears run down your leg. When she's not reading, writing, or sleeping, she's being crowned employee of the month as a stay-at-home mom and housewife trying to prepare her adorable demon spawn to be productive members of society, all while she fantasizes about long walks on the beach with hot chocolate chip cookies.